Praise for the novels of Sherryl Woods

"Skillfully introducing readers to The Devaneys,
Sherryl Woods scores another winner."
—RT Book Reviews on Sean's Reckoning

"Sherryl Woods writes emotionally satisfying novels about
family, friendship and home. Truly feel-great reads!"
—#1 New York Times bestselling author Debbie Macomber

"Woods is a master heartstring puller."
—Publishers Weekly on Seaview Inn

"Woods's readers will eagerly anticipate her trademark
small-town setting, loyal friendships, and honorable mentors
as they meet new characters and reconnect with familiar ones
in this heartwarming tale."
—Booklist on Home in Carolina

"Once again, Woods, with such authenticity,
weaves a tale of true love and the challenges
that can knock up against that love."
—RT Book Reviews on Beach Lane

"In this sweet, sometimes funny and often touching story,
the characters are beautifully depicted, and readers…
will…want to wish themselves away to Seaview Key."
—RT Book Reviews on Seaview Inn

"Woods…is noted for appealing character-driven stories
that are often infused with the
flavor and fragrance of the South."
—Library Journal

"A whimsical, sweet scenario…
the digressions have their own charm, and Woods
never fails to come back to the romantic point."
—Publishers Weekly on Sweet Tea at Sunrise

#1 *New York Times* Bestselling Author

SHERRYL WOODS

The Devaney Brothers

RYAN & SEAN

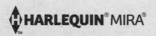

ISBN-13: 978-0-7783-1607-7

THE DEVANEY BROTHERS: RYAN AND SEAN

Copyright © 2014 by Harlequin Books S.A.

The publisher acknowledges the copyright holder of the individual works as follows:

RYAN'S PLACE
Copyright © 2002 by Sherryl Woods

SEAN'S RECKONING
Copyright © 2002 by Sherryl Woods

Recycling programs for this product may not exist in your area.

For questions and comments about the quality of this book, please contact us at CustomerService@Harlequin.com.

Printed in U.S.A.

Dear Friends,

Years ago, I heard a question on *Jeopardy!* about the most successful Disney movies of all time. It stated that they all had something to do with orphans. Well, who am I to argue with the Disney magic? Thus the Devaneys were born—five brothers, separated for years, thanks to a decision by desperate parents.

As each story unfolds and the brothers are reunited, more and more questions arise about why their parents allowed them to be separated. Readers have debated ever since about whether their reasons were valid or impossible to understand. As you come to know the brothers, I hope you'll share your thoughts with me, as well. Put yourselves into the parents' shoes and think about what you might have done under the same circumstances.

In the meantime, I'm delighted that the emotional stories of Ryan, Sean, Michael, Patrick and Daniel are coming back into print. I'll look forward to hearing from you.

All best,

Sherryl

CONTENTS

RYAN'S PLACE

_1_

Ryan Devaney hated holidays. Not only were they lousy for business, but the few people who did walk into his Boston pub were usually just about as depressed as he was. The jukebox tended to blast out its most soulful tunes, which might have reduced him to tears if he hadn't given up shedding them a long time ago. Thanksgiving, with its bittersweet memories, had always been worst of all. And this year promised to be no different.

Outside there was the scent of snow in the crisp air, and back in Ryan's kitchen, his cook was already baking the dozens of pumpkin pies Ryan would be taking to the homeless shelter and also serving to the handful of people who showed up at the pub for a lonely meal tomorrow. Ryan had a very dim recollection of a time when both aromas would have stirred happy memories, but those days were long gone. It had been more than twenty years since he'd had anything at all for which to be thankful.

Even as the thought crossed his mind, he brought

himself up short. Father Francis—the priest who evidently considered saving Ryan's soul his personal mission—would blister him with a disapproving lecture if he ever heard him say such a thing aloud. The priest, whose church was just down the block and whose parish benefitted from Ryan's generosity, had a very low opinion of Ryan's tendency to wallow in self-pity around holidays.

"You have a roof over your head. You have money in your pocket and warm food in your belly," Father Francis had chided on more than one occasion, disappointment clouding his gaze. "You have a business that prospers and customers who rely on you. You have countless others who depend on you for food and shelter, though they don't know it. How can you say there are no blessings in your life? I'm ashamed of you, Ryan Devaney. Truly ashamed."

As if Ryan had conjured him up just then, Father Francis slid onto an empty stool at the busy bar and gave Ryan his usual perceptive once-over. "Indulging again, I see."

Ryan winced at the disapproving tone. "Haven't touched a drop," he said, knowing perfectly well that liquor was the last concern on the priest's mind.

"Ah, Ryan, my boy, do you honestly believe you can get away with trying that one on me?"

Ryan grinned at the white-haired man, who still had a hint of Ireland in his voice. "It was worth a try. What can I get you on this chilly night?"

"Would a cup of Irish coffee be too much trouble? The wind is whipping out there, and my old bones can't take it the way they once did."

"For you, Father, nothing is too much trouble," Ryan told him with total sincerity. As annoying as he sometimes found the priest, Ryan owed him his life. Father Francis had snatched him out of the depths of despair and trouble many years ago and set him on a path that had landed him here, operating his own business, rather than sitting in a jail cell. "Why aren't you home in front of a fire?"

"I've been to visit the shelter. We've a new family in there tonight. Can you imagine anything sadder than being forced to go to a homeless shelter for the first time on Thanksgiving eve, when everyone else is fixing turkey and baking pies and preparing to count their blessings?"

Ryan gave him a sharp look. It had been Thanksgiving eve, seventeen years ago, when Father Francis had taken him to the St. Mary's shelter, scared and hungry and totally alone. Just fifteen, Ryan had been angry at the world and had barely managed to escape being arrested for shoplifting, thanks to the priest's influence with the local police precinct and the outraged shop owner.

"No, I can't imagine anything sadder," he said tersely. "As you well know. What do you want?"

Father Francis smiled, a twinkle in his eye. "Not so very much. Will you talk to them tomorrow? Your own story is an inspiration to many in the neighborhood. Hearing what you've accomplished under difficult circumstances will give them a reason to hope."

"I imagine you think I can find work for at least one of them, as well," Ryan said with a note of resignation in his voice.

There had been a time when he'd had a formal business plan for his pub, complete with goals and bottom-line projections. Taking in Father Francis's strays had pretty much thrown that plan into chaos, but if the priest had asked him to cater a funeral in hell, he would have found some way to do it. Hopefully, this latest request would require less drastic action.

"Well?" he prodded.

"One…or both. The fact of the matter is, I understand the mother is a wonderful cook. Didn't you tell me that you're short-staffed in the kitchen?" Father Francis inquired innocently. Before Ryan could reply, he rushed on, "And with the holiday season coming on, you'll be busier than ever in here as folks gather to warm up a bit after their shopping. And some of the local businesses like to use your back room for their Christmas parties, isn't that right? Perhaps you could use another waiter, at least through New Year's."

Ryan cursed his loose tongue. He was going to have to remember that Father Francis was a sneaky, devious man, always looking to pair up his strays with people who casually remarked on some need or another. There had been one point when half his waitresses had been unwed mothers-to-be. For a brief time, he'd been certain his private dining room was going to wind up as a nursery, but even Father Francis had stopped short of making that request. The priest's grudging acknowledgment that a pub was no place for infant day care suggested, however, that the thought had crossed his mind.

"Hiring an extra waiter is no problem. As for the

woman, can she fix corned beef and cabbage, Irish stew, soda bread?" Ryan asked.

The priest looked vaguely uncomfortable. "Isn't it time for a bit of a change?" He pulled the bright-green, laminated menu from its rack on the counter and pointed out the entrées that had been the same since the opening on St. Patrick's Day eight years ago. Even the daily specials had remained constant. "It's a bit boring, don't you think?"

"This is an Irish pub," Ryan reminded him dryly. "And my customers like knowing they can count on having fish and chips on Fridays and stew on Saturdays."

"But people eventually tire of eating the same old things. Perhaps a little spice would liven things up."

Spice? Ryan studied him warily. "What exactly can this woman cook?"

The priest's expression brightened. "I understand her enchiladas are outstanding," he reported enthusiastically.

Ryan frowned. "Let me get this straight. You're asking me to hire someone to cook Mexican food in my Irish pub?"

He shuddered when he considered how his born-in-Dublin cook was likely to take to that news. Rory O'Malley was going to be slamming pots and pans around for a month, assuming he didn't simply walk off the job. Rory, with his thick Irish brogue and a belly the size of Santa's thanks to his fondness for ale, had a kind heart, but he could throw a tantrum better than any temperamental French chef. Because his kitchen had never run more smoothly, Ryan tried his best to stay out of Rory's way and to do nothing to offend him.

The priest plastered an upbeat expression on his face. "Ryan's Place will become the most talked-about restaurant in the city, a fine example of our melting pot culture."

"Save it," Ryan muttered, his already sour mood sinking even lower, because despite the absurdity and the threat of a rebellion in the kitchen, he was going to do as he'd been asked to do. "Send her in day after tomorrow, but she'd better be a quick learner. I am not serving tacos in this place, and that's that. Does she at least speak English?"

"Enough," Father Francis said.

He spoke with the kind of poker face that had Ryan groaning. "I should let you be the one to explain all this to Rory," Ryan grumbled.

"Rory's a fine Irish lad and a recent immigrant himself," Father Francis declared optimistically. "I'm sure he'll be agreeable enough when he knows all the facts. And surely he'll see the benefit in the positive reviews likely to come his way."

"On the off chance he doesn't take the news as well as you're predicting, I sincerely hope you can find your way around a kitchen, Father, because I have an apron back there with your name on it."

"Let's pray it doesn't come to that," the priest said with an uncharacteristic frown. "If it weren't for Mrs. Malloy at the rectory and your own Rory, I'd starve." He glanced toward the doorway, his expression suddenly brightening. "Now, my boy, just look at what the wind's brought in. If this one isn't a sight for sore eyes. Your good deed is already being rewarded."

Ryan's gaze shifted toward the doorway where, indeed, the sight that greeted him was a blessing. A woman that beautiful could improve a man's mood in the blink of an eye. Huge eyes peered around the pub's shadowy interior. Pale, fine skin had been stung pink by the wind. Waves of thick, auburn curls tumbled in disarray to her shoulders. Slender legs, encased in denim and high leather boots, were the inspiration for a man's most erotic fantasies. Ryan sighed with pleasure.

"Boy, where are your manners?" Father Francis scolded. "She's a paying customer who's obviously new to Ryan's Place. Go welcome her."

Casting a sour look at the meddling old man, Ryan crossed to the other end of the crowded bar. "Can I help you, miss?"

"I doubt it," she said grimly. "I doubt all the saints in heaven can solve this one."

Ryan chuckled. "How about a bartender and a cranky old priest? Will we do? Or is there someone you're supposed to be meeting here? I know most of the regulars."

"No, I'm not meeting anyone, but I'd certainly like an introduction to someone who can fix a flat. I've called every garage in a ten-mile radius. Not a one of them has road service tonight. They all point out that tomorrow's Thanksgiving, as if I didn't know that. I have a car loaded with food, thank you very much, and given the way I hate to cook, I flatly refuse to let it all spoil while I'm stuck here. Of course, since the temperature is below freezing, I'm sure I'll have blocks of ice by the time I finally get home."

Ryan wisely bit back another chuckle. "Do you have a spare tire?"

The look she shot him was lethal. "Of course I have a spare. One of those cute little doughnut things. Don't you think I tried that? I'm not totally helpless."

"Well, then?"

"It's flat, too. What good is the darn thing if it's going to be flat when you need it most?"

Ryan decided not to remind her that it probably needed to be checked once in a while to avoid precisely this kind of situation. She didn't seem to be in the mood for such obviously belated advice.

"How about this?" he suggested. "Have a seat down here by Father Francis. I'll get you something to drink that will warm you up, and we'll discuss the best way to go about solving your problem."

"I don't have time to sit around." She regarded the priest apologetically. "No offense, Father, but I was supposed to be at my parents' house hours ago. I'm sure they're getting frantic."

"Did you—"

She frowned at him and cut him off. "Before you say it, of course I've called. They know what's going on, but you don't know my parents. Until I actually walk in the door, they'll be frantic anyway. It's what they do. They worry. Big things, little things—it doesn't matter. They claim their right to worry about their children came with the birth certificates."

Ryan had a lot of trouble relating to frantic parents. His own hadn't given two hoots about him or his brothers. When he was nine they'd dumped the three oldest boys on the state, then vanished, taking the two-year-old twins with them. If there had been an explanation for their cavalier treatment of their sons, they hadn't bothered to share it with Ryan or his brothers.

He could still remember the last time he'd seen seven-year-old Sean, crying his eyes out as he was led away by a social worker. Michael, two years younger, had been braver by far...or perhaps at five he hadn't really understood what was happening to them. They'd never seen each other or their parents again.

Most of the time, Ryan kept those memories securely locked away, but every once in a while they crept out to haunt him...most often around holidays. It was yet another reason to despise the occasions when anyone without family felt even more alone than usual.

"You're closing in an hour or so, aren't you, Ryan?" Father Francis asked, snapping him out of his dark thoughts. There was a gleam in the old man's eyes when he added, "Perhaps you could give the young lady a lift home."

Before Ryan could list all the reasons why that was a lousy idea, a pair of sea-green eyes latched on to him. "Could you? I know it's an imposition. I'm sure you have your own Thanksgiving plans, but I truly am desperate."

"What about a cab? I'd be happy to call one, and you'd be home in no time."

"I tried," she said. "It's a long trip, and a lot of the drivers have gone home because of the holiday. There aren't a lot of people out and about. Most are home with their families. Both companies I called turned me down."

"Ryan, my boy, if ever there was a lady in distress, it would seem to be this young woman. Surely you won't be saying no to such a simple thing," Father Francis said.

"I'm a stranger," Ryan pointed out. He scowled at her. "Don't you know you should never accept a ride with a stranger?"

Father Francis chuckled. "I think she can take the word of the priest that you're a positive gentleman. As for the rest, Ryan Devaney, this is…?" He glanced at the young woman and waited.

"Maggie O'Brien," she said.

A beaming smile spread across the priest's face. "Ah, a fine Irish lass, is it? Ryan, you can't possibly think of turning down a fellow countryman."

Ryan suspected Maggie had spent even less time in the Emerald Isle than he had on his ventures to learn the art of running a successful Irish pub. She sounded very much like a Boston native.

"I think we can probably agree that Ms. O'Brien and I are, indeed, fellow Americans," he said wryly.

"But you carry the blood of your Irish ancestors," the priest insisted. "And a true and loyal Irishman never forgets his roots."

"Whatever," Ryan replied, knowing that for the second time tonight he might as well give in to the inevitable. "Ms. O'Brien, I'll be happy to give you a lift if you can wait till I close in an hour. In the meantime I'll give you the keys to my car. You can transfer all that food you're carrying to it." He shot a pointed look at the priest. "Father Francis will be happy to help, won't you, Father?"

"It will be my pleasure," the priest said, bouncing to his feet with more alacrity than he'd shown in the past ten years.

"Ms. O'Brien," Ryan called after them as they headed for the door. "Whatever you do, don't listen to a word he says about me."

"I always sing your praises," Father Francis retorted with a hint of indignation. "By the time I've said my piece, she'll be thinking you were sent here by angels."

"That's exactly what I'm afraid of," Ryan said. For some reason he had a very bad feeling about this Maggie O'Brien getting the idea, even for a second, that he was any sort of saint.

"I'm not sure Mr. Devaney is very happy about doing this," Maggie said to Father Francis as they transferred her belongings from her car to Ryan Devaney's. She considered leaving the things in the trunk behind, but snow was just starting to fall, the flakes fat and wet. If it kept up as predicted, it was going to make a mess of the roads in no time. There was no telling how long it might be before she'd be able to come back for the car.

"You mustn't mind a thing he says," the priest said. "Ryan's a good lad, but he's been in a bit of a rut. He works much too hard. An unexpected drive with a pretty girl is just what he needs."

It was an interesting spin, Maggie thought, concluding that the priest was doing a bit of matchmaking. She had to wonder, though, why a man like Ryan Devaney would need anyone at all to intercede with women on his behalf. With those clear blue eyes, thick black hair and a dimple in his chin, he had the look of the kind of Irish scoundrel who'd been born to tempt females. Maggie had noticed more than one disappointed look when he'd turned his attention to her at the bar. Come to think of it, quite a few of his customers had been women, in groups and all alone. She wondered how many of them were drawn to the pub by the attractiveness and availability of its owner. Then again, there had been clusters of well-dressed young men around as well, so perhaps *they'd* been the lure for the women.

"Has Ryan's Place been around a long time?" she asked Father Francis.

"It will be nine years come St. Patrick's Day," he told her.

Maggie was surprised. With its worn wood, gleaming brass fixtures and antique advertising signs for Irish whisky and ales, it had the look of a place that had been in business for generations.

The priest grinned at her. "Ah, I see you're surprised. Ryan would be pleased by that. He spent six months in Ireland gathering treasures to give the pub a hint of age. When he makes up his mind to do something, there's nothing halfway about it." He gave her a canny look. "In my opinion, he'll be the same way once he sets his sights on a woman."

Despite the fact that she'd spent less than a half hour with Ryan Devaney, Maggie couldn't deny that she was curious. "He's never been married?"

"No, and it's a sad thing," the priest said. "He says he doesn't believe in love."

He said it with such exaggerated sorrow that Maggie almost laughed. "Now why is that?" she asked instead. "Did he have a relationship that ended badly?"

"Aye, but not like you're thinking. It was his parents. They went off and abandoned him when he was just a wee lad."

"How horrible," Maggie said, instantly sympathetic, which, she suspected, was precisely the reaction the sneaky old man was going for. "He's never been in touch with them again?"

"Never. Despite that and some troubled years, he's grown into a fine man. You won't find a better, more loyal friend than Ryan Devaney."

"How long have you known him?"

"It's been seventeen years now."

Maggie regarded him intently. "Something tells me there's a story there."

"Aye, but I think I'll let Ryan be the one to tell you in his own time." He met her gaze. "Would you mind a bit of advice from a stranger?"

"From you, Father? Of course not."

"Ryan's a bit like a fine wine. He can't be rushed, if you want the best from him."

Maggie laughed. "Father, your advice is a bit premature. I've just met the man. He's giving me a lift home—under pressure from you, I might add. I don't think we can make too much of that."

"Don't be so quick to shatter an old man's dream, or to dismiss the notion of destiny," the priest chided. "Something tells me that destiny has played a hand in tonight's turn of events. You could have had that flat tire anywhere, but where did it happen? Right in front of the finest Irish pub in Boston. Now, let's go back inside, and you can have that drink Ryan promised to warm you up before the drive home."

Maggie followed Father Francis back to the bar. Ryan's hands were full, filling orders for last call, but Irish coffees materialized in front of them without either of them saying a word. Maggie wrapped her icy hands around the cup, grateful for the warmth.

Next to her, Father Francis had fallen silent as he sipped his own coffee. Maggie hadn't been able to guess his age earlier, but now, with his features less animated, the lines in his face were more evident. She guessed him to be well past seventy, and at this late hour he was showing every one of those years.

Apparently, Ryan spotted the same signs of exhaustion, because the apron came off from around his waist and he nabbed one of the waitresses and murmured something to her, then handed her a set of keys.

"We can be going now. Maureen will close up here," he said, stepping out from behind the bar. "Father, I'll give you a ride, as well. It's far too cold a night for you to be walking home, especially at this hour."

"Nonsense. It's only a couple of blocks," the priest protested. "Since when haven't I walked it? Have you once heard me complain? Walking is how I keep myself fit."

"And you do more than enough of it during the day, when the wind's not so fierce. Besides, the rectory is right on our way," Ryan countered, even though he couldn't possibly know in which direction they were heading to get to Maggie's.

She immediately seized on his comment, though,

to second the offer. "Father, please. I'd love to catch a glimpse of your church. Maybe I'll come to mass there one of these days."

The priest's expression promptly brightened. "Now, there's a lovely thought. St. Mary's is a wonderful parish. We'd welcome you anytime."

Ryan shot her a grateful look, then led the way outside. If anything, the bite of the wind had grown colder in the last half hour. Maggie shivered, despite the warmth of her coat and scarf. To her surprise, Ryan noticed.

"We'll have you warmed up in no time," he promised. "Once it gets going, the car's heater is like a blast furnace."

The promise was accompanied by a look that could have stirred a teakettle to a boil. For a man who didn't believe in love, he certainly knew how to get a woman's attention. A couple of sizzling glances like that and she'd be begging for air-conditioning.

"I really appreciate this," she told him again. "I know it's an imposition."

"Ryan's happy to do it," Father Francis insisted from the backseat as they pulled to a stop in front of a brownstone town house next to a church. Lights were blazing from the downstairs windows, and smoke curled from a chimney. "I'll say good-night now. It was a pleasure meeting you, Maggie O'Brien. St. Mary's is right next door, as you can see. Don't be a stranger."

"Thanks for all your help, Father."

"What did I do? Nothing that any Irishman wouldn't do for a lady in distress. Happy Thanksgiving, Maggie. Be sure to count your blessings tomorrow. Ryan, you do the same."

"Don't I always, Father?"

"Only when I remind you, which I'm doing now." He paused before closing the door and cast a pointed look in Maggie's direction. "And don't forget to count this one."

Maggie had to bite back a chuckle at Ryan's groan.

"Good night, Father," Ryan said firmly.

He waited as the priest trudged slowly up the steps and went inside, then turned to Maggie. "I'm sorry. My love life has become one of Father Francis's pet projects. He's determined to see me settled with babies underfoot. I apologize if he made you uncomfortable."

"I think it's wonderful that he cares so much," Maggie said honestly. "You're obviously very special to him."

"And vice versa," Ryan admitted.

"He told me you've known each other for a long time," she continued, hoping to open the door to the story that the priest had declined to share.

"A very long time," Ryan confirmed, then looked away to concentrate on roads already slippery from the now-steady snowfall.

Or was he simply avoiding sharing something painful from his past? Maggie suspected it was the latter, but she recalled the priest's advice about not pushing for answers. Impatient and curious by nature, she found this difficult. It went against everything in her to keep silent, but she managed to bite her tongue.

She turned away and looked out the window just as the car slowed to a stop.

"Maggie?"

She turned and met Ryan's gaze. "Yes?" she said, a little too eagerly. Was it possible that he was going to share the story, after all? Or perhaps suggest another drink before they made the trip to her family's home in neighboring Cambridge?

"It's going to be a long night unless you give me some idea where I'm headed," he said, laughter threading through his voice.

"Oh, my gosh, I am so sorry," she said, feeling foolish. She rattled off the directions to her parents' home, not far from Massachusetts Institute of Technology, where her mother was a professor.

Ryan nodded. "I know the area. I'll have you there in no time. And I can arrange to have your car towed out on Friday, if you like."

Maggie balked at the generous offer. "Absolutely not. It's not your problem. I'll take care of it."

Even as the protest left her mouth, she realized that her stranded car was her only sure link to seeing Ryan Devaney again. She stole a look at him and felt her heart do an unexpected little flip. Such a reaction was not to be ignored. Not that she believed in destiny—at least the way Father Francis interpreted it—but just in case there was such a thing, she didn't want to be too quick to spit in its eye.

2

Ryan liked a woman who knew when to keep silent. He truly admired a woman who knew better than to pry. To her credit, Maggie O'Brien was earning a lot of respect on this drive, thanks to her apparent understanding of those two points.

He'd seen the flare of curiosity in her eyes earlier. No telling what Father Francis had seen fit to share with her, but there was little doubt in his mind that the priest had done his level best to whet her interest in Ryan. A lot of women would have seized the opportunity of a long drive on a dark night to pester him with an endless barrage of personal questions, yet Maggie seemed to enjoy the silence as much as he did.

Of course, there could be too much of a good thing, he concluded finally. Any second now he was going to start filling the conversational lull with a litany of questions that had been nagging at him ever since she'd walked into the pub.

Over the years, working at Ryan's Place, he'd managed to put aside his natural reticence in order to make the expected small talk with his customers. Few understood how difficult a task it was for him. In fact, there were those who thought he had a natural gift of the gab and many more who were sure he'd kissed the Blarney Stone during his stay in Ireland.

Outside the pub, though, he tended toward brooding silence. That was probably one reason why the handful of women customers he'd asked out over the years were so surprised to find him less than forthcoming on a date. And since he'd generally asked all the personal questions in which he had an interest during those evenings in the pub, it made him less than scintillating company. Since he had little interest in a long-term relationship, it generally worked out for the best all the way around. Few women pestered him for more than a single date. Those who took his moods as a challenge eventually tired of the game, as well.

Since Maggie O'Brien had never set foot in Ryan's Place before, he had all his usual questions, plus a surprising million and one more personal queries on the tip of his tongue. But because asking them might give her an opening to turn the tables on him, he concluded he'd better keep his curiosity under control.

"Mind if I turn on the radio?" he asked, already reaching for the dial.

She seemed startled that he'd bothered to ask. "Of course not. Whatever you like."

"Any preferences?"

"Jazz," she suggested hesitantly. "Not everyone likes it, I know, but I can't get a single jazz station where I live, and I really miss it."

Ryan was surprised by the choice. "Now, I would have pegged you as a woman who likes oldies."

"I do, but there's something about a mournful sax that tears my heart up. It's such a melancholy sound." She regarded him worriedly. "If you hate it, though, it's okay. Oldies will be fine."

Ryan flipped on the radio, and sweet jazz immediately filled the car. He grinned at her. "Preset to the jazz station," he pointed out. "It seems we have something in common, Maggie O'Brien. Wouldn't that make Father Francis ecstatic?"

"Something tells me we shouldn't offer him any encouragement," she said dryly. "The man does perform weddings, after all. He's liable to have us marching down the aisle before we even know each other."

"Not likely," Ryan murmured, then winced at his own harsh response to what had clearly been nothing more than a teasing remark. "Sorry. Nothing personal."

"No offense taken," Maggie said easily.

But Ryan noticed he'd managed to wipe the smile off her face. Once again she turned away to stare out the window, seemingly fascinated by the falling snow.

And he felt about two inches tall.

Even with the soothing sounds of her favorite jazz to distract her, Maggie couldn't help wondering about the brooding man beside her. Time after time during her brief visit to his pub, she had seen him turn on the charm with his customers. She'd also noted the very real affection between him and the old priest and Ryan's quick recognition of the older man's exhaustion.

Now, however, he'd fallen into a grim silence, apparently content to let the radio fill the silence. She could as easily have been riding with an untalkative cabbie.

When she could stand it no longer, she risked a glance at him. Ever since his offhand comment about the unlikelihood of getting trapped into marrying her by the scheming Father Francis, he'd kept his gaze locked on the road as if it presented some sort of challenge. Since the sky south of town was still clear and bright with stars and there hadn't been a patch of ice on the highway since they'd left downtown Boston, she concluded that he was trying to avoid looking at her. Maybe he feared she shared the priest's determination to create a match between them.

Of course, it was probably for the best. From the moment she'd walked into Ryan's Place and looked into the eyes of the owner, she'd felt a disconcerting twinge of awareness that went way beyond gratitude toward a man who'd offered, albeit reluctantly, to bail her out of a jam. Every time she'd ever gotten a twinge like that, it had landed her in trouble. She had a whole slew of regrets to prove it, though few were romantic in nature. Her impulses tended toward other areas. Some had cost her money. Some had gotten her mixed up in projects that were a waste of her time. Only one had been related to a scoundrel who'd stolen her heart.

Still, she couldn't seem to keep her eyes off him. He was, after all, every girl's fantasy of a Black Irish hunk. She noted again that his coal-black hair, worn just a bit too long, gave him a rakish, bad-boy appearance. His deep blue eyes danced with merriment, at least when he wasn't scowling over having been outmaneuvered by Father Francis, a wily old man if ever she'd met one. There was a tiny scar at the corner of his mouth, barely visible unless one looked closely, which, of course, she had. After all, the man had a mouth that any sane woman would instantly imagine locked against her own.

Yes, indeed, Ryan Devaney was the embodiment of every woman's fantasy, all right. A very dangerous fantasy. It would be all too easy to fall in with Father Francis's scheming.

Ryan Devaney was also a man of contradictions. For one thing, he might have his hard edges and unyielding black moods, but she herself had seen evidence of his tender heart in the way he'd bustled the protesting priest out of the bar and into his car for a ride the few blocks to the rectory. Maggie was a sucker for a man with that particular mysterious combination.

For another thing, Ryan was a successful businessman with the soul of a poet. The rhythm of his words, when he'd lapsed for a moment into an Irish brogue to tease a customer, had been like music to Maggie's ears. She sighed just remembering the lilting sound of his voice. She could still recall sitting on her grandfather O'Brien's knee years ago, enthralled by his tales of the old country, told with just such a musical lilt. Listening to Ryan Devaney, even knowing that the accent was feigned, had taken her back to those happy occasions.

She'd known the man less than two hours, and she was already intrigued in a way that had her heart thumping and her thoughts whirling. She blamed at least some of her reaction on her innate curiosity. Her father was a journalist, always poking his nose into things that he considered the public's business, long before the public even knew they cared. Her mother was a scientist and professor at MIT, a profession that managed to combine her curiosity about how the universe worked and her nurturing skills.

Inevitably, living with two people like that, Maggie had grown up with an insatiable desire to understand what made people tick. She had a trace of her father's cynicism, a healthy dose of her mother's reason and an intuitive ability to see beneath the surface.

Among her friends she was the one they turned to when they were trying to make sense of relationships, when a boss was giving them trouble, when a parent was making impossible demands. Maggie always had a helpful insight, if not a solution, to offer.

The only life she couldn't seem to make sense of was her own. She was still struggling to carve out a niche for herself. She had a degree in business and in accounting, but in one of those contradictions that she seemed to like in others, she kept searching for a creative outlet that would feed her soul as well as her bank account.

Her last job certainly hadn't offered that. She'd loved the small coastal town in Maine, which was why she'd persuaded herself that she could be happy doing bookkeeping for a small corporation. In the end, though, the early-morning strolls on the beach, the quaint shops and the friendly neighbors hadn't compensated for the daily tedium in her job. She'd given her notice two weeks ago, on the same day she'd broken off a relationship that had been going nowhere.

Now she was the one in need of direction, but she'd

given herself until after the start of the new year to figure things out. With savings in the bank, she didn't have to rush right into another job. She was going to stay with her parents, brothers and sisters for the next few weeks, then decide if she wanted to return to Maine, where she'd been making her home for the past four years, and look for more satisfying work and a relationship that had more excitement and more promise of a future.

With all that heavy thinking awaiting her, Ryan Devaney and his contradictions offered a tempting distraction. She glanced his way again, noting that his focus on the road was no less intense.

"I'm sorry to disrupt your plans this way," she apologized yet again, hoping to spark a conversation.

"Not a problem," he said without looking at her.

"Most people have a lot to do around the holidays."

"It's okay," he said, his delectable mouth drawing into a tight line.

"Will the pub be open tomorrow?"

"For a few hours. Some of our customers have nowhere else to spend Thanksgiving."

She recalled what Father Francis had said about Ryan having been abandoned by his parents. Obviously, he could relate to customers who were essentially in the same fix—all alone in the world. "It's thoughtful of you to give them a place where they'll feel welcome."

"It's a business decision," he said, dismissing the idea that there was any sentiment involved.

"Your own family doesn't mind?" she asked, deliberately feigning ignorance and broaching the touchy subject in the hope that he would open up and fill in the blanks left by Father Francis's sketchy explanation.

"No," he said tightly.

"Tell me about them," she prodded.

He glanced at her then. "There's nothing to tell."

There was a bleak note in his voice she doubted he realized was there. "Oh?" she said. "Every family has a story."

His frown deepened. "Ms. O'Brien, I offered you a lift home. I didn't offer to provide the entertainment. If you need some noise, turn up the radio."

Maggie hesitated at the sharp tone, but even an armchair psychologist understood that defensiveness was often a cover for a deep-seated need to talk. She wondered if Ryan Devaney had ever talked about whatever he was trying so determinedly to keep from her. Maybe he told his secrets to Father Francis from the shadows of the confessional, or maybe the priest was simply better at prying them loose.

"Sometimes it's easier to tell things to a stranger than it is to a friend," she observed lightly.

"And sometimes there's nothing to tell," he repeated.

Though she already knew at least some of the answers, she decided to try getting them directly from the source. "Are you married?" she began.

"No."

"Have you ever been?"

"No."

"What about the rest of your family?"

He slammed on the brakes and turned to glower at

her. "I have no family," he said tightly. "None at all. Are you satisfied, Ms. O'Brien?"

Satisfied? Far from it, she thought as she gazed into eyes burning with anger. If anything, she was more intrigued than ever. Now, however, was probably not the best time to tell Ryan that. Maybe tomorrow, after she'd persuaded him to stay and spend Thanksgiving with her family, maybe then he'd be mellow enough to explain what had happened years ago to tear his world apart and why he claimed to have no family at all, when the truth was slightly different. They might not be in his life, but they were more than likely out there somewhere.

Even without all the answers, Maggie was filled with sympathy. Because with two parents, three sisters and two brothers, a couple of dozen aunts, uncles and cousins—all of them boisterous, impossible, difficult and undeniably wonderful—she couldn't imagine anyone having no one at all to call family.

Ryan caught the little flicker of dismay in Maggie's eyes when he'd announced that he had no family to speak of. He was pretty sure he'd seen something else, as well, a faint glint of determination.

Maybe that was why he wasn't the least bit surprised when she invited him to stay over once they reached her family's large house off Kendall Square.

"It's nearly two in the morning," she told him. "You must be exhausted. Please stay. I'm sure there's an overflow crowd here tonight, but there's bound to be a couch or something free. If worse comes to worst, I

know there are sleeping bags in the attic. I can set you
up with one of those."

"Don't worry about it. I'm used to late nights. I'll be
fine," he insisted as he began unloading bags from his
trunk. Since she and Father Francis had loaded the car,
it was the first time he'd realized that she must have
half her worldly possessions with her. He regarded her
wryly. "You planning on a long visit?"

"Till after New Year's," she said.

"What about your job? You do have one, I imagine."

"I'm between jobs," she said.

"Fired?" he asked, pulling out the familiar note of
sympathy he used when his customers hit a similar
rough patch.

"Nope. I quit a very good job as an accountant for a
corporation. I'm hoping to find something that's more
creatively satisfying."

"Such as?"

She shrugged. "I wish I knew," she said, then added
with a note of total optimism, "but I'll figure it out."

"Ever considered psychology?" Ryan asked.
"You've got the probing-question thing down pretty
well."

"I can't be too good," she retorted. "You didn't answer most of them."

"So what sort of career do you think you'd find creatively satisfying?" he continued. "Are there any op-
tions on the table?"

She grinned. "Trying to turn things around on me,
Mr. Devaney?"

He laughed. "Every bartender has a bit of the psychologist in him. The difference is, we just ask ques-

tions and listen. We don't dole out advice. Now let's get this stuff inside before we both freeze to death."

"We'll go around back," she said, leading the way. "A lot of this needs to wind up in the kitchen, anyway."

He noted that there was a light on in one of the front windows, as well as another in the kitchen, beaming out a welcome for the latecomer. A little tug of envy spread through him even before a tall woman with a face only barely more lined than Maggie's threw open the kitchen door and held out her arms.

"There you are," she said, enveloping Maggie in a fierce hug. "I've been so worried."

"Mom, I called less than forty minutes ago to let you know I was on my way," Maggie reminded her, amusement threading through her voice. "I'm actually about ten minutes earlier than I predicted."

"Which means you must have been speeding, young man," the woman chastised, turning to Ryan with a twinkle in eyes as bright and as green as her daughter's. "I'm Nell O'Brien. And you must be Mr. Devaney. It was kind of you to bring Maggie to us, even if you did exceed the speed limit getting her here."

"No, ma'am, I can assure you there was no speeding involved," he responded seriously. "I had it on cruise control the whole time."

She laughed at that. "But set at what speed?"

Ryan met her gaze. "You're not a cop, are you?" he teased, liking her at once. She reminded him of… He bit back a sigh. Best not to go there. He'd stopped thinking about his mother on the day she'd abandoned him. Or at least he'd tried to.

"No, but I've had a lot of experience at intimidating

young men," Mrs. O'Brien said. "I have four daughters and two sons, all of whom need to have someone in firm control."

Ryan couldn't help the grin that spread across his face. "If Maggie here is any indication, I imagine that's true."

"Hey," Maggie protested. "I was the dutiful oldest daughter."

"When it suited you," her mother concurred. "Now get in here, both of you. I have coffee made, but if you'd prefer something else, I can fix it in no time."

"Nothing for me," Ryan said, already backing toward the door. The warmth of this big, cheerful kitchen, the teasing between mother and daughter—these were exactly the kind of things he tried to avoid. They brought up too many painful memories. "I need to be getting back to home."

"Absolutely not," Mrs. O'Brien said. "It's much too late to be on the road, Mr. Devaney. You must be exhausted. I'll make up the couch in the den. And before you try arguing with me, remember that I'm older and wiser and I will not be ignored."

"If you're not a cop, you must be a general," Ryan said.

"Just a woman who knows what's best," Nell countered with a serene smile. "You two stay in here and have something to drink and a snack. I'll go on up to bed after I'm done in the den. Your father will want to know you arrived safely, Maggie. Besides, I have to be up at dawn to cook that bird." She winked at Maggie. "Your father bought a huge one that's probably not going to fit in the oven, which means I'll have to surgically dissect the thing, then patch it back together after it's cooked so he won't know."

Ryan saw his chance for escape coming right after Mrs. O'Brien disappeared for the night, but one look at Maggie had him hesitating.

"Don't even think about," she said, her gaze locked with his.

"Think about what?" he asked vaguely, his thoughts scrambling.

"Sneaking away in the dead of night."

"Any particular reason?"

"Because tomorrow's going to be a busy day as it is. I don't want to have to spend a chunk of it hunting you down and dragging you back here."

"So this is purely selfish on your part," he said, taking a step closer to the dangerous fire in her eyes. There was something about her—an exuberance, a warmth—that made him want to take risks he normally avoided.

"It is," she said, her gaze unflinching.

"Maggie, I did you a small favor. You don't owe me anything. Besides, I have plans for tomorrow, and the day starts early. I really do need to be getting back."

Surprise flickered in her eyes then. "You have plans?"

He was vaguely insulted by her obvious shock. "I'm not totally hopeless and alone."

She blinked and backed up a step. "Yes, of course. I should have realized," she said, clearly embarrassed.

Ryan should have let her go on thinking that those plans involved another woman, which was clearly the conclusion she'd reached. That would have been the smart, safe way to go. Instead, he found himself explaining.

"I'm taking food to the homeless shelter run by St. Mary's. Everything has to be set up by noon, which means an early start. And, as we discussed in the car, the pub opens at four for the regulars who don't have anyplace else to go. Not to mention that tonight's paperwork didn't get done, nor were the receipts counted."

She nodded and something that might have been relief flashed across her face. "What a wonderful thing to do," she said, apparently seizing on the planned meal for the homeless. "Can you use some help at the shelter?"

Help was always in short supply, but Ryan hesitated. It would be better to stop things here and now with this woman who had the determination of a pit bull and who seemed eager and able to slip past all his defenses.

"Of course you can," she said, without waiting for his reply. "We'll be at the shelter by ten."

"'We'?"

"My family, except for Mom, of course. She'll need to stay here with that humongous bird, but everyone else will want to pitch in. It works out perfectly. I'll have one of my brothers bring along a spare for my car, too."

Ryan searched desperately for a subtle way to change her mind. "Shouldn't your family be pitching in around here?"

"Mom refuses to let anyone else into the kitchen. She says we just get in the way. Besides, I brought a lot of food tonight that only needs to go in the oven.

Everyone else will bring dishes, too. She really has only the turkey to contend with." Maggie regarded him intently. "Don't even think of turning me down. I owe you."

"You don't," he repeated, even though he knew he was wasting his breath.

Besides, one part of him—a very big part—was suddenly looking forward to Thanksgiving in a way that he hadn't since he was eight years old. That was the last holiday his family had spent together. By Christmas that year, he'd been with a foster family, and he'd had no idea at all where his parents or his brothers were.

And nothing in his life had been the same since.

3

"Late night last night?" Rory inquired as he and Ryan loaded food into a van to take it to the homeless shelter. "You look a wee bit under the weather."

Ryan scowled at his cook's apparent amusement. "I did a favor for Father Francis. It kept me out until after 3:00 a.m."

"And did this favor happen to involve a lovely red-headed lass?"

Ryan gave him a sour look.

"I thought so. Why is it that Father Francis never thinks of me when a beauty like that comes along?" Rory lamented.

"Perhaps because he's well aware of your tendency to break the heart of any woman you go out with," Ryan told him. "You've earned a bit of a reputation in your time among us, Rory, me lad."

"Undeserved, every word of it," Rory insisted.

"Then why do I have a steady stream of women at the bar crying into their beers over you?"

"I can't help it if I'm a babe magnet," the cook said with a perfectly straight face.

The irony was that despite his round shape and fiery temperament, forty-year-old Rory attracted more than his share of women. Ryan suspected it had something to do with his clever way with words and his genuine appreciation of the fair sex. Rory's problem was that he appreciated a few too many females at one time. The drama of the breakups frequently spilled from the kitchen into the pub. Oddly enough, even after the blowups, the women kept coming around. Rory treated each and every one of them with the same cheerful affection.

"I can hardly wait for you to fall head-over-heels in love," Ryan told him. "I truly hope the woman makes you jump through hoops, so I can sit on the sidelines and enjoy the entertainment."

"I feel the same where you're concerned," Rory responded. He regarded Ryan with a speculative look. "So, has this redheaded angel of Father Francis's well and truly caught your eye? Or am I free to pursue her next time she stops in?"

"Stay away from Maggie," Ryan retorted, unable to keep a fiercely possessive note out of his voice. He swore to himself that he was only thinking of Maggie's heart, not his own.

Rory grinned. "So, that's the way of it? Father Francis will be pleased to know that his clever machinations have worked at last. Can it be that our Ryan has finally found a woman who can hold his interest beyond a one-night stand?"

Ryan scowled at him. "Don't be ridiculous. I barely know the woman."

"Has there ever been an Irishman born who doesn't believe that a lightning bolt can strike at any time? Love doesn't always require years of nurturing to blossom, you know."

"Thanks for the unsolicited lesson," Ryan said dryly.

"I have much more wisdom I could impart," Rory claimed cheerfully. "But why should I waste it on a man who's determined to go through life alone?"

"You know, if you don't learn to watch your tongue, I could fire you."

"But you won't," Rory said confidently. "Who would cook your authentic Irish cuisine?"

"Maybe I'll change the menu," Ryan said, thinking of the newest addition to his staff.

"Not bloody likely," Rory said.

"I don't know. I've got someone coming by tomorrow. Father Francis thinks she'll do rather well."

Rory frowned. "Another cook?"

"Yes."

"And would this be the angelic Maggie, by any chance?" Rory inquired hopefully.

"Absolutely not."

"Is she from Ireland, at least?"

"No."

"Well, there you go. How good can she be?"

"I've heard only raves," Ryan said honestly. "She's supposed to be excellent, so of course I hired her sight unseen."

"She's not coming for an interview? You've already

hired a woman you've never even met for my kitchen?" Rory demanded, clearly horrified. "I can't have some stranger—and a woman at that—underfoot all day."

"Why not? Will she be a distraction? Surely you can rise above your need to make a play for anything wearing skirts, especially since this one's married. And just in case you're tempted, you should know that her husband will be working in front." He gave Rory a steady look. "I don't think it will be a problem, do you? There are some lines not even you will cross."

Rory groaned. "These are more of Father Francis's strays, aren't they? I suppose we will find them at the shelter today, am I right?"

Ryan saw little point in denying it. He nodded. He considered telling Rory the rest, that his new helper barely spoke English and prepared only Mexican dishes, but decided his friend had had enough of a shock for the moment. Instead, he simply reminded him that there was a replacement waiting in the wings. "So, let that be a warning to keep a civil tongue in your head. And when you meet her today, be nice."

"When am I not kind to everyone who works at the pub?" Rory demanded indignantly.

Ryan rolled his eyes. "You don't want me to answer that, do you?"

"Okay, okay, I'll be nice." He regarded Ryan curiously. "Are you going to be seeing Maggie again?"

"She says she's going to bring her family to help out at the shelter today," he admitted ruefully.

"Well now, isn't that splendid? Father Francis will have yet another blessing to count on Thanksgiving."

"Go to hell, Rory."

To Ryan's disgust, the big man merely laughed. As far as Ryan could see, this was not a laughing matter. He was apparently surrounded by matchmakers who were going to take a great deal of delight in seeing him squirm. And they'd both handpicked Maggie for the task of accomplishing it, quite possibly because they'd both seen what he hadn't been willing to admit—that he was attracted to her.

The noise level in the O'Brien dining room was at an all-time high, with squealing toddlers scrambling for Maggie's attention and her brothers fighting for the biggest share of her mother's pancakes. It was all music to her ears, even if she couldn't seem to get a word in edgewise.

When her third attempt to interrupt the nonstop bickering fell on deaf ears, Maggie sent a beseeching look toward her mother.

"Enough!" Nell O'Brien said without even raising her voice to be heard above the din. It was her quiet, emphatic tone that caused even the littlest grandchild to fall silent. The skill had to be something she'd acquired in the classroom to control unruly college students. Clearly satisfied by the effect, she said mildly, "I think Maggie has something she'd like to say."

"Since when does Maggie require your intervention?" Matthew asked. "Speak up, sis. You've never been shy about telling us to shut up before."

"You've never been this noisy before, and I'm out of practice," she retorted. "Okay, here's the deal. I more or less promised that we'd spend this morning helping at a homeless shelter in the city."

"Promised who?" Matthew demanded with more curiosity than resentment.

"Must be that handsome man who brought her home last night," her sister Colleen said with a smug expression. "Mom says after meeting him last night, her heart was still all aflutter this morning. I'm sorry I missed him. Count me in, Maggie. I want to get a look at any guy who can make Mom swoon."

"There's definitely a man involved?" their oldest brother, John, asked. "Then we all go, am I right? We can't have a stranger breaking our Maggie's heart."

"This has nothing to do with anyone breaking my heart," Maggie said. "It's about helping those less fortunate on Thanksgiving."

"That may be *your* reason for going," John conceded. "Mine's less pure."

"Mine, too," Colleen said. "My heart hasn't gone pitter-pat over a man in ages."

"Thanks a lot," her husband said, frowning at her.

Colleen grinned at him. "I meant for a man other than *you,* of course."

Daniel leaned over and planted a noisy kiss on her lips. "That's better, love."

"What's this about a handsome man?" Katie, the youngest O'Brien, inquired as she returned from the kitchen with a glass of orange juice. "Where? Can I meet him?"

"He's entirely too old for you," Maggie said.

"That's the truth," her father chimed in. "Our Katie's not to even think of looking at a man until she's at least twenty-five. She's our baby."

Katie rolled her eyes. "Dad, I'm twenty-four, and

I hate to break it to you, but I'm already dating and have been for some years now."

"Dating, yes, but you've a full year to go before you even think of getting serious about anyone. Besides, this Ryan fellow is Maggie's," he said with a grin aimed at Maggie.

"He's hardly that," Maggie protested. "We've just met."

"But you're interested enough to be dragging us all the way to Boston on Thanksgiving," her father said. He turned to her mother. "Nell, what do you think? Is this man worthy of our Maggie's attention?"

With a wink in Maggie's direction, her mother placed her hand over her heart. "If I were just a few years younger..." she began, only to be cut off by her husband.

"Nell O'Brien, shame on you, saying such a thing in front of me, the man who's given you all these fine children, to say nothing of nearly thirty years of my life."

"Darling, I'm old and I'm married, not dead," she teased. "Ryan Devaney is a handsome devil. You'll see."

"So it's settled? You'll all go?" Maggie asked, not as concerned about her brothers' declared motives as she probably should have been. They talked big, but they'd stay in line. Her father would see to it.

"Of course," her father said. "You knew we would." He turned to his wife. "You'll be okay without our help for a few hours?"

"I'll be relieved to have you all out from underfoot," she said.

"What about the kids? You can't be looking after all of them, as well," her father said. He gazed around the crowded table. "Which one of you will stay to help out?"

"Garrett O'Brien, the day I can't look after three toddlers is the day they'll be putting me in my grave," her mother retorted. "I raised this bunch of hellions with little or no help, didn't I?"

"Then it's settled," her father announced. "We'll be leaving in an hour. That will put us there by ten. Is that what you promised, Maggie?"

"Yes, Dad. Thanks." She turned a narrowed gaze on her brothers. "And when you meet Ryan Devaney, I expect you to be on your best behavior. Is that understood?"

"When have we not been perfect gentlemen around your boyfriends?" Matt inquired indignantly.

"Well, there was the time we ran off that Carson fellow," John conceded.

"He was a wuss," Matt countered. "She was better off without him. Okay, aside from that one incident, have there been any others?"

"Just see that this isn't one of those times when your protective instincts kick into gear," Maggie pleaded. She shot a warning look at Katie. "And you remember what Dad said."

A grin spread across her sister's face. "You are staking your claim, then?" She turned to their father. "Told you I could make her admit it. That'll be five bucks, please."

Maggie stared at the two of them. "You already knew about Ryan and you had a bet going?"

"Well, of course we did," Katie said. "It's taken you practically forever to show an interest in anyone."

"I'm picky."

"You're impossible."

"I was beginning to worry that I'd have to explain to my children about their poor old aunt Maggie living all alone up in Maine in a cold and lonely spinster's cottage."

"I ought to make you stay home today," Maggie declared.

"As if you could," Katie responded. "Watching you get all starry-eyed over some man is going to be better than watching you stuffing tissues in the bodice of your prom dress."

"Katie O'Brien, that was supposed to be our secret forever," Maggie said, as everyone at the table hooted.

"Which just goes to prove you should never trust a kid sister," Katie retorted.

"I'll remember that. Just wait till you bring home the man of your dreams," Maggie said direly.

"Now, girls, that's enough squabbling," their father said, ever the peacemaker. "Today's a day to be grateful for family."

"And I am," Maggie said. "At least all family except my traitorous baby sister."

Now not only did she have to worry about Ryan's reaction to her arrival at the shelter, but which one of her family members was likely to be first to try to embarrass her.

The St. Mary's Shelter was just down the block from the church. When Maggie and her family arrived, it was already bustling with activity. Even so, Father Francis spotted her the minute she walked in and came over with a welcoming smile.

"Ryan mentioned you might be here this morning. Thank you for spending part of your holiday with us. It's a generous thing you're doing." He surveyed the group with her and beamed. "And this must be your family."

Maggie introduced the priest to everyone, even as her gaze searched the room for some sign of Ryan. Father Francis caught her.

"You'll find Ryan and Rory in the kitchen," he told her with a grin. "But if I were you I'd stay out from underfoot for now. Our Rory is a bit of a tyrant. He has them on a tight time schedule. He'll not be wanting any distractions. I believe the ladies can use some help with setting the tables." He turned to her father and brothers. "And your help will be welcome in setting up the remaining tables and chairs. We're expecting a large crowd today, so we'll have to keep things moving. The first guests will arrive at noon and the last won't be out of here much before three."

Maggie, Colleen and Katie went to work with the other women, though Maggie was constantly on the lookout for Ryan.

"Where is he?" Katie demanded when there had been not so much as a glimpse of him for more than an hour.

"You heard Father Francis," Maggie said. "He's helping in the kitchen. And where is Colleen, by the way?"

"I haven't seen her for some time now," Katie said.

"*She's* probably in the kitchen where you should be. Can't you think of some excuse to go in there? If you don't, I will."

"Katie O'Brien, you'll do no such thing," Maggie protested. "We came here to help where we're needed, not to gawk at Ryan Devaney."

Katie grinned. "Then you're no sister of mine. I'd rather look at a handsome man any day than make sure the place settings are lined up properly."

"He'll come out of the kitchen eventually," Maggie said. "Until then I'm not bothering him."

"Patience won't earn you sainthood," Katie admonished. "And I'm not sure it's ever done much to snag a man."

"I am not out to snag Ryan," Maggie insisted. "I'm just a little curious about him."

Colleen arrived just in time to overhear her remark. "We're all spending part of our holiday at a homeless shelter just so you can satisfy your curiosity?" she asked skeptically. "I don't think so. We're here because you have the hots for this guy. And since I just came from the kitchen where I got a good look at him, I have to say, way to go, Maggie!"

"You've been in the kitchen?" Katie demanded, looking as if she'd been cheated out of her favorite dessert. "Then I'm going."

Maggie scowled at both of them. "Don't make me regret asking you to come today."

"I just want to see what he looks like," Katie argued. "Where's the harm in that? I'm sure Colleen didn't go in there and create a scene."

Just then the kitchen door swung open and Ryan

emerged, bearing a huge platter of sliced turkey and followed by a large man carrying trays filled with sweet potatoes and dressing. Ryan's hair was tousled, his blue shirt perfectly matched his eyes, and he was wearing snug jeans that hugged his narrow hips. Maggie's mouth went dry, putting to rest any notion that she was here merely to satisfy her curiosity.

"Oh, my," Katie murmured, then gazed at Maggie with approval. "Your taste has definitely improved while you've been away. Not a one of the men you've dragged home in the past held a candle to *this* one."

Before Maggie could respond, Ryan caught sight of her. A slow smile spread across his face, but then his gaze shifted to the commotion at the shelter door, where a long line of people waited impatiently to be admitted. His expression grew troubled, and he turned to murmur a few words to the man next to him, who surveyed the long line, then nodded and hurried back to the kitchen.

Ryan walked in Maggie's direction. Hoping to stave off an embarrassing interrogation, she escaped her sisters and went to meet him.

"I see you're here to do your good deed," he said.

Maggie ignored the faint edge in his voice. "I promised I would be," she said cheerfully.

His gaze clashed with hers. "Not everyone keeps their word."

"*I* do," she said emphatically, returning his gaze with an unflinching look. "I saw you looking at the crowd a minute ago. Is there a problem?"

"The line is longer than I anticipated. I was just asking Rory if he thought we had enough food. He's convinced we do, but he's gone back to the pub to bring over another turkey just in case."

"Is there anything I can do? There are some stores open today. I could make a run to pick up extra food."

"No need. I'm sure Rory has it under control. What about your family, Maggie? Did you convince them to come today?"

"My sisters are over there," she said, noting that Colleen and Katie were staring at them with unabashed curiosity.

Ryan grinned. "Ah, yes, I recognize one of them. She was in the kitchen earlier. I thought she seemed a bit more interested in me than in the whereabouts of the napkins she claimed to be looking for."

"Sorry about that. Nosiness is a family trait, I'm afraid."

"And your brothers? Are they around?"

"Along with my father," she told him. "They're scattered here and there. Father Francis has seen to it that none of us are idle."

A genuine, full-wattage smile spread across his face then. "Watch out for Father Francis," he warned. "He'll have you all signed up for regular duty here before the day's out, if you're not careful. When it comes to caring for his strays, he's totally shameless."

"I can think of worse places to spend my time," Maggie said.

Her answer seemed to disconcert him for some reason. He promptly mumbled an excuse and headed back to the kitchen, leaving her to stare after him.

For the rest of the afternoon, she caught only glimpses of him as he worked. He seemed to know most of the people there. He joked with the men, flirted with the women and teased the children, but there was always a hint of reserve just below the surface. Whenever he happened to catch Maggie watching him, he quickly looked away as if he feared that she might see beneath the superficial charm.

Even her brothers, usually oblivious to such things, noticed the byplay between them.

"Sis, he's all wrong for you," her younger brother warned. "Too many secrets. And don't even think about making him one of your projects. I don't think he'll appreciate it. Something tells me your Ryan is troubled by dark moods."

"When has that ever stopped me?" she replied.

"Unfortunately, never," Matt said. "But this time you could be in way over your head."

"Have you even talked to him?" she asked testily.

"You wanted us to steer clear of him," John reminded her.

"As if my wishes ever mattered to you before," she scoffed. "Well, if you had talked to Ryan, you would see that he's one of the good guys. In fact, you ought to know that just from the fact that he's here today."

She glanced across the room to where Ryan was serving slices of pumpkin pie to a very pregnant woman and her two dark-haired children. The look on his face was impossible to interpret, but she tried nonetheless. Dismay and sorrow seemed to mingle with friendly concern. She had the sense that he was talking to this woman but seeing something else entirely, something from his own past, perhaps.

Drawn by the scene, she found an excuse to head

for the kitchen, slipping in long enough to grab several pies. When she emerged, she was close enough to hear Ryan murmuring encouraging words to the woman. He seemed to be holding out the promise of a job to help her family get back on its feet. A few minutes later he slipped the husband some money and told him to make sure his wife saw a doctor.

"Come to the pub tomorrow," he told the man. "We'll work out your hours then."

The man beamed at him. "*Gracias, señor.* Thank you. Rosita and I will be there. We are very hard workers. You'll see. You will never have reason to regret giving us this chance."

Ryan sighed as the man went to join his wife. Maggie stepped up behind him.

"That was very nice, what you did just then," she said.

Ryan whirled around, almost dropping the plate he was holding. "Where did you come from?"

"I've been here for hours."

He gave her a sour look. "Believe me, I'm well aware of that. I've had to field more than one question about the red-haired angel with the ready smile. You've drawn more attention around here today than the turkey." He didn't sound especially pleased about it. "I was referring to your popping up just now. Were you eavesdropping on a private conversation?"

"Nope, just bringing out more pies," she said, holding up the armload she'd retrieved from the kitchen. "I couldn't help overhearing what you were saying. You're hiring them?"

He shrugged as if it were nothing. "They need work.

I can take on a couple of extra people at this time of year. It's no big deal."

"I'm sure it is to them." Then, to avoid prolonging a topic that obviously made him uncomfortable, she asked, "I understand you're responsible for providing all this food every year. It's very generous of you."

"I have a restaurant. Rory likes to cook for people who appreciate a fine meal," he said. "Why not help out a good cause?"

Once again he'd dismissed his good deed. She probably should have been impressed by his humility, but she found it oddly worrisome, instead. "Why aren't you comfortable accepting a compliment?" she asked.

"Maybe it's because I don't deserve it," he said. "I wasn't the one basting turkeys and pouring pumpkin custard into pie shells all night long. Rory did that, as he has ever since he came to work for me."

"But I imagine you paid for the ingredients and for Rory's time," she countered.

"For the ingredients, yes, but not for Rory's time. He knows, as I do, what it's like to do without on a holiday. We try to make sure that at least some people don't have to know that feeling."

She studied him intently. "How long have you been doing this?"

"Not that it matters, but ever since I opened the pub. And that's enough of that," he said, closing the door on the topic. "I'm sure Father Francis is grateful to you and your family for coming to help out today."

"It's been…" She searched for the right word. While helping out had been rewarding, it was what she'd discovered about Ryan Devaney that had been truly important to her. "It's been enlightening."

His gaze narrowed at her comment. "I'm glad we've been able to provide a bit of entertainment for your holiday," he said with a touch of bitterness. "Excuse me. I have things to do."

He brushed past her, but Maggie reached for his arm. When she touched him, she felt the muscle jerk beneath her fingers. Only when he turned to face her did she speak. "You know that I did not mean that to be insulting," she said quietly. "Who did this to you? Who made you distrust everyone the way you do?"

Ryan hesitated, his expression still angry. "It's a long story, and today's not the time," he said finally, his voice tight.

Maggie's gaze was unrelenting. "Will there be a time?"

His gaze locked with hers, and for the longest time she thought he was going to say no, but eventually he sighed heavily.

"I imagine you'll insist on it," he said.

Maggie laughed at the note of resignation in his voice. It wasn't a very big opening, but it was enough. "Yes, Ryan Devaney, you can count on it."

Because despite all the roadblocks he'd set up and all the alarms going off in her head warning her away, she was very much intrigued with everything about this man.

4

Ryan was still reeling from the fact that Rosita Gomez, the cook who barely spoke English and knew nothing about Irish food, also happened to be seven months' pregnant. Father Francis had delicately neglected to mention that fact to Ryan when he'd been touting her for a job at the pub. Ryan could hardly wait to see Rory's face when he found out. Thankfully, he'd been able to keep the two of them apart at the shelter yesterday. Rory had been too busy to spend much time in the dining room.

But it wouldn't be long now. Rosita and her husband were due at the pub at two to fill out the necessary paperwork. When Ryan heard the tap on his office door, he assumed it was his two new employees. Instead, he found himself staring at Maggie O'Brien. A sigh escaped before he could stop it.

"You again," he murmured.

"I hope this isn't a bad time," she said.

Ryan desperately wanted to think of an excuse to run her off, but none occurred to him.

"No, it's fine," he said, trying to hide his reluctance. "I have a few minutes before my next appointment. Come on in. What brings you into Boston today?"

She held up an armload of shopping bags. "The sales," she said. "Surely you know this is one of the biggest shopping days of the year. Black Friday, when businesses expect to go from red ink to black for the year."

"I believe I have read that somewhere," Ryan said dryly. "An ad or two, maybe? Every TV newscast since last week?"

She laughed. "Probably so."

"That still doesn't explain why you're here. Don't tell me you happened to have another flat outside my pub because your car's overloaded."

"Nope. I have four brand-new tires, thanks to my brother. Matt took the car in this morning, muttering the whole time about how irresponsible I was to let the tires get into such sorry shape in the first place. It made him feel very male and very superior, so I suppose there was a blessing to be had."

"Well—" Ryan began.

"Don't you start. Not when I've coming bearing gifts."

Ryan's gaze narrowed. "Gifts?"

She frowned at him. "Not for you. While my sisters and I were at the sales, we saw a few things we thought Rosita might be able to use for herself and the baby. That is who you're expecting this afternoon, right? I spoke to her briefly after you and I talked yesterday. I know she wasn't able to bring much with her to the shelter. Wait till you see." She poked around in the shopping bags and started pulling out baby clothes, an expression of pure delight on her face. "Aren't these the cutest things you've ever seen? Look at this." She held up a tiny little knit cap in pale yellow. "And this." She retrieved an outfit with ducks embroidered across the front.

When she had his entire desk covered with baby clothes, she sat back. "What do you think?"

"I think you're amazing," Ryan blurted, then regretted it when he saw the smile that spread across her face. "I meant that Rosita is going to amazed. Why did you do it? You must have spent a fortune."

"Everything was on sale," she reminded him. "And we couldn't resist." She held up another huge bag. "There are a few maternity outfits in here for Rosita. These are new, but I have another bag in the car of Colleen's old maternity clothes. She swears she will never need them again, but if you ask me Daniel will talk her into at least two more kids. He wants a huge family. He was an only child."

Ryan's head was spinning. "Colleen is the sister who was ogling me in the kitchen?"

Maggie nodded.

"And Daniel is…?"

"Her husband."

"Was he at the shelter yesterday?"

"He was there, along with my father and both of my brothers, plus my youngest sister, Katie. My other sister lives too far away to get home for Thanksgiving, but they'll be here for Christmas. You can't imagine the chaos."

Oddly enough, he could. After the twins were born,

there had been five children in the Devaney house for two Christmases. Somehow his parents had always seen to it that there were gifts under the tree, even if they were secondhand toys from the thrift shop in the neighborhood. From the moment he and his brothers had crept downstairs to see if Santa had come, the house had been filled with noise and laughter.

At least that's the way it had been for a few brief years. Then they'd all been separated, and after that, Christmas had been one more day to be endured, worse than all the other days, because he'd wondered where his brothers were and if they were happier than he was. As he'd drifted from foster home to foster home, always feeling like an outsider, he'd prayed they were.

"Ryan?" Maggie asked softly, her gaze filled with concern. "Is something wrong?"

"No," he said tightly. "Everything's fine. Why don't you stick around and give these things to Rosita? She should be here any minute."

Maggie shook her head. "I don't want to embarrass her."

"She'll want to thank you, I'm sure."

"Another time. I should go before she gets here," she insisted, already heading for the door.

"Wait. Didn't you say something about having some clothes for Rosita in the car? I'll walk you out," Ryan said, surprised that he wasn't quite ready to see the last of her. She was pushy and intrusive. In fact, she promised to make a nuisance of herself. But she was also warm and generous, a real ray of sunshine. Like a cat seeking warmth on a windowsill he felt himself drawn to her, despite all of his deep-seated reservations about getting involved with anyone.

As he watched her walk to her car, he realized that one of these days he was going to have to decide which mattered more—protecting himself from her prying or accepting her into his heart.

"You weren't in there long," Colleen commented, after Maggie had retrieved the bag of used maternity clothes, given them to Ryan and said goodbye. She had noticed that he'd kept a careful distance between himself and the car once he'd realized that her sister was waiting for her.

"Long enough," Maggie said, satisfied with herself. The meeting had gone precisely the way she'd hoped it would. She had stayed just long enough to remind Ryan that she intended to be a part of his life—at least for the immediate future—but had left before he'd grown weary of her. And with his reluctance so apparent, she hadn't pressed him to say hello to Colleen. Contact with her family seemed to disturb him, either because he was fearful of getting too involved or because seeing them brought back too many painful memories of the family he'd lost.

"What did he think of all the baby things?" Colleen asked.

"I think he was dumbfounded."

"Clever of you to find a way to plant the notion of babies in his head. Now he won't be able to look at you without thinking about having a baby of his own."

"Colleen, that is *not* what this was about," Maggie protested. "Those baby clothes were for Rosita."

Colleen grinned. "But isn't it nice that they served your purposes, as well?"

"I am not scheming to plant ideas in Ryan's head," Maggie insisted.

"Oh, really?"

"Really!"

"Well, intended or not, I'm sure it did the trick. I imagine he's thinking of you in a whole new way now."

"Pregnant?" Maggie asked skeptically. "I doubt that. And don't you think it's a giant leap, anyway? He hasn't even so much as asked me out on a date."

"But you want him to," Colleen guessed.

Maggie thought of the way she felt every time Ryan's blue-eyed gaze settled on her. "Yes, I want him to. He's a very mysterious, complicated man, and you know how I enjoy unraveling a puzzle."

"And if he doesn't ask you out?"

Maggie shrugged. "He owns a pub. I can pretty much see him whenever I want to."

Colleen seemed surprised by her response. "You would do that? You'd just hang around the pub until he notices you?"

"I might. It's a great place. You should have come in with me just now. Even at this hour the jukebox was playing and there were groups of people laughing."

"I figured three would be a crowd."

"Well, if you had come in, you'd know what I'm talking about. I felt right at home there the second I walked in the other night. It's not like some sleazy bar. It's just the way Mom and Dad have always described the pubs in Ireland."

"I can't wait to hear what Mom and Dad are going

to have to say about this. You know how Dad always warned us to steer clear of bars."

"You'll never meet the man of your dreams in a bar," they both said in a chorus.

Maggie laughed. "How could I forget? But how can they object with Father Francis sitting right there most evenings? Besides, didn't you pay attention to what I said not five seconds ago? This is a pub, not a bar—there's a difference."

"I hope you don't mind if I sit in while you try explaining that to Dad," Colleen said.

"Dad's already well aware of the difference, so I won't even try explaining it to him. Besides, I've always believed in being honest with Mom and Dad about what I'm doing, and expecting them to trust my judgment. They usually do."

"So when are you going back? Tonight?"

Maggie shook her head. "Even *I* know that's too soon. I thought I'd give Ryan a day or two to wonder what's happened to me. I'm thinking I'll go back the first of the week. Want to come along for a girls' night out?"

"Something tells me Daniel would object to babysitting so I could go hang out with you while you try to pick up a man. If you need a chaperone, take Katie."

Maggie thought of the way her sister had practically swooned at the sight of Ryan. "Never mind."

Colleen shot a knowing look at her. "She's your sister. She would never try to steal your guy."

"It's not her I'm worried about. Have you taken a good look at our baby sister? She's gorgeous, something she doesn't even realize."

"And you think Ryan might prefer her?" Colleen asked. "Come on, Mags. He never even gave her a second glance yesterday."

Maggie regarded her sister with surprise. "He didn't?"

"Sweetie, he never took his eyes off you. Didn't you know that?"

Maggie shook her head. "I had no idea. I thought maybe I was fighting an uphill battle."

"You may be," Colleen warned. "He doesn't strike me as someone who wants to fall in love. He may not even believe in it."

"That's what Father Francis said, as a matter of fact," Maggie admitted.

"Well then, at least you know what you're up against. But a powerful attraction has a way of making a man take risks he never intended. It's all a matter of patience and persistence."

"I was blessed with one—" she thought of her total lack of patience "—but definitely not the other."

"Then Ryan promises to be good for you in more ways than one, doesn't he? Just keep reminding yourself—if he's the one, then he's worth waiting for."

"You might have to do the reminding," Maggie said.

Her sister chuckled. "Oh, sweetie, that will be my pleasure."

Throughout what seemed like the longest weekend on record, Ryan's gaze kept drifting toward the door each time it opened. He kept expecting—hoping—to see Maggie coming in with each blast of icy air. He was so obvious that there was little chance that Father

Francis or Rory hadn't taken note of him doing it, but they'd remained oddly silent.

Monday the pub was closed. That was the day Ryan usually spent running errands and catching up on paperwork, but he couldn't seem to concentrate today. He finally gave up in disgust around four-thirty and headed out to take a brisk walk to clear his head. Maybe that would push images of Maggie out of it.

Instead, when he opened the door, he bumped straight into her. He stood there staring like an awkward teenager. "Maggie, what are you doing here?"

She swallowed hard and backed up a step. "I came by for a cup of coffee or two. I'm freezing."

"The bar's closed today, but I'd be happy to fix you one," Ryan said, stepping aside to let her in.

"Closed?" she asked blankly.

He grinned. "As in not open for business," he explained patiently. He pointed toward the carved wooden sign posted by the door, where it plainly stated that the pub was closed on Mondays.

"Oh," she said, her cheeks flaming. "I never even looked at the sign. I just assumed, I guess, that you were open every day, but of course you'd need time off. I'll come back another time." She whirled around.

"Maggie?"

"Yes."

"I thought you were freezing."

She faced him with a defiant lift of her chin. "It's nothing. I'll just turn up the car heater."

He should let her go. He certainly shouldn't be inviting her in when there was no one around to serve as a buffer, no other customers needing his attention.

Still, he found himself saying, "I wouldn't mind having some coffee myself. I was going for a walk to clear the cobwebs out of my head, but coffee will accomplish the same thing." Never mind that he'd already drunk gallons of it and Maggie was the only thought cluttering his brain.

She beamed at him. "Well, if you're sure."

Ryan wasn't sure of anything, not when she looked at him like that. "Come on in," he said, "before it's as cold inside as out."

When she was in, he closed the door and flipped the lock, then retreated behind the bar. He figured it would give him the illusion of safety, maybe keep him from reaching for her and kissing her until her cheeks flamed pink from something other than the chilly air.

When he'd fixed a fresh pot of coffee and poured two cups, he handed one to her, then took a sip of his own.

"Do you need to stay behind the bar?" she asked. "Can't you come out here and sit next to me? Or maybe we could go to one of the booths?"

"I'm fine here," he said. "This is where I'm used to being."

"And we definitely wouldn't want to drag you out of your comfort zone," she said, her eyes sparkling with undisguised amusement.

He scowled at that. "There are reasons why people have comfort zones," he said. "Why mess with them?"

"It's called living," she pointed out. She patted the bar stool next to her. "Come on, Ryan. Take a risk. We'll save the cozy booth for another day."

He sighed and gave in to the inevitable. He walked

around the bar, but when he sat, he carefully left one stool between them. She bit back a grin.

"Oh, well, that's progress anyway," she teased. "No need to rush things."

"Maggie, why are you here? It's not as if this is the only place in town where you can get a coffee."

"But it's the only place where I know the owner," she said. "By the way, since you are the owner and it's your day off, what are you doing here?"

"Catching up on this and that," he said evasively.

"Doesn't sound like much of a day off to me. Have you ever heard of taking a real break?"

"To do what?" he asked, genuinely baffled.

She regarded him with blatant pity. "Whatever you want."

"I want to catch up on all the things I don't get to do when this place is busy," he said defensively. "Paperwork, bookkeeping, checking supplies."

Maggie shook her head. "Don't you have a hobby?"

"No."

"Something you enjoy doing to relax?" she persisted.

Uncomplicated sex relaxed him, but Ryan seriously doubted she wanted to hear about that. And today sex had been the last thing on his mind. Okay, not exactly true, he mentally corrected. Sex with Maggie had been very much on his mind, which he'd concluded was a really, really bad idea.

Even so, he couldn't quite keep himself from giving her a blatant once-over that had her blushing.

"Not that," she said, evidently grasping his meaning with no trouble at all.

"Too bad," he teased. "I do find that relaxes me quite a bit."

Her gaze locked with his. "Perhaps another time," she said in a deliberately prim little voice.

Ryan choked on the sip of coffee he'd just taken. "What did you say?" When she started to reply, he cut her off. "Never mind. Let's not go there."

Now it was her turn to regard him with a knowing look. "Oh? Why is that?"

"Maggie, what do you want from me?" He couldn't seem to prevent the helpless, bewildered note in his voice.

Her expression faltered at the direct question. "Honestly?"

He nodded.

"I'm not entirely sure," she replied, as if she found the uncertainty as disconcerting as he did.

"Then you're playing a risky game," he warned.

"I know," she agreed, meeting his gaze. "But I can't seem to stop myself. I keep finding myself drawn here. There's something about this place, about you..." Her voice faltered and she shrugged. "I can't explain it."

Gazes locked, they both fell silent. Finally Maggie sighed and looked away.

"Can I ask you something?" she said eventually, still not meeting his gaze.

"Sure."

"Father Francis told me something. He said that you don't believe in love."

"Father Francis has a big mouth, but he's right. I don't," Ryan said grimly.

"Why?"

Rather than answering, he said, "I gather you do believe in it. Why?"

"Because I see it every single day. I see it between my parents. I've felt their love since the day I was born. I see it with my brothers and their wives, with Colleen and her husband. There's nothing they wouldn't do for each other or for their families."

Ryan listened, trying to put his skepticism aside. He tried to imagine being surrounded by such examples. He couldn't. His own experience had been the exact opposite. There'd been a time when he'd thought his parents loved him and his brothers, but then they'd vanished without a trace. He'd been forced to question whether their love had ever been real.

"Have you experienced it yourself?" he asked.

"No, but I know it exists because I can feel it just by walking into a room with my family. It's in their laughter, in the way they look at each other, in the way they touch each other. How can you dismiss that when it's right in front of you?"

"No," he said quietly. "It's in front of *you*. I've never seen it."

Because he didn't want to get into a long, drawn-out argument over the existence of love, he deliberately stood up. "I'd better finish running those errands now."

Maggie looked as if she might argue, but then she put down her cup and picked up her coat. "Thanks for the coffee."

"No problem." He jammed his hands in his pockets as he followed her to the door.

She opened the door, then hesitated. This time her

gaze clashed with his in an obvious dare. "I'll keep coming back, you know."

An odd sense of relief stole through Ryan at her words—part warning, part promise.

"Unless you tell me to stay away," she challenged, her gaze steady.

"Whatever," he murmured as if the decision were of no consequence.

Her lips curved up. "I'll take that as an invitation."

Before he realized her intention, she stood on tiptoe and pressed her lips to his cheek.

"See you," she said cheerfully, then disappeared down the block before he could gather his thoughts.

Ryan stared into the shadows of dusk, hoping for one last glimpse, but she was gone.

"That was a touching scene," Rory said, stepping out of the shadows.

"Have you been reduced to spying to get your kicks?" Ryan asked irritably.

"Hardly. I just stopped by to see if you'd like a blind date for tonight. My date has a friend. I've met her. She doesn't hold a candle to your Maggie, but I imagine she could provide a much-needed distraction."

"I don't think so," Ryan said. He doubted if both Julia Roberts and Catherine Zeta-Jones rolled into one could distract him tonight.

Rory grinned at him. "Which says it all, if you ask my opinion."

"Which I did not," Ryan said.

"Well, I'm offering it, anyway. A woman like Maggie comes along once in a man's life, if he's lucky. Don't be an idiot and let her get away."

"I don't even know her," Ryan argued. "Neither do you. So let's not make too much of this."

"Are you saying the woman doesn't tie you in knots?"

Ryan frowned at the question. "Whether she does or she doesn't is no concern of yours."

"In other words, yes," Rory interpreted. "So, get to know her. Find out if there's anything more to these feelings. What's the harm?"

Harm? Ryan thought. He could get what was left of his heart broken, that was the harm. Maggie's words came back to him then.

It's called living.

Ryan tried to balance the promise of those words against the reality of the heartbreak he'd suffered years ago and vowed never to risk again. Bottom line? There was nothing wrong with his life just the way it was. It was safe. Comfortable. There were no significant bumps, no nasty surprises.

"See you," he said to Rory. "I've got things to do."

Rory's expression brightened. "You going after her?"

"Nope."

"Why the hell not?"

"Better things to do."

"What could be better than an evening with a beautiful woman?"

"A couple of games of racquetball and an ice-cold beer," Ryan retorted.

Rory laughed. "That's called sublimation, my friend."

"Call it whatever you want to. It's my idea of a great way to spend a few hours."

"That's only because you haven't been on a real date with a woman who might actually matter to you in all the time I've known you," Rory said.

Ryan couldn't deny the accusation. "You live your life. Let me live mine."

"That's the problem, Ryan, me lad. What you're doing's not living, not by any man's definition."

Nor by Maggie's, Ryan was forced to admit. But neither her opinion nor Rory's mattered. His was the only one that counted, and he was perfectly content with his life.

At least he had been till a few days ago, when Maggie O'Brien had blown into the pub on a gust of wind and made it her mission to shatter his serenity. From what he could tell, she was doing a darn fine job of it, too.

5

Maggie was beginning to hate the defiantly silent phone at her parents' house. Ryan was definitely not taking the hint. She'd all but thrown herself at him, and he was still maintaining the same aloof, distant air. Without her fairly secure ego, she might have found it humiliating.

If she'd honestly believed that he wasn't the least bit interested in her, she might have accepted that and moved on, but she didn't believe it. Not only did she know Colleen's impression regarding his interest, but her own instincts on her last visit to the pub had told her he was attracted to her. She'd seen the immediate rise of heat in his eyes when he'd found her outside, the too-brief flicker of desire before he'd forced a neutral expression onto his face.

Maybe if she hadn't quit her job, if she had a million things to do, she could have let it go, rather than obsessing about him. The truth was, though, that she was bored with all this time on her hands, and Ryan was the most fascinating element in her life at the moment. The vacation she'd been looking forward to when she'd left Maine was turning tedious. She was not used to being idle. And though she was supposed to be contemplating a future career path, all she could think about was Ryan Devaney. Maybe her personal life had been neglected for too long and needed to be dealt with before she considered her next job.

"What are you frowning about?" her mother asked as she poured herself a cup of coffee and joined Maggie at the kitchen table. "Or do I need to ask? Is this about Ryan?"

"I know it's ridiculous," Maggie said. "I barely even know the man, but I can't stop thinking about him. He seems so lost and lonely."

Her mother smiled. "Ah, yes, two traits that are guaranteed to fascinate a woman. So, when are you going to do something about it?"

"Such as?"

"Invite him here for dinner."

"Here?" Maggie asked, unable to hide her dismay at the idea of exposing an already jittery Ryan to an inquisition from her parents.

Her mother chuckled at her reaction. "Your father and I are capable of being polite and civilized when necessary," she teased. "Didn't you tell me Ryan had a difficult family background? Maybe being around a normal family would be good for him."

"You think we're normal?" Maggie asked with obvious skepticism.

"Of course I do. A little rambunctious at times, but pretty typical. There are no major dysfunctions I can think of," she added dryly.

"I suppose you're right, but I don't think Ryan would accept the invitation. Frankly, I think normal makes him uncomfortable. Besides, it's obvious to me that he's happiest on his own turf."

"Meaning the pub," her mother guessed. "Then we'll go to him. I'd like to see this young man of yours again. How about tonight? Your father should be home early, and since it's Friday, neither of us has to work tomorrow. It's been ages since we've had a night out in Boston."

The prospect of descending on Ryan's Place with Nell and Garrett O'Brien in tow made Maggie decidedly uneasy, but her family was a big part of her life. She might as well find out now if Ryan could cope with that.

"Are you sure?" she asked her mother.

"Of course I'm sure. It's a great excuse to spend the evening out with my husband. And didn't you say there's an Irish band at the pub on weekends? That will be lovely," she said, then quickly amended, "as long as we can keep your father away from the microphone."

Maggie grinned. Her father's enthusiasm for singing was a family legend. Sadly, though, he couldn't carry a tune, but that had never kept him silent.

"Keeping Dad away from the stage will be your job," she told her mother. "I can't have Ryan threatening to bar us from the premises."

Her mother chuckled. "Yes, that would pretty much ruin your grand scheme, now wouldn't it?"

Ryan had been lured over to the homeless shelter by a frantic call from Father Francis. When he arrived, he found the priest trying to console a heavyset African-American woman who was clutching a crying boy about ten years old. As he got closer he could see that the boy had some sort of medical problem that had left his complexion ashen and his eyes listless.

When Father Francis spotted Ryan, he gave the woman's hand a pat, then left her to join Ryan.

"What's the problem?" Ryan asked.

"That poor woman is beside herself, and who could blame her?" the priest said. "A few weeks ago the doctors told her that her son has a congenital heart problem that requires surgery. He also mentioned that it's probably something he inherited from his father. Apparently, the news was so distressful for the father that he quit his job and took off, leaving them with no income and no insurance."

Ryan felt his gut tighten with knee-jerk anger at a man who would do that to his family. He pushed the reaction aside to deal with the real crisis. "I suppose you want money for the surgery," he said. "I'll make the arrangements tomorrow. You could have told me about it tonight at the pub. Why bring me over here?"

"Because that boy needs his father," the priest said. "He can't go into such a risky surgery believing that his own father doesn't care about him. Though you never faced a major illness, I'm sure you can relate to how he must be feeling."

Unfortunately, Ryan could relate to it all too well. "You can't expect me to find his father."

"I do." Father Francis regarded him with a steady look. "I think your own experience will motivate you to help. And if finding his father can't be accomplished in a matter of days, then I want you to step in and be his friend."

Ryan had no difficulty offering financial assistance, even in hiring a private detective to conduct a search, but involving himself emotionally in the boy's situation was out of the question. "What's wrong with *you* being his friend?" he asked testily.

"I'm a priest, and I'm an old man. It wouldn't be the same," Father Francis insisted. "Come. Meet the boy and his mother. You'll need to talk to them to get the information you'll need for the search."

"You're assuming I'll go along with this," Ryan grumbled.

"Well, of course you will," Father Francis said without a trace of doubt. "That's the kind of man you are. You put aside your own feelings to do what's needed for someone else."

Ryan was growing weary of living up to such high expectations, but he dutifully followed the priest. The woman watched their approach with a wary expression.

"Letitia Monroe, this is Ryan Devaney. He's here to help." Father Francis patted the boy's hand. "And this is Lamar."

Ryan nodded at the mother and shook the child's icy hand. "Nice to meet you, Lamar. You, too, Mrs. Monroe."

"You can help us find my husband?" she asked, her cheeks still damp with tears.

"I'll see what I can do," Ryan promised. "I have some friends who are pretty good at finding people who are missing."

She looked alarmed at his words. "Not the police," she said urgently.

"No, not the police," he reassured her. He hunkered down so he could look Lamar in the eyes. "You a Celtics fan?"

The boy's eyes lit up. "They're the greatest," he said, his voice weak.

Ryan had to steel himself not to feel anything, not pity, not anger. "Well, once you've had your surgery, we'll see about getting you tickets to a game. Would you like that?"

"Really?" Lamar whispered.

"That's a promise. Now let me talk to your mom for a minute. Father Francis will keep you company. Just don't play checkers with him," he warned, then confided, "he cheats."

"What a thing to say about your priest," Father Francis scolded, but there was a twinkle in his eyes.

Ryan spent a few minutes with Mrs. Monroe, trying to garner enough facts to pass along to a private investigator who visited the pub most evenings on his way home.

"Do you really think you can find him?" Mrs. Monroe asked. "It will mean the world to Lamar to have his daddy at his side when he has this surgery."

"And to you, I imagine," Ryan suggested.

"Me?" she scoffed. "I don't care if I ever set eyes on his sorry behind again. What kind of man runs out on his family at the first sign of trouble?"

Ryan couldn't think of any acceptable excuse for it, either, but he tried. "Father Francis said Lamar's condition could be hereditary. Perhaps your husband simply feels guilty."

She seemed startled by the suggestion. "You think that's it?"

"I don't know your husband, Mrs. Monroe. You do. But if it were me, I'd be struggling with a lot of emotions about now. Maybe you should wait till you talk to him before you give up on him."

She nodded slowly. "I'll think about what you said. And I'm grateful for whatever you can do."

"Let's pray I'll be back to you with some news in a day or two. In the meantime, you make the arrangements for Lamar's surgery. You won't have any problem at the hospital."

"But they said—"

He met her gaze. "Trust me. There won't be a problem."

A relieved smile spread across her face. "Mr. Devaney, I don't know how to thank you."

"There's no need," he insisted, casting a look toward the boy who was giggling softly at something Father Francis had said. "Let's just make sure Lamar is back on his feet soon. I'm looking forward to going to that ball game with him."

Before he knew it, he was enveloped in a fierce hug.

"You'll be in my prayers every night of my life," she told him.

"I'd return the favor, but I think you'll have better luck letting Father Francis do the honors," he said wryly. "I've got to get back to work now, but I'll be in touch. You can count on it."

Ryan slipped out of the shelter before Father Francis

could waylay him with some other mission of mercy. Outside, he shivered, though it was less a reaction to the temperature than to the sad plight of the Monroe family.

He was still thinking about them when he walked into the pub and headed for the bar, where Maureen had been filling in while he was gone.

"Everything okay?" she asked, regarding him with concern.

"It will be," he said with grim determination. "Has Jack Reilly been in tonight?"

"Haven't seen him," she said. "But there *is* a familiar face in that booth by the stage."

"Oh?" he said, puzzled by the mysterious glint of amusement in her eyes. One glance at the booth was explanation enough. Maggie was seated there with her parents. They each had the night's fish-and-chips special and a pint of ale. He glanced at Maureen. "Cover for me a few more minutes?"

"Of course," she said at once.

He walked across the room, greeting several regulars along the way, then paused beside Maggie. "Good evening. Welcome to Ryan's Place," he said, his gaze directed first at Nell O'Brien, then at her husband. He nodded at Maggie.

"Ryan, I love your pub," Nell said with enthusiasm. "It reminds me of a place in Dublin that Garrett and I visited on our honeymoon."

"The Swan," Garrett said at once. He regarded his wife with a warm expression. "I believe we can credit a night there for our firstborn son."

Nell blushed. "Garrett O'Brien, what a thing to be saying in front of a stranger."

"Ryan's no stranger. He's a friend of our Maggie's. Isn't that right, Maggie, me girl?"

Maggie grinned at her father. "He still might prefer not to know all the intimate details of John's conception."

Ryan chuckled. "Actually I'm fascinated," he said, just to keep the color high in her cheeks. "And what about Maggie's? Is there a story behind that, as well?"

Maggie shot a warning look at her father. "If you tell it, I will never forgive you."

"Now I really am intrigued," Ryan said. "Make room, Maggie." He settled in the booth beside her, thigh-to-thigh, in a way that had his blood heating. "Come on, Mr. O'Brien. Tell the story."

Garrett O'Brien opened his mouth, then grunted, apparently when Maggie's foot made contact with his shin. "Sorry, lad. I've been persuaded to keep silent. Even in today's tell-all society, I imagine there are some things that are best kept private."

Ryan turned to Maggie. "I suppose I'll just have to pester you until *you* tell all," he said. "Right now, though, I'd better get behind the bar before Maureen rebels." And before he gave in to the urge to spend the entire evening right here with Maggie so close he could feel her breath on his cheek when she spoke.

"Join us again if you can spare the time," Nell invited.

"I'll do that," Ryan promised, casting a last, lingering look at Maggie before striding across the room and trying to block her presence from his thoughts.

He didn't get to keep his promise. Instead, it turned into an impossibly long night. Fridays were always busy because of the popularity of the band, but this was busier than most. It didn't help that his new waiter was struggling a bit to keep up with the unfamiliar orders, but Ryan had to give Juan credit for trying. Still, it meant that Maureen was carrying more than her fair share of the load and that Ryan was spending extra time soothing ruffled feathers and keeping an eye out for Jack Reilly so he could ask for his help in tracking down Lamar's father.

Suddenly Maggie was beside him. "It looks as if you could use an extra pair of hands behind the bar," she said, already donning an apron.

He stopped filling an order for ale from the tap and stared. "What are you doing?"

"Pitching in," she said, moving away to smile at a new arrival. She'd taken the man's order and placed a pint of ale in front of him before Ryan could blink. She came back to him with a satisfied smile on her face. "Any objections?"

Ryan weighed uneasiness against pragmatism. Pragmatism won. "Not a one," he said. "I can use the help."

Just then he spotted her parents heading toward the door. They gave him a cheery wave as they exited. Gaze narrowed, he turned to Maggie. "Wasn't that your ride home that just walked out of here?"

She grinned at him. "Not if I'm lucky," she said, then vanished to take another order.

"Meaning what?" he said when she reappeared.

"I figure you'll owe me," she said. "A drive home's not too much for a volunteer waitress to expect, is it?"

Ryan shook his head, aware that he'd just fallen into a tidy trap. "No, I suppose not, but I ought to make Rory take you."

Her smile faltered at the suggestion, and Ryan grinned despite himself. "Not what you had in mind, hmm?"

She met his gaze evenly. "Definitely not."

"Then I suppose I'll have to be the one, if only to see exactly where this plan of yours is headed."

"You won't be disappointed," she promised.

She said it with a look that had his temperature soaring.

And a lifetime's worth of defense mechanisms slamming into place.

Maggie figured she would owe her mother for a really long time for coming up with the idea of leaving Maggie behind to help out in the pub. Nell had overcome all of Garrett's objections by reminding him that it would give the two of them several hours at home alone. After that, her father couldn't leave the pub quickly enough. Years of having six children underfoot had taught him to snatch any opportunity for privacy.

Sticking around uninvited had been a risky notion. Ryan could very well have found someone else to give her a lift home, just as he'd threatened. The fact that he'd backed down and decided to take her himself was definitely a good sign. Unfortunately, she wasn't at all convinced they were ever going to get out of the place.

It was past midnight, and the last customer had been

gone for twenty minutes, but Ryan was still tallying the receipts, dragging out the process, if she wasn't mistaken. Maggie was sitting in a booth, rubbing her aching feet. It had been a long time since she'd spent so many hours as a waitress and bartender. She'd forgotten how exhausting it could be.

Oddly enough, though, a part of her felt exhilarated. She'd made over fifty dollars in tips, which was the only money she intended to take for her efforts. More important, she had thoroughly enjoyed talking to the customers. She'd missed that kind of interaction with people in her old job. Being the senior accountant for a corporation might have carried more prestige than waiting tables, but it hadn't been nearly as much fun.

She glanced across the room and saw that Ryan had disappeared into his office. Maybe she could hurry him along, if she went over there and looked pathetic, which wouldn't be all that difficult given the way she was feeling.

Groaning, she stood up in her stocking feet and walked over, carrying her shoes, coat and purse. She found Ryan behind his desk, jotting figures in a ledger.

"I'll be with you in a second," he said without looking up. "I like to get these numbers entered at night, so the day's cleared out and I'm ready to start fresh tomorrow."

"You're keeping your records in a ledger?" she asked, staring at the cumbersome book with surprise. She glanced around the office and saw no evidence of a computer.

"Sure."

"Why aren't you computerized? It would take less

time, and you'd have everything you need at your fingertips when tax time comes around."

"This works," he said, dismissing the idea.

"But—"

He glanced up with a grin. "You selling computers in your spare time, too?"

"No, but this is something I know a little bit about. I could set up a system for you in no time. And I noticed tonight that if you reorganized the liquor supply, it would be easier to keep track of what's running low."

"Maggie, I don't need a system. I already have one," he explained patiently.

"An outdated one, but I suppose that's to be expected," she said.

He frowned at that. "Meaning?"

"You're pretty much stuck in your ways across the board," she said.

For a minute it seemed he might take offense, but then he grinned. "It must seem that way to you, being the kind of modern woman that you are."

"It *is* that way," she insisted, ignoring the teasing. "But I won't push you to change tonight. I'm too exhausted to waste the energy." She grinned back at him. "But, as they say, tomorrow is another day."

"I'm *not* changing the way I do things around here," he said emphatically.

"We'll see," she said blithely.

"Maggie!"

"Don't worry about it," she soothed. "I'll just sit right over here, quiet as a mouse, while you finish up. You won't even know I'm here."

"I doubt that," he muttered.

She settled into the easy chair in the corner of his office, curling her feet up under her. Two minutes later she was sound asleep.

Ryan compared his figures one last time, then uttered a sigh of satisfaction. The orderliness of numbers pleased him. There was nothing messy or questionable about totals written down in black and white. Emotions, however, were another matter entirely.

And speaking of emotions, what was he to do about Maggie? He glanced across the room and found her sound asleep in his easy chair. At some point during the evening, she'd scooped her hair into some sort of ponytail, but there were curls escaping now to feather against her cheeks. Her dark-green sweater had twisted and ridden up to expose a tantalizing inch-wide strip of pale-as-cream skin. His heart hammered a little harder at the sight. If only he had the right to skim a finger along that delicate band of flesh, to slide his hand beneath the sweater to cup softly rounded breasts. His throat went dry at the thought.

He swallowed hard. He had to get her out of here and safely home before he did something stupid and acted on one of these increasingly frequent impulses of his.

Crossing the room, he hunkered down beside the chair. Despite his best intentions, he couldn't seem to resist reaching out to smooth a wayward curl from her cheek, then lingering to feel the way her skin heated at his touch.

"Maggie?" he whispered, his voice suddenly husky. "Time to wake up."

She moaned softly and stirred, but didn't open her eyes. Ryan bit back a groan as images of her stirring just like that in his bed slammed through him. Visions of tangled sheets falling away from long, bare legs taunted him.

"Maggie," he repeated with more urgency. "Time to go home."

He said the latter to remind himself that home was where she belonged—her home, not his.

Another moan. Another stretch. And then a sigh as her eyes flickered open. A smile curved her lips. "Hi," she said softly.

"Hey, sleepyhead."

"I guess I fell asleep. What time is it?"

"After one. I need to get you home."

She kept her gaze steady on him. "I could stay here. Save you the trip."

Ryan stood up and backed away so fast he nearly tripped over his own feet. "Not a good idea."

She seemed amused by his reaction. "Surely you have a sofa I could sleep on," she said, her expression innocent. "Where do you live, by the way?"

"Upstairs."

"Well then, that's a whole lot handier than driving all the way to my place."

"Maybe so, but something tells me I don't want to tangle with your father and your brothers, who might find the idea of you staying at my place a little premature."

She grinned. "Premature, not out of the question?"

"Maggie." It came out as part protest, part plea.

"I just want things to be absolutely clear between us," she said.

"And I'll be happy to let you know when I have them figured out," Ryan retorted.

"You're assuming you're the only one who gets to have a say," she accused lightly. "Wrong, Devaney. I'm part of this equation."

"Didn't you tell me that your life is in a bit of a muddle right now?" he asked. "You don't need to add to that by getting mixed up with me."

She rose gracefully from the chair and crossed the room until she could reach up and place a hand against his cheek. Ryan felt that touch straight through to his toes.

"What if I want to get mixed up with you?" she asked.

"Why would you want that? I'm not an easy man to be with, Maggie. I don't let people in. I like my privacy. I like the status quo."

She laughed. "If that was supposed to scare me off, it missed the mark. You've just made the game more interesting."

"Is that all it is to you, a game? Because if that's it, maybe we have something to talk about after all. But if it's more you're after—" he captured her gaze and held it "—I'm the wrong man."

Her gaze never faltered. "I suppose time will tell about that, won't it?"

She stood on tiptoe and touched her lips to his, a quick brush of soft heat that invited more. Too much more.

Before Ryan could stop himself, he'd dragged her

back for another kiss, this one deeper and more urgent. He was only dimly aware of the soft-as-satin texture of her mouth under his, of the faint taste of coffee and the heady scent of perfume. What truly captured his attention was the jolt to his system, the rush of blood and lick of fire that had him wanting more…needing more. Her body—soft and pliant—molded to his, as close as a second skin, as tempting and dangerous as anything he'd ever known.

He was on the brink of dragging her straight upstairs, not to his sofa but to his bed, when reason kicked in. Breathing hard, he backed away and dragged a shaky hand through his hair.

"I'm sorry," he apologized.

"I'm not," she said, sounding more triumphant than shaken. "I've been waiting my whole life for a kiss like that."

Warning bells went off in Ryan's head. "It was just a kiss," he said, regarding her uneasily.

"That's like saying the Revolutionary War was just a little disagreement over tea."

Despite his wariness, the analogy amused him. "There was the Boston Tea Party," he reminded her.

"Tip of the iceberg," she countered. "It's okay, though, if this was just a kiss for you. Maybe then you won't mind doing it again."

He heard the teasing note in her voice and decided to ignore the challenge. "Not tonight. Grab your coat and let's get out of here."

"Chicken," she murmured as she passed him.

"Damn straight," he replied without apology. Anything else and he'd be making the kind of decisions a man would only live to regret.

6

When Maggie finally crept into the house, it was nearly three in the morning. No sooner had she crossed the threshold into the kitchen, though, than the light was switched on. Maggie nearly jumped out of her skin.

"A little late, aren't you?" Katie inquired, looking thoroughly pleased at having scared the daylights out of her big sister.

"What are you doing up?" Maggie asked irritably. "Come to think of it, what are you doing *here?* I thought you'd gone back to your own place."

"Since my big sister's visiting, I thought I'd spend some time at home," Katie said. "Imagine my surprise when I arrived and found that no one was home. I waited for hours before Mom and Dad got here."

Maggie thought of her parents' delight at the prospect of going home to be alone. "I'm sure they were thrilled to find you here," she said dryly.

Katie frowned. "Actually, they did seem a bit taken aback. What was that about?"

Maggie smothered a grin. "Just think about it, okay?" She glanced at Katie's mug of hot chocolate. "Is there more of that?"

"There are packages in the cabinet. I zapped it in the microwave." When Maggie shuddered, she added, "Dump enough marshmallows on the top and you can't tell the difference." She stood up. "Here, I'll do it. You sit down and put your feet up. You look beat. What did you do tonight?"

"Mom and Dad didn't tell you?"

"They made some cryptic remark about you being with Ryan."

"That's right. Actually, I helped out at the pub."

Katie paused with the cup halfway into the microwave and stared. "I thought you swore you would never wait tables again after you worked out at the Cape that summer during college."

"This was different."

Katie grinned. "Because Ryan was there," she guessed. "Ah, the things we do for love."

"I'm not in love with him," Maggie protested. She was fascinated, curious, in lust…but love? No way. She might believe in it, but she wanted to get the rest of her life in order first.

"Just halfway there?"

"Not even halfway," Maggie insisted, though the memory of that bone-melting kiss they'd shared sent heat shimmering through her all over again. "He's an attractive man and a decent, complicated guy. I want to get to know him."

"In the carnal sense, I imagine," Katie said slyly.

"Katie O'Brien, you shouldn't say such things," Maggie protested indignantly.

"Well, if you don't, you're crazy." She handed Maggie the mug of nuked chocolate with four marshmallows jammed on top.

"Let's drop the topic of Ryan Devaney for the moment," Maggie said. "What about you? With everyone around, we hardly had a chance to talk over Thanksgiving. Any man in your life?"

"Not even one on the horizon," Katie said. "It makes Dad very happy."

"But you like your job, right? You're happy teaching?"

Katie grinned. "I love the kids, even if Dad does think that teaching kindergarten is little more than glorified babysitting. They're so eager to learn at that age. And the school is small enough that I can really get to know each child and figure out the best way to get through to him."

"You're more like Mom than any of the rest of us. You have endless patience and a real knack for making learning fun."

"Thanks," her sister said, clearly pleased by the praise. "But it's going to be way too easy to wind up in a rut. Next thing I know, I'll be forty and single and wondering what happened. It doesn't help that most of the people I know these days are female teachers and moms."

"Oh, please," Maggie scoffed. "I don't think you need to worry about that yet."

Katie regarded her with a knowing expression. "Isn't that what brought you home? Didn't you wake up one day and realize that you were dissatisfied with your life?"

Maggie thought about it. "In a way, I suppose. I wasn't meeting interesting people, and the work was boring. I wasn't making use of half the skills I learned when I got my MBA. I needed a new challenge."

"Like I said, you were dissatisfied. Any idea what you'll do next? Will you go back to Maine?"

"I've kept the house for the time being, but I don't know. It's going to be hard to find the kind of work I really want."

"Which is?"

"Something where I can make better use of my degree and my people skills."

"Like running a pub?" Katie inquired slyly.

Maggie laughed, thinking of her earlier attempt to convince Ryan to update his accounting methods or even to reorganize his inventory. "If I decide on that, I suspect I'll have to find someplace other than Ryan's," she said wryly. "He balks at the prospect of changing the least little thing."

Katie laughed. "You've already tried, haven't you? What did you do, start messing with his accounting procedures?"

"I just recommended that he consider computerizing his bookkeeping."

"And he told you to buzz off?"

"More or less."

"So, of course, the next time you go, you'll take along a few sample spreadsheets and show him how simple it would be," Katie guessed.

Maggie took the joking suggestion seriously. "Actually, not a bad idea."

"Oh, Mags," Katie said with a shake of her head. "Telling a man he's doing something all wrong is not the way to win his heart. Of course, maybe you'd rather have a job than his heart."

"Why does it have to be an either-or situation?"

"Because he's a man," Katie said wisely.

Maggie sighed. "He is definitely that."

Katie regarded her speculatively. "Have you kissed him?"

At Maggie's blush, she hooted. "You have, haven't you? Was it great?"

"Oh, yes," Maggie murmured. "Better than great."

"Then forget about the man's financial system. Concentrate on what's important."

"And that would be?"

"If you don't know," Katie said with a pitying expression, "then nothing I can say will help."

She stood up, gave Maggie a peck on the cheek and announced, "I'm going to bed. You coming?"

Maggie shook her head. "Not just yet."

A worried frown creased Katie's brow. "Mags, don't analyze this to death."

"More advice from the woman who doesn't have a man in her life?"

"Yes," Katie said, her expression serious. "Take it from someone who analyzed the love of her life right out the door."

She swept out of the room before an openmouthed Maggie could comment. This was the first Maggie had heard about her baby sister losing the man of her dreams. Had anyone in the family known? As far as Maggie knew, everyone had assumed Katie was happily playing the field, years away from wanting to settle down, just as their father preferred. Apparently, they were all wrong. None of them had even suspected that she'd met the man of her dreams, much less lost him.

Adding worry about Katie's unexpected revelation to her already churning thoughts about Ryan's kiss, Maggie concluded it was going to be a very long night.

Since Jack Reilly hadn't stopped by the pub on Friday night, Ryan set out to track him down first thing Saturday morning. He was actually relieved to have something to do that might keep his mind off of Maggie, at least for a couple of hours. He doubted there was anything that could banish her from his thoughts permanently, not after that kiss they'd shared.

He found the private investigator on a basketball court a few blocks away, shooting hoops with a bunch of neighborhood kids. When he spotted Ryan, he passed the ball to one of the boys and loped over to meet him.

"Thank heavens you came along. They were wearing me out," he said, bending down to catch his breath. "Don't know when I got to be so out of shape."

"Too many nights on a barstool?" Ryan asked.

"I don't think a couple of ales account for it. Probably the cigarettes." He grabbed a towel from a bench and wiped his face. "What brings you over here? Were you looking for me?"

Ryan nodded. "I need your expertise." He explained

about Letitia Monroe and her son. "Think you can track down the father?"

"If he's using credit cards or gotten a new job, I can probably locate him by the end of the day," Jack said, then held up his hand when Ryan started to say something. "But if somebody really wants to get lost, there won't be much I can do to find them."

"I doubt he gave this enough thought to hide out for long," Ryan said. "I think it was an impulsive decision. He probably just got scared and ran. Sooner or later he'll have to do something for money. They didn't have much. Now Mrs. Monroe and the kid are at the St. Mary's shelter."

One of the boys, taking a break to drink some water, overheard. "You talking about Lamar's dad?"

Ryan nodded. "You know him?"

"Yeah. He used to work with my old man till he quit his job and took off."

"Has your dad mentioned anything about where he might have gone?" Jack asked him.

The boy regarded him warily. "He ain't in no trouble, is he?"

"Not the way you mean," Ryan assured him.

"Then you might try checking around down by the docks. Sometimes you can pick up day work there. My dad said that's what he told him. He said old man Monroe just needed some time to think."

Jack gave the boy a high-five. "Thanks, Rick. I owe you."

"Does that mean you'll give me another lesson on that fancy computer of yours?" the boy asked hopefully.

"Meet me at my place at five. I can spend an hour or so with you then," Jack promised.

A grin split the boy's face. "All right!"

Jack shook his head as the gawky kid, who kept tripping over his own feet, moved back onto the basketball court. "Never seen a kid so eager to learn. I find him on my doorstep half a dozen times a week, hoping I'll show him how to do things on the computer. He's getting so he can do a search and turn up things I never even thought to look for. Pretty soon, *he'll* be giving *me* lessons."

"You think there's anything to his suggestion about looking for Lamar's dad down by the docks?"

"No way of telling till I go down there. I'll go now, then stop by the pub and let you know what I find out. When's the kid's surgery?"

"It's not scheduled yet, but I imagine it'll be in the next week or two. It's a risky procedure. The boy needs to know his father's there for him."

"Then we'll find a way to make that happen," Jack said confidently.

"You need a retainer?" Ryan asked.

"No way. This one's on me. Just make sure there's a cold ale waiting for me when I get there later."

"Thanks, Jack."

"Hey, not a problem. I can't have the neighborhood thinking you're the only good guy around. I need my share of those babes who are always circling around you. Hell, I'd even take one of Rory's rejects."

Ryan laughed. "You pick out any woman in the pub and I'll introduce you."

"I saw a redhead in there the night before Thanksgiving…" Jack began.

Ryan stiffened. "Except her," he said.

Jack's gaze narrowed. "What's up with that? Is she married?"

"No."

"Engaged?"

"No."

A grin spread across Jack's face. "Yours?"

Ryan hesitated, then sighed. "Could be." Whether he wanted it that way or not.

Maggie walked into the pub shortly after three in the afternoon lugging a laptop, a portable printer and a package of paper. Rory came out of the kitchen, took one look at her and rushed over to take some of the load.

"You trying to get a hernia?" he demanded. "What is all this stuff?"

"I wanted to make a point with Ryan. Is he around?"

"He went by the shelter. He should be back soon." He paused in the middle of the room. "Where do you want this?"

"In his office," she said at once.

Rory shook his head. "I don't think that's such a good idea."

"Why not?"

"Nobody goes in Ryan's office without an invitation."

"Why is that?"

"Because he says so," Rory said simply. "And since something tells me he's not going to be real happy to see all this fancy technological stuff, anyway, maybe you better not start off on the wrong foot by busting in there when he's not around."

Maggie considered the advice. "You could have a point. Set it on the end of the bar. There's bound to be a plug nearby."

Rory shook his head again. "If I were you, I'd pick a real dark corner."

Maggie laughed. "The bar will do."

He shrugged. "Suit yourself. Hope you don't mind if I go back in the kitchen. I want to be out of the line of fire when he gets back. Can I get you a drink or something before I go?"

"No, thanks. Besides, I worked the bar last night. If I get thirsty, I can fix something."

A look of delight split his round face. "Taking over here, are you? That's the girl. Poor Ryan's head must be spinning."

She grinned at that. "I certainly hope so."

"Well, I'll leave you to it, then. You need any advice from a man who knows him well, you come to me. There's little about Ryan Devaney that I don't know. He's the best friend a man could have. And something tells me if a woman can win his heart, he'll be the best husband, as well. The trick lies in the winning. You won't do it overnight."

"I'll keep that in mind," Maggie said, finding it interesting that Rory's impression so closely mirrored Father Francis's.

While she waited for Ryan to arrive, she set up the computer and printer, then opened her business finance program. She began filling in all the inventory categories she could think of for a pub. Satisfied that she'd hit on most of them, she looked up to find Ryan standing over her, a scowl on his face.

"What's this?" he inquired, as if she'd brought a dangerous foreign object into his pub.

"A free demonstration," she said cheerfully. "Come see."

"I don't have the time. I've a business to run. And I'm getting a late start as it is."

"What I'm suggesting would make it easier," she said.

"Can it serve drinks?"

She frowned at the mocking question. "No, but—"

"Then I'm not interested," he said flatly. He reached for an apron and tied it around his waist, then vanished to the far end of the bar, leaving her to stare after him.

"Don't mind Ryan," Father Francis advised, appearing out of nowhere and sliding onto the stool next to her. "He'll come around. After a childhood that was filled with the unexpected, he works hard to keep things steady and familiar, now that he's grown. It takes him a while to warm up to new people and even longer to listen to new ideas."

"And I'm pushing at the boundaries of his comfort zone," Maggie assessed thoughtfully, considering his reaction from a fresh perspective. "Maybe I should back off."

"Now, why would you be wanting to do such a thing?" Father Francis demanded. "Change is what keeps us all alive. Ryan does too little of it."

"If you're so fond of change, why don't you invite her over to the church to meddle in your business?"

Ryan inquired sourly as he plunked an Irish coffee down in front of the priest. "I imagine you have ancient systems there that could use an overhaul."

"Perhaps I will," Father Francis said readily. "In fact, I think I'll see if we have the budget for it. Would you be interested, Maggie?"

Maggie was more interested in the fact that Ryan's expression turned even darker at the priest's acceptance of his challenge. Still, she turned to Father Francis. "I'd be happy to take a look and see if I have any suggestions," she told him. "The consultation's on the house. After that, we'll see if there's anything I can contribute, and discuss terms."

"Well, isn't that just perfect?" Ryan snapped, retreating to the opposite end of the bar, where he slammed a few mugs around so hard, it was amazing that they didn't shatter.

Maggie sighed. "I'd better talk to him. I owe him an apology for pushing so hard."

"No, child," Father Francis said at once. "He's the one who needs to apologize. Give him a minute. He'll come around on his own. He knows when he's being unreasonable, and he's generally honest enough to admit it."

Maggie sat back down, but the wait seemed interminable. Finally, though, Ryan approached the two of them with a look of remorse on his face. "Okay, I was out of line." He frowned at the priest. "But you were deliberately pushing my buttons, and you know it."

"Do I now?" Father Francis said, his expression innocent.

"Of course you do. You take great pleasure in it,

which makes me wonder why I put up with you." He turned to Maggie. "As for you, I truly am sorry. I know you were trying to be helpful. It's just that I don't need that kind of help. I've been running this place for a while now. I know how to do it. It might not be the most efficient operation, but it works for me."

"And there couldn't possibly be a better way?" she challenged.

He grinned. "There could be, but I'm satisfied with things as they are. When I'm not, I'll let you know."

Maggie knew a brick wall when she slammed into one. "I'll be waiting to hear from you."

"When it comes to this particular topic, you could be in for a long wait," he warned.

"I have the time," she told him.

"And why is that? Shouldn't you be starting that search for a new job?"

"Not just yet. I'm taking the next few weeks to think things through and decide what I want to do. I have an MBA that's going to waste."

He frowned. "Just so you don't get it into your head that this is the place to put it to use," he said. "You're overqualified."

"Okay, okay, I get it. I'll back off," she said, then murmured under her breath, "for now."

He scowled. "I heard that."

Maggie beamed at him. "Just a fair warning," she said cheerfully as she slid off her bar stool.

"You leaving?" he asked.

She grinned at the faint disappointment in his tone. "You should be so lucky. Actually, I'm getting an apron. In case you haven't noticed, the place is packed, and Maureen and Juan have their hands full again."

Ryan shook his head. "A lot of people think a vacation is best spent on a beach in the Caribbean this time of year, not waiting tables in a pub."

"I'm not one of them," she said, grabbing an order pad and heading for a table of couples across the room.

"Bless you," Maureen said as she passed Maggie. "I don't know where everyone came from tonight, but they're all tired and cranky and starving."

"More holiday shopping," Maggie suggested. "And it's only going to get worse when desperation sets in."

"Now there's a cheerful prospect," Maureen said, lifting her gaze heavenward. "Saints protect us from the truly desperate."

Maggie took orders from the three couples, along with a request for the band that was just setting up. She left that and a tip with the lead guitarist, then took the dinner order in to Rory.

The cook beamed when he saw her. "You're still in one piece, I see. Tell me, did you win Ryan over to your way of thinking?"

"Hardly. The man's head is like a rock."

"Aye, that it is. I've been wanting to experiment a bit with the menu, but all of my pleas have fallen on deaf ears," he said, sounding resigned.

"Speaking of changes to the menu, where's Rosita and her recipe for enchiladas?" Maggie asked.

"I sent her home," Rory said.

Maggie regarded him indignantly. "Just like that? She needs the job."

He frowned at her. "Did I say anything about firing her? Her ankles were swelling. And don't you be telling Ryan, either. There's no need for him to dock her pay. As you said yourself, she needs every bit of it to prepare for the baby."

Relieved, Maggie grinned at him. "Why, Rory, I believe the reports of your temper have been greatly exaggerated. You're a softie."

"Only when it comes to mothers-to-be, so don't be getting any ideas about testing my patience," he said. "I expect the waitstaff around here to deliver my meals to the tables while they're still hot. Maureen's order's ready. You can take it."

"Yes, sir," she said, loading her tray with the steaming plates and heading for the door.

For the rest of the evening, there was little time for idle chitchat with anyone. As she rushed from table to table, Maggie felt Ryan's steady gaze following her. Just before midnight he nabbed her arm and dragged her to a stool at the end of the bar.

"Sit. Maureen and Juan can handle things from here on out. Have you eaten a bite all evening?" he asked.

"No time," she said, sighing as she kicked off her shoes.

He uttered a sound of disgust and headed for the kitchen. He came back with a plump ham and cheese sandwich and a bowl of Rory's thick potato soup.

"I can't eat at this hour," she protested.

"You can and you will," he said. "I will not be responsible for sending you home half-starved. I won't risk Nell and Garrett's wrath coming down on my head."

Maggie grinned at him. "I'm a grown woman. I take responsibility for my own actions."

"Do they know that? Aren't these the very same parents who worry frantically if you're so much as a few minutes late? Didn't you tell me that yourself on the first night you came through my doors?"

"At least there's one thing I've said that you listened to," Maggie retorted.

"I hear every word out of your mouth," Ryan countered. "I just pick and choose what to ignore." He gestured toward the untouched sandwich. "Now when you've eaten that, I'll drive you home."

"I have my car."

"Then I'll follow you home. It's too late for you to be driving around the streets of Boston all alone. And yes, I know you're a grown woman, but you're not a foolish one. You'll accept my offer and be gracious about it. Otherwise, I'll be the one worrying through the night."

She met his gaze. "Really? You would worry if I drove home alone?"

He sighed heavily. "Yes, really."

Pleased, she relented. "Then you may follow me home, if you agree to come in for coffee when we get there. Deal?" She held out her hand.

Ryan regarded her steadily, reluctance written all over his face. Eventually, though, he clasped her hand in his. "Deal."

It was such a silly, simple agreement, but Maggie felt as if they'd taken a giant leap forward. Now all that remained was to see how many steps backward would follow.

7

Ryan approached the O'Brien house filled with trepidation. He'd expected to find most of the lights off and the family in bed, but instead it looked as if there were a party going on. He said as much when he joined Maggie in the driveway.

"I probably shouldn't intrude," he told her. "It looks as if your parents are entertaining."

"Nonsense," she said, slipping her arm through his. "I imagine some of the family dropped by and they got to playing cards or something. You'll be welcome. Besides, we had a deal. You can't back out now."

It had been a stupid deal. He'd known that when he made it. He should never have agreed to come inside this house where there was so much warmth. It made him yearn for things he'd never had.

He dreaded the prospect of going inside and getting caught up in the kind of teasing camaraderie he'd witnessed when the family had helped out at the homeless shelter. That kind of situation always made him uncomfortable. It caused him to feel more alone, more like an outsider than ever.

He sighed and looked down to find Maggie regarding him with sympathy.

"It will be okay," she reassured him.

"I'll stay long enough for a cup of coffee. That's it," he said. "That was the deal."

"That was the deal," she agreed, leading the way to the kitchen door.

Inside—to his surprise, given the late hour—they found bedlam. Six people were sitting around the kitchen table, poker chips piled in front of them, making enough noise for twenty.

"You cheated," Katie accused her father, barely sparing a glance for Maggie and Ryan as they walked in.

"He most certainly did," one of Maggie's brothers agreed.

Garrett O'Brien rose to his feet, practically quivering with indignation. "The day my own children accuse me of cheating is a sad day, indeed."

"Oh, sit down," Nell ordered. "You did cheat. I saw you myself."

Garrett—most of the fight drained out of him—turned to Ryan for support. "Can you imagine a man's own wife saying such a thing?"

Ryan grinned, his nervousness dissipating. He could imagine Nell O'Brien saying whatever she wanted to whomever she wanted and expecting to be taken seriously. "Well now, I imagine she's a woman who always speaks her mind," he said cautiously, not sure exactly how welcome his opinion might be.

"And always truthfully," Katie added. "Pull up a chair, Ryan. These guys are just about tapped out. We need deep pockets to join the game."

Ryan felt Maggie's gaze on him.

"Are you willing?" she asked. "Can you stay for a bit?"

Ryan weighed his reluctance against the prospect of a few good poker hands. "I can stay."

"Bring the chairs from the dining room, then," Garrett said. "We'll push over to make room. Maggie, get the man a beer."

"Coffee would be better," Ryan said. "I have to drive back into Boston after this."

"Nonsense," Nell said. "Not when there's a perfectly good guest room that's unoccupied tonight."

"We'll debate that when the time comes," Ryan said, refusing to commit to staying under this roof, especially with the tempting Maggie just down the hall.

Maggie set his coffee in front of him, then slipped onto her own chair right next to him and leaned closer to whisper, "That's the last act of kindness you can expect from me. When it comes to poker, I play a take-no-prisoners game."

"Listen to her," her brother Matt said. "Our Maggie liked to stay up and play with Dad's cronies as she was growing up. Dad allowed it because she split her winnings with him."

Ryan laughed, regarding Maggie with new respect. "Well, we'll just have to wait and see if you've lost your edge, now won't we?"

"Trust me, there are some things a woman never

forgets," she retorted, dealing the cards with quick, professional efficiency.

Ryan drew a scowl from Maggie and hoots from her family when he won the first hand. When it was his turn to deal, he made an elaborate show of allowing her to cut the cards. "For luck," he declared.

"Thank you," she replied, though there was an edge to her polite tone.

"I believe you misunderstood," he said as he dealt. "The lucky cut was for my benefit."

"Oh, my, he's a smug one," Garrett remarked happily.

"With good cause, I'd say," Katie said when she threw in her hand.

Nell, John and Matt followed suit, as did John's wife. Garrett added his cards to the pile with a muffled curse.

Ryan leveled a look into Maggie's eyes. "It looks as if it's just you and me."

Her gaze never wavered. "I'll see your bet and raise you a dollar."

"Uh-oh, our Maggie has that glint in her eyes," Matt said. "Watch yourself, Ryan."

Ryan was already all too aware of the dangers he faced anytime he was around Maggie. This card game was just the tip of the iceberg. "I'll see your raise and call you," he said, watching her expectantly.

"You're absolutely sure you want to do that?" she asked. "There's still time to take it back."

He nodded. "My bet's on the table."

"Okay, then." She fanned her cards out on the table. She had a full house, jacks high.

"Very nice," Ryan complimented her.

She smiled and reached for the pot. "I thought so."

He placed his hand on top of hers. "Just not nice enough." His own full house had kings high.

Maggie frowned as he scooped up the money.

Ryan leaned in close and whispered in her ear, "Don't pout. I told you luck was going to be with me."

Matt winced. "Oh, brother. You've really done it now, Ryan. You've won and, worse, you've gloated about it. She's going to be out for blood."

Maggie gave them all a serene smile. "I am, indeed."

Ryan thought they were joking, but to his amazement Maggie took the next four hands in a row. He regarded her with amusement. "Feeling better now?"

"Much," she said, a satisfied gleam in her eyes.

"Why do I have the feeling this game has gotten personal?" Katie inquired. "I think I'll just slip off to bed while I still have two cents to my name."

"And I have to be getting home before my wife disowns me," Matt chimed in.

John exchanged a look with his wife. "I guess we're out of here, too."

Within ten minutes, the entire room had been cleared. In the silence that followed, Ryan stared at Maggie.

"That was fun," he said.

She seemed surprised. "Even though you lost?"

"Only because I lost to you. You take the game so seriously. Next time, though, I'll know what to watch for. You won't be so lucky."

"What does that mean?"

"It means when you're bluffing, you get this little nervous tic by the corner of your eye. Right about here," he said, touching a finger lightly to her cheek. "And this corner of your mouth starts to tilt up into a smile, but you fight it." He skimmed a caress along her bottom lip to emphasize the point.

Maggie swallowed hard. "Ryan, what are you doing?"

"Just explaining how you give yourself away. I'm surprised the others haven't noticed. Then again, I doubt any of them are as fascinated with your face as I am."

The pulse at the base of her neck jumped. "Ryan..." Her voice trailed off.

He leaned forward and covered her mouth with his. He'd been wanting to do that from the moment they'd started to play, had been so obsessed with the idea, in fact, that he'd lost his concentration in the third hand. That was why she'd won so many rounds. His mind hadn't been on the cards at all.

"You taste so good," he whispered against her lips. "And you smell like flowers."

"Roses," she said, sounding breathless. "My favorite perfume."

Shaken by the emotions racing through him, he sat back, sucked in a ragged breath and raked his hand through his hair. "I need to get out of here."

"Mom invited you to stay."

"She wouldn't have, if she'd known what was on my mind," he said.

Maggie's eyes sparkled with curiosity. "Exactly what *is* on your mind?"

"You," he said, opting for total honesty. Maybe that would scare her into being wary around him. "Getting you out of those clothes so I can touch you. Making love to you for the rest of the night."

"Oh, my," she whispered.

He stood up. "Which is why I need to get out of here now."

"No, don't. Stay," she pleaded.

"That's a really bad idea," he said, reaching for his coat.

He leaned down and kissed her one last time. "Good night, Maggie."

"Good night," she said with obvious reluctance. She stood up and walked with him to the door. "Will you call me when you get home?"

"And wake the household? I don't think so."

"I'll worry if you don't."

He stopped and stared. She'd sounded totally sincere. "You can't be serious," he said, struggling with the unfamiliar sensation her words stirred in him.

"Well, of course I will. It's late. Who knows what could happen on the road at this hour? I'll keep the phone right beside me in the bed. I'll pick up on the first ring. No one else will be disturbed."

It was the first time in decades that anyone had expressed the slightest concern over his whereabouts or his safety. Ryan expected to rebel against it, but instead her plea made him feel warm deep inside. "Okay then, I'll call," he said eventually.

She reached up and touched his cheek. "You're not used to anyone worrying about you, are you?"

"No."

"Well, that's about to change. I'm an O'Brien and we worry about everything," she said lightly.

"Then it's nothing personal?" he said, hiding his disappointment.

"Oh, in your case, it's very personal. I just don't want you freaking out about it."

"I don't freak out."

"Of course you do," she teased. "But that's okay. I understand. You'll get used to me and the others in time."

In time? Ryan wondered about that on the drive back into Boston. Would he ever get used to having someone care what happened to him? Or had his past destroyed any chance of that?

"Who called in the wee hours of the night, or was it morning?" Katie inquired sleepily as the family sat around the breakfast table before church.

"My money's on Ryan," Nell said. Her gaze came to rest on Maggie. "Am I right?"

"I asked him to let me know he made it home safely," she said.

"You couldn't persuade him to stay here?" her mother asked.

"He didn't think it was a good idea," Maggie said.

"Probably afraid we'd catch him sneaking into Maggie's room," Katie said.

"Mary Kathryn O'Brien, watch your tongue," their father scolded. "I don't like to hear such talk from my very own daughter."

Katie refused to be daunted. "Only because you're terrified it could be true and it would ruin forever your image of us as your darling girls, rather than grown-up women."

"That's true enough," he said easily. "And what is wrong with a man thinking his girls behave as angels, at least until the very day they say their wedding vows?"

"Nothing," Nell soothed. "As long as he's prepared to admit he's been wrong. Now let's drop this before we end up in an argument before mass. Maggie, are you coming with us this morning?"

"I was thinking of going to a mass at St. Mary's," she admitted.

"You think you'll be bumping into Ryan there?" her mother asked.

"I can always hope," Maggie admitted candidly.

"Well, if you do, bring him back with you for Sunday dinner."

"It takes a brave man to face this crowd two days running. I doubt I'll have much luck convincing him, but assuming I see him, I'll try."

Unfortunately, she didn't get the chance. There was no sign of him at the church, but when she ran into Father Francis after mass, he was happy to tell her that Ryan could be found at the shelter. "He likes to spend some time with the children on Sunday morning. I imagine you'll find him with Lamar Monroe this morning."

"Lamar? He hasn't mentioned that name," Maggie said.

"He's a lad Ryan's taken an interest in. He's having surgery later this week."

"I see," Maggie said, sensing there was far more to

the story than Father Francis was sharing. Whatever it was, though, it was also clear she'd have to pry it out of Ryan himself.

She found him, as predicted, sitting on the edge of a cot with a young boy crowded next to him, the boy's fascinated gaze locked on the book Ryan held. Maggie remained in the shadows watching the two of them as Ryan read the story in a voice filled with so much animation that he had the child laughing.

"He's a wonder with my boy," a woman said quietly as she joined Maggie. "I'm Letitia Monroe."

"Maggie O'Brien."

"You're a friend of Ryan's?"

Maggie wondered if she could legitimately make that claim. She asked herself if a few kisses added up to friendship, when it was evident that there was so much about Ryan Devaney that she didn't know.

"I'm hoping to be," she said finally.

Letitia Monroe grinned. "So, that's the way of it, is it? The man is playing hard to get?"

"Try impossible," Maggie said fervently.

"You know what they say about anything worth having," Mrs. Monroe reminded her.

"That it's worth waiting for."

"That's right."

Watching as Ryan coaxed yet another chuckle from the obviously ill boy, Maggie realized with a sudden burst of insight that she would willingly wait for as long as it took.

He looked up then and spotted her. "Hey, Maggie," he said, then turned and said something in an undertone to Lamar that had the boy grinning. Ryan patted a spot next to him. "Come join us. I have to finish reading this story. I can't leave Lamar in suspense."

"Maybe she should do the girl's part," Lamar said. "You sound kind of funny doing it."

"Hey," Ryan protested, "is that any way to treat a man who has humiliated himself to keep you entertained?"

Maggie sat down and reached for the book. "Allow me," she said with a wink at Lamar. She finished reading the last few pages, then sighed as she read, "The end."

"You were real good," Lamar said, approval shining in his eyes.

"Better than me?" Ryan demanded.

Maggie rolled her eyes at the question, causing Lamar to giggle. "Tell him he was better or he'll be grumbling all day," Maggie advised him.

"Mr. Devaney, you were the best," Lamar said dutifully. "Thanks again."

"Anytime, kid. I'll see you before you go to the hospital, okay?"

"Okay," Lamar said, his smile fading. He regarded Ryan fearfully. "You think you're gonna be able to find my dad by then?"

"I'm working on it," Ryan assured him. "I'm going to do everything in my power to make sure he's here with you and your mom before then."

"Thanks. It'll be okay if you don't find him, though. I'm not too scared. And my mom and me will be okay, long as we have each other."

Maggie had to bite her lip to keep from crying at the boy's obvious attempt to appear brave.

"I know that," Ryan told him. "But I'll try hard, just the same." He looked at Maggie. "You ready?"

"Sure." Impulsively, she bent down and gave Lamar a kiss. "You take care of yourself."

"I will. Come back sometime, okay? I wouldn't mind hearing you read another story. My mom doesn't always have the time, and listening is even better than reading to myself."

"I will. I promise."

Outside, Maggie drew in a deep breath. "How risky is this surgery of his?"

"It's heart surgery, so there's bound to be some risk," Ryan said, his expression grim. "It'll go a lot better, though, if he's feeling optimistic."

"Which is why you're trying to track down his dad," she guessed.

Ryan nodded. "He took off when he found out about the surgery. Since he quit his job, that cut off their insurance and their income. That's how they ended up at the shelter."

"Father Francis turns to you a lot in cases like this, doesn't he?"

"He knows I'll do what I can."

"Does it make up for what happened to you?" she asked.

He frowned at the question. "What are you really asking?"

"I notice you're eager to help Lamar find his dad. Have you ever looked for your own?"

She could see the tension in his face as his jaw tightened. "Why the hell would I want to?" he asked heatedly.

"For the same reason you're trying to find Lamar's father for him—because your dad broke your heart when he abandoned you."

Ryan shrugged, clearly refusing to concede the obvious. "I got over it."

"Did you?"

"Yes," he said emphatically, his scowl deepening. "And I don't talk about that time in my life. Not ever."

"Maybe you should."

"And maybe you should mind your own damned business!"

He left her on the sidewalk staring after him, stunned by the force of his anger.

"Well, hell," she muttered, swiping at the tears spilling down her cheeks.

She was still standing in the exact same spot, debating whether to go after him, when Ryan reappeared at the corner. She watched as he sucked in his breath, squared his shoulders and walked toward her.

"I'm sorry," he said. "I shouldn't have bitten your head off like that."

"No," she agreed, "you shouldn't have, even though I understand why you did."

"My family's a sore subject."

"I gathered that."

"Then you won't bring them up again, right?"

She met his gaze evenly and shook her head. "I can't promise that, not when it's so apparent that what happened with them shaped your whole life."

He regarded her with obvious exasperation. "Dammit, Maggie, what do you want from me? You come busting into my life and act as if I'm suddenly your personal mission."

"Maybe that's exactly what you are," she said. "There has to be some reason why I keep coming back to see a man as cranky and ill-tempered as you are."

His lips twitched slightly. "You have a thing for cranky, ill-tempered men?"

"Apparently so," she said with a deliberate air of resignation.

His lips curved into a full-fledged grin then. "Lucky me."

She grinned back at him. "Try to remember that."

"Oh, I imagine you're going to give me plenty of occasions to question it," he said.

She nodded. "It is my mission, remember?"

"Maggie—"

She touched a finger to his lips to silence him. "Just accept it. I'm here to stay."

"But why?" he asked, obviously bewildered.

"It's that cranky, ill-tempered-man thing," she reminded him. "I'm a sucker for a challenge." She hooked her hand around his neck and drew his head down till she could kiss him. "It doesn't hurt that you're a great kisser." She winked at him. "Gotta get home. You're invited for Sunday dinner, by the way. Mom insisted."

He shook his head. "Not today."

"Better things to do?" she asked, not surprised by the refusal and determined not to push for once.

"Nope. Safer things to do," he told her.

Maggie laughed. "See you, then."

She was halfway to her car, rather pleased with

herself despite his refusal to come to dinner, when he called after her.

"Hey, Maggie!"

She turned back, regarding him with a questioning look.

"Drive carefully."

"Always do."

"And call me when you get home, okay?"

Well, well, well, the man was learning, she thought. "Will do," she promised.

She noticed he was still standing on the sidewalk, watching her car when she finally turned the corner and drove out of sight. He looked so lonely, she almost went around the block and demanded that he come with her. She could have persuaded him if she'd really tried.

"One step at a time," she murmured to herself. Right now they were frustrating baby steps, two forward, half a dozen back, but after this morning she had a feeling a giant leap forward was just around the corner.

8

For the next few days Maggie was careful not to push too hard. She didn't want to risk the progress she'd made so far. That didn't keep her away from Ryan's Place, though. She turned up most nights, always finding some way to make herself useful. One of these days Ryan would discover he couldn't get along without her.

At the same time, she cleverly avoided any further mention of his accounting system. There was no sense in antagonizing him when they were making such nice advances in other areas. Sooner or later he'd trust her enough to listen to her financial advice. She didn't stop to question why she was so determined to make herself indispensable to a small business when she ought to be out looking for a big corporate position that would make use of her MBA.

In the meantime, there were the books at St. Mary's to be straightened out. Father Francis had none of Ryan's reticence when it came to utilizing Maggie's expertise. In fact, he seemed delighted to have someone take over the task of sorting through the chaotic system the church had been using for decades.

As for the shelter, it had no system at all. If there was a need, donations were found to help. Money came and went in a haphazard manner that would have set an IRS agent's teeth on edge. Maggie didn't doubt for a second that not one cent was spent on anything other than legitimate expenses, but there were few records to prove it.

She stared helplessly at the pile of unorganized receipts that had been crammed into a drawer. "What were you thinking?" she asked Father Francis. "Do you have any idea what kind of dangerous path you've been following? If there was ever an audit…" She shuddered just contemplating it.

"It's a bit of a tangle, isn't it?" Father Francis admitted, seemingly not the least big chagrined. "But I don't see the need for a lot of fuss. We've more important things to do. If the money's there, we spend it on those who need our assistance. If it's not, we go out and find what we need. Why complicate things?"

Maggie groaned at his logic. "Have you even filed for nonprofit status?"

"It's an outreach of the church," he said, as if that settled the matter.

"But none of the shelter's funds or activities are on the church's books."

He refused to see the point, clearly trusting that the shelter's mission and good intentions would exempt it from scrutiny.

Maggie tried again. "You might increase the level of giving if people could claim a tax deduction. Instead, you're relying on special collections at the church. Why not reach out to the entire community? Why not build up a solid bank account so there are funds available for an emergency? If you'd had such a fund, you wouldn't have had to turn to Ryan to help with Lamar's surgery. And Ryan could have claimed that money as a deduction on his taxes."

"Ryan doesn't help for the rewards," the priest insisted, his expression set stubbornly.

"I know that," Maggie said, totally exasperated. "But it could be a win-win situation."

"Is that an improvement over an unselfish act of kindness?" the priest asked reasonably.

Maggie sighed. How could she argue with the logic of that? "You won't even consider letting me set up a system?" she asked, then sighed again when he shook his head. "You're turning out to be as impossible as Ryan."

That, apparently, was an accusation he couldn't ignore. Father Francis's sigh was just as deep as Maggie's. "You really think it's important?"

"I do."

"Who's going to take care of all the record keeping it will entail?"

"I will."

For the first time since they'd begun, he beamed. "Well then, if you're promising to take charge, go ahead. The shelter can always use a volunteer." He gave her one of those canny looks that she'd come to consider suspect. "Perhaps you'd like to help a few of the children with their math, while you're here. The math tutor we had recently moved away."

"I didn't offer—" she began, but the priest cut off her protest.

"I know you didn't offer," he conceded. "I'm asking. Your help would be a blessing for the children."

Maggie shook her head at his clever manipulation. "No wonder the shelter hasn't needed a formal fund-raising drive. I'll bet you could single-handedly squeeze money out of Scrooge."

"Actually, it's the Lord who provides," he said with pious innocence. "I just give a gentle nudge here and there to point the way. Will you help the children?"

"When?" Maggie asked, resigned.

"I find after school on Tuesday is good for tutoring. Many of their tests are later in the week. And they haven't yet grown bored with studying, as they have by Thursday or Friday."

"Fine. I'll be here on Tuesdays. I'll come early and work on the books."

He feigned a troubled expression. "That won't interfere with your work, will it? I wouldn't want to interfere with your need to earn a living."

"I'm not working now, as you perfectly well know. Once I do find a job, we'll make whatever adjustments we must."

"You're a good girl, Maggie O'Brien."

"Or an idiot," she murmured.

He grinned at her. "Never that. You've had the good sense to fall in love with Ryan Devaney, haven't you?"

She regarded him with dismay. "Nobody said anything about me falling in love with Ryan."

"Nobody had to. The look is shining in your eyes whenever you're in the same room."

"If that's the case, no wonder he panics when he sees me coming," she said, no longer making any attempt to deny the obvious. She'd fought against putting a label on her feelings, more for Ryan's sake than her own. Maybe it was time she admitted that fascination had turned to something deeper.

The priest patted her hand. "The panic will wear off in time. Ryan's no more a fool than you are. He'll see what's staring him in the face eventually."

"From your lips to God's ear," Maggie said fervently.

Father Francis regarded her serenely. "Aye, child, that's the way of it."

Ryan was beginning to get used to having Maggie turn up at the pub every evening just before suppertime. Sometimes she sat at the bar, blatantly flirting with him. Sometimes she huddled in a booth with Father Francis, scolding him about the church's accounting methods and casting surreptitious glances Ryan's way. And increasingly, whenever it was especially busy, she grabbed an apron off the hook in the kitchen and waited on tables, refusing to accept anything more than whatever tips were left by the customers. Rory and Maureen considered her part of the staff. Juan and Rosita thought she was an angel. As for him, he was still struggling with what to make of her.

"Are you independently wealthy?" Ryan inquired one night a week before Christmas, when she'd turned down his offer of money yet again.

"Hardly, but I have some savings. Besides, this isn't a job," she insisted once again. "I have time on my hands right now, anyway. I enjoy being here. Your customers are the friendliest people I've ever met. And as long as I am here, I may as well pitch in. It's obvious you can use the help."

"I can't deny that," he said.

She looked into his eyes in an expectant way that had his knees going weak and the rest of him going hard.

"If you were to steal a kiss from time to time, it would go a long way toward making it worth my while to be here," she taunted.

The woman could tempt a saint, he thought as she held his gaze. Unable to resist, Ryan tucked an arm around her waist and dragged her close. "Now, that is something I can do," he said, covering her mouth long enough to send a shudder rippling through them both.

It was a risky game they were playing, though. He wanted so much more. His yearning for her had deepened each day, until every minute was a struggle not to haul her up to his apartment.

He'd vowed, though, that he wouldn't let her tempt him into making a mistake they'd both regret. No matter how she got under his skin, he was going to be the sensible one and keep his hands to himself. Still, he couldn't help wondering what it would be like to strip away those thick, soft sweaters she wore, to peel away her skintight jeans and the lacy panties he fantasized about, and bury himself deep inside her. He hadn't wanted to experience that kind of closeness with a woman—real intimacy that went beyond sex—in a long time, if ever.

Instead, he settled for the occasional kiss, deliberately keeping them brief enough to permit him to cling to sanity. For once in his life, he was trying to do the right thing.

Not that Maggie did anything to help. She had absolutely no reservations about using her own hands to torment him. She was always skimming a caress across his knuckles, patting his cheek and on one especially memorable occasion, linking her fingers through his and pressing an impulsive kiss on their joined hands, while gazing deeply into his eyes in a way that had him losing track of everything, including his own name. Oh, yes, Miss Maggie was a toucher, and it was driving him flat-out crazy.

Father Francis clearly found the whole situation highly amusing. Whenever he thought Ryan might not be tormented enough, he drew Ryan's attention back to Maggie with one observation or another meant to remind him of just how desirable she was. The priest had turned into a determined matchmaker, who had absolutely no shame about the methods he used. Rory was just as bad. And even Maggie's family seemed to have bestowed their approval on the match, turning up singly or a few at a time to sit at the bar or in a booth. They seemed to have adopted Ryan as one of them without waiting for the link between him and Maggie to be formalized.

With so many people giving their blessing, Ryan might even have been tempted to get involved in a fling with Maggie-of-the-roving-hands...if she'd been another kind of woman. But Maggie was all about happily-ever-after. One look at her family was evidence enough of that.

Unfortunately, Ryan knew better than anyone that

there was no such thing. Someday a man would let her down and she'd know the truth, but it wasn't going to be him.

Besides, he couldn't help thinking that she'd adopted him as she might a bedraggled kitten she pitied. One day she'd tire of him and move along to a man whose heart wasn't cast in stone. Since abandonment had been a sore subject with him for some years now, he didn't intend to risk it a second time.

None of that kept him from his yearning, though. Right now, she was across the room, chatting with a customer, her auburn hair flowing to her shoulders in shiny waves, her face devoid of any makeup beyond a touch of pale lipstick, and beautiful just the same. Ryan stared at her and barely managed to contain a sigh.

"You wouldn't be so frustrated, lad, if you'd make a move on the lady," Rory observed.

"You've hit on the problem," Ryan responded, his gaze not shifting away from Maggie. "She's a *lady*."

"But I think you'd find her more than willing."

Ryan didn't doubt it. In fact, there were so many signals and unspoken invitations sizzling in the air, it was a wonder half his customers didn't wind up singed. "That's not the point," he said testily.

"There won't be any rewards for saintliness in this instance," Rory said.

"I'm not looking for rewards. I'm trying to be sensible. I have nothing to offer a woman like Maggie."

"She seems to think otherwise."

"Because she doesn't know me that well," Ryan said. She didn't know that he had no heart, no love at all to give. Quite likely, even with what she did know, she'd dismissed the possibility that he would never allow himself to fall in love, would never marry and risk disappointing a family as his parents had disappointed him. She was deluding herself, because she wanted to believe the best of him.

"Again, I say she thinks otherwise," Rory said. "She seems to know all she needs to."

"Then it's up to me to protect her from herself."

"She won't thank you. Women seldom appreciate a man doing their thinking for them."

Ryan gave him a rueful look. "It's not her thanks I'm after. A man protects a woman he cares about because it's the right thing to do."

"We're back to that bloody try for sainthood again," Rory chided. "You're a mere mortal, Ryan. Why not act like one?"

"Is that what you do? Is that why any woman who crosses the threshold in here is fair game to you?"

"Whatever happens between me and any woman is a mutual decision," Rory countered. "That's because I think of them as equals and respect that they know their own minds. Perhaps you should give Maggie some credit for knowing hers."

There was sense to what Rory said. Ryan could admit that, but he couldn't dwell on it. If he did, the game would be lost. He and Maggie would have their momentary pleasure, but the regrets would pour in on its heels.

No, his way was better…even if he was having the devil's own time remembering why.

* * *

Lamar's surgery was scheduled for Friday morning. As of midnight on Thursday, Jack Reilly had had absolutely no luck in finding the boy's father. Ryan decided he was going to have to take matters into his own hands. If there was even a chance that Monroe was anywhere around the Boston harbor, he was going to find him before that boy went into the operating room in the morning.

"You can't be serious," Jack said when Ryan asked him to describe every single place he'd already searched. "If I haven't found him, he's not there."

"I refuse to accept that," Ryan said, aware that Maggie had joined them and was blatantly eavesdropping. "Now, are you going to tell me and save me some time, or do I have to spend the entire night covering ground you've already covered?"

Jack sighed. "Never mind. I'll come with you. Maybe we'll get lucky."

"I'm coming, too," Maggie announced, running to grab her coat and purse.

Ryan stopped her in her tracks, frowning at her. "It's late. You have no business wandering around down there at this hour."

"You're going, aren't you?" She scowled right back at him. "And if you point out that you're a man, I'm going to have to dump a pitcher of ale over your head." She was already reaching for it to emphasize the point.

"Maggie," Ryan protested, then sighed in the face of her determined expression and her firm grip on the pitcher. "Okay then, let's go. We don't have the time to waste arguing."

"Such a gracious capitulation," she noted as she set the pitcher back on the bar and swept past him.

Jack gave him a pitying look. "She's a woman with a mind of her own, isn't she?"

"Tell me about it," Ryan said dryly.

Together, the three of them combed the bars along the waterfront. They spoke to fishermen and dock-workers as they began to arrive for work in the pre-dawn hours. When people seemed reluctant to talk to them, Maggie stepped in and charmed them into opening up. Despite her best efforts, though, no one recalled a man fitting Jamal Monroe's description.

"Dammit, that boy cannot go into surgery thinking that his own father doesn't care enough to be there," Ryan said when they'd retreated to a small, crowded café filled with the raucous banter of men who spent their lives on the water. He cupped his hands around a mug of strong coffee, grateful for the warmth after being out for hours in the damp, cold air.

"We're going to make sure that doesn't happen," Maggie soothed with unwavering confidence.

Suddenly a shadow fell over the table. Ryan glanced up into chocolate-brown eyes that glinted with anger and suspicion. The man was dressed warmly, in worn yet clean clothes, but he was too thin. And undeniable exhaustion and strain were evident on his dark face.

"I hear you've been asking a lot of questions about Jamal Monroe," he said. "Why?"

Ryan suspected that this was Lamar's father, though the man hadn't admitted it outright. He gestured to-ward the fourth chair at their table. "Join us. How about a cup of coffee and some breakfast?"

The man hesitated, but the lure of the hot drink and food apparently won him over. With a respectful nod toward Maggie, he sat down, though he kept his jacket on as if he wanted to be ready to take off at once if the need arose.

Ryan didn't say anything until the waitress had brought coffee and taken the man's order. Then he looked him directly in the eye. "We've been bumping up against a brick wall for hours now. I don't suppose you have any idea how we can find Monroe?"

"Could be," the man said cautiously. "But you still haven't said why you're so anxious to find him. You friends of his?"

"No, we've never met," Ryan admitted, keeping his gaze locked on the man's face. "It's about his son, Lamar."

There was a definite flicker of recognition, maybe even something else. Fear, perhaps.

"You know his boy?" the man asked.

Ryan nodded. "And his wife. They've been staying at the St. Mary's homeless shelter."

This time there was no mistaking the reaction. "Why are they there?" he asked with more emotion in his voice. "They had a halfway decent apartment when I—" He looked flustered at the telling slip and hurriedly corrected it. "When *he* left."

At Ryan's nod, it was Maggie who continued, her tone gentle. "They needed help. Without Mr. Monroe at home, they couldn't make it. And Lamar needs surgery, but once Mr. Monroe quit his job, their insurance was cut off."

The man's shoulders slumped, and his eyes filled

with tears. "Damn, I never meant it to come to that," he said, his voice thick. "I thought I'd be back in time to make things right. I just needed some time away to think."

Ryan and Jack exchanged a look.

"Then you are Jamal," Ryan said gently.

He nodded. "Even if I am a sorry excuse for a husband and a father, I love those two."

"Then why did you take off?" Ryan asked, barely managing to keep an accusatory note out of his voice.

"If you know about the surgery, then you probably know Lamar's medical condition is hereditary. He got it from me," Jamal said, his tone filled with guilt.

"Through no fault of your own," Maggie insisted fiercely, resting her hand on his. "You didn't know you had the problem, so how could you know you could pass it along to your son? Nobody is blaming you."

"I blame myself," Jamal said heatedly, " 'cause the honest truth is, I did know. Soon as that doctor started talking, I remembered the problems I had when I was a kid."

"You had a heart problem that required surgery?" Ryan asked, stunned.

Jamal nodded. "I was younger than Lamar is now, and I spent a lot of time in the hospital. My folks never explained much about what was going on, and I was too little to understand if they had. I wasn't even in school yet, so I must have been three, maybe four years old. Once I had the surgery, I could do anything I wanted. Didn't take me long to put all of the bad times out of my head. Years go by, and it's like it happened to some other person, if you remember at all. Never crossed my mind that I could pass it along to a child of mine."

"That's perfectly normal," Maggie reassured him, shooting a warning look at Ryan. "People don't always consider all the genetic ramifications before having kids. They fall in love, get married and start a family. Unless they've had to confront a congenital illness all their lives, it's the last thing on their minds. Letitia doesn't blame you for Lamar being sick. Lamar certainly doesn't blame you. If they don't, how can you go on blaming yourself? And it's time to forgive yourself, too, for being human and running out. The important thing is to be there for Lamar now."

Jamal shook his head. "Letitia's bound to be fit to be tied. That woman has a temper when she's riled, and she has every right to be furious with me. She probably won't let me anywhere near the boy."

"You're wrong," Ryan said. "The only thing on her mind now is what's best for Lamar, and he needs to see his daddy before he goes into surgery."

Jamal seemed startled. "Thought you said he couldn't have it, because they lost their insurance."

Ryan carefully avoided Maggie's gaze. "The shelter was able to help," he explained. "The surgery's this morning. If you're willing, we can take you to see him. I know if I were a father, there's nowhere else I'd be today."

Maggie gave Jamal's hand a squeeze. "Please. Lamar needs you. He's scared. Having you there will go a long way toward reassuring him that everything's going to turn out all right, especially once you tell him that you had the same surgery a long time ago."

Jamal seemed to struggle with himself, but he finally nodded and pushed back from the table. "Take me to see my boy."

Ryan paid the check and led the way back to the car. It was still early enough that they didn't get tangled up in rush hour as they made their way to the children's hospital where Lamar's surgery was scheduled for eight o'clock. He pulled up at the front entrance.

"Maggie, why don't you take him to Lamar's room while I park the car? I'll be up in a few minutes."

She regarded him with a penetrating look. "You are coming in, though, aren't you? Lamar will want to see you, too."

"I'll be there," he said, overcoming his reluctance to give her the answer she was all but demanding.

She bent down to whisper in his ear. "Five minutes, Devaney. If you're not there, I'm going to come looking for you."

Ryan didn't doubt for a second that she would do just that. "I gave you my word," he said.

"And promises mean as much to you as they do to me?" she asked.

He gazed into her eyes. "I don't make them unless I mean to keep them. If anyone knows the devastation of broken promises, it's me."

She rested her hand against his cheek. "I'll see you inside, then."

Ryan watched her walk away with Jamal.

"She's a remarkable woman, isn't she?" Jack noted.

"Yeah, she certainly is."

"If I were you, I wouldn't let her get away."

Ryan scowled. "Not you, too," he protested. "Geez,

if I get any more matchmaking advice from people who hang out at the pub, I'll have to turn the place into a lonely-hearts club."

"Not a bad idea," Jack said. "And if there are any more out there like Maggie, send ' em my way." He reached for his door handle. "I think I'll catch a cab and head for home."

"You're not going to stick around to make sure I go inside?" Ryan inquired. "I thought maybe you'd nominate yourself to see to it I don't let Maggie down."

"If you let her down, you're an idiot," Jack said succinctly. "And frankly, if you're that dumb, I don't want to know about it. Right now I'm feeling all warm and fuzzy toward you for helping Lamar."

Ryan laughed. "Go. I'll give you a call once he's out of surgery."

Jack nodded. "You do that." He grinned. "Or give Maggie the honor. I wouldn't mind waking up to the sound of her voice in my ear."

"Go to hell," Ryan said. If Maggie was going to be whispering in any man's ear, it was going to be his. And it was looking more and more as if that was going to be inevitable.

9

Maggie knew precisely why Ryan had let her be the one to escort Mr. Monroe into the hospital to see his son. He hadn't wanted to be a part of an emotional family reunion, even if he was the one responsible for making it happen. Because there had been no reunion for him and his brothers, the prospect of this one made him uncomfortable.

He needed to be there, though. He needed to put his discomfort aside if he was ever to know that happy endings were possible.

As Maggie and Jamal Monroe stepped off the elevator, she turned and looked at him. "I know I have no right to ask this, especially after insisting that you get right over here, but would you mind waiting a few more minutes before you see Lamar?"

He regarded her with surprise. "You want to go in and make sure they want to see me?"

"No, I know how happy they'll be that you're here. In fact, that's the point."

He studied her knowingly. "This has something to

do with Mr. Devaney, doesn't it? You seemed real anxious that he not take off. You still worried he might not show up?"

"No, I'm sure he'll be here any second, and I think he should be a part of this."

"So he gets the credit he's due for tracking me down?"

She smiled at the all-too-cynical reaction. "No, so he can see for himself the look in Lamar's eyes when you walk through the door."

At her explanation, his natural suspicion gave way. He nodded in apparent understanding. "I suppose a couple more minutes won't make any difference," he said. "And I do owe the man for his trouble."

"He doesn't want your thanks or your sense of obligation," Maggie was quick to assure him. "He just wants you and your son to be together. I can't explain why this meeting is so important to him, but it is. Trust me."

They were still standing by the elevator when Letitia Monroe emerged from Lamar's room and spotted them. An entire spectrum of emotions flashed across her face, from anger to love to relief. Her husband took a few hesitant steps in her direction, then paused and waited. She hurried down the corridor and straight into his arms. Her shoulders shook with sobs as he tried ineffectively to console her.

"Jamal Monroe, I ought to slap you silly for putting us through all this worry," Letitia said finally, sniffing loudly and wiping her eyes with a tissue Maggie provided. "But I'm too relieved to see you. The rest will have to wait." She glanced around. "Where's Mr.

Devaney? I know he had something to do with you being here."

The elevator doors whooshed open just then, and Ryan emerged. Letitia threw her arms around him in a fierce hug that almost knocked him off his feet.

"I will be indebted to you for the rest of my life," she declared. "Thank you for finding Jamal and getting him here in time."

"The truth is, he found us," Ryan said modestly. "All I did was poke around and ask a few questions."

"But I don't doubt for a minute that it was all that poking around that stirred things up and flushed him out," she said with conviction. She slipped her hand into her husband's. "Let's go see our boy."

They started down the hall, but Ryan held back. Maggie regarded him with a questioning look, but it was Letitia who turned around and said impatiently, "Hurry up. Lamar's expecting you. And I imagine Father Francis has heard about all of the boy's pitiful jokes he can stand for one morning."

"I shouldn't intrude," Ryan said, looking around desperately for someplace to flee.

"Intrude, nothing. You're part of this family till the end of time," Letitia said emphatically. "And I don't want to hear anyone saying otherwise, including you."

Maggie grinned at the woman's belief that she had the right to boss Ryan around. Maybe she should steal a page out of Letitia's book. Ryan appeared a little shell-shocked.

"I guess she told *you*," Maggie teased.

Ryan seemed a little bewildered at being summarily made a part of the Monroe family, but he snagged Maggie's hand and followed Letitia.

"You know," Maggie began casually. "It's an interesting thing about families."

He regarded her warily. "Oh?"

"Some people spend a lifetime surrounded by blood relatives they don't get along with much. Some have wonderful families like mine." She gave him a pointed look. "And some get to choose the people they consider family."

He gave her a wry smile. "I get it, Maggie."

"I hope so," she said softly. "I really do." She figured their future depended on it.

Ryan hesitated again once they reached Lamar's room. Despite Letitia's insistence that he belonged there, he felt like an interloper at what should be a very private moment. But even if he'd wanted to hang back, there was Maggie watching him with that beseeching, hopeful expression. He couldn't let her down. And he wasn't too keen on being the recipient of one of Father Francis's disappointed looks, either, to say nothing of another outburst of Letitia's temper.

"You go in first," Letitia instructed. "Tell my baby you have a surprise for him."

"Me? Shouldn't you be doing that?"

She glanced at Maggie, then regarded him with a steady look. "Something tells me it's important that you do it."

Recognizing that he was defeated, Ryan sucked in a sharp breath, then walked into the room. His nervousness eased the instant he saw Lamar's face light up. Father Francis smiled at him and stepped aside to give Ryan room at the boy's bedside.

"You came!" Lamar said. "Mom said you would, but it was getting late. They've already given me some kinda shot. I'm getting real sleepy."

Ryan rubbed his knuckles over the boy's head. "Don't go to sleep just yet. I have a surprise, and you're going to want to be wide-awake for it."

Lamar's eyes widened. "A surprise? For me? What is it?"

Ryan nodded toward the door. "Look over there."

Just as he said it, Jamal stepped into the room.

"Dad," Lamar whispered, reaching for Ryan's hand and gazing up at him with a grateful expression. "You found my dad. I knew you would."

As Jamal reached the side of the bed, his eyes filled with tears. "Hi, son. I'm sorry for worrying you, for letting you and your mom go through all of this alone."

"It's okay, Dad. I knew you'd come back. I just knew it."

Jamal bent down, his tears spilling onto his son's face as he hugged him. "I love you, boy. Don't you ever forget that. And once you've had this surgery and are good as new again, you and I are gonna do all the things we've always talked about. That's a promise."

Lamar looked at Ryan, his eyes shining. "And my dad never breaks his promises. Not ever." He glanced toward his mother. "Ain't that right, Mom?"

"*Isn't* it, right," Letitia corrected. Wisely, she didn't mention the promise Jamal had made to her to be there in sickness and in health, in good times and bad. "Your daddy's here now. That's all that matters."

Just then the nurse came into the room with an orderly. "Time to go, Lamar."

He clung to his father's hand. "You'll be here after the operation, right? You're not going to go away again?"

"I'll be right by your side when you wake up," Jamal assured him.

The next few hours passed in a blur of lousy coffee, tasteless food and pacing. There were a dozen times when Ryan would have made an excuse and escaped, but one glance at Maggie kept him right where he was. From the moment they'd met, she'd seemed to expect the best from him, the same as Father Francis. Now there were two people in his life Ryan hoped never to disappoint. He was surprised he didn't feel more pressured by it, but the truth was, it felt good to know there were people counting on him and that, so far at least, he had never let them down.

Across the room Letitia and Jamal sat side by side, hand in hand, drawing comfort from each other the way they should have all these weeks.

"Looks like Letitia has forgiven him already," he said to Maggie, unable to keep the surprise out of his voice.

"Human beings make mistakes," Maggie said quietly. "Wise human beings understand that and forgive them."

"How the hell do you forgive someone for walking out when he's needed the most?" Ryan demanded, his chin jutting forward.

Maggie regarded him with a penetrating look. "Are we talking about Jamal now, or your parents?"

Ryan ground his teeth. "Jamal, of course," he said tightly.

"Ryan—"

"Don't," he said, shooting to his feet and walking away from the lecture so evidently on the tip of her tongue. He didn't need anyone, not even Maggie, telling him that there could be any possible justification for what his parents had done to him and his brothers. He certainly wasn't going to entertain the notion of forgiving them for dumping three boys into the foster care system before taking off to who-knew-where.

He moved to the window and stared outside, only halfway aware that snow was falling, leaving a coating of white on the ground. Christmas was fast approaching, and it was his second most hated holiday of the year, right after Thanksgiving. He never failed to spend the day trying to imagine where his brothers might be, what they might have endured. If their holidays had been anything like his, they must hate the season, as well.

"I take it Maggie dared to say something about your parents," Father Francis said, coming to stand beside him.

"What makes you think that?" Ryan asked.

"Little else puts such a scowl on your face," the priest replied. "Besides, it's natural for you to think of them on a day like this. Seeing Lamar reunited with his father must make you wonder a little about your own father."

"I am not thinking of my parents," Ryan insisted. "Or at least I wasn't until the two of you decided to pester me about them."

Father Francis waited until Ryan eventually turned to face him, then said, "Are you going to allow two people you claim to have no feelings for, at all, control the way you live the rest of your life?"

"What the devil are you talking about? They control nothing!" Ryan declared.

"Oh, really? Have you given one second's thought to a future with Maggie?" The priest held up a silencing hand when Ryan would have responded. "And don't waste your breath telling me you're not attracted to her, because anyone with eyes can see that you are. Yet you do nothing about it, because in your heart you know it would have to lead somewhere, to a place you won't allow yourself to go."

"Shouldn't you be praying for Lamar, instead of giving me advice on my love life?" he inquired sourly.

"I'm a modern man. I've learned to multitask," Father Francis said.

Despite his irritation, Ryan bit back a laugh. "And who taught you that term? Maggie, I imagine."

"The girl's an inspiration, to be sure," Father Francis said cheerfully. "But then, even you can see that, can't you?"

Ryan sighed as the priest retreated to sit with Letitia and Jamal, apparently satisfied that he'd gotten his message across. Ryan glanced over at Maggie, saw the worry in her eyes as she watched the door, then the lingering flicker of hurt when she caught him staring at her. Resigned, he went back to her side.

"I'm sorry for snapping your head off before," he said. "And I'm sorry I keep doing things that necessitate so many apologies."

"It's okay," she said with another display of that ready forgiveness she seemed willing to dispense, no matter how unreasonable he'd been. "We're all under a lot of stress this morning."

"That's no excuse." He noted the dark circles under her eyes, the strain around her mouth. "Maggie, you must be exhausted. Why not let me drive you home?"

She shook her head. "Not until we hear something."

"Okay then, at least rest for a bit." He sat beside her and slipped an arm around her shoulders, giving her a gentle tug. After a moment's resistance, she gingerly put her head on his shoulder. "That's better. Now close your eyes. If the doctor comes, I promise I'll wake you."

She didn't respond, and moments later he felt the tension in her shoulders ease. Soon after, her breathing deepened, and something inside him eased, as well. He had only the dimmest memory of feeling this protective toward anyone, quite likely because he hadn't wanted to remember that, when it was truly important, he hadn't been able to protect his brothers from the worst hurt of all.

Maggie couldn't recall when she'd ever felt so safe. In her dream, she was in a house that was being buffeted by a powerful northeast wind, but she was safe and warm, tucked in Ryan's arms in front of a cozy fire. She had the sense that as long as she was in his embrace, nothing could ever harm her.

She shifted sleepily, cuddling closer to all that strength and heat, only to hear his voice whispering urgently in her ear.

"Come on, Maggie. Wake up, darlin'. The doctor's here."

It was the last, more than the term of endearment, that penetrated. Her eyes snapped open, and she immediately spotted the surgeon in his operating room attire standing beside Letitia and Jamal. Her gaze shot to Ryan.

"Have you heard what he's saying? Is it good news?"

"I can't hear from here."

"What about his expression? How did he look?"

Ryan regarded her blankly.

"Was he happy? Sad? What?" she prodded. "You read people's moods every single night at the pub. Can't you read his?"

"Maggie, we could find out everything if we went over there," he suggested with exaggerated patience.

"I don't want to intrude."

"Look at it this way—if the news is good, they'd want us to share in it," he said. "If it's bad, they're going to need our support."

She blinked at that, struck by the fact that a man who professed no emotional entanglements could still have the most amazingly sensitive insights. He should give himself credit for them more often. "Of course you're right." She stood up and grabbed his hand, pulling him along with her.

As they reached the small gathering, Letitia turned to them, her eyes brimming with tears. Maggie's heart stopped. "Oh, no," she whispered, her hand tightening around Ryan's.

"No, no," Letitia said, gathering her into a hug. "It's good news. He's going to be fine. My boy's going to be fine." She turned to Ryan, hugging him, as well. "And it's all because of you, not just because you paid for the surgery, but because you got his daddy here. That gave Lamar the will to live. I know it did."

"Now, it's still going to be a critical twenty-four to forty-eight hours," the doctor cautioned. "But I have every reason to believe Lamar will come through this with flying colors."

"It's a miracle, that's what it is," Letitia declared, her cheeks damp.

"It is, indeed," Jamal said. He turned to Ryan. "Thank you."

"I'm glad I was able to help," Ryan said, clearly uncomfortable with their gratitude. "And now that we know Lamar's made it through the surgery, I'm going to get Maggie home. She was out with me most of the night trying to find you, Jamal. She's beat."

"I'll come by later, though," Maggie promised, too tired to waste any breath on a futile argument. "And if you need anything, anything at all, you call me." She pressed a slip of paper into Letitia's hands.

"Bless you, girl. You, too, Mr. Devaney."

Outside in the crisp air, Maggie drew in a deep breath, then turned to Ryan. "I can't begin to tell you how relieved I am. You must be, too. And if we are, just imagine what Letitia and Jamal must be feeling."

"They love their son. Of course they're relieved," Ryan said.

Maggie regarded him intently. "You know, Ryan, it's possible that your parents did what they did because they loved you and your brothers."

"Don't be absurd."

"How will you ever know if you don't try to find them and make them explain?"

"Why the hell would I ever want to see them again?"

"So you can put the past to rest."

"If you knew the whole story, you'd never suggest such a thing," he said fiercely.

"Then tell me."

He sighed, a lost, lonely expression on his face. "Maybe one of these days I will."

"Why not now?" she pushed.

"Because we're both exhausted."

"Buy me a strong cup of coffee and I can listen."

He smiled wearily at that. "Trying to get me when my defenses are down?"

"Absolutely," she said without hesitation.

He leaned down and covered her mouth with his. The kiss was sweet and all too brief. "Ah, Maggie, what am I going to do with you?"

"Are you seriously asking for suggestions?" she teased.

His gaze captured hers and held, amusement darkening into desire, then giving way to regret. "Maybe one of these days," he said.

She bit back her own regrets. "I'll hold you to that, Ryan Devaney."

He laughed. "I don't doubt that for a second. In fact, I'm fairly certain you have a whole list of things I'm expected to make good on."

"None you can't handle," she said with confidence.

10

Ryan had absolutely no intention of allowing Maggie to drive all the way home in her current state of exhaustion. Since he wasn't one bit better off, there was only one answer: she'd have to stay at his place. Proposing that, while making it clear it was an innocent suggestion, was going to be a neat trick.

He pulled to a stop in a parking space down the block from the pub and glanced over at her. She was struggling to keep her eyes open. He left the car and circled to open the passenger door.

"Okay, come with me," he said, his tone firm.

"My car's right across the street," she said, when he steered her toward the pub.

"And if you get behind the wheel and drive as far as the corner, you're likely to fall asleep and crash into something. I won't have that on my conscience."

She tilted her head and regarded him curiously. "Then what are you suggesting?"

"You'll sleep at my place," he said, trying to be grimly matter-of-fact about it.

"How intriguing!" A smile tugged at her lips. "Just minutes ago you vetoed that idea."

Ryan laughed at her typically give-an-inch-take-a-mile response. "No, that is not what I vetoed. You'll be sleeping in the bed. I'll be on the sofa."

A glint of amusement lit her eyes. "Now, where's the fun in that, Ryan Devaney?"

He managed a severe expression. "Don't you be tempting me, Maggie O'Brien. What would your fine father and brothers think of that?"

"They have nothing to do with my personal life," she assured him airily.

"Do they know that?" he inquired with skepticism.

She sighed heavily. "Probably not."

"Then perhaps we'd best do this my way for now," he said as he led the way upstairs to his apartment over the pub.

When he walked through the doorway, he tried to view the room through Maggie's eyes. The windows across the front let in a lot of light and the bare wood floors gleamed softly, but beyond a sofa, a comfortable chair and the television that he never bothered to flip on, there wasn't much to recommend it.

To the left, the kitchen had new appliances he'd used no more than a handful of times because he took most of his meals downstairs in the pub. Even his coffeemaker was in like-new condition.

"The minimalist style, I see," Maggie observed, still standing in the entry. "I imagine most people think they get a better sense of you from the pub downstairs."

Her thoughtful comment made him wary. "And you don't?"

"No, I think this gives away more. No clutter. No personal objects to give any hint about the man you are. All your secrets are protected here." She met his gaze. "Is the bedroom any better?"

"Not if you're looking to unravel any secrets," he said with an edge of defensiveness.

He showed her the way, then stood back as she surveyed the king-size bed with its dark-green quilt tossed haphazardly over sheets in a paler shade of green, the oak dresser with nothing beyond a pile of loose change on top, the digital clock on the bedside stand and an antique rocker in the corner. She blinked when her gaze fell on that, then turned to him, her face alight with curiosity.

"A family heirloom?" she asked, crossing over to rub her hand over the oak wood with its soft sheen.

"Hardly."

"You're fond of antiques, then?"

"Not especially," he said, the defensiveness back in his voice. He should never have brought her here. He could see that now. She liked digging beneath the surface of things to the raw truths beneath.

"Back problems?" she persisted unrelentingly.

"No, and what does that have to do with having a rocker in my room?"

"They say President Kennedy had a rocker because of chronic back problems. I've seen pictures of it."

Ryan nodded. "Okay, yes, I guess I have heard something about that, but it's got nothing to do with this. I saw it in a shop and I liked it. End of story."

Her gaze narrowed with obvious disbelief. "Did your mother rock you when you were little?"

Ryan bit back a curse at the accurate guess. "How the hell would I remember a thing like that?" he asked derisively.

Maggie's gaze never left his face. "She did, didn't she? That's why you bought this chair. It reminds you of one your family had."

The truth was, he suspected it might have been *this* chair. On the one occasion he'd ventured back to his childhood neighborhood, he'd found the rocker in a shop not all that far from where they'd lived. He'd been drawn to it at once, and despite his claim that he wanted nothing at all to do with the past, he hadn't been able to put it out of his mind. He'd gone back the next day and bought the rocker, but only after asking the shop owner what he knew about the original owner. Unfortunately, the man had bought the shop from someone else, and the rocker had been a part of the inventory. He'd known nothing at all about its history, not even the year in which it had been purchased.

"Maggie, drop it, okay? It's just a chair."

"And if someone were to take an ax to it, it wouldn't bother you at all?" she inquired innocently.

Hands jammed in his pockets, he shrugged. "It would be a waste of a beautiful piece of craftsmanship, nothing more," he asserted.

She sighed at his response. "If you insist."

"I do." He gestured toward a door across the hall. "The bathroom's over there. There are towels in the closet. If you need anything else, let me know."

"Just a phone. I need to call home and let them know what's going on."

He felt guilty for not having suggested it right away. "Given the way they worry, they must be frantic by now."

She shook her head. "I doubt it. I called them last night and told them I was going to be with you."

Ryan couldn't have been more stunned if she'd punched him in the gut. "You told them that? In those words?"

She grinned at his discomfort. "Maybe not those precise words, but that was the gist of it, yes."

Curious despite himself, he asked, "How did they react?"

"Mother said I need to bring you home to dinner tonight."

"That's it?"

"Oh, I imagine she'll have quite a bit to say when you get there, but last night that's all she said," Maggie replied, clearly enjoying herself.

"Then let's postpone that dinner for a while—like maybe ten years from now."

She laughed. "If you think that will work, you don't know my mother at all. She's counting on tonight. No excuses accepted."

"You'll just have to extend my apologies," Ryan insisted. "Tonight's out of the question."

"A prior engagement?"

"Nope. Just a healthy desire to live."

"I don't think it will come to that," Maggie said soothingly. "My folks haven't killed a prospective son-in-law yet. And before you panic—which, by the way,

I can see that you're doing—you should know that they regard any male of an appropriate age as prospective marriage material. It's not as if they're getting invitations printed as we speak."

"I should hope not," he said fervently.

She frowned at him. "You know, if I were a less confident woman, I might be offended."

"Maggie, you know where I stand on this. I don't do commitment. I don't do love."

"So you've mentioned."

She didn't seem particularly dismayed. Either she didn't care or she didn't believe him. "It's not something you should forget," he told her, to make the point clearer.

"As if you're likely to let me," she scoffed.

Ryan still wasn't at all convinced she was taking him seriously. However, prolonging the subject struck him as a decidedly lousy idea. "Get some sleep," he muttered, then left the room and closed the door behind him.

The woman was dangerous. As if she couldn't tempt him with a glance, now she was deliberately taunting him every chance she got. One of these days, his willpower was going to snap and his common sense was going to fly right out the window, and then nothing would keep him from joining her in that bed of his. In fact, right now, with the image of her snuggled beneath his sheets firmly implanted in his brain, it was almost more than he could cope with.

Just to be sure he didn't give in to the desire swirling through him, he left the apartment and locked the door securely behind him. Of course, short of his tossing the key in the river, there was nothing to prevent him from unlocking the door and going right back in there an hour from now and struggling with the same neediness. To prevent any chance of that, he went downstairs in search of coffee and Rory's company.

The cook glanced up when he walked in. "I thought I heard you moving about upstairs," he said, and gestured toward a pot of coffee. "The coffee's fresh and strong."

"Thanks," Ryan said, pouring himself a cup.

Rory gave him a sly look. "Of course, I also thought I heard another set of footsteps and a lovely feminine voice. Those wouldn't belong to our Maggie, would they? Have you finally come to your senses where she's concerned?"

"I never lost my senses, which is why I'm down here and she's up there," Ryan retorted.

Rory regarded him with disappointment. "You're breaking my heart, lad. You're a disgrace to all the males of Ireland."

Ryan thought of what Maggie was offering him, of everything he was fighting so hard to resist. He weighed that against a lifetime of noble restraint that had earned him nothing but loneliness. He sighed heavily.

"It's entirely possible that you're right," Ryan conceded.

"Then do something about it."

That image of a naked Maggie sliding beneath his sheets slammed into Ryan's head again. It was getting harder and harder to remember why he needed to resist.

"One of these days, maybe I will," he said, a note of wistfulness creeping into his voice.

"No time like the present," Rory reminded him.

Ryan shook his head. "Some things can't be rushed."

"Would Maggie view you coming back upstairs as rushing her?"

"No," he admitted ruefully. "I'm the one who's slowed the pace of things. I can't afford a mistake."

"What sort of mistake?" Rory asked, clearly bewildered.

Ryan didn't answer. How could he explain to a man who made a habit of loving and leaving women that once Ryan allowed Maggie to touch him, she'd be a part of his soul?

And that would give her the power to destroy him if she were ever to walk away.

Maggie was relieved to hear the answering machine when she called home to let her family know the outcome of Lamar's surgery and to tell them she was still in town. She wasn't quite ready to try to explain Ryan's continued reticence to come to dinner. Knowing her mother, Maggie suspected Nell wasn't going to take the refusal lightly. When it came to self-proclaimed missions, Nell O'Brien was even quicker to rush in than her daughter. Maggie had a feeling that would be more pressure than Ryan could handle.

She thought of his reaction to her guess that the rocker had reminded him of his mother. He'd obviously been dismayed that she'd hit on the truth. Clearly he didn't like the fact that she was chipping away at that protective wall he'd erected around himself and could see into his heart. Maggie recognized that she needed to be careful, especially since her preference would be to take a sledgehammer to what was left of that wall. Rather than poking and prodding about the Devaneys, she was going to fill Ryan's head with stories of the O'Briens until he grew comfortable with the idea of *her* family, even if he couldn't deal with his own.

Sighing, she snuggled more securely around the pillow that still held Ryan's faint, masculine scent. For now, this was the only way she was likely to get close to him, but that would change eventually. Maggie could be patient when she had to be…especially now that she thought she knew how to break down that wall.

It was afternoon when she woke. Sun was streaming in the bedroom window. Maggie yawned and stretched, then listened for some sound to indicate that Ryan had returned to the apartment. All she heard were street sounds and the distant clatter of pots and pans, coming no doubt from the pub kitchen downstairs.

Wrapping herself in one of Ryan's shirts that she found hanging on the back of the door, she slipped across the hall to the bathroom and showered, then dressed. Using his hair dryer, she did what she could to coax some waves into her hair, then ventured downstairs, where she found the pub empty.

The sound of voices in the kitchen drew her. Poking her head around the door, she scanned the room for Ryan, but saw no sign of him. Rory, however, was chopping the vegetables for Irish stew, while Rosita sat nearby, her feet up.

"Taking a break?" Maggie asked with a grin.

"Señor Rory not let me help," Rosita responded,

sounding thoroughly disgusted. "I can chop, *si?* That is not so difficult."

"You need to stay off your feet," Rory countered.

Rosita rolled her eyes. "He is worse than Juan."

"Does Ryan realize he's paying her to rest?" Maggie inquired.

"I'm in charge of the kitchen," Rory claimed defensively. "I see no need to tell himself how I'm running it or who's doing what. As long as there's food for the customers, he's got no cause to complain."

Maggie chuckled. "You're an angel, Rory."

"You'd best be keeping that to yourself, Maggie. I have a reputation as a tyrant to protect."

"Don't worry. I won't give away your secret. Where *is* your boss, by the way?"

"In the pub."

"I didn't see him."

"Check the booth in the back corner. He was asleep on the bench last time I checked."

"Why on earth would he sleep down here when there was a perfectly good sofa upstairs?" she asked. "To say nothing of half a bed."

Rory's eyes sparkled with amusement. "Now that's a question you should be asking him, but I think you can figure it out if you put your mind to it."

"It's because I was in the other half of that bed, wasn't it?" she asked, astonished that her presence had actually scared the man out of his own home.

"You never heard me say such a thing, now did you?" Rory replied, a grin splitting his face.

"He doesn't trust himself around me," she concluded with a sense of wonder. She'd suspected it, but the confirmation was music to her ears.

"That would be my impression," Rory agreed. He studied her intently. "What do you intend to do about this power you have over him?"

Rather than replying, she met his gaze. "Any suggestions?"

"Now if a woman affected me the way you affect our Ryan, I wouldn't mind if she were to make an outright pass at me," the Irish cook said, then sighed heavily. "But sadly, Ryan is a better man than I. I think a subtler approach is called for."

"Meaning?"

"Persistence and patience," he recommended. "Whatever you've done to rattle him, do that and more of it." An unrepentant grin suddenly crossed his face. "Ah, here is the very man in question, looking oddly unrefreshed from his nap."

"Go to hell," Ryan muttered as he crossed to the coffeepot and poured himself a cup. Only then did he glance at Maggie. "Want some?"

"I'd love a cup," she said, noting that Ryan's gaze fell on Rosita as he poured the coffee. He hesitated, then gave a resigned shake of his head before handing Maggie her coffee.

"Okay," Rory declared, "there are too many people in my kitchen. You two, out. I'll fix you an omelette and bring it out, or would you prefer a sandwich since we're well into afternoon now?"

"An omelette sounds lovely," Maggie said.

"Perhaps Rosita could fix it," Ryan suggested.

"She's on a break," Rory retorted emphatically.

"Come on," Maggie encouraged before Ryan could debate the topic.

"I knew hiring that woman was a mistake the instant I saw she was pregnant," he complained as they went to a booth. "If nothing else, Rory is gallant. I knew he'd never let her do a lick of work."

"If it's any consolation, I think Rosita is as frustrated as you are."

"That doesn't actually help. I hired her because Rory claimed to need help."

"And now he's satisfied. Maybe all he really needed was company."

"I am not paying someone to sit in there and chat with him. Besides, she doesn't know enough English to carry on a conversation."

"Oh, I think she knows enough," Maggie said, then captured and held his gaze. "So, Rory tells me you slept down here. Mind telling me why?"

"I sat down for a minute and fell asleep," he said defensively. "There's nothing more to it."

"But why were you down here in the first place? You were as exhausted as I was. I thought you were going straight to sleep on the sofa upstairs."

He shrugged. "I changed my mind."

"I hope it wasn't because of me."

He didn't look away as she'd anticipated. Instead, he turned the challenge around.

"Now why would you have anything to do with it?" he asked.

"Oh, I don't know," she said with an offhand shrug. "Maybe because you were tempted to crawl into your bed with me."

"Absolutely not," he said.

Maggie laughed at the too-quick response. "Liar, but I'm going to let that pass this time."

"How gracious of you," he said sourly. "Did you explain to your mother that I couldn't come to dinner?"

"She wasn't home. I left her a message to that effect. Just to prepare you, though, don't be surprised if she comes in here to demand an explanation."

He frowned at that. "Can't anyone in your family take a simple no for an answer?"

"Not usually," she said cheerfully. "You should probably try to get used to it."

"Why? Eventually you'll go back to Maine, and that will be that. I'll probably never see you or any of your family again."

Maggie shook her head at the note of resignation in his voice. "That's not how it works with us. Face it, Devaney, we're here to stay."

"What about Maine?" he asked, a faint note of desperation in his voice. Apparently, he'd been clinging to the notion that she would be leaving after the holidays so he could let himself off the hook and never have to deal with his all-too-apparent feelings for her.

"I've decided not to go back," she announced, making the decision on the spot. Whatever happened between her and Ryan, she wanted to remain in Boston. And, if she had her way, she would work right here, by his side. Eventually maybe he'd even let her get her hands on his accounting system so she could bring him into the twenty-first century.

His gaze narrowed. "Why not?"

"There's nothing for me there," she said.

"And here?"

"That remains to be seen."

Ryan sighed heavily at her response, but Maggie was almost certain there was a slight flicker of relief in his eyes. It wasn't much, but she was going to cling to that with everything she had.

A week later, with Christmas only days away, Ryan was still cursing the fact that he hadn't done everything he could to persuade Maggie that she belonged in Maine. The only trouble would have been that he didn't believe it. It was more and more evident to him that she belonged right here, making him laugh with her stories about her family.

Making him yearn.

Even so, he caught himself before he allowed her to weave a spell around him that couldn't be broken. Though the invitations to join the O'Briens for dinner came almost daily, he determinedly turned down every single one. He was pretty sure he was finally getting through to Maggie that what they had now was as far as he was going to allow things to go.

Of course, just when he was feeling confident, he looked up and spotted her mother coming through the pub's door with a determined glint in her eyes. Maggie had warned him about precisely this, but as the days had gone by, he'd put the possibility of a direct confrontation with Nell O'Brien from his mind. Now, on Christmas Eve, she was standing squarely in front of him, hands on hips and a no-nonsense expression on her face.

"I am going to pretend that you haven't rudely

turned down every single invitation Maggie's offered," she said, eyes flashing. "I will not allow you to say no to having Christmas dinner with us tomorrow. Father Francis is invited, as well."

"The shelter—" Ryan began, only to have his words cut off.

"Dinner at the shelter is at noon. I checked," she told him. "We'll eat at five. That should give you both plenty of time to get there." She tilted her head in a way that reminded him of Maggie. "Any questions?"

Ryan knew when he was beaten. "No, ma'am."

"Then I'll see you tomorrow?"

"Yes, thank you. Can I bring anything?"

"Just Father Francis and a pleasant attitude," she said, then kissed his cheek. "And a small token for Maggie, perhaps. I know she has a little something for you."

Ryan sighed. He'd already seen the perfect gift for Maggie, but he'd kept himself from buying it. He'd told himself that any present at all would carry implications of a connection he was trying not to encourage. He should have known it was another bad decision on his part, should have realized that she would have no such reticence about buying him something.

"Maureen, watch the bar," he called to his waitress. "I have an errand to run."

"We're filled to overflowing and you want to run an errand?" she asked, regarding him with astonishment.

"Last-minute Christmas shopping," he said.

A grin spread across her face. "And if I'm not mistaken, that was Maggie O'Brien's mother who just came breezing through here. Does that mean you're going to buy something special for Maggie?"

"You can jump to whatever conclusions you want," he said, "as long as I can get out of here before the stores close."

"Go," Maureen said. "Besides, I imagine Maggie will be along any minute now to help out. Shall I tell her you're out shopping for her?"

He scowled. "You'll do no such thing, or your bonus for this year will turn out to be ashes and switches."

Maureen laughed at the empty threat. "You gave me my bonus last week."

He sighed. "Next year, then."

As if the holidays weren't stressful enough for him, why was it that every female he knew had suddenly decided this was the perfect season to drive him crazy?

11

"It's a good thing you're doing," Father Francis assured Ryan as they drove to Maggie's house on Christmas afternoon after a busy morning at the shelter during which Ryan had played Santa to dozens of children. "It's about time you spent a holiday with a real family, rather than just the lost souls at the shelter or the strays who wander into the pub."

"This from a man who is usually among those strays," Ryan retorted.

"Only because I worry about you," the priest responded. "And because Rory is the only man I know who can make a decent Christmas pudding."

"Then why are you so agreeable to missing it this year?" Ryan asked.

"Because we've had a better offer. Christmas pudding is not the most important part of the holiday, after all."

"Besides which, I'm sure Rory agreed to save you some," Ryan guessed.

"Aye, that he did," the priest agreed unrepentantly.

A few minutes later Ryan found a parking space half a block from the O'Brien home. Judging from the number of cars in front of the house and lining the driveway, there was a full house. Even though he was likely to know almost everyone there, Ryan suffered a moment of panic at the prospect of facing them. However, one look from Father Francis had him cutting the engine and climbing out.

At the door Maggie greeted them warmly, reserving a smug grin for Ryan. "They've been taking bets inside on whether you'd show up," she told him. "I believe my haul should be more than twenty dollars. Mother gets the other half."

"Do you all bet on everything?" he asked as Father Francis laughed.

"Just about," she said, standing on tiptoe to give Ryan a slow, deliberate kiss that made his head spin.

Before he could gather his wits, Ryan heard Father Francis mutter, "About time." Then the priest disappeared in an obvious attempt to give them some privacy.

Ryan felt Maggie's lips curve into a slow smile against his. When he pulled away, there was amusement dancing in her eyes. "What?" he demanded crankily.

"Nothing," she insisted. "Did you hear me say a word?"

Ryan gave a nod of satisfaction. "Keep it that way. This situation is not amusing, Maggie. I can't seem to make myself stay away from you, but that doesn't mean I've changed my mind. I'm the wrong man for you."

She surveyed him so thoroughly he almost squirmed, then shook her head. "I don't see it."

"See what?"

"You being wrong for me." Her gaze lit on the small gift bag in his hand. "Is that for me?"

With a sigh, he handed it to her. A part of him wanted her to open the present right then, but a part of him dreaded it. He didn't have a lot of practice picking out gifts, but this one had seemed so right. If she hated it, he was going to feel like an idiot.

Maggie had no such hesitations. She was pulling tissue from the bag with the excitement of a child. Her eyes lit up when she saw the small, square box. For a moment she fumbled with the lid, then impatiently handed it to him. "I'm all thumbs. You open it."

"It's your present," he protested.

"Please."

Ryan took the box, slit the tape holding it closed, then lifted the lid just enough to make opening it the rest of the way easy for her. "Okay, all yours," he said, anxious to be rid of it. Even so, he couldn't tear his gaze away as he awaited her reaction.

Maggie carefully unfolded the tissue in the box, then sighed. "Oh, my," she whispered, her eyes shining. "Ryan, they're beautiful." She removed the antique marcasite hair clips from the box with a look of reverence. The clips were made in the shape of shamrocks, and each had a tiny emerald chip in the center that was the exact color of Maggie's eyes. "I have to put them on."

Ryan stood as if frozen while she moved to a mirror on the foyer wall. Once the sparkling clips were in her hair, she turned to him with a smile. "They're perfect, the very best present anyone ever gave me. Thank you."

Ryan didn't know how to cope with either her gratitude or the too-obvious love shining in her eyes. It was all too much for a man who'd rarely been the recipient of either, at least not from anyone who'd truly mattered. Panic rushed through him. Not five minutes ago he'd told her that he was wrong for her, and now, apparently, she was more convinced than ever that they were exactly right for each other. He'd never realized before that a gift could speak volumes, could even contradict words, no matter how emphatically they'd been expressed.

"Maggie, I'm sorry. I can't do this," he said, turning toward the door. Before he could bolt, however, she stepped in front of him.

"Do what?" she asked.

He gestured toward the rest of the house, which was crowded with O'Briens. "The family thing. I'm no good at it."

Her gaze locked with his, unrelenting, yet tempered with understanding. "If that's true—and I'm not saying I believe it for a minute—then it's time you told me why. The whole story, not bits and snatches."

Ryan sighed at her reasonable request. "Yes, I do owe you an explanation, but not today. Your family's waiting for you in there."

"They're waiting for both of us," she corrected. "There are plenty of appetizers and Dad's eggnog. They won't mind waiting a little longer."

So, he thought, this was it. "Is there someplace we can talk privately?"

"My room," she said at once.

Ryan balked as if she'd suggested going upstairs to make love. "I am not going to your room with you, in front of your entire family. Are you nuts? What will they think?"

"That we're looking for someplace private," she replied reasonably. "In case you haven't noticed, there's a crowd in the kitchen keeping my mom company while she cooks. There's a crowd in the den watching football. The kids are in the rec room downstairs. And there are at least a half-dozen people in the living room listening to every word we're saying right now. Do you have a better idea?"

He latched on to her hand, grabbed a coat off the rack by the door and dragged her outside to his car. He turned the heater up full blast, then turned to look at her. Only then did he realize that he'd mistakenly grabbed a coat belonging to someone much larger. She looked lost and more delicate than ever in the folds of dark-blue wool. Her wide eyes watched him warily as if she were uncertain what sort of storm she'd unleashed.

Before he could drag her to him and kiss her the way he desperately wanted to, he forced himself to take a deep breath and tell her everything—about the way his parents had run off, about the devastating day he'd been separated from his brothers, about the roller-coaster ride he'd taken through the foster care system, about Father Francis catching him just as he'd been about to break into a neighborhood quick-mart for something to eat on a bitterly cold Thanksgiving eve.

"It wasn't the first time I'd broken into a store, and probably wouldn't have been the last," he told her, his gaze unflinching. "I was a thief."

"You were a hungry kid," she countered, her eyes overflowing with sympathetic tears.

"Don't excuse what I did because you feel sorry for me," he retorted sharply, hating that she seemed so eager to overlook the truth. "And don't you dare pity me. I didn't deserve it then, and I certainly don't now. I knew right from wrong."

"You were a boy," she insisted, still fiercely defending him. "You were obviously desperate."

"I was old enough to know better," he countered just as harshly. "I was just a no-good brat. Obviously, my parents knew that." He took a deep breath, then blurted the secret guilt he'd kept hidden in his heart for so long. "It's why they left, why I could never fit in with any of the foster families."

Maggie stared at him in shocked disbelief. "No," she said, flatly refusing to accept his explanation. "Whatever the reason your parents left, it wasn't that."

Ryan was startled by the depth of her conviction. He wished he were half as convinced that he'd had no role to play in their leaving. What else was he to think, though? He'd been the oldest. If only he'd taken on more responsibility, behaved better, perhaps things would have been different.

"I've asked this before, but you've avoided answering. Have you ever tried to find them or your brothers?" she asked, her voice suddenly gentle.

He shook his head.

"I've asked before, but I'll ask it again—why not?"

"Isn't it obvious? They wanted no part of me or my brothers. Why should I go crawling after them?"

"If it were me, I'd want to know why they did it," she said simply. "I'd have to know."

"Some things defy explanation."

"And some things are less painful when you're old enough to understand the truth."

"That's nothing more than a bunch of psychological mumbo-jumbo and you know it," he accused. "I don't need it."

"Then what *do* you need from me?"

He regarded her sadly. "Nothing," he insisted, lying through his teeth. "Absolutely nothing."

Maggie didn't say a word, but she looked shattered. Before he realized what she intended, she was out of the car and running up the sidewalk. Ryan sat there, the open passenger door letting in the freezing air, and realized that never, not even on the day he'd been abandoned by his parents, had he felt quite so alone.

The pounding on the door to his apartment would have awakened the dead. Ryan scowled but didn't budge from his chair. The drink he'd poured himself when he'd returned from Maggie's was still full. Even as he'd filled the glass, he'd known the solution to his problems wasn't alcohol. Unless he drank the whole blasted bottle it wouldn't grant him the oblivion he sought.

"Dammit, I know you're in there," Rory shouted. "Open the door or I'll have to break it down."

Ryan sighed. He knew Rory was not only capable of such a thing but, given the heat in his voice, probably even eager to do it. He crossed the room in three long strides and threw open the door.

"What is your problem?" he demanded.

"I'm not the one with the problem," Rory said.

"Oh?"

"Maggie called. She's worried about you."

"She shouldn't be," Ryan said.

"Then call her and tell her that."

"I don't think so." As horrendous as this pain in his chest was, he knew that dragging Maggie back into his life wasn't going to work. It was better that they end this with a clean break.

Rory noted the glass of scotch beside his chair. "I thought you didn't drink."

"I *rarely* drink. There's a difference," Ryan said. "And if you nose around a little more closely, you'll see that I haven't touched that drink, either."

Rory gave a nod. "That's okay, then. Want to talk about what happened?"

"No."

"Interesting. Maggie didn't say much, either."

"How discreet of her," Ryan said sarcastically. "It's a pleasant change."

Rory frowned at him then. "Maligning Maggie won't fix whatever's bugging you."

"Don't you think I know that?"

"Talking it out might help."

"I am *not* discussing this, not with you, not with Maggie," Ryan said forcefully, his gaze leveled at his friend. "Are we clear on that?"

"Whatever you say," Rory said. "I suppose I'm expected to call her and tell her you're still among the living?"

Ryan shrugged. "Up to you."

"Perhaps I should drive out to console her," Rory suggested slyly.

Ryan felt his gut tighten. "Don't expect me to object."

"Okay, that's it," Rory declared, plopping down on the sofa. "I'm not leaving here until you tell me what happened. The day you say it's okay for me to pay a visit to Maggie is obviously the next-to-last day of the world."

Despite his foul mood, Ryan felt his lips twitch. "It's nothing that dire. It's just that it's over," he told Rory, keeping his tone surprisingly even. "Not that there was anything to begin with, just the promise of something."

"And you ended it, I suppose."

Ryan thought back over the scene outside of Maggie's. He'd said the words that had ended it, but it was Maggie who'd walked away. There was equal blame, if he wanted to be honest about it. No, he corrected, the blame was all his. He'd done what he was so good at doing. He'd shut her out, this time with a declaration she couldn't ignore.

"Yeah, I suppose I ended it," he admitted.

"Why the devil would you do a lame-brained thing like that?" Rory demanded, clearly dumbstruck. "And on Christmas, too? Have you no heart at all?"

Ryan met his friend's scowling gaze. "No," he said evenly. "And isn't that the point?"

"Sure, and if that's so, then why does it appear to

me that it's not your hard head that's suffering so to-night? It seems to me it's your heart that's broken," Rory said, then headed for the door. "Think about that one, why don't you?"

When the door clicked shut, Ryan closed his eyes against the tide of anguish and regret washing over him. He tried once again telling himself that he'd done the right thing, but being in the right was cold comfort.

The remainder of Christmas day passed in a blur for Maggie. She managed to keep a smile on her face, but she didn't really fool anyone. She knew, because they all tiptoed around Ryan's sudden disappearance, not a one of them asking why he'd gone. Matt quietly offered Father Francis a lift back to the city, and the priest left after giving Maggie's hand a sympathetic squeeze. Obviously, not even he intended to try to explain away Ryan's abrupt departure. Of course, Maggie already knew the answer to that. He'd left because he couldn't bear to spend another minute in her company...and because she'd run at the first sign of trouble.

The fact that her call to Rory had been as pointless as every other attempt to get through to Ryan only made her heartache worse. He'd called back to confirm that Ryan had gotten home, adding nothing more, not even a glimmer of hope that Ryan's brooding state was likely to change come morning.

After several restless, sleepless nights, by the following Monday morning Maggie had convinced herself that *she* ought to search for the Devaneys if Ryan wasn't going to do it. They were the key to this.

Downstairs, though, in the clear light of day, she

knew that finding Ryan's family wasn't up to her. No matter how important she thought it was for Ryan to confront the past, he was the only one who could make the decision to do so.

"Maggie?" her mother said, studying her worriedly. "What's troubling you? I haven't wanted to pry, but did you and Ryan have a fight the other day? Is that why he left?"

Had it been a fight? Not really. He'd simply told her he didn't need her, that he never would. She'd walked away without a word.

"No," she said wearily, stirring sugar into the tea her mother set in front of her.

"Then what?"

"I can't talk about it, not just yet," she said.

"I saw the hair clips he gave you. They're lovely."

Maggie smiled. "Aren't they? He couldn't have picked a more perfect gift."

"Did you give him his present?"

She shook her head. "I never had the chance."

"Will you take it to him?"

"I honestly don't know."

"Because you don't want to be the one to take the first step toward mending fences? Pride's a lonely bedfellow," her mother reminded her. "If it were me, I'd take it today and resolve whatever disagreement you had so you can start the new year fresh."

Maggie sighed. It wasn't pride that had her considering staying away from the pub. It was a matter of protecting her aching heart.

But deep inside, she knew that staying away was impossible. The two most important people in Ryan's life had turned their backs on him at a critical time. She was not about to be just another person who loved him and let him down.

And she did love him. She'd accepted that weeks ago. She'd also accepted that she'd found her niche at the pub. She liked working side by side with Ryan. She loved making the customers feel welcome, loved the homey feel of the place, the impromptu singing that livened the atmosphere on many a night. Who would have thought that Father Francis would have a voice like an angel?

Maggie was not going to give up any of that without a fight. She stood up, then bent to kiss her mother's cheek. "Thanks."

"For what?"

"For reminding me what's important," she said.

"Did I do that?" her mother inquired innocently.

Maggie grinned. "You and Dad do that every day, just by being who you are."

A serene smile stole across her mother's face. "If we've given you an understanding of what marriage can be at its full potential, then we've done well by you. Now run along. I have faith that you can teach Ryan the same lesson with a little patience and a lot of love."

"I hope so," Maggie said. "Because I do love him, Mom."

Her mother gave her a hug. "I know you do. I also know he probably doesn't make it easy. But if you ask me, he returns those feelings. I just don't think he recognizes it quite yet, perhaps because it's such a new experience for him."

Maggie thought about her mother's words on the drive into Boston. She held tightly to them as she braced herself, put on a sunny smile and walked into the pub as if she'd never been away. She dropped his present casually on the bar, then moved on to hang up her coat. Before she turned away she saw the surprise in Ryan's eyes and something else, possibly a hint of relief.

Determined to act as if nothing were amiss, she grabbed her apron and immediately went to work, grateful that the place was packed and she could delay actually speaking to Ryan.

When Maureen caught up with her, she said, "Maggie, thank God you're back."

"I can see you're swamped," Maggie said.

"It's not the crowds I can't handle, it's Ryan. He's been grouchy as a bear since Christmas. It's a wonder he hasn't driven all the customers away, to say nothing of the staff. Even Rory's giving him a wide berth."

That news gave Maggie more confidence. When she eventually passed behind the bar, Ryan caught her hand and held her still, his blue eyes searching her face.

"I'm sorry for what happened on Christmas," he said finally. "I behaved like an idiot."

She studied his dear, familiar face and saw the genuine remorse. She touched a hand to his cheek. "I know."

"I'm glad you came back."

She permitted herself a small smile. "I know that, too."

He drew in a deep breath as if gathering his courage, then declared, "I've had nothing to do but think the past few days, and I've come to a conclusion. I want you, Maggie O'Brien, and if you say you know that, as well, I'll have to kiss you, right here in front of everyone."

Her smile spread. "I know everything about you, Ryan Devaney. Get used to it."

It was tantamount to a dare and they both knew it. Heat flared in his eyes right before his mouth covered hers. This was no coaxing, tentative kiss. It was a crushing, demanding kiss that had her blood turning to fire. The new urgency and neediness turned the kiss even more dangerous than all the others that had gone before. His tongue swept inside her mouth, and Maggie felt the world spin.

The only thing that stopped the kiss from lasting an eternity was the cheer that erupted from the entire bar. Ryan backed away from her as if he'd been burned.

"I'm sorry," he said, his voice husky.

Maggie scowled at his words. "Don't you dare apologize," she said.

He grinned at the ferocity of her response. "We'll finish this later," he promised.

"The kiss or the discussion?"

"Probably both," he admitted with a rueful grin.

It was all the opening she needed. Maggie's gaze locked with his. "It could be a good night to close early," she suggested with a wink.

Ryan shook his head, suddenly all practicality and reason, as he grabbed a cloth and began polishing the bar. "Monday-night football."

She'd already learned not to let reason kick in with

him. It kept him safe, not alive the way a man should be. He needed to work on his spontaneity.

She glanced around at the sea of mostly familiar faces and said loudly, "Don't any of these people have televisions at home?"

The question was greeted with laughter and a sudden flurry of activity, and the place cleared out in ten minutes flat. Even Maureen had vanished with a promise to come in early to count the receipts in the morning.

"You can sleep in," she said to Ryan with a wink.

After Maureen had gone, locking the door behind her, Ryan gazed around with a stunned expression, then faced Maggie with feigned indignation. "You trying to ruin my business?"

She shook her head. "Nope. Just trying to get your clothes off."

He swallowed hard at that, then turned out all the lights except for the neon shamrock in the window, picked up his unopened gift and grabbed her hand. "Well, then, since it looks as if I have the night off, let's go upstairs and see what we can do about that."

Maggie gave him a considering look. "What's wrong with right here?"

"You want me to strip in the middle of the pub?"

"I'm a risk taker. How about you?"

"The condoms are upstairs."

Maggie hesitated, then glanced around the room with regret. "I'm not that much of a risk taker. Upstairs it is."

"Don't look so sad," Ryan teased. "I'll make it worth your while."

She grinned at him. "I'm counting on it."

12

Ryan kept expecting to wake up from a dream. Instead, each brush of Maggie's hands over his chest, each deeply satisfying kiss, felt very real. The roar of his blood, the heat generated by each caress, the demanding need, couldn't possibly have been matched by a mere dream, no matter how sweet.

He opened his eyes, saw the flesh-and-blood Maggie before him and knew the greatest sense of satisfaction he'd ever felt in his life. This—*she*—was real. She was in his arms, just as she was in his heart.

For better or for worse.

Right now, though, he could only think of the positives, of the way the light turned her pale skin a soft gold, the way her curves fit him, the way she came alive with each touch, the way her back arched when he cupped her breast in the palm of his hand.

There was nothing halfway about Maggie. She was open and giving, and demanded as much as she gave.

Ryan lifted his head and gazed into her sea-green eyes. "You are a revelation."

"Oh?" She eyed him with sleepy sensuality. "What were you expecting?"

"Caution. Restraint. A hint of modesty, perhaps."

She laughed. "From me? I've been all but begging for this moment for weeks now. There wasn't much caution or restraint in that."

He gave her a sheepish shrug. "I honestly thought it was all talk."

"Are you disappointed that it wasn't?" she asked, a faint hint of worry in her eyes.

Ryan pressed a kiss at the base of her throat, felt the quick flash of heat beneath his lips. "Absolutely not. An eager woman can be a real turn-on, especially when it's unexpected."

She grinned at that. "Then you won't mind if I do this," she said, reaching for the snap on his jeans. "I think this break has lasted long enough."

Ryan jerked as her knuckles skimmed his abdomen. With her gaze locked with his, she lowered the zipper on his jeans, then slid them down his legs. He kicked them aside.

"Anything else you're anxious to strip off me?" he inquired in a lazy tone, curious to see what she'd do next.

"Those shorts have to go sooner or later," she said with a considering look that sent his temperature soaring. She lifted her gaze to his, a half smile on her lips. "But not just yet."

Ryan couldn't breathe. "Oh?"

"Don't think I don't know the fine art of building anticipation, Ryan Devaney. Haven't I been patient for weeks now, while you've been making up your mind? Hasn't it almost driven me to distraction?"

"Really?" he asked, pleased beyond measure that she'd been as anxious as he for this moment. "You've had your revenge, though. You've done your best to torment me every minute."

"Well, of course I have," she said smugly. "Isn't that the point? How else was I to make you want me so desperately you'd forget all your silly reservations?"

His mood sobered at once at the teasing question. "They weren't silly, Maggie. And I still have a slew of them."

She shook her head. "Not tonight, you don't. And tonight is all that matters. One night, Ryan." She grinned. "And then possibly another."

It was the give-an-inch-take-a-mile attitude with which he'd become increasingly familiar, and which had made him increasingly wary.

"I can't promise tomorrow," he said, needing to be clear about that even though he'd begun dreaming of weeks and months from now.

"Have I asked you to?" she inquired lightly.

"No," he admitted. "But you deserve all the promises of tomorrow a man can make."

"If it's right, they'll come in time," she said readily. "For now, I think it's best if we concentrate on the moment."

She lifted her sweater over her head, then shimmied out of her jeans, revealing all the fancy, delicate lace he'd fantasized about. She might tend toward an unremarkable wardrobe of sedate jeans and sweaters, but beneath she clearly indulged her feminine side.

Her body was perfect with its narrow hips, long, long legs and breasts that filled the cups of her bra to overflowing. He could have stared at her forever, but she was having none of that. She moved closer, looped her arms around his neck and hooked one leg around his, bringing all that satiny skin and heat in contact with his own suddenly burning flesh.

"Make love to me, Ryan," she whispered against his lips. "Now."

He pushed aside the last nagging cautions, lifted her up and settled her on his bed. Then he stripped off his shorts and joined her, making quick work of getting rid of those remaining scraps of lace. For the moment he was content to explore every inch of her with lingering caresses, discovering the secrets of her body, his gaze locked on her expressive face as her arousal grew and her movements turned restless.

"Now," she pleaded, her back arching, her hips lifting off the bed in time to the rhythm of his fingers probing deep inside her. "Please, Ryan. I want you inside me."

"It's okay," he said as her body tensed. "Go with it, darlin'. Let it come."

"But—" The rest of the protest was lost as the climax ripped through her.

Only when the last shudder had died away did he slowly enter her, thrusting deep, then waiting as her body adjusted to him. The welcoming heat wrapped itself around him, and her last fluttering contractions made him even harder.

Then, looking into her eyes, he began to move, the steady, pulsing rhythm as old as time as it built to a higher and higher peak. The wonder on Maggie's face would have been enough, but there was more. There were the sweet cries deep in her throat, the demanding rise of her hips to meet his, the glow of perspiration on her skin as she strained to reach that elusive, final pinnacle. Her eyes drifted closed, as if to increase her concentration on the struggle, but Ryan was having none of that, not when they were so close to the end.

"Maggie, look at me," he commanded. He needed to know that she was with *him* and no one else. He could feel her body starting to shudder, could feel his own tensing for one last thrust and an exquisite release. "Look at me!"

She opened her eyes just as the rush of his climax rocked through him. Her hips rose one last time, and then she, too, was catapulting over the brink,

The aftershocks seemed to go on forever. Ryan rolled on his back and pulled her on top of him, cradling her close, as his breathing finally slowed. Maggie was limp in his arms, her own breathing ragged.

Eventually she lifted her head and met his gaze. "That was...remarkable."

Ryan grinned at the stunned note in her voice. "I told you I'd making coming upstairs worth your while."

Her mouth gaped at the reminder, and then, to his shock, she began to laugh.

"What?" he asked, bemused by the reaction. He'd certainly found nothing to laugh about in the last hour or more.

"We came up for the condoms," she reminded him. A sense of dismay washed over him at the implication. "And forgot them," he said slowly. "Oh, my God, Maggie, I'm sorry. It never crossed my mind."

"Nor mine," she reminded him.

"But I'm always responsible." He raked a hand through his hair. What had he been thinking? Of course, that was precisely the problem, he hadn't been thinking. Not with his brain, anyway. And the rest of his anatomy clearly wasn't to be trusted. What the hell was he supposed to do if she got pregnant? He couldn't—he wouldn't—abandon her. But what kind of father could he possibly be? What kind of husband? All of the questions he'd spend a lifetime thinking he'd never have to deal with came crashing down around him, demanding answers.

Even as the questions set off panic, a tiny part of him marveled at the possibility that they had created a child together. The fear of committing to that—to Maggie—wasn't nearly as horrendous as it would have been even days ago.

Maggie touched a finger to his brow. "Uh-oh. Worry lines. Stop it, Ryan. I'm not going to get pregnant."

"You can't possibly know that. People get pregnant all the time, even when they use protection."

"Well, it won't be your problem if I do," she insisted, her jaw set stubbornly.

If that was meant to be reassuring, it failed miserably. Instead, it infuriated him. "And whose would it be? Is there someone in this bed I'm not aware of?"

"I just meant—"

"I know what you meant. You're trying to let me off the hook…again," he said, all but shouting. "And let's get one thing very clear, if there's a baby, I'm responsible. It *is* my problem, and we'll deal with it together. Understood?"

"I won't have you trapped into a marriage you don't want, Ryan," she said, her voice cool. "That's something you need to understand. Any baby we conceived wouldn't be a problem, not to me. It would be a blessing." She regarded him wistfully. "Do we have to fight about this now?"

"Isn't it better to be clear about things now, rather than put them off till we've a crisis?" he asked.

"No," she said emphatically. "Because I've just had the best night of my life, and you're ruining it with all this talk of doom and gloom." She frowned at him. "Now let me be clear about something—I won't have it."

He grinned despite himself. "Okay then, no more doom and gloom. Would I be out of line if I suggested another kiss?"

"Perhaps." Her expression turned thoughtful. "Try it and we'll see."

"I prefer not to take chances, especially with a woman who's in such a dangerous mood."

She laughed, and the dark mood was broken for good. "Come here and kiss me."

He chuckled and rolled toward the nightstand. "If you don't mind, I think I'll grab the condoms first. With you, one kiss has a way of leading to another."

Maggie had waited so long for this moment she thought her heart would burst from sheer joy. She was not going to allow Ryan's momentary panic about the possibility of a baby ruin it. Truthfully, she could think of nothing more wonderful than having his child, but she could understand his fears.

To her those fears were just one more reason why he needed to act and do whatever it took to put the past to rest, but she was done with nudging him. It hadn't gotten her anywhere so far.

She rolled over and stared at him, admiring his long, lean body and well-defined muscles.

"Is there something here you like?" he inquired, his voice threaded with amusement.

"I'm debating," she said.

"Very funny."

She met his gaze then, her expression serious. "Did I mention to you that last night was the best night of my life?"

"Once or twice," he teased.

"Well, it was, and I see no point in denying it."

He grinned. "I'd be the last one to want you to. So, Miss Maggie, what plans do you have for the day? The new year is fast approaching. Have you given any thought to what you'll be doing come January?"

"Trying to get rid of me?" she asked, attempting to inject a light note into her voice. But even she could hear the hint of edginess.

"Never that," he said, his expression unguarded for once. "I want you here, Maggie. More than I should."

She relaxed then, relieved that he'd asked, after a fashion, anyway. "Then this is where I'll be."

He studied her. "For how long?"

"Now who's pushing for more than one day at a

time?" she teased. "Is it a commitment you're asking for, Ryan Devaney?"

He seemed to struggle with himself before finally sighing. "What if I were?"

"Then you'd have it," she said without any hesitation at all.

He seemed taken aback by her ready response. "Just like that?"

"Just like that." She regarded him with a steady look. "But you're not asking yet, are you?"

He reached over and brushed a wayward curl from her cheek. "Not yet, Maggie," he said with obvious regret. "But I'm beginning to believe that one of these days I will."

She rose on one elbow to kiss him. "Then I'll be waiting for that day. And in the meantime, I'll be poking into your business at the pub as much as you'll let me."

He chuckled. "Which won't be much," he warned.

"We'll see."

"Aren't the books at St. Mary's enough to keep you occupied?"

"Hardly. I had those straightened up the first week. The only thing giving me any trouble is getting Father Francis to follow the rules about collecting receipts for what he buys for the shelter and taking note of the donations so a proper acknowledgment can be sent."

"I can see where that might be a challenge," he said. "Since he's not a stupid man, has it occurred to you that he's being impossible just to make sure you keep coming around?"

Truthfully that had never crossed Maggie's mind. "You think so?"

"If it were me, I would."

She grinned at him. "In other words, you won't let me touch your business records because you're holding them in reserve as an incentive to keep me here?"

"You never know," he teased.

"What if I were to promise to stick around, anyway—would you let me work on them then?"

He seemed to consider the question thoughtfully, then shook his head. "Afraid not."

"Why not?"

He shrugged. "Too much experience with broken promises."

Maggie sighed. They were back to his family again. "Ryan—"

He held up a hand. "No. Don't go there. For once, let's just forget all about my family."

"Okay," she said with a nod of agreement. "I can do that." She leveled a look directly into his eyes. "Can you?"

Maggie's challenge lingered in Ryan's head for days. He knew he was in way over his head with Maggie if he was even considering for a second looking for his parents. And he *was* thinking about it, not because he wanted to find them, but because it mattered so damned much to her. He'd give her just about anything on earth she wanted. From the moment he'd made love to her, he'd known he was lost.

With her open, generous heart, Maggie offered everything he'd been denied all his life—love, a sense of belonging, joy. And with Nell and Garrett O'Brien and the others, she was also offering him the chance to be connected to a real family. That should have been more than enough for a man who'd had so little in the way of love.

But as happy as he was with their growing relationship, he was forced to admit that there was still something missing from his life, something that Maggie could never replace. Perhaps, if he was brave enough, they could marry and have children, but no matter how many people she brought into his life, it would never entirely make up for those he'd lost. From the moment she'd uttered that challenge, she hadn't said anything more about finding his family, but she, too, clearly believed that they were the missing part of his heart. If he hadn't known it before, he couldn't mistake it once he'd finally opened her Christmas present—a frame with his picture and room for five more. He'd known those empty spaces were meant for photos of his brothers and parents.

Despite all that, Ryan couldn't seem to bring himself to do anything about initiating a search. He wasn't entirely sure why he was so terrified to try. Was he afraid of being disappointed? Or afraid of another rejection?

Whenever his head was filled with questions and no answers, he always headed for the shelter. There were people there with worse problems than his, people who survived despite whatever tragedies had befallen them.

When he arrived at midmorning, he was surprised to find Letitia at work in the kitchen preparing lunch for the children. She was making peanut butter and jelly sandwiches at a rapid clip, but her expression was distracted.

"Everything okay?" Ryan inquired after watching her for several minutes.

She looked up from her task, and her face broke into a smile. "Mr. Devaney, what are you doing here?"

"I came by to spend some time with the kids. They usually need a distraction during the holidays. With no school and some of the parents out looking for jobs, they can get a little rambunctious. What are you doing here? I thought you'd be at the hospital."

"Jamal's with Lamar." Her eyes lit up. "Did you know he's getting out of the hospital later this week? The doctors say he's making fantastic progress. Looks like my boy has a bright future ahead of him."

"That's wonderful. Will you be coming back here?"

She shook her head, her smile widening. "Jamal went back to his old boss and explained what had happened. He agreed to take him back after the first of the year. He even gave him an advance on his salary, so we could make a deposit on an apartment. We move in tomorrow so we can get it all fixed up before Lamar comes home."

She put down the jar of jelly and crossed the room to hug him. "I have my life back, and it's all because of you."

Ryan was growing more comfortable with the impulsive show of affection, but not with the praise. "Letitia—" he began.

She cut off his protest. "I won't hear none of that," she scolded. "You did a good thing. Now accept my thanks."

He grinned. "You're welcome."

She studied him intently. "Is there something else on your mind? You've got the look of a man with troubles. Is it Maggie?"

"Maggie's fine," he said.

"You treating her right?"

He grinned at the protective note in her voice. "As right as I know how."

"What's that mean?"

"It's a long story. I won't bore you with it."

She frowned at that. "Let me get these sandwiches out to my babies out there, and you tell me the story."

Oddly, Ryan couldn't seem to make himself turn down the offer. Maybe what he needed was an entirely fresh perspective. For so long now he'd simply tuned out Father Francis's advice and, more recently, even Maggie's, because he hadn't wanted to deal with the past at all.

Letitia made short work of delivering lunch to the children in the dining room, then came back and poured them each a cup of coffee. "Now sit down over here and tell me what's on your mind," she instructed him in a no-nonsense tone.

Ryan began the story with the day his parents left and he was separated from his brothers. Tears welled up in Letitia's eyes as he talked, but she didn't say a word. She just listened until he had told her everything, right on up to Maggie's belief that he needed to find his family if he was ever to have any real peace.

"I'm beginning to think she's right," he admitted. "I've been living in some sort of emotional limbo for too long now."

"Seems that way to me, too," Letitia said. "And there's one more thing you're not considering."

"What's that?"

"Just think for a minute about what happened to Lamar because his daddy and I didn't know Jamal's medical history and what it could mean for our boy. You haven't said if you're thinking of marrying Maggie, but if that thought has crossed your mind, you need to know something about this whole genetics thing."

Ryan seized on that as if he'd been presented with a lifeline. "You're absolutely right," he told Letitia. For the first time, he had a purely practical reason for conducting a search for his family—one he could embrace without risking his heart.

Letitia looked troubled by his reaction. "That shouldn't be the only reason you go looking for them," she cautioned, as if she'd read his mind.

"I know," he acknowledged, but it was reason enough. A nice, *safe* reason. He stood up and bent down to kiss her cheek. "Thank you."

"I didn't do a thing," she said.

Ryan grinned at her. "Accept my thanks graciously," he chided.

Letitia laughed. "It's good to see a man who's not too old to learn a thing or two. Now, get on out of here and take care of business. And remember—I expect an invitation to the wedding."

He hesitated at the suggestion. "I never said anything about a wedding."

"The day will come," she said confidently. "Unless you're a fool, and I've seen nothing to suggest that."

"Thanks, I think. I'll try to see Lamar before he

leaves the hospital, but in case I don't, make sure I know how to find you."

"You can count on that. Like I told you, you're family now," she said, giving his hand a squeeze. "And I never lose track of family, not for long, anyway."

Ryan left the shelter feeling blessed. Only a few short weeks ago he'd been satisfied with a handful of friends and a ton of acquaintances. Now he seemed to be collecting families who were determined to draw him in. Maybe if his own family rejected him for a second time, it wouldn't be quite so painful.

Now that the decision to find his biological family had been made, Ryan was anxious to get started. Unfortunately, he had no idea where to begin. He had no clue how to conduct a search for people missing for so many years. Hiring a private eye seemed like the best option, but the prospect of sharing the story with a stranger was painful. Turning to Jack Reilly once again made it easier.

To Ryan's surprise, telling the whole sad tale to Jack turned out to hurt less than it had when he'd told it to Maggie, or even to Letitia. Jack was a professional. He was used to listening without comment, and he'd probably heard far more sordid tales than the one Ryan had to tell. Throughout the conversation, the investigator was completely matter-of-fact, taking notes and asking questions about facts and places, not about emotions.

When Jack had everything he needed, Ryan said, "One last thing—don't say anything about this to Maggie, okay?"

"You're the client," Jack said readily. "Anything you tell me is strictly confidential."

Ryan was relieved. He didn't want her to know until he had something solid to report. Besides, there was still the very real chance that even once he'd found his parents or siblings, he wouldn't be able to confront them. Why get Maggie's hopes up, only to back out?

"How long is this likely to take?" he asked Jack.

"Hard to say. The trail's been cold for a long time. Since you were all fairly young when you went into foster care, it's possible that the youngest boys were adopted. Their names could have been changed. If that happened and the records are sealed, it'll take a miracle to find them."

"And my parents?"

"Easier, I'd say, depending on where they ran off to. I'll have a better idea once I've run a few simple checks on credit reports, that kind of thing. As soon as I know anything, I'll let you know." He studied Ryan curiously. "It's been a lot of years. Is there some reason you're in a rush all of a sudden?"

"I'm not in a rush," Ryan said. "Not exactly."

But until he'd found these missing pieces to the past, he couldn't begin to think about the future with Maggie that he'd begun to yearn for.

13

Something was up with Ryan. He was edgy and distracted, and he seemed to be spending a lot of time huddled in a booth with Jack Reilly. Whenever Maggie approached, they both fell silent. It was getting on her nerves.

She was behind the bar taking inventory, something Ryan had grudgingly allowed her to do, when he came back after one of those secret talks. She saw the evident frustration in his eyes and decided to confront him.

"Okay, that's it," she said, putting down the legal pad and pen she'd been using to take notes. She scowled at him. "What is going on?"

Ryan stared at her blankly. It was a pretty good act. Even she could admit that. He looked as if he had no idea at all what she was talking about.

"You and Jack," she said, to clarify things. "What's up with all the whispering?"

"It's about a case he's working on."

"Why can he talk to *you* about it?" she asked, not

buying it for a minute, "yet the two of you clam up whenever I come around."

"It's nothing for you to worry about," Ryan said dismissively, picking up the legal pad and scanning her notes. "How's our supply of Irish whisky?"

Maggie frowned at the deliberate evasiveness. "We have an entire case, which you should know, since you ordered it day before yesterday."

He gave her a sheepish grin. "So I did." He stepped closer. "Must be you. You have a way of making me forget everything except my name." He tucked a finger under her chin and kissed her thoroughly. "Now that's something I've been waiting to do ever since you walked through the door tonight."

Her gaze narrowed at the touch of blarney in his voice. "Ryan Devaney, you're keeping something from me," she accused. "And you're being patronizing about it, as well. Just so you know, I don't like it."

"Is that so?" he asked, still not taking her nearly seriously enough. "I thought you were a woman who was fond of secrets."

"I'm a woman who is fond of *unraveling* secrets. There's a difference. I don't like things being *kept* from me."

"Is it not possible that some things don't concern you?" he inquired.

"Of course it's possible," she retorted impatiently. "But something tells me that's not the case right now."

He beckoned her closer. "If you were to put aside all those doubts and questions, I could close up now and we could go upstairs."

"You shouldn't use sex as a distraction," she chided,

but her mood was definitely shifting. Maybe she didn't have to have answers to all those burning questions just yet. Tomorrow might be soon enough. "Though if it were a promise of outrageously wicked sex you were making, I could be persuaded to go along with it."

He leaned down and whispered in her ear. His husky voice and the promise of something absolutely sinful shot the last of her resolve to smithereens. When he was in this kind of dangerous mood, he was practically irresistible.

"Lock the door," she said, her voice breathless.

His expression turned smug. "You're a surprisingly predictable woman at times, Maggie O'Brien."

Maggie glowered at him. "Not a compliment," she warned.

He didn't seem disturbed. "There are other times, though—and far more of them, I might add—when you're so unpredictable you make a man's head spin."

Pleased by that assessment, she kissed him. "Much better. Which am I tonight?"

He gave her a considering look. "Now that remains to be seen, doesn't it?"

Heat shot through her at the speculative gleam in his eyes. She headed for the stairs. "If you dawdle over closing up, I'll have to come down here and have my way with you on the bar."

He laughed. "You've been begging to do that since the first night we made love. One of these nights I'll have to accommodate you, though it seems to me that a bed is a more practical, comfortable choice."

"Sometimes the thrill of accepting a dare offsets

whatever discomfort is involved," she teased. "But tonight the bed will do."

In fact, just about any place where she could feel Ryan's arms around her and his body joined with hers was a magical place indeed. And with each and every day that passed, Maggie was growing more and more confident that Ryan felt the same.

If only there weren't this faint shadow threatening her happiness.

Two days later Maggie looked up from behind the bar and spotted her entire family coming through the door. Her mother shot her a rueful look as they made their way to the biggest table in the room. Maggie sighed. She might not be able to kick them right back out, but she could certainly avoid them, at least for a while. She turned to Maureen.

"That crowd that just came in," she said, nodding in her family's direction. "They belong to me, but I think I'll give you the pleasure of waiting on them. I have the feeling they're here on a mission."

"What sort of mission?" Maureen inquired curiously.

"I haven't been home for a few days now."

Maureen's gaze shot to Ryan, who was just emerging from the kitchen. "I see. How lovely!"

"I imagine that depends on your point of view," Maggie said, eyeing her family warily. "Go and keep them occupied, while I warn Ryan."

Maureen laughed. "Judging from that panicked look in his eyes, he doesn't need warning," she said, but she took her order pad and made her way to the table.

Ryan joined Maggie behind the bar. "Exactly how dire is this situation?" he asked, his gaze locked worriedly on the O'Brien entourage.

"I imagine that depends," she said. "If you can cope with a few questions about your intentions, and assuming they're honorable enough, I imagine the weapons will remain sheathed."

Ryan swallowed hard. "Well now, there's an incentive to race over to St. Mary's and pray. Where's Father Francis when I need him? They'd never attack with a priest beside me."

"Don't count on it," Maggie said. "There is one other choice. I could go over there, announce that I'm the happiest I've been in years, and tell them if they do one single thing to mess that up, I'll never forgive them."

Ryan nodded. "I like that choice."

"Of course you do," she said. "It keeps you out of harm's way."

"True enough," he admitted. "But before you go, mind telling me something? Is it true what you just said?"

"What?"

"That you're happy?"

She regarded him with shock. "How could you possibly question that?"

He shrugged. "It's a habit, I guess." Avoiding her gaze, he added, "Whenever something seems too good to be true, I'm always waiting for it to be snatched away."

His tone was so bleak and there was such sadness behind the words that Maggie made a decision. She latched on to his hand with a firm grip. "You're coming with me," she said, as she dragged him toward the table.

When she reached her family, she pinned her gaze on her mother. "I imagine you came tonight to hear the band," she said. "It's a wonderful group just over from Dublin."

"The music be damned," John said, scowling at Ryan. "We came because you've all but vanished from the house. We wanted to see if you were all right."

"And why wouldn't I be?" Maggie inquired. "I'm with Ryan, aren't I?"

"That's what we've been worrying about," Matt said. "Do you really know what you're doing? Has he made any promises?" His gaze was locked on Ryan, even though he'd addressed the questions to her.

Maggie rolled her eyes at the growling note of protectiveness in his voice. "I haven't asked for any," she said. "And what goes on between Ryan and me is our business. He makes me happy. That's all that should concern any of you."

Ryan met John's gaze, then Matt's. "I can understand your concern," he said. "If I had a sister like Maggie, I'd want to do everything in my power to keep her from getting hurt, too."

"So?" John pushed.

"I'm not going to hurt her," Ryan said. "Not intentionally, anyway."

When her brothers seemed about to leap on the opening he'd left himself, Maggie's mother interceded. "That's good enough for me," she said cheerfully. "Shouldn't you back off now, Matthew? John?" It was quite clearly not a request but an order.

"I haven't heard a word about marriage," John said, defying her.

Ryan looked him in the eye. "And you're not the one I'd be proposing to, either."

Katie and Colleen smothered laughter at John's look of indignation.

"I'd say he has you there," Matt said, relenting a little. He looked back at Ryan. "Just know that we're keeping an eye on things."

"That's as it should be," Ryan agreed, accepting the warning.

Maggie's father had kept silent through the entire exchange, but he gave a nod of satisfaction now. "That's that, then. I'll have a glass of your finest ale. Can you join us, lad?"

"I'm needed at the bar just now, but I'll be back," Ryan promised. "Maggie, why don't you join your family for dinner? It's on the house."

"You cannot be giving away dinner to a crowd like this," she retorted, thinking of the dent it would make in his bottom line for the night. "What kind of business practice is that? Next thing you know, all your regulars will be coming in with their families and asking for the same deal you gave the O'Briens."

Her brothers hooted. "Now isn't that what every man needs, a woman with a head for business standing beside him?" John said.

"But at the moment, it is my business," Ryan said, his gaze clashing with hers in a test of wills with which she was increasingly familiar. "And I'm of a mind to buy dinner for your family."

"Then we'll be grateful for it," her mother said, giving Maggie a pointed look. "Won't we, Maggie?"

Maggie uttered a sigh of resignation and pulled up a chair beside her mother. She knew better than they exactly what Ryan was doing. He was hoping to pacify the wolves with a hearty meal…and just in case it didn't work, he was throwing her to them.

Keeping Maggie from learning the truth about his meetings with Jack Reilly was getting to be increasingly difficult for Ryan. When the P.I. came to him a few days later with the news that he had a lead on Ryan's brother Sean, Ryan was relieved on several levels. If nothing else, it meant he finally had something concrete to share with Maggie.

"What did you find out?" he asked the detective as an image of his dark-haired brother came to mind. "Where is he? Is he okay?"

"He's right here in Boston, working as a firefighter," Jack told him. "The trail led to his last foster family, but I had the devil's own time getting a word out of them. They were afraid that you'd just be stirring up bad memories. Finally I convinced them to contact him. I gave them my number, and he called earlier today."

"And?"

"He wants to see you. Here's the address and the phone number. The number's unlisted, so don't lose track of it."

"Did you tell him anything about me?"

Jack shook his head. "I wasn't sure if you wanted me to, so I just said you'd been anxious to find him and that I was sure you'd be in touch soon."

Ryan sighed. So, this was it? he thought, staring at the piece of paper with Sean's address. It was only a couple of miles away. It was hard to imagine, but they could have passed on the street a thousand times and not even known it.

"You going to call him now?" Jack asked.

Ryan shook his head. "I need to tell someone first."

"Maggie?"

"Yes."

"Well, I'll leave you to it, then. Do you want me to keep looking for the others?"

No matter how this reunion went, Ryan knew he needed to find the rest of them now. He had to play this out to the end. "Of course."

"I'll be in touch, then." Jack glanced toward the door and smiled. "And here comes Maggie now. Just in time, I'd say."

He waved to Maggie, then took off. Maggie's gaze followed him from the bar before she came over and joined Ryan. "Another of those top-secret meetings? It must be quite a case he's handling."

Ryan slipped the piece of paper in his pocket. Despite Jack's advice, he wasn't ready to share the news yet. He needed to absorb it.

"Where have you been off to?" he asked, deliberately ignoring her question.

She regarded him with disappointment, but let the matter drop. "I went to see Lamar," she said.

"How is he?"

"Getting stronger every day. He wants to see you."

"I'll get by there this week. Is the new apartment okay?"

"A little small, but it's clean and in a nice neighborhood. Letitia says it's a palace compared to the place where they were forced to stay before she gave up and moved to the shelter. We looked over her budget and found a way for her to put a little aside from Jamal's paycheck each week toward a down payment on a house. Once Lamar is back on his feet, she's going to look for work, too." Maggie eyed him speculatively. "I suggested she find a book of Irish recipes at the library and practice a bit, then invite us over for dinner."

Ryan shook his head. "As if Father Francis weren't bad enough, now you're going to be bringing me new employees?"

"I never said anything about you hiring her," Maggie said, her expression perfectly innocent. "But it's a great idea, don't you think? Besides, Rosita will be having her baby anytime now, so there'll be an opening in the kitchen."

"As if Rosita has done a lick of work since she came," Ryan grumbled.

"Only because Rory is a gentleman," Maggie replied.

"Okay, fine. Whatever. If Letitia needs a job, we'll work it out."

Maggie studied him with a narrowed gaze, as if she suspected his capitulation had been too easy. "Is everything okay? Is there something you're not telling me?"

Ryan frowned at the question. "Who says I'm keeping anything from you?" he asked defensively.

"Nothing's really changed, has it?" she asked. "You still can't let me all the way into your life."

He heard the unmistakable hurt in her voice. Regret washed through him, but he couldn't make himself share the truth. Not just yet. "I'm sorry, Maggie. I'm trying, but I'm not there yet. Be patient, okay?"

She sighed heavily. "Since I'm in love with you, it seems I have no choice."

Her easy claim of love startled him. He'd known her feelings for him were growing, but to have her admit that she actually loved him caught him off guard. Even more surprising was the fact that it didn't terrify him. Rather, it made him want to admit that his feelings were growing deeper as well.

He took her hand in his, swallowed hard, then fumbled until he found the right words. "If it's any consolation, I love you, too." The admission had been easier than he'd expected, but he couldn't help adding a quick disclaimer. "At least as much as I know how to love anyone. Can that be enough for you?"

A faint glimmer of a smile appeared on her lips. "For now," she said, her eyes shimmering with unshed tears. "It is for now."

Ryan must have looked at that slip of paper with Sean's address on it a dozen times a day. Each time he picked up the phone to call his brother, then settled the receiver back into its cradle. For two solid weeks that paper taunted him, as did the worried frown puckering Maggie's brow. He evaded all the questions Rory and Father Francis had about his dark mood, as well. He was driving them all away, and all because he was afraid to tell them the momentous news that he'd found one of his brothers.

At night, lying awake in bed next to a sleeping Maggie, he questioned why he was having such a difficult time with this. It didn't take long for him to figure out the answer. He was desperately afraid of how seeing Sean again might change things.

What if his brother hated him for standing by and watching him walk away with strangers that day and doing nothing? For all Ryan knew, Sean could have found their parents and discovered that Ryan's worst fear was accurate, that he had somehow driven them away. He knew it was a boy's fear, not that of a rational grown-up, but he couldn't seem to turn his back on it just the same. He'd lived with that guilt burning inside him for too many years.

Greater than the fear of all that, though, was this mounting panic that if he didn't do something, Maggie would eventually slip away. Despite her promise to give him all the time he needed, it was already happening. She was growing more reserved as he insisted on keeping his secret. The openness he prized in her was giving way to brooding silences. He couldn't let that go on or he would lose her forever. He sighed heavily.

"Ryan?" she murmured, rolling toward him. "Are you awake?"

He nodded, then realized she probably had her eyes closed. "Yes. Go back to sleep. I didn't mean to disturb you."

Instead, she propped herself on her elbow and studied him sleepily. "What's wrong?"

"I have a lot on my mind."

"Please tell me."

He hesitated, then drew in a deep breath. This was the moment he'd been waiting for, here in the dark, where she couldn't read his expression so readily.

When he didn't speak right away, she said, "Is it so hard to talk to me? There's nothing you can't say now. I want to be here for you, but I can't be if you won't let me in."

She was right and he knew it. "Okay, here it is. I've had Jack looking for my family," he said quietly.

"Really?" Maggie remarked, her voice surprisingly neutral, as if she didn't want to risk getting excited. "And?"

Relieved by her calm, accepting reaction, he went on. "He's found one of my brothers."

"Oh, my God," she murmured. "Which one?"

"Sean. He's two years younger than I am."

He felt her tears fall on his bare chest. "Oh, Ryan, that's wonderful! How long have you known?"

"A couple of weeks now."

"And you haven't said a word? Why not?"

"I'm not entirely sure why I haven't," he admitted candidly.

"Have you been to see him?"

"No…."

"Why on earth not? Is he here in Boston?"

He shrugged, feeling helpless. "Only a couple of miles away, as a matter of fact. And to be honest, I don't know why I haven't called or gone to see him. He must be wondering about it, too, since Jack told him I was looking for him."

"Oh, Ryan, put yourself in his shoes," Maggie said

urgently. "It must be awful waiting for a call that hasn't come. It must be a little bit like reliving what he went through after your parents took off. I'm sure all of you kept expecting to get a phone call any day."

"Oh, God," Ryan whispered, struck by her words. "I never looked at it that way. You're right, Maggie. It was months before I finally accepted the fact that they weren't calling and weren't coming back." The memory still haunted him. How many hours had he stayed near the phone wherever he was, waiting, trying desperately not to hope when it rang, fighting tears when it wasn't for him.

"That's when I started getting in trouble," he told Maggie. "Once I knew that it didn't matter where I was, because they were never going to look for me, I didn't care if I was moved from foster home to foster home. I didn't want to get attached to any of those families, so whenever I felt myself letting down my guard, I'd do something to get sent away."

He felt Maggie's hand on his cheek.

"It must have been so awful for you," she said sympathetically. "And now you have a chance to get back something you lost. Don't wait another day. Call Sean. Go to see him."

Ryan wasn't sure he could do it alone. "Would you...?" He looked into Maggie's eyes. "I want you to come with me."

To his dismay she shook her head. "Ryan, after all these years this should be private, just the two of you."

He searched his heart for the strength, but it wasn't there. Besides, having Maggie with him, since she'd been the one to encourage the search, felt right. "No, I need you to be there. If we're going to be family, that's how it should be."

She stared at him, clearly stunned by the casual mention of a future for the two of them. "Are we? Are we going to be family?"

He was just as shocked that she hadn't known that that was what they were leading up to, that it was the reason for everything he'd done lately to deal with the past. He was desperately trying to tie up all the loose ends so he could move forward with a clear conscience.

"That's why I'm doing this," he explained. "I want to find them all, to make sure that, you know, there are no problems you ought to know about before you marry me."

"Problems?" she asked, clearly bewildered.

"Illnesses, that kind of thing," he said, avoiding her gaze.

Maggie sat straight up in bed and regarded him with unmistakable dismay. "You're looking for them to see if everyone's *healthy?*"

"Of course," he said defensively. "That's the responsible thing to do."

"And that's the only reason?" she asked, disbelief still written all over her face.

"It's important, dammit!"

"Oh, Ryan," she whispered, fresh tears tracking down her cheeks. "It shouldn't be about that."

And then, to his shock, she climbed out of bed, dragged on her clothes and left the room without so much as a glance in his direction. And somehow, despite the terrible, aching emptiness inside him, he couldn't find a single word to call her back.

14

Ryan didn't get it. He'd done what Maggie wanted. Maybe he hadn't found his whole family, but he'd found one of his brothers. That was a start, dammit! What did she want from him? If she was expecting the Devaneys to suddenly turn all warm and fuzzy like the O'Briens—well, it wasn't going to happen. There was too blasted much water under the bridge for that.

"Ryan, you've the look of a man with a lot on his mind," Father Francis said, sliding onto a stool at the bar. "Anything I can help with?"

"Not unless you can explain the way a woman's mind works," Ryan retorted.

Father Francis grinned. "Now that is a mysterious thing," he agreed. "Are we talking about any woman's mind, or is it Maggie's that has you looking as if there's a dark cloud hanging over your head?"

"Maggie's, of course."

"I notice she hasn't been coming in as regularly as she was," Father Francis said. "It's been a few days since her last visit, hasn't it?"

"Close to a week," Ryan admitted despondently.

"Have you spoken to her?"

He shook his head. What was the point of calling, when he didn't know what to say?

Father Francis looked dismayed. "Now there's your first mistake, it seems to me. Whether he's right or wrong, a man should take the first step toward making things right." He gave Ryan a canny look. "Unless, of course, you're happy with the way things are."

"No, of course not, but I don't know the first thing about smoothing this over. I have no idea what Maggie expects. She's the one who walked out." It was a disingenuous statement, and Ryan knew it. He knew precisely why Maggie was so furious. She was outraged because he cared more about making sure his family health history was problem free than he did about some phony family reunion.

Father Francis studied him intently. "She left without giving you any clue at all about why she was upset?" the priest asked doubtfully. "That doesn't sound like Maggie."

"Are you calling me a liar?" Ryan asked edgily.

"No, of course not. Have you thought of asking her to explain, then?"

"It's not that simple."

Father Francis clearly wasn't convinced. "Why, because Maggie won't be honest?"

"Of course not," Ryan said at once. "Maggie's the most honest person I know."

"Is it because she won't be able to tell you what's in her heart?"

Ryan sighed. "No."

"What then?"

"It's because I still won't be able to give her the answers she wants."

"About?"

"My family." Ryan regarded the priest helplessly. "How can I tell her I care about seeing them again, when the truth is that I don't?"

"Ah, so that's it," Father Francis said. "Have you finally decided to search for them, then? I imagine Maggie's had a hand in helping you reach that decision. Are you not comfortable with it now that you've made it? Are you considering backing down?"

"Too late for that," Ryan said wryly. "Actually, Jack Reilly's been looking for a while now. He's found one of my brothers—Sean, the one two years younger than me, which would make him about thirty now."

The old man's face lit up. "That's brilliant news. Have you seen him?"

"I can see that your expectations are the same as Maggie's," Ryan said. "You're expecting me to be overjoyed."

"And you're not?"

"I'm just looking for answers."

"What sort of answers? You do realize that if he was younger than you, Sean may not have the answers you need. Unless he's found your parents, it's unlikely he knows what went wrong."

Ryan shook his head. "That's not it at all. I want to be sure everyone's in good health, so if Maggie and I ever decide to marry and have a family, I won't be unwittingly passing any hereditary conditions along to our children."

Father Francis sighed heavily. "I imagine this is because of Lamar," he said. "And you told this to Maggie, that your search is all about genetics?"

"Yes," Ryan admitted.

The priest gave him a pitying look. "It's a wonder she didn't take a skillet to your head. I'm thinking of it myself," he said with disgust. "You clearly know how to rob a moment of its meaning."

"If you're trying to accuse me of not being a sentimental jerk, then you're right. I'm not. This is a practical search for answers I need to have before I decide whether it's right to take the next step with Maggie."

"No," the priest said flatly. "It's a way of protecting yourself from being hurt again. You're taking no chances that your brother—or the others when you find them—might not want to be a part of your life even now."

Ryan felt the undeniable sting of truth in his words. "What if I am? Can you blame me?"

"Of course not, but life is about risks, about being open to possibilities. Have you not been happier these last weeks with Maggie than you ever have been before?"

There seemed to be little to gain by lying when the answer was obvious. "Yes. What's your point?"

"If you'd continued to keep the door to your heart tightly shut, you'd have had none of that," Father Francis reminded him. "Life would have gone along on its nice, even keel with no ups and downs. It would have been safe. But you'd have missed all the joy Maggie has brought into your life. Wasn't that worth the risk of letting down your defenses?"

Much as Ryan wanted to protest that he'd been better off before, he knew it wasn't true. Maggie had opened up his heart, and there was no turning back.

"And you think that seeing my brothers and even my parents again could turn out as well?" he asked skeptically. "Despite the fact that I've spent all these years with bitterness and resentment churning around inside me?"

"You'll never know unless you try...and for the right reasons. And you'll need to be willing to let go of the bitterness and resentment and be ready move on. Surely your brother's not the one you've been angry with. Wouldn't that be a good place to start? I'm sure he's been grappling with many of the same resentments that you have."

"Okay, you win. I'll call Sean in the morning."

"It's not about what I want or about me winning. It's about you. And is there any reason for not calling him right now?" Father Francis pushed.

Ryan frowned, but he reached for the phone.

With the priest's steady gaze on him, he dialed his brother's number. Unfortunately, it was an answering machine that picked up. Hearing his brother's voice after all these years—his deep, grown-up voice— threw Ryan. Sean sounded so much like their dad, it was uncanny and disturbing. But before he could lose his nerve, he left a message.

"Sean, this is Ryan...um, your brother Ryan." He considered hanging up then, but after a glance at Father Francis's expectant, encouraging expression, he plunged on. "I'd like to see you. If it's okay, I'll stop by tomorrow around ten. I have the address. If I miss you then, I'll come by another time." He searched his brain for something more, but nothing came to him. "Um, I guess that's it. Bye."

To his shock, his hand was shaking as he replaced the receiver in its cradle. Father Francis covered his hand to steady it.

"You've taken a first step, lad, the first of many."

Ryan swallowed past the lump in his throat. "I just wish to hell I knew where they were going to lead."

Maggie had been for an hour-long walk, but it hadn't done a thing to steady her nerves or calm her temper. Nor had any of the other walks she'd taken since she'd walked out of Ryan's apartment and out of his life. She'd been expecting him to call, but the phone had remained stubbornly silent. It shouldn't have surprised her. If he hadn't reached out to his family in all these years, why was she expecting him to reach out to her? Back then he'd been too young to fight for what he needed. Now he was evidently too scared.

Back at the house, half-frozen, she poured herself a cup of tea, then sat at the kitchen table, brooding over the way things were turning out. She'd been so sure that Ryan was the one, that her love could give him the strength to face his past and move on. Maybe it was impossible after what he'd been through. Maybe she'd been expecting too much once again, just as she had when she'd wanted more passion from her last relationship. Maybe her expectations simply couldn't be met, at least never all at once.

She was still thinking that over, debating whether

there was more she could have done to get through to him, when her mother walked into the kitchen.

"I thought I heard you come in," Nell O'Brien said, pouring herself a cup of tea, then putting a few freshly baked shortbread cookies onto a plate before sitting down opposite Maggie.

"Uh-oh, you've brought out the cookies," Maggie teased. "You must be anticipating a serious talk."

"I am, indeed. I've waited patiently for you to tell me what happened between you and Ryan, but you haven't said a word. I've lost patience," her mother said. "And since Father Francis called a while ago with a rather cryptic message, I've concluded that it's time to get to the bottom of things."

Maggie sat up a little straighter. "Father Francis called? What did he want?"

"He said Ryan was going to try to see his brother at ten this morning. He seemed to think you'd be interested in that, that you might want to be there."

"No way," Maggie said fiercely. "I am not going to help him do this, not when he's doing it for all the wrong reasons."

"What reasons are those?" her mother asked.

"The stupid idiot thinks I'm worried about his genes," Maggie grumbled. "Can you imagine anything more ridiculous? I don't give two figs about that."

"Aren't you assuming it's all about you?" her mother asked mildly. "And isn't that a bit presumptuous?"

"I'm not assuming anything. That's what Ryan said. He said he needed to know if everyone was okay, if there were any medical skeletons in the closet, before he could contemplate a future with me."

Her mother gave her a pitying look. "And you took that at face value?"

"He said it, didn't he?" Maggie replied defensively, even as her conviction began to waver.

"Have you considered for an instant that maybe that's the only way he can let himself think?" she asked Maggie. "If he lets himself be vulnerable, if he lets himself envision being reunited with his family, what happens if he's rejected again?"

She let that image sink in before she continued. "Can you imagine what it must have been like for him to be abandoned when he was only nine? It was devastating enough to shape the rest of his life. Can't you remember how skittish he was just being in the same room with all of us, as if being around a big family scared him to death? It's only because of your persistence that he's let the walls around his heart come down at all."

As she listened to her mother's interpretation, shame flooded through Maggie. How could she not have seen that, when her mother had grasped it at once? Of course, that was it. This was a way for Ryan to cover emotions far too fragile for him to deal with.

"Go with him this morning," her mother encouraged. "Don't let him do this alone. Be there for him no matter how it turns out. He's taking a first step, Maggie. And he may say he's only doing it for you and for all sorts of practical reasons, but he's doing it for himself, as well. Whether he admits it or not, there has to have been an empty place inside him all these years. He's about to reach out and try to mend at least some of the hurt. That must be a very scary thing to a man whose heart's been broken the way his has been. Some people never truly recover from deep childhood hurts."

"You're right," Maggie said. "I'm the one who's been an idiot. What time did Father Francis say he was going over there? Can I still make it?"

"He said Ryan had left a message saying he'd be there at ten. Here's the address. You should have just enough time, if you hurry." She smiled. "He's a good man, Maggie."

"I know that. I think I was just expecting him to be a saint." She recalled what Ryan had said to her the night they'd first met, that he wasn't the man Father Francis was likely to make him out to be. If only she'd listened then, perhaps her expectations wouldn't have been so unreasonable.

Ryan had so many qualms about going through with this meeting that he'd almost turned right around and driven back home a half dozen times. It was the prospect of facing Father Francis's disappointment—and Maggie's, assuming she ever started speaking to him again—that kept him going until he reached the street on which Sean's apartment was located.

It was in an older neighborhood, where brownstones had been converted into multifamily dwellings. It wasn't exactly shabby, but it wasn't an area that had been gentrified either. Even so, it was head and shoulders above the neighborhood they'd lived in as kids.

He spotted Sean's building, drove around the block, then found a parking space just down the street. But once he'd cut the engine, he couldn't seem to make himself leave the car. Suddenly he was awash in memories.

Because they'd been the oldest, barely two years apart, he and Sean had been best friends. Sean had been his shadow from the moment he learned to walk. He'd even insisted Ryan walk with him on his first day of school, rather than their mother, because he hadn't wanted to look like a baby. They'd played baseball together at the small park down the street. Ryan had taught him to ride the secondhand bike he'd managed to buy from a church thrift store with the pocket change he'd earned by helping elderly neighbors carry their groceries or wash their cars.

None of that had changed when Michael came along. Ryan and Sean had welcomed their new brother, waiting impatiently until he was old enough to go with them everywhere. They were brothers, and that's what brothers did.

But when the twins were born, everything changed. They were fussier babies, and the mere fact that there were two of them in a an increasingly crowded apartment added to the tension. Tempers flared more often. Ryan couldn't count the number of evenings he and Sean had fled from the apartment in tears because of the shouting between his parents. Michael, too little to follow, had huddled in his bed and cried just as hard as the babies.

In retrospect, he probably shouldn't have been surprised when their family collapsed under the weight of all that stress. But coming home after school to an empty apartment, standing inside the deserted rooms with Sean's hand tucked in his, had been a shock.

They'd been there only moments when the neighbor caring for Michael came in with him in tow, her face pale and tears welling up in her eyes. She'd still been trying to explain that their parents had disappeared with the twins when the social worker arrived to take over.

They'd gone to an emergency foster care home together that first night. Michael had finally cried himself out and fallen asleep, but Ryan and Sean had huddled together in bed, whispering, trying to make sense of what had happened, trying desperately not to be afraid.

They hadn't been allowed to go back to their old school, which was across town. Instead, while the social worker tried to locate their parents, they had waited, terrified to ask what would happen if their parents weren't found.

The memory of what happened next was burned forever into Ryan's brain. The social worker had lined them all up on the sofa in the foster family's living room and explained that for now they were going to be wards of the state, that they would be going to new families who would care for them until all the legal issues could be resolved.

Ryan had faced her defiantly. "We're staying together, though, right?"

"I'm sorry," she said with sympathy, "but no. We don't have a home that can take all three of you."

Sean had stood up then, his arms across his chest. "Then I'm not going," he said. "I want to be with my brothers."

"Me, too," Michael had whispered, his eyes filling with tears, his hand tucked in Ryan's.

"I wish that were possible," she replied, her gaze on Ryan. "It will be okay. We'll look for a place where you can stay together, but it may not be for a while."

Ryan had heard the finality in her tone and known it was useless to argue. Still, with Sean's gaze on him, he'd felt as if he had to try. "You don't understand. Sean and me need to look out for Michael. He's still little and he's our responsibility." It was a lesson that had been ingrained in them from the first time their brother had left the house with them to play. They were to protect him against any eventuality, but they'd never envisioned anything like this.

"I'm sorry," she said. "Sean and Michael will be coming with me now. You'll stay here tonight. I'll have a new family ready for you tomorrow." She'd turned to his brothers and spoken briskly. "Get your things, boys."

"No," Sean said, still defiant.

Ryan had looked into the woman's unrelenting gaze and known it was over. "You don't have a choice, Sean," he'd said, defeated. "We have to do what she says."

Ryan would never forget the look of betrayal in Sean's eyes as he left. Ryan had watched through the living room window as they drove away, but Sean had never looked back. All of his attention had been focused on Michael, who was sobbing his eyes out.

Ryan hadn't cried that night or the next, when he'd been transferred to his first official foster home. For weeks he'd asked about his brothers, but the replies had been evasive, and eventually he'd given up. Even at nine he'd known that he was no match for a system run by adults. He'd fought back the only way he knew how—by stirring up trouble everywhere he went.

It had been a childish form of retaliation against people who'd only wanted to help. He could see that now, but back then it had become a way of life, his only way of lashing back.

Now, staring up at Sean's apartment, he sighed. How could Sean possibly forgive him when he couldn't forgive himself for not finding his brothers years ago, for not reuniting them? It didn't matter that he'd only been nine. As the years passed, he could have found a way.

Maybe Sean hadn't forgiven him. Maybe the reason Sean had passed along his address was simply because he wanted an opportunity to vent years of pent-up rage. Ryan thought he might even welcome such a reaction. It couldn't possibly be worse than the anger he'd directed inward all these years.

There was only one way to find out how Sean felt, though. He had to cross the street, walk up the stairs and knock on his door. And he'd do just that…any minute now.

Maggie clutched the address of the apartment across town where Ryan was going to meet his brother. She drove there with her heart in her throat. When she found the block, even though it was after ten o'clock, she spotted Ryan sitting in his car, his shoulders slumped, his gaze locked on the building where his brother lived.

She crossed the street and tapped on his window. "Want some company?"

He rolled the window down, even as he shook his head. "Too late."

"You've already seen him?"

"Nope. I've decided this is a bad idea."

Maggie walked around to the passenger side and slid in. "You'll never forgive yourself if you get this close and don't follow through."

"I'm used to it. There are a lot of things I've never forgiven myself for."

"Such as?"

"I should have stopped them from leaving."

"Who? Your parents?" she asked incredulously. "You think you could have changed their minds?"

"I should have tried."

"Did you even know what they were planning?"

"No."

"Well then, how were you supposed to stop it?"

"I was the oldest. I should have figured out what was going on."

"You were nine!"

He turned a bleak expression on her. "What if Sean can't forgive me?"

"First you have to give him a chance. If he doesn't, then at least you've tried."

He studied her face, then finally drew in a ragged breath, and nodded. "Okay, let's do it."

The walk up that sidewalk and into the building was the longest Maggie had ever taken, because Ryan's tension was palpable. When he knocked on the door, it was opened by a man who was almost his spitting image. His hair was shorter. He didn't have the scar on his mouth. But there was no mistaking the fact that these two men were brothers.

Maggie held her breath as they stared at each other, sizing each other up, maintaining a reserve that no brothers should ever feel.

"Sean?"

The younger man nodded.

Ryan swallowed hard, then said in a voice barely above a whisper. "I'm Ryan. Your brother."

For what seemed like an eternity, Sean didn't reply, but finally, when Maggie was about to give up hope, he opened his arms. "Ah, man, what the hell took you so long?"

15

Ryan clung to his brother, fighting tears of relief and surprising joy. Never in a million years had he expected to feel this way. He'd anticipated looking into the face of a stranger, feeling no more than a faint twinge of recognition perhaps. Instead, it was as if they'd never been apart, as if on some level the deep connection between them as children had never been broken.

Finally Ryan stood back and surveyed his brother, noting that Sean's hair was shorter but still had a defiant tendency to curl, just as his did. The eyes were the same as well, though perhaps the blue was a shade deeper.

"I guess you've never been in my pub after all," he said at last. "I'd have known you anywhere. You look like Dad."

"I look like *you*," Sean said, making no attempt at all to hide his bitterness at the mention of their father. "Come on in. The place isn't fancy, but it's clean— though only because I've been straightening up ever since I got your message last night." He shrugged. "Couldn't sleep."

Ryan grinned. "I didn't get much myself."

"That must be why you've been sitting out there in your car for the past half hour," Sean said with a touch of wit as wry as Ryan's. "Did you fall asleep?"

"You knew I was there?" Ryan asked, startled.

"I've been watching out the window all morning. I saw you drive up."

"Why didn't you come out?"

"Stubbornness mainly," Sean admitted. "I was still mad at you."

"Past tense?" Ryan asked.

Sean turned his gaze to Maggie, then said, "Only if you introduce me to this beautiful woman who's been waiting patiently for you to remember her."

Ryan reached out and clasped Maggie's hand, pulling her forward. "Sean, this is Maggie O'Brien. She's the reason I'm here."

Sean started to shake her hand, then pulled her into a hug instead. "Thank you. I owe you for turning up and getting him out of that car."

"It went beyond that," Ryan told him. "But, yes, she did persuade me I'd come too far to turn back this morning."

"I'm so glad it worked out," Maggie said, swiping at a tear tracking down her cheek. "I should let you two spend some time alone. You have a lot of catching up to do."

"No," Ryan said at once. "Please stay." He wanted her there as a buffer…and because she deserved to be a part of this reunion.

She glanced from him to Sean. "Is that okay with you?"

"Absolutely. I've made a huge pot of coffee. And I bought a pecan coffee cake from the bakery down the street," he said.

Ryan felt a sharp stab of pain. "Pecan coffee cake was Mom's favorite," he said, suddenly remembering.

Sean nodded. "She baked one for every special occasion—our birthdays, Christmas morning, Easter."

Ryan sighed. "You still think about that, too?"

"I guess so. I've been buying coffee cakes all these years."

He led the way into the kitchen, then handed a knife to Ryan. "You cut the cake. I'll pour the coffee. Maggie, have a seat."

For the next hour Ryan and Sean exchanged news about their lives. When Ryan described his pub, Sean glanced at Maggie. "And that's where the two of you met?"

She nodded and told about her flat tire on Thanksgiving.

"Now she's trying to take over the place and run my life," Ryan said.

Sean laughed. "You don't sound as if you object all that strenuously."

"I'm getting used to the idea," Ryan admitted, giving her hand a squeeze.

"On that note I think I really will leave," Maggie said. "You two stay right here. I can find my way out."

Ryan's gaze caught hers. "Will you be at the pub later?"

Maggie smiled. "Of course. Haven't you just said

I'm taking over? Guess that means I can finally start fiddling with your financial records."

"Don't even think about it," Ryan said with feigned ferocity.

"You don't scare me," she retorted over her shoulder.

"Hey, Maggie," he called. When she stepped back into the kitchen, he met her gaze. "I'm glad you came this morning."

"Any time you need me, chances are I'll be around somewhere."

After she'd gone, Ryan saw his brother studying him.

"So, this thing with you and Maggie is serious?" Sean asked.

"As serious as I've ever allowed any relationship to be. I love her."

"Marriage?"

"It's looking that way," he admitted.

"I'm really glad for you. She seems like a great woman."

"You have no idea," Ryan said. "What about you? Anybody serious in your life?"

"Afraid not. I have *issues,* according to the women I've dated."

Ryan laughed. "Yeah, join the club. Maggie didn't seem to care. She badgered me until the issues didn't seem so damned important anymore. You'll find someone like that one of these days. Start dropping by the pub. I've got some regulars there who'd probably swoon at the sight of you."

"I'm not interested in your rejects," Sean retorted,

grinning. "I can find my own women. I just can't keep 'em." His expression suddenly sobered. "Have you ever looked for the others?"

"Not until now. You?"

Sean shook his head. "I didn't think I ever wanted to see any of you again till I heard your voice. Michael's the one I really wonder about. He was so scared the last time I saw him, and he couldn't stop crying. He kept trying to run back to me, but they wouldn't let him. It's an image I've never been able to shake. All these years I kept praying that he adapted, maybe even ended up with an adoptive family. He was still so little, I told myself that he'd forget all about us. Do you think he did?"

"I try not to think about it," Ryan said tightly.

"Maybe we should think about it," Sean said. "I know how I've felt all this time, as if I was waiting and waiting for someone to come looking for me and pretending it didn't matter when no one did."

Ryan was filled with that familiar sense of overwhelming guilt. "I'm sorry, Sean. It should have been me. I should have looked a long time ago."

His brother shook his head. "No, man, Mom and Dad are the ones who should have looked. Hell, they never should have left in the first place. What were they thinking?"

"I have no idea, and to be perfectly honest, I don't give a damn."

Sean blinked at the vehement response. "Really? You honestly don't care why they did what they did?"

"The point is, they did it. The reason hardly matters."

Sean let the matter drop. A grin tugged at his lips. "I still can't believe you have your own pub and it's only a couple of miles from here."

"We have great Irish music on Fridays and Saturdays. Will you come by this weekend?"

"Will your Maggie be around to keep me company?" he asked.

"You heard her. She'll likely be there, but don't be getting any ideas about her."

"I didn't see a ring on her finger," Sean teased.

Ryan chuckled. "You always did want whatever I had, and most of the time I let you have it. Not this time. Stay away from Maggie."

"I imagine you have to give that warning to a lot of men."

"More than you can imagine," Ryan agreed.

"Then marry her and end the problem," Sean encouraged. "I saw the love shining in her eyes earlier. I don't think you'll get any argument from her."

Ryan thought of his intention to find the rest of his family and reassure himself that there were no hidden health risks. "One of these days I will," he said.

"Don't wait too long," Sean warned him. "One of the things I've learned as a firefighter is just how short life can be. It's not something to be wasted."

"Look at you," Ryan teased, "giving advice to your big brother."

"I was always the smart one," Sean retorted.

"Yeah, right. The truth is, Michael was smarter than both of us."

Sean sighed. "He was, wasn't he? Remember how he used to plan strategies for winning whenever we played war games? He was only four, and a runt at that, but he was the only kid I ever knew who could maneuver us into a trap in the blink of an eye, even when we were watching out for it." He looked at Ryan. "Is your detective looking for him?"

Ryan nodded. "No luck so far." Reluctantly he glanced at the clock and realized that he needed to get back. The pub would be opening soon. Besides, he needed to get away and spend a little time absorbing the miraculous way this morning had gone. "I need to get to work. You'll come by soon, though, right?"

"I'm working this weekend, but next Friday for sure. I want to hear that Irish band you've been bragging about. I haven't heard a really good rendition of 'Danny Boy' since Dad used to sing it in the shower."

Ryan grinned despite himself. "He did like to sing, didn't he? And he had a voice that could make people weep, it was so beautiful." He regarded Sean with surprise. "You know, I think that's the first time I've thought of him in years without a lot of anger welling up inside me."

"I got tired of hating him years ago," Sean admitted. "But I never could bring myself to look for him, or any of the rest of you. Probably stubbornness as much as anything. I'm glad you took the initiative. One of these days that detective of yours will come through."

"Let's just pray we don't regret it," Ryan said.

"How could we? It's turned out pretty good so far, hasn't it?"

Ryan drew his brother into a hug. "Yeah, better than good, in fact."

* * *

Maggie kept glancing at the door of the pub, hoping that Ryan would appear. When the time came to open and he still wasn't back, she consulted with Rory and Maureen, and they insisted on opening without him.

"I suppose you're right," she said, but it didn't feel right.

It was dinnertime and the pub was hopping when Ryan finally walked through the door. He didn't seem the least bit surprised to see that everything was running as smoothly as usual. He simply took his place behind the bar.

As relieved as Maggie was, she still wanted to smack him for worrying her. The first chance she had, she swung by and announced, "I have a few choice words for you, mister."

To her surprise he grinned. "Are any of them 'I love you'?"

"That's at the end of the list," she said.

He sighed dramatically. "Then, you might as well start now, so we can get to the end."

"I would, but in case you haven't noticed, the place is packed. I have customers who are already wondering where I am with their drinks."

He gave her a wry look. "Then you might be wanting to give me their order."

Maggie frowned and handed it over, tapping her foot impatiently while he filled it. Eventually he slid the tray toward her, then tucked his finger beneath her chin. "Thank you for worrying about me."

"Who said anything about worrying?" she grumbled.

"I might not have much experience with it, but I do recognize it," he said. "I'm sorry I was late. I needed to think."

"That's all?"

"That's all. As you can see, I did not run my car in a ditch. There's not a scratch on me."

"And your cell phone? Is the battery on that dead?"

"I ought to say it is," he said, his gaze locked with hers, "but I won't lie to you, Maggie. Not ever."

She gave a curt nod. "That's something, then."

She hurried away with the drinks, not because the customers were truly likely to be impatient, but because she didn't want him to see just how happy his explanation had made her. He needed to sweat a little longer for making her worry herself sick. He needed to understand that what he did—or didn't do—mattered to her.

It was hours before they had another free minute. Maggie's feet and back were aching from hauling the heavy trays around all evening, but it was a good kind of exhaustion, the kind that came from doing satisfying work.

She was just about to collapse into a chair and put her feet up, when Rory emerged from the kitchen, his face ashen.

"Um, you guys," he said in a choked voice, "I think Rosita's having the baby."

"Now? In the *kitchen?*" Juan asked, racing for the door.

Maggie took one look at Rory's panicked expression and stood up. "Sit before you faint." She pushed him onto a chair.

He gave her a pained look and popped right back up. "I'm not going to faint. And nobody has time to sit. She's in labor, and I do not want that baby born in my kitchen. Is that clear?"

Ryan patted him on the back. "Nobody's going to have a baby here," he said. "I've already called for an ambulance. Maggie, why don't you go in there and make sure Rosita's okay?"

She frowned at him. "Sure, when it comes to babies, you big, strong men want to leave it all up to us," she grumbled, but she headed for the kitchen.

She found Rosita on the floor, clutching her stomach, her face contorted as another contraction washed over her. "How far apart are the contractions?" Maggie asked.

"Very fast," Juan answered, clutching Rosita's hand and looking dazed. He slipped into Spanish, then caught himself. "This is the second one since I've come in here."

Maggie swallowed hard. That meant they had to be less than two minutes apart. Unless the paramedics arrived in record time, they were going to be delivering the baby here, after all. She knelt beside Rosita and took her other hand. Forcing a reassuring note into her voice, she said, "Don't worry. It's going to be okay." She looked at Juan. "Tell Rory to get in here to boil some water. Tell Ryan to bring down all the towels he has upstairs."

Within a minute the kitchen was bustling with activity. The last customers had been told to send the paramedics in the instant they arrived, but by the time that happened, Rosita's baby—a boy with a full head of dark hair—was already slipping into Maggie's hands.

"Oh, my. Look how beautiful he is," she whispered, her eyes filling with tears as she handed him to the emergency medical technician, who made quick work of getting a lusty wail from him. She felt Ryan's arm slide around her waist.

"Is everything okay?" she asked the EMT.

"Looks fine to me," he said, grinning at her. "You might want to consider a new career."

"I don't think so," she said shakily, then looked at Ryan. "The only births I want to handle from here on out will be my own kids."

Her words brought a surprising smile to his lips. "We'll have to talk about that when things settle down," he said.

It didn't take long for the paramedics to whisk Rosita and Juan off to the hospital.

"I need a drink," Rory announced, his color finally returning.

"Buy one for everyone out there," Ryan told him, his gaze on Maggie.

"Where are you going?" Rory asked.

"Upstairs. Maggie and I have things to talk about."

Maggie felt her heart flutter at the heat in his gaze, but she shook her head. "Not before we toast the baby," she insisted.

He looked disappointed. "One drink, then."

She grinned. "I think a sip will do."

He laughed. "That's much better. By all means, let's have a toast to the baby."

Maggie looked into his eyes. "And to all the babies to come around here."

Rory frowned at that. "Watch your tongue, woman. There are confirmed bachelors in the room."

Ryan grinned at him. "Only one I can see."

A huge grin spread across Rory's face. "Well, isn't that lovely, then? Congratulations, Ryan, me lad."

"Hold it," Maggie interrupted. "Has anyone heard me say yes yet?"

"Now that you mention it, I haven't even heard a proper question," Rory said.

"Some things are meant to be done in private," Ryan retorted. "And in their own good time."

Maggie promptly lifted her glass. "Here's to the baby," she said, taking a quick swallow of her drink before setting it on the bar and heading for the stairs.

"Seems a bit anxious," Rory noted as she left.

She turned and winked at him. "This night's been a long time coming."

"It's been a long day. You must be exhausted," Ryan said when he joined Maggie upstairs.

"Ryan Devaney, don't think you're getting out of making good on your promise downstairs by turning all sweet and concerned. I'm not so tired that I can't listen to what you have on your mind."

From the moment he'd seen Sean that morning, Ryan had felt as if he'd discovered a piece of himself. He'd also realized that the only way to make himself completely whole and give Maggie the kind of man she deserved was to go all the way and find the rest of the family. He hadn't planned on officially proposing to her until he'd taken care of all that. But the way events had unfolded tonight had pretty much turned that plan on its ear. That didn't mean they had to rush into marriage, though.

"Shall I make a pretty speech, then?" he teased her. "Or do you know what's on my mind?"

"I think I know," she said, sitting there with her hands folded primly in her lap. "But I want all the pretty words."

"You know I love you," he began.

"I've had an inkling about that for some time," she agreed.

He regarded her sternly. "Do you intend to keep interrupting? If so, I may never get through this."

"Sorry," she said without much evidence of remorse.

"You're the most amazing, exasperating woman I've ever met. You're beautiful and strong and intelligent... and before you say it, I know I put that backward. It's because I get all tongue-tied just looking at you."

"Ryan Devaney, you've never been tongue-tied a day in your life," she said.

"I am now," he insisted. "I'm terrified I won't find the right words to convince you to spend the rest of your life with me."

She rested her hand against his cheek. "Any words will do," she told him quietly.

"Okay, then," he said, feeling an irresistible urge to make her laugh before things got too serious. "Will you marry me and keep the books for the pub for the rest of our days?"

As he'd anticipated, she began to chuckle. "So it's a bookkeeper you're really after, not a wife?"

He cupped her face in his hands and looked deep into her eyes. "I'm not sure I know what to do to keep a wife happy," he said with total honesty.

"I don't know about any other wife," Maggie said, regarding him seriously. "But all you need to do with me is love me for the rest of our lives."

"That I can promise you," he said.

She held out her hand. "It's a deal, then."

This time Ryan was the one laughing. "No, you don't, Maggie O'Brien. This is the sort of deal that can only be sealed with a kiss." He grinned at her. "And perhaps a bit more."

Hours later, when the deal was well and truly sealed, and Maggie's warm body was curved against his, he sighed with a feeling of pure contentment.

"Now all that's left is finding the rest of my family, and then we can plan our wedding," he murmured against her hair.

She shot up and stared at him, looking as if he'd announced a delay in the arrival of Christmas or any other cherished holiday. "You want to find them first?"

"Well, of course. Don't you want that, too?"

"Absolutely not," she said fiercely. "Don't get me wrong. I want you to locate each and every one of them for your sake, but that could take a long time, and I'm not waiting."

Ryan's heart sank. "You won't wait for me?"

"I won't wait to get married," she corrected. "Then we'll find the rest of your family together."

He stared at her. "You're asking me to marry you now?"

"Actually, I'm insisting on it. The sooner the better."

He grinned, but she noticed he wasn't arguing.

"Pushy woman, aren't you?" he teased.

"When I have to be," she confirmed with evident pride.

He pulled her back into his arms. "You're really sure you're willing to take me on without knowing everything there is to know about me?"

"I already know all the important stuff," she insisted. "For instance, you're a great kisser."

He regarded her with amusement. "Am I really?"

"Really great," she confirmed. "And a fantastic lover."

"You think so?"

She hesitated. "Come to think of it, I do have a couple of nagging little doubts. They could probably be wiped right out if you were to take me downstairs and make love to me there."

He laughed. "You're really not going to be happy till I make love to you on top of the bar, are you?"

"Try it and let's see," she dared him. "I'm pretty sure I'll be ecstatic."

He called downstairs to make absolutely certain that everyone had cleared out, then carried Maggie downstairs and did his absolute best to see that she was every bit as ecstatic as she'd been anticipating all these months.

When he held her afterward, he promised to keep right on making her happy for the rest of their lives.

"If you don't, my brothers will beat you up," she warned.

Ryan thought of the way Sean had taken an instant liking to Maggie. "If I don't, *my* brother will beat me up."

"Then I guess you're highly motivated," she teased, deliberately wiggling her hips beneath him.

"Highly motivated," he agreed, right before he set out to show her just how motivated it was possible for a man to be.

Epilogue

Despite Maggie's initial insistence on marrying before Ryan found the rest of his family, she was finally persuaded by her mother to at least wait until fall to give them time to plan a proper, lavish ceremony befitting the oldest O'Brien daughter.

"In fact," Nell had said with a sly gleam in her eye, "if you want to teach Ryan a bit more about romance, a wedding on the anniversary of your first meeting would certainly be a good way to start."

Maggie had been convinced, especially since it meant that the Thanksgiving season would mean something special to Ryan and possibly even chip away at his general hatred of holidays.

Besides, a fall color palette for the bridesmaids' dresses had made her sisters happy. With the trademark O'Brien auburn hair, they all looked fabulous in shades of bronze and gold velvet.

Maggie's dress, a heavy white satin sheath with simple pearl trim at the low neckline and a dip in back, was far more elegant and sophisticated than she'd originally envisioned, but she'd fallen in love with it the instant she'd seen it. She made a slow turn in front of the dressing room mirror, still not quite believing that her wedding day was finally here after a wait that had seemed to last an eternity. In less than an hour she would be Mrs. Ryan Devaney.

When she made one last turn, she met her mother's gaze and saw that Nell O'Brien was trying valiantly to smile through her tears.

"Mom, are you okay?"

"You're just so beautiful. They say every bride is radiant, but I swear I don't think I've ever seen one who glowed with happiness as you do right this minute."

"That's because Ryan makes me very happy."

Her mother smoothed an errant curl back into Maggie's upswept hairstyle. "He's a complicated man, your Ryan. That won't change just because he's been convinced to make a commitment to you."

"I know that. I don't think he'll ever truly be at peace until he finds the rest of his family."

"How's that search going? Anything new?"

Maggie shook her head, sharing in Ryan's frustration. Jack was concentrating on finding Michael at the moment, and he'd run into one brick wall after another.

"Ryan and Sean are ready to give up looking for their brother, Michael, but I've been pushing them to continue. I keep imagining that little boy they've described sobbing his heart out as they were separated. I know he'd be happy to see them again, that he's been waiting for them all these years."

Her mother smiled. "You just want happy endings these days," she teased.

"Well, of course I do," Maggie said. "I've found mine."

"And Ryan's found his."

"I'm part of it," Maggie agreed. "But he needs his family."

"You know, it wouldn't be so awful if he didn't locate them," her mother said. "He has all of us now and Sean and the Monroes. And Rory and Father Francis. I'd say his life is full."

"He says that, too," Maggie said. "But I want more for him."

"You want it, but does he?"

Maggie thought about it. "Yes, I think he does deep down. Finding Sean was a turning point. Before that, it might not have mattered as much to him, but he's been a changed man since he located Sean." Maggie smiled. "Of course, some of that is because Sean has a wicked sense of humor and a zest for living that can drag Ryan out of his dark moods. I wonder if it was always that way, if Ryan was the serious, responsible big brother and Sean the cutup or if they changed after their parents left."

"You've never asked?" her mother said with a surprised expression.

"They don't like talking about their childhood. Sometimes they'll start, but it always leads back to that day they came home from school and no one was there." Maggie sighed. "Enough sad talk or I'll start crying and have to do my makeup all over again. Have you seen Ryan yet? Is he as handsome as I imagined in his tux?"

"Not as handsome as your father," Nell said with a

smile. "But he'll definitely do." She touched Maggie's cheek. "Your father and I want nothing more than your happiness, but I must say I'm thrilled that you've found it here rather than in Maine. It's going to be good having you nearby. We missed you."

"Now I'll be underfoot all the time," Maggie said. "You'll get tired of seeing me."

"Never," her mother said. "And I'm looking forward to all the grandchildren you'll bring over, as well."

Maggie laughed. "Let's not rush things. Ryan's still getting used to the marriage concept."

Her mother glanced at her watch. "Then we'd better not keep him waiting. I'll send your sisters in and then go into the church. Your father's waiting for you in the foyer, probably wearing a hole in the carpet, as he did with your sisters. I love you, Mary Margaret O'Brien."

"And I, you. No woman ever had a better mother."

"And no woman will make a better wife and mother than you," Nell said, tears welling up. "Here, I go again. Let me get out of here."

Maggie's sisters came in as her mother departed and offered her the traditional something old, something new—a lace-edged handkerchief carried by every O'Brien bride for three generations, a brand-new blue garter from Frannie and a pair of Colleen's pearl earrings, loaned for the occasion.

"I think that's it," Colleen said, standing back to study her. "Mags, you're even more beautiful than I was, dammit."

"But not as gorgeous as I'll be," Katie insisted.

"What an ego, baby sister," Frannie chided.

Maggie laughed. "Come on, guys, let's go march

down the aisle and show everyone just how beautiful *all* the O'Brien women are. We'll make Mom and Dad proud."

"They're not proud of us because we're pretty," Colleen began.

"But because we're smart," the rest of them said in a chorus.

Maggie didn't say it, but she thought she might be the smartest one of all, because she'd seen through Ryan's brooding moods and tough demeanor to the wonderful man beneath. And today she was making him hers for the rest of their lives.

"Stop fidgeting," Sean commanded Ryan, "or I will never get this tie on straight! The person who invented these things ought to be taken out and shot. Had to be a woman, since they're the ones always anxious to get a noose around our necks."

Ryan frowned at his brother. "A fine thing to be saying to me on my wedding day."

"Well, it's true. Your Maggie is a wonderful woman, the finest I've ever met, in fact, but making a commitment to her for the rest of your lives requires a kind of courage I can't begin to imagine."

"You're a firefighter, for heaven's sake!"

"I'd risk a burning building a thousand times before saying I do," Sean said with feeling.

"We'll see about that," Ryan retorted. "If I could fall, so can you."

"Never!" Sean insisted.

Ryan laughed. "As an Irishman, don't you know better than to tempt fate that way? The gods are prob-

ably up there right this second laughing as they plan
your downfall."

Sean shot him a sour look. "Don't go getting any
ideas about helping them along."

"Doubt I'll have to," Ryan replied. "Destiny does a
pretty good job all on its own."

"Tell that to all the people who meddled in your life
to get you to this point."

The door cracked open as if on cue, and Father
Francis came in with Rory right behind him.

"Are you thinking of getting married today or next
month?" Rory asked irritably, running a finger inside
the tight collar of his tux. "I don't know how much
longer I can stand this thing."

"Then by all means let's not make you wait," Ryan
said, before turning to the priest. "Is Maggie ready?"

"Waiting in the foyer for the wedding march to
begin," he confirmed. "And looking like an angel."

Ryan sighed. "Then by all means, let's get this show
on the road."

They started from the room, but Ryan caught Sean's
arm. "I'm glad you're here to be my best man," he told
him. "It makes today feel right."

"From here on out, nothing's ever going to keep us
apart again," Sean said, pulling him into a hug. "If the
world tangles with one Devaney, it has to deal with
both of us. We're a team."

Ryan fought back unexpected tears and forced a
smile. "Moving words, but I'm still not sharing Maggie with you. She's mine."

Sean grinned. "No question about that. I've seen

the look in her eyes when you're in the room. You'll never have any cause to question her love."

Ryan sighed as a rare feeling of pure contentment stole through him. A ceremony wouldn't change the truth of his brother's words. Maggie O'Brien well and truly loved him.

And that made him the luckiest man on earth.

The ceremony was everything Maggie could have hoped for, though it passed in a bit of a blur. She had a feeling the wedding pictures were going to be disastrous, because one person or another was either bursting into tears or laughing. And the reception at Ryan's Place was filled with music and laughter and dancing.

Through it all Maggie could think of nothing besides the wedding night ahead, which they were spending upstairs before going off on a honeymoon trip to Ireland first thing in the morning. By midnight she was trying to shoo everyone out of the pub.

"She seems a bit anxious for us to leave, don't you think?" her brother Matt asked. "Why is that? It's not as if this night is any different from the others the two of them have shared, now is it?"

"Don't be telling me about that," her father retorted. "Now come along. You didn't find Maggie lingering with you on your wedding nights, did you?"

"Actually, I'm pretty sure she was the one involved in short-sheeting the bed in the hotel on *my* wedding night," John replied.

"Not our saintly Maggie?" Colleen said, feigning shock.

Maggie frowned at the lot of them. "Ryan, as your first official duty as my husband, make them go away."

He laughed. "Aren't you the one who's always telling me about the importance of family?"

She scowled at him. "And it is important, just not tonight."

Her mother finally took pity on her. "Come along, you hooligans. Let's leave the newlyweds alone."

Even with that encouragement, it took another half hour to get everyone out of the pub, the doors locked and the lights turned off. When it was all done, Maggie sighed and turned to Ryan.

"Now, then, Mr. Devaney, we are officially on our honeymoon."

"Is there something special required of me?" he inquired, his expression innocent.

"First you have to carry me upstairs and across the threshold," she instructed.

When he'd done that, she gazed into his eyes. "Now you have to get me out of this dress."

He grinned. "With pleasure, though it's a lovely dress. I could go on admiring it for hours."

"No, you can't," she said. "It's in the way."

"In the way of what?"

She touched his cheek. "You making love to me for the first of a million times as my husband."

"A million times, huh? Won't I be too worn-out to do anything else?"

Maggie laughed. "Precisely. Which is why I'll have to take over everything else around here."

"Is this your devious plan to poke your nose into my accounting ledgers?"

She nodded. "Pretty clever, don't you think?"

"Come here," Ryan said, his gaze already heating. "Let's see how tonight goes, and tomorrow and the day after that. We'll talk again after the five-hundred-thousandth time."

Maggie slipped into his arms. "I can live with that."

"Must be your fine head for negotiating that recognizes a win-win compromise when it's presented," Ryan declared approvingly.

Maggie laughed. "I knew that MBA would be good for something one of these days."

Ryan leveled a long, serious look into her eyes. "You do know I didn't marry you for your MBA, don't you?"

"Why did you marry me—aside from wild, passionate love, of course?"

He touched her face. "Because you're the real family I've needed all my life."

* * * * *

SEAN'S RECKONING

1

Sean Devaney's eyes were stinging from the smoke at the still-smoldering ruins of a tumbledown Victorian house that had been converted into low-rent apartments. Bits of ash clung to his sweat-dampened skin and hair. Even after stripping off his flame-retardant jacket and coveralls, Sean continued to feel as if he'd just exited an inferno...which he had. The acrid smell of smoke was thick in the air and in his clothes. Even after ten years with the Boston Fire Department, he still wasn't used to the aftermath of fighting a blaze— the exhaustion, the dehydration, the stench.

He'd been young and idealistic when he'd joined the department. He'd wanted to be a hero, craved the rush of adrenaline that kicked in when an alarm sounded. Saving lives had been part of it, but so had the danger, the thrill of putting his own life on the line to do something that mattered. In fact, it seemed Sean had spent most of his life trying to matter in one way or another.

Now, though, with the adrenaline wearing off, all he wanted was a warm, pounding shower and about sixteen straight hours of sleep. Unfortunately, until these last hot spots were thoroughly dampened and the location made secure, Sean was destined to stay right here just in case there was another flare-up.

The landlord was damn lucky no one had been killed. Indeed, from what Sean had observed inside, the landlord of this building himself ought to be shot. Even in the midst of battling heat and flames, Sean had noticed that there were so many code violations, he couldn't begin to count them all. Though it would be another twenty-four hours before investigators pinned down the cause of the blaze, in Sean's opinion it was most likely the outdated and overloaded electrical system. He hoped the landlord had a healthy insurance policy, because he was going to need it to pay off all the suits from his tenants. Most had lost just about everything to flames or to extensive smoke and water damage.

Sean scanned what remained of the crowd that had gathered to watch the inferno to see if there was any sign of a likely landlord, but most of the onlookers appeared to be more fascinated than dismayed by the destruction.

"Hey, Sean," his partner, Hank DiMartelli, called out, a grin splitting his face as he gestured toward something behind Sean. "Looks like we've got a new helper. He's agile enough, but I doubt he meets the department's age and height requirements."

Sean turned around just in time to catch a kid scrambling inside the fire truck. By the time Sean latched on to him, the boy was already reaching with unerring precision for the button to set off the siren.

"Whoa, fella, I think this neighborhood's heard enough sirens for one afternoon," Sean said, lifting the boy out of the truck.

"But I wanna do it," the child protested, chin jutting out in a mulish expression. With his light-brown hair standing up in gelled spikes, he looked a little like a pint-size member of one of those popular boy bands.

"Another time," Sean said very firmly. He set the boy on his feet on the ground and was surprised when the kid didn't immediately take off. Instead he stood there with his unrepentant expression and continued to cast surreptitious glances toward the cab of the engine. Sean had a hunch the boy would be right back up there unless Sean stuck close by to prevent it.

"So," he said, hoping to drag the boy's attention away from his fascination with the siren, "what's your name?"

The kid returned his gaze with a solemn expression. "I'm not supposed to tell it to strangers," he said automatically, as if the lesson had been drilled into him.

Sean hated to contradict such wise parental advice, but he also wanted to know to whom the kid belonged and why he was wandering around the scene of a fire all alone. "Normally I'd agree with that," he assured the boy. "But it's okay to tell me. I'm Sean, a fireman. Police officers and firefighters are good guys. You can always come to us when you're in trouble."

"But I'm not in trouble," he responded reasonably, his stubborn expression never wavering. "Besides, Mommy said never to tell *anyone* unless she said it was okay."

Sean bit back a sigh. He couldn't very well argue with that. "Okay then, where is your mom?"

The kid shrugged. "Don't know."

Sean's blood ran cold. Instantly he was six years old again, standing outside a school waiting for his mom after his first day of first grade. She had never come. In fact, that was the day she and Sean's father had disappeared from Boston and from his life. Soon afterward, he and two of his brothers were sent into foster care, separated forever. Only recently had Sean been found by his older brother, Ryan. To this day, he had no idea what had become of his younger brother, Michael, or of the twins, who'd apparently vanished with his parents.

Forcing himself back to the present, Sean looked into the boy's big brown eyes, searching for some sign of the sort of panic he'd experienced on that terrible day, but there was none. The kid looked perfectly comfortable with the fact that his mom was nowhere around.

Pushing aside his own knee-jerk reaction to the situation, he asked, "Where do you live?"

"I used to live there," the boy said matter-of-factly, pointing toward the scorched Victorian.

Dear God in heaven, was it possible that this child's mother was still inside? Had they missed her? Sean's thoughts scrambled. No way. They had searched every room methodically for any sign of victims of the fire that had started at midafternoon and raged for two hours before being brought under control. He'd gone through the two third-floor apartments himself. His partner had gone through the second floor. Another team had searched the first floor.

"Was your mom home when the fire started?" Sean asked, keeping his tone mild. The last thing he wanted to do was scare the boy.

"Don't think so. I stay with Ruby when I get home from school. She lives over there." He pointed to a similar Victorian behind them. "Sometimes Mommy doesn't get home till really, really late. Then she takes me home and tucks me in, even if I'm already asleep."

The kid kept inadvertently pushing one of Sean's hot buttons. Another wave of anger washed through him. How could any mother leave a kid like this in the care of strangers while she cavorted around town half the night? What sort of irresponsible woman was she? If there was any one thing that could send Sean's usually placid temper skyrocketing, it was a negligent parent. He did his best to stay out of situations where he might run into one. The last time he'd worked a fire set by a kid playing with matches while his parents were out, he'd lost it. They'd had to drag Sean away from the boy's father when the man had finally shown up, swearing he'd only been away from the house for a few minutes. Sean had really wanted to beat some sense into him. A few minutes was a lifetime to a kid intent on mischief.

"Is Ruby around now?" Sean asked, managing to avoid giving any hint about his increasingly low opinion of the boy's mother. He even managed to keep his tone neutral.

The boy bobbed his head and pointed down the street. "Ruby doesn't have a phone, 'cause it costs too

much. She went to the store on the corner to call Mom
and tell her what happened. I went with her, but then
I came back to see the truck."

Great! Just great, Sean thought. The babysitter had
let the kid run off alone, too. He had half a mind to
put in a call to Social Services on the spot. The only
thing stopping him was his own lousy experience in
the system. Plenty of kids were well served by foster care, but he hadn't been one of them, not until the
last family had taken him in when he was almost ten.

The Forresters had been kind and patient and determined to prove to him that he was a kid worthy of
being loved. They had almost made up for his having
had his real parents walk out on him and two of his
brothers. The Forresters had made up for some of the
too-busy foster parents who hadn't had the time or the
skills necessary to reassure a scared kid who was fearful that every adult in his life was going to leave and
never come back. Foster care, by its very temporary
nature, only fed that insecurity.

Since this child, despite wandering around on his
own, showed no other apparent signs of neglect, Sean
decided to check things out a bit more before taking
a drastic step that could change the boy's life forever.
He looked the kid in the eye. "So, how about I call
you Mikey? I had a kid brother named Mike a long
time ago. You remind me of him. He was pretty ad-
venturous, too."

"That's not my name," the boy said.

Sean waited as the kid hesitated, clearly weighing
parental cautions against current circumstances. He
was probably trying to calculate the odds that Sean

would let him back into that fire truck if they were on a first-name basis.

"You really don't think my mom would be mad if I told you my name?" he asked worriedly.

"I'm pretty sure she'd tell you it was okay, since I'm a firefighter," Sean reassured him. "You can at least tell me your first name."

The boy's brow knit as he considered that. "Okay," he said at last, his expression brightening. "I suppose it would be okay if you called me Seth."

Sean bit back a grin at the reluctant concession. "Okay then, Seth, why don't we sit right here on the curb and watch for Ruby to come back?"

Seth regarded him eagerly. "I could go get her. She'd probably want to meet you. Ruby's really beautiful and she's always looking for a new boyfriend. Are you married?"

"Nope, and I think it's best if we wait right here," Sean said, praying for protection from the too-available Ruby and her pint-size matchmaker. "So, Seth, you haven't told me about your dad. Is he at work?"

For the first time, the boy showed evidence of real dismay. His lower lip trembled. "I don't have a dad," he said sadly. "He went away a long, long time ago when I was just a baby. I'm almost six now. Well, not till next March. I know that's a long time from now, but being six is going to be really cool, 'cause I'll be in first grade."

Sean struggled to follow the conversation. He wasn't sure what to say to the announcement that the boy's father had abandoned him, but Seth didn't seem to notice. He kept right on chatting, spilling the details of his life.

"Mom says my dad loved me, but Ruby says he was a no-good son of a something. I'm not sure what." He regarded Sean with hopeful eyes. "Do you think Mom's right?"

Old emotions crowded in, and Sean bit back a string of curses. "I'm sure she is," he reassured the boy. "What dad wouldn't love a great kid like you?"

"Then how come he went away?" Seth asked reasonably.

"I don't know," Sean told him with total honesty. It certainly wasn't something he could understand. Not in Seth's case, not in his own, even with an adult's perspective on it. He told Seth the same thing he'd been told on countless occasions. "Sometimes things happen that can't be helped. And sometimes we never find out why."

Sean sighed. He certainly hadn't. And until Ryan had come back into his life, he had told himself he didn't care. In fact, he'd gone out of his way not to be found, in case his folks had ever gotten around to looking. He'd stayed in Boston, but he'd maintained a deliberately low profile—an unlisted phone number, no credit cards. Anyone looking for him would have had to work hard to find him. That way, when no one had come knocking at his door, he'd been able to tell himself it was because he'd been all but impossible to find. He'd never had to deal with the possibility that no one had cared enough to look.

His brother Ryan had apparently erected the same sort of walls around his heart. Then he'd fallen in love with Maggie, who had prodded him into searching for the family he'd lost. Sean's safeguards hadn't been enough to stop a determined investigator from finding him, which told Sean that his parents had more than likely never bothered to try. Most of the time he could convince himself that that didn't hurt, but there were times like this when the wounds felt as raw as they had more than twenty years ago.

Just when he was about to sink into a disgusting bout of self-pity, a dark-haired woman wearing a waitress's uniform came racing down the street, her expression frantic. She was trailed by a sexy blonde wearing tight jeans, a bright pink tank top and spike heels.

"Mom," Seth shouted, leaping up and racing straight for the petite, dark-haired woman.

She scooped him up, smothered his face in kisses, then held him out to examine him from head to toe. Only then did she speak. "What are you doing back here, young man?" she demanded, her expression stern. "You know you're never supposed to go anywhere unless Ruby's with you."

"I came to see the fire truck," he said, then pointed accusingly at Sean, who'd risen to join them. "He wouldn't let me play with the siren, though."

The woman turned toward Sean and held out a hand. "I'm Deanna Blackwell. Thanks for keeping an eye on him. I hope he wasn't any bother."

"Sean Devaney," he said tightly. Looking into huge brown eyes filled with sincerity, Sean couldn't bring himself to deliver the lecture that had been forming in his head from the moment he'd run across the kid. Before he could say anything at all, the second woman stepped forward and slid a hand provocatively up his arm. The muscle tensed at her touch, but beyond that he was pretty much immune to the invitation in her eyes.

"I'm Ruby Allen, the babysitter," she said, regarding him seductively. "I've always wanted to meet a real, honest-to-goodness firefighter."

Deanna rolled her eyes at the provocative come-on. "You'll have to excuse Ruby," she apologized. "She's basically harmless."

A lot of men would fall for Ruby's sex-on-the-run attitude, but Sean wasn't even tempted. His dates tended to be smart, independent types who weren't looking for a future. Ruby had desperation written all over her. She might act as if she were looking for nothing more than a roll in the hay, but instinct—and Seth's innocent remark—suggested otherwise.

Deanna Blackwell was another story entirely. With her fragile features and huge eyes emphasized by dark curls that had been cropped very short in a no-muss, no-fuss style, she looked about as innocent as her kid. The stay-out-all-night playgirl mom he'd been anticipating was, instead, an angel with smudges of exhaustion under her eyes. *That* was a combination that could get under his skin. That was one reason he avoided the type at all costs.

At the sound of a shout across the street, Deanna suddenly turned toward the house that had apparently been her home. The relief at having found her son gave way to a shock so profound, her knees buckled.

Sean caught her before she fell, inhaling a faint whiff of some soft, feminine perfume that made his pulse leap. The skin of her arms was soft and smooth as satin against his rough palms. When he gazed into her eyes, they were filled with tears and a level of dismay that almost broke his heart. No matter how many times he saw people hit between the eyes by that sudden recognition of everything they'd lost, he'd never been able to steel himself against their pain.

"I'm sorry," he said, reaching for a fresh bottle of water inside the truck and holding it out for her. "Sit down for a minute and drink this."

She sank onto the fire truck's running board. "I had no idea," she whispered, looking from him to Ruby and back again. "I thought…I don't know what I thought, but it wasn't this. What am I going to do? We didn't have much to begin with, but everything we owned was in there."

Sean exchanged a look with Ruby, whose helpless expression encouraged him to take over and reply.

"But you and Seth are safe," he said, dredging up a familiar platitude. It was a reminder he'd delivered a hundred times, but he knew it was small comfort to someone who'd seen everything they owned— all the sentimental keepsakes from the past—go up in flames. There was always a gut-wrenching sense of loss even when they understood that life was more important than property.

He held her gaze. "You know that's what really matters, don't you?"

"Yes, of course, but—" She shook her head as if something had confused her. "You said something about Seth?"

"Your boy."

She turned to the child in question, an unexpected grin suddenly tugging at her lips. "Why did you tell him your name is Seth?"

"Because I'm never supposed to tell my name to strangers," he said dutifully. He slid a guilty look toward Sean. "I'm sorry I lied."

Sean was surprised at having been taken in by a pint-size con artist. "You're not Seth?"

The kid shook his head.

"Then who's Seth?"

"He's my friend at school," the boy admitted. "I wanted to do what Mom said, but I figured you had to call me something if we were gonna be friends."

"At least one lesson stuck," Deanna Blackwell said gratefully, then met Sean's gaze. "His name is Kevin. I hope you won't hold this against him. He was trying to do the right thing."

Sean chuckled at the clever deception. He'd deserved it for pushing so hard. Maybe she was doing a better job with the kid than he'd been giving her credit for. Maybe she was just a struggling single mom doing the best she could.

"No problem," he reassured both of them. "Look, if you need a temporary place to stay, there are services available that can help. I can make a call to the Red Cross for you. Your insurance will kick in in a few days."

She shook her head. "No insurance."

He should have guessed, given the sorry state of the building even before the fire. Anyone forced to live here probably couldn't afford insurance. "The landlord probably has some," he suggested.

"On the building, not the contents," she said. "He made that very clear when we moved in."

"Even so, if he's found liable through some kind of negligence, he can be sued."

"You're assuming I could afford a lawyer to handle the suit," she said despondently. "I know what they charge, and I couldn't even afford an hour of their time."

Sean desperately wanted to find something that would put some life back into her eyes. "What about your family? Can they help?"

She shook her head, her expression grim. "That's not possible," she said tightly. "Look, this isn't your problem. You've done more than enough just by keeping Kevin out of mischief, when there are probably far more important things you ought to be doing. We'll manage."

"Stop worrying, Dee. You two can stay with me," Ruby volunteered, giving Deanna Blackwell a reassuring hug. "It'll be crowded, but we can make it work. You're hardly ever home, anyway, and Kevin's already with me every afternoon. I can loan you some clothes, too."

Sean tried to imagine Deanna wearing Ruby's tight-fitting clothes, but the image wouldn't come. Impulsively he reached for his wallet and peeled off a hundred dollars and tucked it into her hand. Before Deanna could protest, he said, "It's a loan, not charity. You can pay me when you get back on your feet."

He saw pride warring with practicality, but then she glanced down at Kevin. That seemed to stiffen her resolve. She faced Sean. "Thank you. I will pay you back."

"I'm not worried about it," he told her.

"But I always pay my debts. It's important to me. Where can I find you?"

"At the fire station three blocks over most of the time," he said, though he was mentally kissing that money goodbye. Years ago he'd learned the lesson never to lend anything if he couldn't afford to lose it. He'd taken very few possessions with him when he'd left home, and since then he hadn't bothered to accumulate much that had any sentimental value. As for money, it was nice to have, but he wasn't obsessed with it. And he had few material needs that couldn't be met with his next paycheck.

"Bring my pal Kevin by sometime, and I'll let him try out the siren," he suggested, giving the boy a solemn wink.

"All right!" Kevin said.

Satisfied at last that Kevin was in better hands than he'd originally assumed, Sean jogged back across the street to check on the progress being made at the fire. Only an occasional wisp of smoke rose from the ashes. They'd be out of here soon and he'd be off in a couple of hours. Sleep beckoned like a sultry mistress.

"Way to go, Sean!" Hank said, enthusiastically slapping him on the back. "I saw you with the only two females under the age of seventy in this entire neighborhood. Did you get the number of the hot blonde?"

"Like I really wanted it," Sean scoffed. "She's your type, not mine."

Hank regarded him with disappointment. "How about the brunette with the kid?"

"Nope."

"Two gorgeous women and you struck out completely?" Hank asked incredulously. "Man, you *are* slipping."

"I didn't strike out," Sean told him patiently. "I never even got in the game."

"Why the hell not?"

Sean wondered about that himself. Maybe it was because one woman was definitely not his type and because the other one struck him as being just a little too needy and vulnerable, despite that streak of stubborn pride. It was one thing to rescue someone who'd just lost her home. It was quite another to allow himself to get emotionally entangled. He always tried to keep his protective instincts on a short leash.

Hank sidled up to him and held out a metal toy fire truck. "It's not too late," he consoled Sean. "This probably belonged to the kid. Hang on to it. Unless you're a whole lot dumber than I think you are, something tells me one of these days you're going to be looking for an excuse to see his mom again."

"No way," Sean said fiercely.

But even as he uttered the denial, he took the truck and tucked it into his pocket. He told himself it was a reflexive gesture simply to keep it out of Hank's hands, but the truth was, his partner had him pegged. Despite all the alarm bells in his head, Deanna Blackwell's vulnerability tugged at him like an invisible rope.

He glanced back toward the spot where she'd been

standing, but she was gone. He was surprised by the intensity of his disappointment.

Then he caught a glimpse of the flashy blonde disappearing into a building across the street, and something akin to relief spread through him. If—and that was a really huge *if*—he ever lost his mind and decided he wanted to see Deanna Blackwell again, Ruby would know where to find her.

He grinned as he considered whether Ruby would be inclined to give up that information, or whether, like Kevin, she'd choose to be tight-lipped. Only one thing to do if that happened, he concluded. He'd introduce her to Hank, who could wheedle information out of any female on earth.

Now there, he thought with a chuckle, was a match made in heaven. Maybe one day when he was really bored, he'd get the two of them hooked up together just to watch the sparks fly. And if he ran into Deanna Blackwell in the process…well, that would just be an accidental act of fate.

2

"That man was so into you," Ruby teased Deanna as they climbed the steps to Ruby's third-floor apartment, which was going to be home for who knew how long.

"He was not," Deanna said, grateful for the teasing because it was, temporarily at least, keeping her mind off the fire and her uncertain future. "No man ever looks at me twice when you're around."

"This one did," Ruby insisted, leading the way into her one-bedroom apartment with its tiny kitchen and a bathroom no bigger than a closet, which it probably had been before the house had been converted to apartments. She grinned at Deanna. "And you've got something I don't have."

It was hard to imagine anything that the sexy, self-confident Ruby didn't possess, especially when it came to the sort of attributes that appealed to men. Sadly, far too few of them took the time to look beneath Ruby's flashy looks and impressive chest. It infuriated Deanna that they never saw the kind, generous woman who would do anything in the world for a friend, something she was proving right now by inviting Deanna and Kevin to stay with her.

Deanna regarded Ruby with curiosity. "What on earth could I have that you don't?"

Ruby ducked her head into the refrigerator so that her reply was muffled, but Deanna had no trouble hearing her.

"Kevin," she said. She stood up, held out a soda and met Deanna's gaze. "I watched the two of them together out there. Fireman Sean is definitely daddy material. Something to think about, don't you agree?"

Deanna sighed and accepted the soft drink. "Ruby, we've been over this a million times. Unlike you, I am not looking for a man to make my life complete."

Ruby scowled at her. "Not complete, just easier."

"I can take care of myself and Kevin," Deanna insisted.

"When it comes to being a loving, wonderful mom, you're the best," Ruby agreed. "But the way I see it, Kevin could sure use a daddy to replace that scumbag who left the two of you. Not that I don't think you're better off without Frankie, but he has left a huge hole in Kevin's life. Even you have to see that. The kid asks a million and one questions about his dad on a daily basis. That one snapshot he has of Frankie is practically worn bare from his constant handling."

"I know," Deanna admitted. If she hadn't seen it for herself, she had Ruby to point it out with disgusting frequency.

"Well then, don't you owe it to Kevin to take another look at fireman Sean?"

"I'm not getting involved with some guy just so my

son has a father figure in his life," Deanna said impatiently. "Besides, he has Joey."

Ruby nearly choked on her soft drink as she let out a hoot of laughter. "You want Joey Talifero to be your son's role model? Are you nuts?"

"There's nothing wrong with Joey." Deanna reacted defensively as she always did when Ruby said something disparaging about her boss. "He's a perfectly respectable businessman."

"I'll give you respectable, if by that you mean he probably hasn't deliberately broken any laws lately. But he has a tenth-grade education, if that. He owns a two-bit restaurant and spends all his spare time betting on the ponies," Ruby countered.

"He has a heart of gold, and he and Pauline treat me like family," Deanna retorted.

"If you mean Joey overworks you and underpays you, I agree," Ruby replied. "And I notice you didn't mention your other boss as having hero potential."

Deanna and Ruby both worked at a small law firm in the neighborhood, Deanna as a full-time receptionist, Ruby as a part-time clerk. Their boss, Jordan Hodges, was not the kind of man who invited a lot of personal chitchat on the job. He was all business. Deanna wasn't even entirely sure he was aware she had a son, and she did her best to make sure that Kevin didn't interfere with her job performance. She needed that minimal salary and her tips from working at Joey's in the evenings just to scrape by.

"Mr. Hodges would be a great role model," she said stiffly, "assuming he was the least bit interested in being one."

"Yeah, right," Ruby scoffed. "Come on, Dee. Think about it. Don't you think a friendly fireman would be a better choice in the hero department than either Joey or stiff-necked Hodges?"

Deanna thought about the man who'd befriended her son that afternoon. Goodness knows, even covered with soot and sweat, he'd been the most handsome male she'd run across in years. Coal-black hair, blue eyes, square jaw, well-defined muscles. Definitely the stuff of fantasies. He'd been kind to Kevin. He'd even loaned her money. Beyond that, though, she knew absolutely nothing about him. How much could you really tell about a man's character in a twenty-minute encounter? She'd known Frankie Blackwell for a year before she'd married him, and look how that had turned out. Better the devil she knew—Joey, or even Jordan Hodges—than the one she didn't.

Besides, Joey would never in a million years hit on her. His wife would strangle him. Deanna wasn't so sure about this Sean Devaney. If what Ruby said about the way he'd looked at her was true—and Ruby definitely had reliable instincts where men were concerned—how long would it be before he wanted more from her than she was interested in giving? And how long after that before she made the second-worst mistake of her life by starting to count on him, just as she had once foolishly counted on Frankie Blackwell? Nope, the status quo was definitely safer. Since Frankie had walked out on her and their son, she'd learned to rely on no one except herself. Ruby was the one exception.

Studying her friend's tight jeans and stretched-to-the-limits tank top, Deanna understood why people got the wrong idea about Ruby. But Deanna knew better. She would trust Ruby with her life. She did trust her with Kevin's safety almost every single afternoon and evening. Ruby had never let her down. Deanna counted herself blessed to have such a friend in her life.

"I have more pressing things to worry about than a role model for Kevin," she said, dismissing the entire uncomfortable topic. "In case it's slipped your mind, I've lost my home and everything I own."

Suddenly the enormity of that had her knees buckling for the second time that day. This time there was no strong firefighter there to keep her from collapsing. Instead, she sank onto the sofa, blinking back the hot sting of tears.

"Ruby, what am I going to do?" she asked, relieved that Kevin had stopped off downstairs to play with a friend. He clearly didn't understand just how dire things were, and she didn't want him to witness her distress. There were more than enough uncertainties in his life as it was, things she had no more control over than she did the rise and fall of the moon each day.

"You're going to do exactly what you always do," Ruby said with complete confidence. "You're going to draw on that unlimited reserve of strength that has gotten you through in the past, and I'm going to do everything I can to help you. We'll manage. That's what friends do in a crisis. You were there for me when my world crashed down around me. Now it's my turn to return the favor."

Ruby's reassuring words barely registered. Deanna was mentally calculating dollars and cents for the bare necessities. Even with Sean's hundred dollars in her pocket and a tiny bit of savings in the bank, she was going to come up short. Way short. She sighed wearily.

"I was barely making it as it was. How can I find a new place, pay a security deposit, furnish it and buy all new stuff for Kevin and me?" she asked, over-whelmed by the task ahead of her. "We don't even have a toothbrush."

"Stop worrying. Kevin has a toothbrush here. He also has clothes and toys here," Ruby reminded her. "And you wear those blah uniforms at Joey's. At least one's got to be at the laundry, right? You can pick up a couple of skirts for your job at the law firm with that cash Sean loaned you. And my blouses will fit you. You can borrow anything in the closet. As for finding a place to stay, we've already discussed that. You'll stay right here."

"For a night or two, maybe, but you can't have us underfoot indefinitely."

"Why can't I?" Ruby asked indignantly.

"For one thing, you only have one bedroom."

"So? We can share it, and Kevin can sleep on the sofa," Ruby insisted, determinedly putting the best possible spin on the situation. "He's been falling asleep there on the nights you work late, anyway."

"I'm grateful for the offer, I really am, but won't that play havoc with your social life?"

Ruby shot her a wry look. "It's not like it's all that hot at the moment, anyway. An excuse for a break will do me good. I can use the time to reevaluate the way I'm going about choosing the men I date. Clearly I'm doing it all wrong."

Ruby sounded totally sincere, but Deanna studied her worriedly. "Are you sure? Really sure?"

"This is what friends do in a crisis," Ruby repeated. "Now quit worrying about it. We're going to be fine."

"I don't know how to thank—"

"No thanks are necessary, and if you keep it up, I'm going to get cranky. Now, I just got paid for helping Mrs. Carlyle clean her apartment, so I recommend we get Kevin and go out for pizza."

Deanna shook her head, struggling to her feet. "I have to get back to work."

"You most certainly do not. Joey knows what happened. I explained when I called. And I've already told him you won't be back in until at least tomorrow, possibly the day after."

"This is no time for me to miss work," Deanna protested, as panic rose up in her belly. "He could fire me."

Ruby grabbed her shoulders and shook her gently. "Hey, wake up. Not even Joey is dumb enough or mean enough to fire you under these circumstances. You're half the reason people keep coming back there. It's certainly not for his gourmet cooking. Now listen to me. You've just been through a trauma. In my experience the only thing to do in this kind of situation is eat comfort food. In fact, I think we ought to follow the pizza with hot-fudge sundaes."

Despite her dismay over the wild spin her life was taking, Deanna laughed. "I'm the one with the crisis. How come you get to indulge?"

"I'm giving up men." Ruby winked at her. "In my book, *that* is a genuine trauma."

For Deanna, who'd given up on men after being dumped by Kevin's dad, it didn't seem like any sacrifice at all, but she wasn't Ruby. Ruby might have been devastated by her divorce, but she'd bounced right back into the game. She made no apologies at all for the fact that she enjoyed having a man in her life.

"You could always take Kevin to the fire station. Try your luck with Sean Devaney again," Deanna suggested, ignoring the surprising pang of dismay that swept through her at the prospect of pushing Ruby and Sean together.

"And have that gorgeous hunk reject me twice? I don't think so. A woman has to have some pride." Ruby regarded Deanna slyly. "Of course, when *you* take Kevin over there, I might just tag along and see what the rest of the pickings are like."

Deanna sighed heavily. "I suppose that's how I'm going to pay you back for taking me in."

"Absolutely."

An image of Sean Devaney crept into her head. The man *was* seriously gorgeous. What healthy woman wouldn't want to sneak another look at him? It didn't mean she was actually interested in anything more. And she did owe Ruby big-time.

"Done," she agreed eventually.

And based on the way her hormones dipped and swayed in jubilation even as she uttered the word, she'd better make very sure that all of her carefully honed defenses were firmly in place.

"And Mom said I shouldn't bother you because you're probably really busy, but I was thinking that if you weren't busy, maybe you could come over in the fire truck and take me for a ride," Kevin Blackwell was saying earnestly to Sean.

The call had come in on the nonemergency line at the fire station about five minutes earlier. Sean had barely gotten a word in edgewise. The kid definitely had a lot to say, and he was saying it all in such a rush that Sean could barely keep up with him.

"Hey, Kevin, slow down, okay?" he said, laughing.

"Oh, okay. I thought you might be in a hurry."

"Not right this second," Sean reassured him. "How did you know how to find me?"

"It was easy. Ruby found the number in the phone book."

Ah, so the notorious Ruby was promoting this idea. For whose benefit? Sean wondered. The kid's or her own? Or was she by any chance matchmaking? That possibility intrigued him far more than it should.

"Is she there now?" Sean asked, hoping to clarify things before he agreed to anything.

"Uh-uh. I'm at the pay phone outside the laundry. Ruby's inside. She'll be out in a minute, though. She said it was okay if I called. It is, isn't it? You're not mad, are you?" he asked worriedly.

"No. I'm not mad. I'm glad to hear from you," Sean said, realizing it was true. He'd thought about the boy and his mother—a lot the past couple of weeks. He'd dismissed the thoughts as perfectly normal under the circumstances. He often worried about people whose homes had been destroyed, though few of them haunted his dreams the way Deanna Blackwell had.

"How are you and your mom doing?" he asked.

"Okay, I guess. Staying with Ruby is kind of cool," Kevin said. "She keeps way better stuff in the refrigerator than Mom did."

Sean bit back a chuckle at the boy's standards. "Such as?"

"Ice cream and sodas and a whole bag of candy. Mom says I'm not supposed to touch that 'cause it's Ruby's crisis food, whatever that is. But I don't think she'd mind if I ate one candy bar, do you?"

"No, I don't imagine she would, as long as you asked permission first." More curious than he cared to admit, Sean asked, "Does Ruby have a lot of crises?" And what kind were they? he wondered. The kind no five-year-old should know about?

"I don't know," Kevin told him. "Maybe you could ask her. She just came out."

"In a minute," he said, hoping to put off a conversation with Ruby until he had plenty of backup to distract her, namely Hank. "I can't get away from here, but maybe you and Ruby can come on over to see the fire truck, like I promised."

"Wow, that would be cool," Kevin said enthusiastically. "You talk to her, okay? She'll do it if you ask. Here."

Sean heard the flurry of excited conversation on the other end, then finally Ruby took the phone.

"You sure know how to win a kid's heart," she said.

Sean ignored the compliment. "What about it? Can you bring him by?"

To his surprise she hesitated. "How about in a couple of hours? Will you be around after seven?"

"Never can tell when we'll get a call, but I imagine we will be. Any particular reason you want to wait?"

"Deanna will be home then. I know she wants to come along. I think she has some money she wants to pay you."

"I told her that there was no rush on that," he said, feeling unreasonably irritated that Deanna was in such a hurry to pay him back. Since he never liked being indebted to anyone himself, he realized he should be more understanding, but it rankled nonetheless. "It's only been a couple of weeks. She can't possibly be on her feet financially already."

"She isn't, but you don't know her," Ruby said, sounding every bit as exasperated as Sean felt. "She's got this mile-wide stubborn streak and more pride than any woman ought to have. She won't rest until she's paid you back every cent." She lowered her voice and confided, "Frankly, I think she's on the verge of collapse from exhaustion. She was already working two jobs. Ever since the fire, she's added extra hours at the restaurant. Tonight's her first night off, and she wouldn't have taken that if I hadn't called and told Joey he had to insist on it."

"You called her boss?" Sean asked, not sure whether to be impressed or shocked. "What did you do? Did you have to blackmail him?"

"Pretty much," she said cheerfully. "I told him if he didn't let her out of there, I'd come over and tell his customers he was a total creep for making her work all these extra hours when she's practically asleep on her feet." She paused. "And I might have mentioned something about spreading the word about a case of food poisoning I had recently."

Sean grinned at the thought of a vengeful Ruby descending on the hapless Joey. Whoever the poor man was, it was unlikely he would be a match for her.

"What about Kevin?" he asked. "Does Deanna have any time for him these days?"

"Kevin's okay. He's with me," she said, her voice immediately taking on a defensive edge, as if she understood the implied criticism of her friend.

"A boy needs his mom," Sean said fiercely, perfectly willing to risk Ruby's wrath to make his own point.

"Yeah, well, he needs a roof over his head, too," she retorted, switching gears to take her friend's side. "And Deanna's determined to give him that. I keep telling her she doesn't have to make it happen tomorrow, but she won't hear it." She hesitated, then added thoughtfully, "Maybe you can get through to her."

"Damn right I will," Sean muttered.

"What?"

"Nothing. But if you all come by, I'll talk to her."

"We'll see you in a couple of hours, then," Ruby said with what sounded like a hint of satisfaction in her voice.

Listening to her, Sean felt his gut tighten. He had his answer for sure now. The woman was matchmaking, no question about it. If he had half a brain in his head, he'd develop a sudden case of the flu and be long gone before they got to the station.

But an image of Kevin Blackwell's excited expression as he'd crawled up into that fire truck crept into

Sean's head. Add to that the boy's obvious yearning for a man he could look up to, and Sean knew he wasn't going anywhere. There were plenty of men in the world who didn't think twice about disappointing a kid, whether their own or someone else's, but Sean would never be one of them. He'd lived with way too many disappointments of his own.

Deanna was still irritated by the way Joey had summarily dismissed her just as the dinner hour was getting into full swing. No matter how hard she'd argued that she needed the tips, he'd kept right on shooing her toward the door.

"Wednesdays are always slow," he'd said, despite the fact that every table was occupied. "How much would you make tonight, anyway?"

"Every little bit helps," Deanna had countered.

He'd opened the register, pulled out a twenty and slapped it into her hand. "This will make up for some of it, then. You need some sleep. You need to spend some time with your boy."

Deanna's gaze had narrowed at that. "You've been talking to Ruby, haven't you?"

"Ruby who?" he'd inquired with completely phony innocence.

"You know perfectly well who I'm talking about," she'd responded. Jocy and Ruby had taken an almost instant dislike to each other years ago. They tried not to let it show in front of Deanna, but it was hard to miss. "Okay, if you and Ruby have actually reached an agreement about something, I know better than to argue with you. I'll go home. I'll spend some time with Kevin. I'll sleep."

Joey gave a nod of satisfaction. "And tomorrow you'll be back with a smile on your face for all the customers, so they'll double their usual tips."

"If only," Deanna had muttered. Most of Joey's customers were senior citizens living on fixed incomes. That was one reason they came for Joey's early-bird specials in the first place.

Now that she was actually on her way home, Deanna found her feet dragging. Exhaustion clawed at her. She would give just about anything for an hour in the tub, a glass of iced tea and twelve uninterrupted hours of sleep.

Instead she found Ruby and Kevin waiting for her on the front steps.

"You've got five minutes to go inside and make yourself beautiful," Ruby announced.

"Why?"

Kevin bounced up and down in front of her. "We're going to the fire station to see Sean. He invited us, didn't he, Ruby?"

Instantly suspicious, Deanna glanced at her friend. "Sean called?"

"Well, the truth is that Kevin called him, but Sean did ask us to come by. I spoke to him myself."

Deanna sensed a plot, one she wanted no part of. "Then why don't the two of you go on over there? You don't need me. You can take that cash I have for him."

Kevin's face fell. "But we waited for you, Mom. You've got to come."

"That's right," Ruby agreed, giving Kevin's hand a

squeeze. "Sean's expecting all of us. You don't want to disappoint him, do you?" She glanced pointedly at Kevin to indicate that Sean wasn't the only one who was going to be disappointed if Deanna refused to go.

Pushing aside her exhaustion and her suspicions, Deanna forced a smile. "Okay then. Give me ten minutes to shower and change."

Kevin's expression promptly brightened. "Hurry, Mom. We don't want to keep him waiting too long. He might get too busy to see us. Or he might go home."

Deanna pressed a kiss to her son's forehead. "I'll hurry," she promised.

As she passed Ruby on her way up the steps, she leaned down and whispered, "And I'll get even with you for this."

Ruby chuckled. "I doubt it. In fact, if things go the way I'm anticipating, someday you'll thank me. I left my red halter top on the bed. I think it's just the thing for you to wear on a hot night like this."

"Don't count on it."

"Mom!" Kevin whined.

"I'm going," she said, slipping inside and trudging up the stairs. Going to the fire station was absolutely the last thing she wanted to do tonight.

Unfortunately, she couldn't say quite the same thing about seeing Sean Devaney…and that reaction scared her to death.

3

Sean tried to pretend that he wasn't watching for Deanna's arrival at the firehouse. He kept his nose buried in a book. As a kid he hadn't been much of a reader, but during the endless hours between calls at the station, he'd picked up a fantasy novel one of the other firefighters had just finished and he'd been hooked. He'd enjoyed the pure escape from reality into realms where good always triumphed over evil.

He was currently finishing up the latest Harry Potter book, enjoying the way the beleaguered kid stood up to the bullies around him. He couldn't help wishing he'd had Harry as a role model when he'd been a kid. Tonight, however, even though he was as engrossed in the latest adventure as he had been in all the others, his attention kept drifting to the sidewalk outside.

"Looking for anyone in particular?" Hank inquired, dropping into a chair next to him.

"Who says I'm looking for anyone?" Sean replied, testy at having been caught.

"Usually when you get lost in one of those books

of yours, this place could burn down around you and you wouldn't notice, but tonight you seem distracted. You keep glancing toward the street."

Sean considered lying, but since he was going to need Hank's help to get some alone time with Deanna, he decided to come clean. "Deanna Blackwell's on her way over with her kid."

A grin spread across Hank's face. "I knew it!" he said triumphantly. "She's the doll from that fire a couple of weeks back, right? You've been seeing her all along on the sly, haven't you, you sneaky dog? I knew you were lying through your teeth when you claimed you weren't interested."

Sean frowned at him. "I have not been seeing her. The kid called today and wanted to come by to see the fire trucks. I said okay. It's no big deal."

"It's worth fifty bucks to me," Hank gloated.

Sean studied his friend's expression, looking for even the tiniest hint of guilt. "You actually had bets going on whether I'd see her again, didn't you?" he asked. Hank didn't even flinch.

"Well, of course I did," Hank said with no evidence of remorse. "Your love life—or lack thereof—is the subject of much speculation around here. All the guys keep wondering why you're not married, since every woman you meet falls madly in love with you."

"I don't see anyone long enough for them to fall in love with me," Sean contradicted.

"Which I explained to the guys, but they think you're just holding out on us, that you've got some gorgeous babe stashed away and that you sneak off to spend every spare minute making passionate love to her."

Sean groaned. "You all clearly have too much time on your hands."

Hank grinned. "True enough. So, is the delectable Deanna bringing her hot friend with her?"

"If you're referring to Ruby, the answer's yes."

"Then I am forever in your debt," Hank said solemnly. "I have had a few incredibly steamy dreams about that woman."

"You have steamy dreams about every woman you pass on the street," Sean pointed out.

"This is different," Hank insisted.

Sean rolled his eyes at the familiar refrain. "I doubt that, but you can do me a favor. I need a few minutes alone with Deanna. Can I count on you to show Ruby and Kevin around?"

"When have you not been able to count on me?" Hank demanded indignantly. "No matter how trying the task, do I not step up to the plate when you ask?"

Sean chuckled. "Then I take it the answer is yes, even though this is one of those *trying* occasions?"

"Yes," Hank said, then added with exaggerated politeness, "And thank you for thinking of me. Those of us in the Boston Fire Department are here to serve and protect in whatever way we're called upon to do so."

"Try to remember that when you're thinking about hitting on Ruby," Sean cautioned, thinking of the way she'd neatly blackmailed Deanna's boss. "Something tells me she could bring you to your knees if you get out of line."

Hank made a show of swooning ecstatically. "This

just keeps getting better and better. You know how I love a challenge."

"Don't make me regret this," Sean said.

"Have I ever let you down?"

Ah, Sean thought, that was the thing. For all of his fooling around and his penchant for chasing anything in skirts ever since his divorce, Hank DiMartelli was the best buddy a man could have. There was no one in the department Sean would rather have at his side going into a raging inferno. Hank was fearless and loyal and smart. He'd won more citations for bravery than anyone else at the station, Sean included.

Sean punched him in the arm. "Never," he agreed. "But there's a first time for everything, and in your case this better not be it."

Hank's gaze narrowed and his expression turned serious. "Why all the paternal concern for a woman you barely know and aren't interested in?"

Sean wasn't precisely sure himself. "She's Deanna's friend," he said, which was the closest he could come to summing it up. "And something tells me Deanna would be royally ticked if she thought I was throwing Ruby to the wolves, or to one wolf in particular. People seldom spot your finer qualities through all the bull."

"Then by all means, I'll be on my best behavior," Hank assured him. "I won't even try to cop a feel of those gorgeous breasts of hers."

Sean grinned at the concession despite himself. "Something tells me that's the last thing I need to worry about. I'm pretty sure Ruby can handle some-one with roving hands. She's probably had a lot of practice. Maybe you should consider getting to know her for her mind."

"That body, and she has a mind, too?" Hank asked, his expression incredulous.

Sean scowled at his joking. "Go to hell."

Hank laughed. "But if I do, who'll show Miss Ruby and the kid around and get them out of your hair so you can practice seducing the lovely Deanna?"

"It's not about seduction, and I'm sure I can manage on my own, if it comes to that," Sean said. "In fact, showing them all around myself might be the smarter way to go."

"Forget it. Ruby's mine. You can have the single mom with the vulnerable look in her eyes. Just one question, though. I thought that was the type you tended to avoid like the plague. So what's up with this Deanna? How did she get under your skin?"

Sean sighed, not even bothering to deny Hank's claim that Deanna had gotten to him. "I wish I knew."

The walk to the fire station a few blocks from the apartment hadn't taken nearly as long as Deanna would have liked. She'd wanted to postpone this encounter with Sean Devaney for as long as possible, but with Kevin running ahead and demanding that she and Ruby hurry, they'd made it to the station in record time.

All the way over she had tried to prepare herself for the physical impact the sexy firefighter was likely to have on her again. She told herself that appreciating a man's body wasn't a crime, that it certainly wasn't anything that required some sort of commitment. She even consoled herself that her stomach probably wouldn't even flutter when she saw him again. It had probably been a one-time thing brought on by her overwrought condition on the day of the fire. Maybe he was really a toad.

But when Sean walked into view in his snug jeans and tight T-shirt, looking like a walking advertisement for testosterone, that weak-kneed effect slammed into her again. Deanna was forced to face the possibility that it hadn't been seeing the burned-out wreckage of her home that had drawn all the air out of her lungs that day. Maybe she'd just been subconsciously looking for an excuse to fall into this man's powerful arms.

Beside her, Ruby sucked in a breath. "My God, he's every bit as gorgeous as I remembered," she said in a stage whisper that Sean could easily hear.

"Stop it," Deanna whispered, her cheeks flaming. "You're embarrassing me."

"A work of art that impressive is meant to be appreciated," Ruby retorted with a grin, her gaze never wavering as Sean sauntered toward them. "And if you tell me that you don't see it, then I'm giving up on you and taking another shot at him myself."

"Okay, yes, I see it," Deanna admitted. "Now hush."

Ruby ignored her plea and leaned down to whisper, "I still say he has the hots for you. Just look at that glint in his eyes. He hasn't even glanced at me once."

"It's probably there because he knows you're talking about him," Deanna retorted with exasperation.

Fortunately, Kevin raced ahead to literally launch himself at Sean. Deanna noticed he caught her son without breaking stride, and after one last glance in her direction, he focused all of his attention on Kevin. Deanna's heart instantly melted. She liked the fact that he treated Kevin as if what he had to say was important. Ruby had been right. Sean was a man who understood a boy's desperate need for attention. She was forced to admit it was a trait that could get to her if she let it.

Because she was so shaken by the discovery that any man could have that sort of impact on her after years of general immunity to the male segment of the species, she resorted to brisk politeness when Sean finally reached them. When he held out his hand, rather than shaking it as he'd obviously expected, she slapped an envelope of cash in it.

"I really appreciate what you did for me," she said, the words stiff and formal and not nearly as grateful as she'd meant them to be. "This is half of what I owe you. I'll have the rest in another week or so."

He gazed directly into her eyes. "Yeah, well, that's something we should talk about."

Deanna blinked at his somber tone. "Meaning?" she asked, noting that he didn't put the envelope into his pocket. In fact, he looked as if he had every intention of giving it right back to her.

Sean didn't reply. Instead he glanced across the room. "Hey, Hank," he called to another fireman, who looked to be a year or two older. His craggy features weren't as handsome as Sean's, but there was a confidence about him and an irrepressible grin that would definitely appeal to most women. "How about showing my man Kevin here and his friend Ruby around the station, while Deanna and I talk? We'll catch up with you in a few minutes."

Hank's appreciative gaze swept over Ruby and his eyes lit up. Deanna noted that Ruby looked equally intrigued.

"No problem," Hank said at once, then forced his attention to Kevin. "You really like fire trucks, huh, kid?"

"You bet," Kevin said eagerly.

"Personally, I prefer the men who drive them," Ruby said, regarding Hank with frank appreciation.

Deanna took note of his broad shoulders, dark-brown eyes and only a dark shadow of hair on his shaved head. He was definitely Ruby's type—unrepentantly male.

He grinned at Ruby. "Is that so?"

Deanna shook her head as the three of them left. "Your friend is a brave man. Ruby's a wonderful friend, but she's fickle. She has a habit of discarding men like tissues when they don't live up to her ideals, and they seldom do."

Sean chuckled. "Then I think they were made for each other. Hank is a notorious flirt."

Deanna shot a look at him. "He's not married, is he?"

Sean looked hurt by the question. "Of course not. What kind of guy do you think I am? And even if he were, what's the harm in asking him to show Ruby and Kevin around the station? I didn't set them up on a date."

"Sorry," she said at once. "I overreacted. It's just

that Ruby's a lot more vulnerable than she looks. Most men miss that."

Sean stared after them, his expression thoughtful. "Yeah, I imagine they do. She looks as if she could handle anything that comes along."

"When her guard's up she can," Deanna agreed.

"But she lets it down too often and too quickly?" he guessed, surprising Deanna with his insight.

"Exactly."

Sean turned back to her. "I doubt anything much can happen between her and Hank with Kevin along as a chaperon."

Deanna nodded. "You're probably right. Why did you make such a point of getting rid of them, by the way?"

"Like I said, I wanted to talk to you about the money thing." He held out the envelope. "I want you to take this back."

Deanna's hackles immediately rose. "Not a chance. And there is no 'money thing,'" she responded edgily. "You made a loan, which was extremely generous of you, by the way. I'm paying you back. It's a business matter."

"It's not as if we signed loan papers and there's some huge penalty if you miss a payment," he retorted. "It was a hundred bucks, not a thousand. I wish it could have been more. After the fire destroyed everything you owned, I thought a few extra dollars might help you get back on your feet, buy a few essentials. I certainly didn't need it back right away."

"Maybe in your world a hundred dollars doesn't amount to much, but it was a lifeline for me."

"That's exactly my point. You need it right now. I don't. It's certainly not worth working yourself into exhaustion to pay me back."

Deanna groaned. Now she understood why he'd gone all worried and protective on her. "Ruby's been blabbing, hasn't she? Did she tell you I was working too much?"

"She mentioned two jobs and extra hours on top of that," he admitted. "That's crazy."

"It's not crazy if I want to start over and get out of her apartment."

"Is she complaining?"

"No, of course not."

"Well then, what's the rush?"

"It's a matter of principle."

"Is the principle worth more than your son's happiness?"

Deanna stared at his suddenly harsh expression. "What kind of question is that?" she demanded heatedly. "*Nothing* is more important to me than Kevin's happiness and well-being. And what right do you have to question that? You don't even know me."

Despite her sharp response, he didn't back down. "Maybe not, but I can see what's staring me right in the face. Kevin needs his mom, not an extra few bucks for groceries."

"Maybe if you'd gone hungry you'd feel differently," she snapped.

"I have," he said bluntly. His unflinching gaze clashed with hers. "And I've gone without a mother. I'm here to tell you that there's no comparison. I would have gone hungry every night of my life, if it had meant seeing my mother again."

Deanna felt as if he'd landed a punch squarely in her gut. Even without details, that revelation explained a lot. No wonder he was taking her situation so personally.

"I'm sorry," she said at once, shaken by the raw pain in his voice. "What happened? Did she die?"

"No," he said tightly. "She and my dad walked out on me and my brothers. My brother Ryan was eight. I was six. And Mikey was four. As far as I know, they took the twins, who were only two, with them. We never saw them again."

"Oh, God, how awful," she whispered, trying to imagine a six-year-old having his entire family torn apart. What could possibly have driven his parents to do such an awful thing? Hadn't they understood the permanent emotional scars likely to be inflicted on the boys they'd left behind?

Even when she'd been at the lowest point in her life, when Kevin had been screaming all through the night with colic, and she hadn't known where their next meal was coming from, Deanna had never once considered walking away from him. He was the reason she'd had for going on. She wouldn't have allowed anything to split them up.

She started to reach out to touch the clenched muscle in Sean's arm, but after one look at his shuttered gaze, she drew back before she could make contact. "I really am sorry."

"I don't need your pity. I only told you that so you'd realize that I know what I'm talking about. Don't short-change your kid on what really matters." He shoved the envelope back at her. "Keep the money until you really do have it to spare."

Years of stubborn pride told her to refuse to take it, but the look of despair in Sean's eyes made her relent. She put the envelope back in her purse. At the same time, it took every bit of restraint Deanna possessed not to reach out and hug the man standing beside her. He looked as lost and vulnerable as if his mother had walked out days, rather than years, ago.

"Just so you understand that Kevin's situation is not the same as yours. I'm not abandoning him," she said softly. "I would never in a million years walk out on my son."

"If he hardly ever sees you, it's the same thing," Sean insisted, clearly still drawing comparisons with his own background.

"I love my son."

"I'm sure you do. I even believe my mother loved me. That doesn't change the fact that she was gone." He regarded her with sudden urgency. "Please think about what I'm saying. I was only a year older than Kevin when my folks walked out. It's not something a kid ever gets over."

"I'll keep it in mind," she promised. "And I'm not just saying that. I really will."

Sean's intense gaze held hers. Finally he gave a nod of satisfaction. "That's good, then." But, as if he feared he'd given away too much, his expression suddenly went blank. "We should probably try to catch up with Hank. I imagine he's wondering what happened to us."

Deanna laughed at that. "I doubt he or Ruby even realize we're missing."

Sean's lips twitched, and then a slow grin spread across his face. In that instant the last of the tension between them was finally broken. "All the more reason to catch up with them," he said. "They're liable to forget that they have an impressionable kid tagging along."

"Does Kevin strike you as a boy who allows himself to be ignored for long?" she asked. "He's probably boring Hank to tears with a million and one questions about being a fireman. Ever since the day of the fire, it's all he's talked about. If he could sign up now, he would."

No sooner had the words left her mouth than the siren on one of the engines split the air with its loud wail.

"A call?" Deanna asked worriedly, glancing around for signs of men rushing to pile onto the trucks.

"Nope. I think Hank just showed Kevin how to turn on the siren," he said, leading the way to the truck in the next bay.

Instead of Kevin in the driver's seat, though, it was Ruby. Kevin was sitting next to her, giggling.

"Told you that would get them over here," he said, pointing to his mother and Sean as they approached. "Can I do it now?"

Hank turned and winked at them, then returned his gaze to Ruby. "If Ruby's willing to give you a turn, go for it, kid."

Ruby didn't budge. "I don't know. I kind of like it up here. I understand why you guys get off on this kind of thing."

"It's not driving the truck that does it," Hank explained patiently.

Ruby regarded him doubtfully. "So you don't get some macho kick out of making all that noise and tearing through the streets?"

"I never said that. But we make noise and tear through the streets to get to the fire faster," Hank said. "It's not some macho game. We're trying to save lives and property."

Ruby nodded solemnly. "Then it's the danger? You like putting your life on the line?"

"It's not as if we deliberately risk our lives for the fun of it," he retorted, his genial expression suddenly fading.

"No, for the thrill of it," Ruby corrected.

Hank regarded her with obvious exasperation. "It's about doing a job. If we do it right, there's only a tiny, carefully calculated risk involved."

Ruby grinned. "Then all those medals for bravery I heard about inside, you didn't really deserve those?"

"Oh, brother," Sean muttered. He turned to Deanna. "Want to grab Kevin and go out for a soda or something? My shift's over, and I have a hunch those two will be arguing about this for a while. Ruby's pushing all of Hank's buttons. His wife left him because she thought he was a danger junkie."

"Ouch," Deanna said. "Maybe I ought to warn her."

Sean shook his head. "Don't. His ex was right, and so is Ruby. He needs reminding occasionally." He met her gaze. "So, how about that soda?"

Deanna knew the smart thing would be to refuse, but she couldn't seem to make herself say the words.

She simply nodded, then added, "But you're not going to get Kevin away from here till he gets to turn on that siren."

"Good point." Sean climbed up on the opposite side of the truck, whispered something to Kevin, then helped him to reach the button to turn on the siren. Ruby looked vaguely startled, but she never tore her gaze away from Hank. He looked equally captivated, despite his apparent frustration at the turn their conversation had taken.

"We're leaving now," Deanna announced.

"Whatever," Ruby said.

"I'll get Ruby home," Hank said absently.

"I'm perfectly capable of getting home on my own," Ruby shot back. "I walked over here, didn't I?"

Hank shot a bewildered glance toward Sean. "Was that offer an insult? I thought I was being a gentleman."

"Don't ask me," Sean said. "Everyone knows I don't understand women. You're the expert."

"Hah!" Ruby muttered.

"I heard that," Hank said.

"I meant for you to hear it."

Sean chuckled. "Okay, children, play nice. The grown-ups are leaving now."

He scooped Kevin up and settled him on his shoulders, then beckoned to Deanna. "Let's get out of here before we get caught in the cross fire."

"I don't get it," Kevin said. "Ruby really, really likes guys. How come she's been fighting with Hank the whole time we've been here? She hardly even knows him."

"Sometimes people just don't hit it off," Deanna said.

"Then how come she's staying here instead of coming with us?" Kevin asked, his expression puzzled.

"He's got you there," Sean said, amusement sparkling in his eyes.

Deanna frowned at his obvious reference to the sizzling sexual chemistry between their friends. "I don't think there's an explanation that's suitable for a five-year-old, do you?"

"How come?" Kevin asked.

"You'll understand when you're older," Sean told him, winking at Deanna.

"But I need to know now," Kevin persisted. "My teacher says you gotta ask questions if you're gonna learn stuff."

"Hard to argue with a teacher," Sean agreed. "Deanna? Care to give it a shot?"

She frowned at him. "Ruby is staying because she wants to," she told Kevin, hoping it was the kind of simple explanation that even a five-year-old could grasp and accept.

"But why?" Kevin glanced back toward Ruby. "Look. They're still arguing. What fun is that?"

"Some people think a lively argument is stimulating," Sean said. It was apparent that he was barely holding back a laugh.

Deanna regarded him with exasperation. He was clearly enjoying her discomfort with the entire topic. "Care to find out if we're among them?" she asked testily.

He did laugh at that. "Nope. I'm a nonconfrontational kind of guy."

Kevin peered quizzically at both of them. "I still don't get it," he said, sounding disgusted. His expression brightened when they reached a drugstore with an old-fashioned soda fountain inside. "Can I have a chocolate milk shake?"

Deanna would have let him have anything he wanted if it would take his mind off the byplay between Hank and Ruby that had evidently been building to some sort of sexual crescendo all evening long.

"A milk shake's fine," she said.

"What about you?" Sean asked, regarding her with continued amusement. "Something nice and tame, like a vanilla cone?"

It was obvious he was deliberately taunting her. Instantly an image of provocatively licking that ice cream just to torment him flashed through her mind. "Yes, as a matter of fact. An ice-cream cone would be lovely."

The three of them slid onto stools at the counter, with Kevin strategically set up as a buffer in the middle. Sean ordered two milk shakes and the vanilla cone.

When the order came, Deanna deliberately swiveled her stool around until she was facing Sean. He was just responding to something Kevin had asked when he caught sight of her slowly swiping her tongue over the scoop of ice cream. He literally froze, his gaze locked on her. Satisfaction and a hint of something far more dangerous swept through her.

How long had it been since she'd felt that kind of power over a man? How long since her blood had heated to a delicious sizzle under an intense gaze? Too long apparently, because panic promptly set in.

What was she doing? Was she crazy? She didn't play this kind of game. Games were Ruby's territory. Deanna didn't even understand the rules half the time.

"Mom!"

Kevin's urgent tone shook her out of her daze. "What?"

"Your ice cream's melting," he said.

Little wonder, she thought since her temperature had obviously shot into the stratosphere in the past two minutes. Instead of licking at the dripping cone as she might have done scant minutes ago, she swiped at the drips with a napkin, trying not to notice Sean's knowing expression.

"Hot night," he observed mildly.

"Yes," she agreed, her voice oddly—annoyingly— choked.

Kevin looked from one of them to the other, then shook his head. "You guys are as weird as Ruby and Hank."

Deanna was very much afraid her son had gotten it exactly right.

4

Sean wondered what the hell had ever made him think that Deanna was innocent as a lamb? The woman was a temptress, possibly even more dangerous than the incomparable Ruby, because Deanna's seductiveness came from out of the blue.

Ever since she'd played that little game of hers with the ice-cream cone, the image had been locked in his brain. Granted, she'd looked a little rattled by the episode and had backed off almost instantly, but she'd definitely known what she was doing when she'd gazed straight into his eyes and run her tongue slowly over that melting ice cream. Even now, just thinking about it made him go hard as a rock.

He'd been working out at the gym practically nonstop on his days off, but it hadn't relieved the sexual tension one iota. There was probably only one surefire way to deal with it, but the thought of going out with some other woman—using her—to forget about Deanna was too crummy a notion to even consider. Sean tried never to behave like a complete jerk where the women in his life were concerned, no matter how willing they claimed to be to take whatever he was interested in offering.

He'd been deliberately avoiding Hank the past couple of days, as well. He didn't want to hear about any conquest that involved Ruby. Part of that was some ridiculous sense of loyalty to Deanna and her friend, part of it was self-serving. Hearing about Hank's sexual exploits would only remind him of the self-imposed drought in his own life. Moreover, he wasn't ready for the kind of probing questions Hank was likely to ask about him and Deanna. Not that there was anything to tell.

Sean finished his workout, showered and changed into comfortable jeans and a gray department-issued T-shirt. He was already thinking about the pizza he was going to order while he watched the Red Sox game when he ran smack into Hank coming in the door of the gym. His partner was unshaven and looked as if he hadn't slept a wink in days. The stubble on his shaved head was longer than he usually allowed it to get, too.

"Hey," Sean said, dragging him back outside and studying him with concern. "What's up with you? You look like hell."

"No sleep," Hank muttered, avoiding his gaze.

Sean was relatively certain he knew why. Ruby, no doubt. Dammit, just for once, why couldn't Hank have behaved in a less predictable way, maybe shown Ruby a little respect, instead of jumping her bones the first chance he got?

"Yeah, well, that's never been a problem before," he said, careful to avoid any mention of his suspicions.

"I've never been in a situation like this before," Hank said, his expression grim, rather than gloating. "Look, I need to get in there and work out for a couple of hours. Maybe if I'm exhausted enough, I'll get some sleep."

"No date tonight?"

"No," Hank said in a tone that didn't invite further questions.

"Want to come over and watch the game when you're done?" Sean asked. "I'm going to order a pizza. I'll even let you get anchovies on your half."

Hank shrugged without enthusiasm. "Sure. Why not? I'll cut it short here and be there by seven-thirty." His gaze narrowed. "No prying questions, though. Are we clear on that?"

Sean bit back his disappointment, but he nodded. Since he was no more interested in talk than Hank appeared to be, he could hardly complain about the embargo. "See you then," he said, staring after his friend as Hank trudged into the gym with all the energy and enthusiasm of a man walking toward the gallows.

Something wasn't quite right here, but Sean couldn't put his finger on it. However, given Hank's edict about keeping all his questions to himself and his own determination not to discuss Ruby with Hank, he was at a loss.

He thought about all the possible explanations for Hank's mood on the drive back to his apartment. No matter which way he looked at it, it all came back to Ruby.

Of course, there was one subtle way to get some answers, he concluded, picking up the phone before he could change his mind. And didn't he owe it to his friend to try to pinpoint the problem? Indeed, he did, he thought nobly. He had a duty to make the call.

At the sound of Deanna's voice, his mouth went dry. What the hell was wrong with him? No woman had ever rendered him tongue-tied before.

"Um, Deanna, this is Sean."

"Hi. How are you?" she said, not even sounding particularly surprised to hear from him, much less shaken by the sound of his voice.

"Fine. Just fine. You?" he asked irritably.

"Fine."

"And Kevin?"

"He's fine."

Sean nearly groaned. Could this be any more awkward? He couldn't imagine how. "Look, I wanted to ask you about something. It's probably none of my business, but I have to admit I'm a little worried."

"About?"

"Hank," he blurted before he could think better of it.

"Oh?" she said, a wary note in her voice. "What about him?"

"Has he been seeing Ruby, I mean since the other night at the station?"

"Why don't you ask him?"

Good question, Sherlock. "Because I'm asking you," he said, unable to keep a testy note out of his tone.

"I'm not really comfortable discussing Ruby's social life with you," she said.

Sean could hardly blame her. He'd known when he picked up the phone that he was crossing some sort of line and that he was asking her to do the same. "It's just that I'm really worried. I've never seen him like this."

"Like what?"

"I can't explain it. I ran into him at the gym about a half hour ago. He's not himself. He looks as if he's been on a two-day bender, if you want to know the truth, but Hank doesn't drink more than an occasional beer, so I know it wasn't that."

"You really are worried, aren't you?" she asked, sounding surprised.

"Yeah, I really am. It occurred to me that it might have something to do with Ruby, and that if it did, you would know about it."

"The truth is, I don't know what's going on between them," Deanna admitted, her own frustration plain. "Ruby hasn't said much since the other night. She's been going out as soon as I get home, then getting in late, but she hasn't said who she's with. I don't like to pry. Usually I don't have to. She pretty much tells me whatever's going on."

"Sounds like Hank."

"Sean, they're both adults," she said reasonably. "I'm sure they can handle whatever's happening between them without any interference from us."

He hesitated. "You don't think maybe we should get together, see if we can figure out what's going on? They're our friends. We pretty much threw them together."

She laughed at that. "Please. Those two flew together like magnets. They're not our responsibility, though I must say I'm impressed by your concern."

Her words echoed, annoying him. *Impressed by*

your concern? Now wasn't that just about the most boring compliment any woman had ever paid him? Sean was absurdly offended, despite the sincerity in her voice.

He sighed. What reaction had he been expecting? Had he hoped that this ridiculous excuse he'd dreamed up just to hear the sound of her voice was going to set off all sorts of bells and whistles that would have her swooning over him?

Maybe he ought to switch gears, focus on her for a change. "Okay, let's forget about Hank and Ruby for the moment. What about you? You're not working too hard, are you?"

"I imagine that depends on who you ask," she said wryly.

Sean could hear the smile in her voice. "What if I asked Ruby?"

"I thought we just agreed to leave Ruby out of this conversation."

He laughed. "Ah, then she would say you're still working too hard, wouldn't she?"

"More than likely," Deanna admitted.

"You're home early tonight."

"Joey insisted on it. I suspect Ruby got to him again. I honestly don't know how she does it, but if I ever find out, I'll put a stop to it." She sounded annoyed.

"Good for Ruby," Sean enthused. "Tell me about this restaurant. Is it any good?"

"The food's filling, and there's plenty of it. Actually the meat loaf isn't bad. And everyone seems to love the spaghetti special."

Sean pounced on the mention of his favorite food.

"What night is that? I love spaghetti. My mom's was the best," he said, a wistful note creeping into his voice.

There were only a handful of things that could drag him right back to his childhood. Spaghetti was one of them. Ironically, when he'd first gone to his brother's pub, he'd noticed that spaghetti wasn't on the menu there. Of course, it was an Irish pub, but still, spaghetti had virtually become a universal menu item. Ryan had claimed it wasn't on the menu because he hated it. He'd also sworn that he didn't remember their mom making it. Either Ryan was lying or he'd suppressed the memory. Since Sean had done his share of that, he'd kept silent.

"You still remember your mom's spaghetti?" Deanna asked, her voice suddenly soft.

"Yeah. Silly, isn't it, when I've forgotten just about everything else about those early years. But when it comes to spaghetti, I've never had any that was better."

"Then, by all means, come by and try Joey's sometime. It's the Thursday-night special."

He thought about his schedule. "I'm on duty Thursday," he told her. "But maybe I can talk the guys into coming by."

"You can leave the station?"

"As long as all of us go and take our gear with us," he said. "We have to be ready to roll if there's a call."

"Well, you'll probably run into Ruby and Kevin, if you come. It's their favorite night, too."

"I imagine if I tell that to Hank, no one will be able to keep us away."

"Unless they've had a fight," Deanna said, sounding thoughtful. "They could have."

"Then this will be one way to find out," Sean said. "He's coming over in a few minutes. I'll mention Thursday to him."

"Okay, then. Maybe I'll see you on Thursday."

"Good night, Deanna."

"Bye."

Sean hung up the phone, then sat staring at it as if it somehow still connected them. It was an odd sensation, one he wasn't especially happy about. It had been a very long time, decades in fact, since he'd allowed himself to feel connected to anyone. Since he and his brother had hooked up, he had felt a renewed bond with Ryan, though it was still a bit on the uneasy side. And he and Hank were pretty tight, but that was it. Even the connection to his foster parents was tenuous. He still saw the Forresters from time to time, but he told himself that was because he owed them, not because he harbored any sentimental feelings toward them. The fact that there seemed to be some sort of invisible pull between him and a woman he barely knew was disconcerting.

He tried to dismiss it but knew he was only lying to himself. Why else had he called Deanna in the first place? It wasn't like him to poke around in his friend's life behind his back. It had been an excuse, pure and simple, designed to let him off the hook emotionally. He could tell himself the call had nothing to do with a ridiculously fierce longing to hear the sound of Deanna's voice.

Lies, all lies. Filled with self-disgust at the pitiful

ruse, he forced himself to face facts. He was drawn to Deanna Blackwell. He shouldn't be. It was completely unwise and out of character, but there it was. He liked her. He liked her son. He was worried about the two of them.

Deanna needed a friend, he concluded. Okay, she had Ruby. But who couldn't use more than one friend? He could be that friend. And he could hang out with the kid from time to time, sort of like a big brother. It didn't have to go beyond that. He wouldn't let it go beyond that.

Satisfied with his decision, he called and ordered the pizza. But as he waited for Hank and their food to arrive, he thought of the spontaneous combustion Deanna had set off the other night simply by licking an ice cream cone, her gaze locked with his.

Friendship? *That's* all he was interested in? Yeah, right. The lies just kept piling up.

"I'll drop Kevin off at Joey's around six-thirty, and then take off," Ruby said casually as she and Deanna ate breakfast on Thursday morning.

Instantly suspicious, Deanna stared at her. "You're not having dinner? I thought you looked forward to Joey's spaghetti all week long."

Ruby shrugged. "I'm not in the mood for spaghetti."

"And at 7:00 a.m. you know that's how you're going to feel in twelve hours?"

"Yep. I'm pretty sure I'm not going to change my mind. I've been thinking about cutting back on pasta for a while now. Too many carbs."

Deanne peered at her intently. "This wouldn't have

anything to do with the fact that I mentioned Hank and Sean might come by, would it?"

"Why would that matter to me?" Ruby asked, studying her cereal as if she'd never seen a bran flake before.

"That's what I'd like to know," Deanna said.

"Leave it alone," Ruby said, pushing away from the table and dumping her cereal down the garbage disposal. "I've got to get to work."

Since Ruby's job was only part-time assistant in the same neighborhood law firm where Deanna worked days as a receptionist, something was off here. Deanna could have let it alone, but it wasn't in her nature. She might not pry into Ruby's social life, but she did pay attention when her friend was behaving weirdly.

"We never leave the house before seven-thirty," she pointed out. "We're not due at the office till eight. It takes us five minutes to walk to work. What's the sudden rush? Are you trying to avoid talking to me?"

Ruby evaded Deanna's direct gaze. "I'm filling in for Cassandra this week, remember?"

"So?"

"I've got a lot of typing piled up. I'm not as fast as she is, and I still need to get out so I can be home when Kevin gets here after school."

Deanna's gaze narrowed at the mention of her son. "Is babysitting Kevin getting to be a problem?"

"Of course not!" Ruby said, staring at her indignantly. "Don't you dare think that. You know I love that kid as if he were my own. Heck, I've been around since the day he was born."

"Well, something's going on here," Deanna said, studying Ruby thoughtfully. She decided to go for broke and throw her suspicions on the table. "You haven't been yourself for days now, not since the night you got together with Hank at the fire station."

"One thing has nothing to do with the other," Ruby insisted, her jaw set stubbornly.

Deanna wasn't buying it, but she couldn't very well drag the truth out of Ruby if she wasn't willing to share it. "Okay," she said at last. "I'll drop it for now, on one condition."

"Anything that will get you to back off," Ruby agreed.

"Have dinner at Joey's tonight."

"Dee!" Ruby protested.

Deanna held firm. "That's it. That's my condition. Otherwise, you'll never be able to convince me that Hank's not at the bottom of your weird mood."

Something that might have been a tiny flicker of relief passed across Ruby's face, then gave way to an air of resignation. "Okay, okay. Geez, you are such a nag."

Deanna grinned at her. "I should be. I learned from the best."

Ruby shook her head. "Obviously I should have kept that lesson to myself."

Sean and five other firefighters in uniform piled into Joey's Italian Diner around six o'clock. Deanna was just coming out of the kitchen with an order when they arrived. She heard her son's whoop of delight, but missed the fact that he was racing straight across the restaurant toward Sean. He bumped into her at full throttle, knocking her off balance and sending the tray of spaghetti dinners tilting toward disaster.

"Whoa!" Sean said, rescuing the tray in midair and managing to keep Deanna upright at the same time. He stared down into her eyes. "Are you okay?"

Deanna gazed up into blue eyes bright with amusement and felt her knees go weak again. "Having you come to my rescue is getting to be a habit," she told Sean, then turned to her son and scolded, "Kevin, you know you're supposed to watch where you're going in here."

"Sorry, Mom!" Kevin said. "I didn't see you. I was excited to see Sean."

Deanna could relate to the feeling. A part of her hadn't expected him to actually show up, not because he was likely to change his mind but because of the unpredictability of his job. "There should be a table for six opening up in a minute," she told him as she reached for the tray. "Let me serve these dinners, and as soon as it's clear, I'll get it ready for you."

Sean held tight to the tray. "Where do you want this? It weighs a ton."

"I'm used to it," she protested.

His stubborn gaze clashed with hers. "Where?"

She shrugged and gestured toward a stand across the room. "Over there, by that table in the corner. Kevin, go on back to your table, before someone else gets tripped up."

Kevin regarded her with disappointment. "But, Mom…"

"I'll see you before I go," Sean promised him. "If your mom says it's okay, you can come have dessert with me and the guys."

Kevin's eyes lit up. "Really? And you'll tell me all

about fighting fires? I want to be a fireman when I grow up, so I need to start learning stuff."

This wasn't the first Deanna had heard about her son's career plans, but she wondered how Sean was going to respond to Kevin's blatant hero worship. Glancing at him, she realized she needn't have worried. He grinned and assured Kevin he could ask all the questions he wanted. The last traces of Kevin's scowl promptly faded. Deanna had to admit, Sean had a definite way with her son. Still balancing the heavy tray on one hand, he ruffled Kevin's hair with his other hand.

"Do what your mom said," he urged Kevin. "I need to take this tray where she wants it, before she docks my pay."

Kevin giggled. "You don't work here."

"Not usually," Sean agreed. "But it's always good for a man to help out a lady, even when she doesn't think she needs any help."

Deanna caught the subtle message about her independent streak. She didn't say another word as Sean carried the tray across the room. She noted that several fascinated gazes followed his progress. Well aware of how the elderly regulars liked to take an interest in her social life, she knew she'd be hearing about the incident for days to come.

"I can take it from here," she told him when he'd set the tray down.

Sean glanced at the tray, which held only specials. He winked at the elderly woman closest to him. "I imagine this is yours," he said, then leaned down to whisper. "She doesn't think I know what I'm doing, so help me out here okay?"

Mrs. Wiley beamed at him. "Crazy girl," she said with a *tsk* for Deanna's benefit. "I can't imagine what she's thinking, turning down the help of a big, strong firefighter. You put that plate right here, young man."

Deanna stood back while he served all four women, who were giggling at his teasing as if they were thirty years younger. When all the dinners were on the table, he stood back and surveyed the results with evident pride.

"Not such a bad job, if I do say so myself," he said. "I didn't spill a drop."

"Only one problem," Deanna noted mildly, barely containing a grin. "These dinners were destined for that table over there."

She gestured toward two couples who were watching the scene from the next table. Three of the four looked amused, but the fourth looked as if he were about to burst a blood vessel.

Mrs. Wiley patted Sean's hand. "Oh, don't mind them, young man. You did a fine job. We'll send over a bottle of Joey's house wine and they won't complain."

Sean looked chagrined. "I'll buy the wine," he said, turning to the other group. "Sorry. I was trying to be helpful."

Amazingly, Mr. Horner, who usually complained about everything, simply shrugged, his anger defused. "Long as you don't expect a big tip, I imagine we can wait."

Sean winced and turned to Deanna. "Sorry."

She was tempted to make him squirm, but he looked so miserable, she relented. "He's a lousy tipper, anyway," she whispered. "By the way, I see that Joey has cleared that table for you. It might be a good idea if you went over there now before I lose all my tips for the night."

Sean retreated to the table where the other fire-fighters had been seated. Deanna had deliberately sent them to a table that was not part of her station, so she could escape Sean's watchful gaze. Let Adele cope with them. There hadn't been a customer born who could fluster her.

The tactic was only partially successful. Deanna still felt Sean's gaze following her as she worked her way between tables, joking with the customers, carrying orders from the frantic kitchen and helping to clear tables for the line of customers waiting to be seated.

It was so busy for a couple of hours that she was only dimly aware that the firefighters didn't seem to be in any big rush to leave. Hank had slipped away from his table and joined Ruby, trading places with Kevin, who was basking in the undivided attention of Sean and the other firefighters, all of whom were being incredibly patient with his endless barrage of questions.

By eight, the crowd finally started to thin out. Those remaining were lingering over coffee and Joey's chocolate cannoli. Satisfied that things in the dining room were under control for the moment, Deanna slipped onto a stool in the kitchen and kicked off her shoes with a sigh of pleasure.

"It's about time you had a break," Sean said, appearing beside her with a frown on his face. "Have you eaten?"

"I grabbed something earlier," she told him.

"Earlier when?" he asked, his skepticism plain. "Lunchtime?"

"Actually I had some salad not more than twenty minutes ago."

"Meaning she grabbed a carrot on her way through the kitchen," the cook chimed in helpfully.

Deanna scowled at Victor, who was ogling Sean with frank appreciation. "Traitor," she accused him.

Victor grinned. "Given a choice between you and your gorgeous friend, whose side did you think I'd be on?"

Deanna chuckled as Sean regarded Victor uneasily. "Don't panic," she advised Sean. "He's almost as harmless as Ruby. He's also been in a long-term relationship with the same man for years now."

"Good to know," Sean said. "Now let's get back to you. You need to eat. Victor, can you fix something for her?"

Deanna bristled at his commanding tone. "*If* I wanted something to eat, which I don't, I could fix it myself. Victor doesn't have to wait on me."

Sean frowned at her. "Don't be stubborn. You have to be starving."

"Sean, I've been taking care of myself and my son for a long time now. Neither one of us is malnourished. Doesn't that tell you something?"

Victor looked from Sean's set jaw to Deanna's equally set expression and immediately headed for the door. "Think I'll go ask Joey to fix me a cappuccino. You two decide you want anything, help yourselves."

"We won't," Deanna said tightly.

As soon as they were alone, she whirled on Sean.

"What do you think you're doing coming into a place I work and bossing me around?"

He looked bemused by her reaction. "All I did was suggest you should have something to eat."

"*Suggest?* That's not how I heard it. You practically ordered me to eat. I don't get it. Why are my eating habits any of your business?"

He jammed his hands in his pockets and backed off a step. "Okay, you're right. They're not."

"Then what's going on?"

"Someone needs to look out for you."

"Someone *does,*" she retorted. "Me. That's how it's been for a long time now."

"Well, pardon me for caring," he snapped defensively.

Deanna was taken aback by his choice of words and by the expression on his face. He looked as if he hated how he was acting almost as much as she did.

She bit back her irritation and managed to keep her voice level as she asked, "Sean, what's really going on here?"

"I wish to hell I knew," he muttered. "You obviously don't want me interfering in your life. I really don't want to be in your life, yet here I am."

"I didn't ask you to come here tonight," she reminded him. "It was your idea."

He scowled. "Don't you think I know that?"

"Then I'm afraid I don't get it." She looked into his eyes and saw evidence of the internal struggle he was waging with himself. She softened her voice. "Sean?"

He kept his gaze locked with hers for what seemed to be an eternity. She could hear the tick of the clock on the kitchen wall, the sighing of the refrigerators switching on, the clink of ice in the automated ice maker.

"Oh, what the hell?" he murmured, reaching for her and slanting his mouth over hers.

He caught her by surprise. The kiss was the absolute last thing she expected when he was so clearly exasperated with her and annoyed with himself. He claimed her lips with a heady combination of heat and urgency that had her breath snagging in her throat and her senses spinning wildly.

Then, almost as quickly as it had started, it was over. Sean raked a hand impatiently through his hair and regarded her with regret.

"I'm sorry," he said, turning on his heels and leaving before Deanna could gather her wits to reply.

She stared after him, wondering what the apology was for…their argument or the kiss.

Please don't let it be for the kiss, she thought wildly, touching a shaky finger to her lips. It had been a very long time since any man had kissed her like that, and she'd been perfectly content to let it stay that way.

Until now. With one kiss Sean Devaney had unwittingly awakened a sleeping need in her. She might not want him telling her what to do or fretting over her eating habits, but, heaven help her, she definitely wanted him to kiss her again. Soon.

5

Kissing Deanna had to qualify as one of the ten dumbest things he'd ever done in his life, Sean concluded on the ride back to the station. He hadn't meant to kiss her. He hadn't wanted to kiss her.

The shouts of *liar* that echoed in his head at that claim were way too loud to be ignored. Okay then, he had *wanted* to kiss her from the very first instant when he'd had to steady her and that tray after her near run-in with her son. Two seconds of contact with all those soft, yielding curves and he'd wanted even more than a kiss. He'd wanted to drag her into his arms and discover every single secret of her delectable body. It had been a long time since he'd felt that kind of instantaneous rush of pure lust.

But he'd dealt with that impulsive, totally male response during dinner. He'd lectured himself on the sheer folly of any intimate contact with her. He'd joined in the speculative jokes his buddies were making about Hank and Ruby. He'd focused intently on Kevin's apparently endless barrage of questions. He'd teased their waitress, pleaded for Joey's surprisingly incredible recipe for spaghetti sauce. He'd done everything he could think of to get his mind completely off Deanna.

He'd done all that, but he hadn't been able to keep his eyes off her. She was always at the periphery of his vision. The sound of her laughter was always teasing him, drawing his focus away from his friends. Hell, he could almost swear he could even pick out the scent of her perfume when she was two aisles away. How pathetic was that?

Given all that, it was little wonder he was destined to cave in to insanity when he followed her into the kitchen. One instant he'd been defending himself against her fury over his overbearing attitude, the next he'd been hauling her into his arms to silence her with a mind-numbing kiss. He was surprised she hadn't slugged him.

Of course, that could be because she'd been too stunned, he thought, a grin tugging at his lips. He recalled her dazed expression when he'd brusquely apologized and walked away. A tiny, satisfied sensation stole through him. God, he was such a *man,* he thought with disgust, taking pleasure in having caught a woman off guard and having gotten her to respond to him. Responses earned that way didn't mean anything. Not really, anyway.

"What's your problem?" Hank asked, joining him in the sleeping quarters where Sean had retreated when they got back to the fire station.

"Nothing," Sean lied, deliberately stretching out

on top of the sheets as if he'd just come in to catch a quick nap.

"Woman troubles," Hank assessed knowingly. His own mood seemed to be much improved. "You and Deanna have a fight?"

Sean ignored the question. "You and Ruby make up?"

"Ruby and I never fought."

"Could have fooled me," Sean said.

Hank's gaze narrowed. "And you're deliberately changing the subject. Why is that, I wonder? You've been uptight as hell ever since you came out of the kitchen at the restaurant. Did Deanna tell you to get lost?"

That could be one interpretation of her angry diatribe about his meddling in her life, Sean decided. But if her words had held him at a distance, the way she'd returned his kiss had been the exact opposite.

Geez, what was happening to him? He was hanging around his bunk pondering the implications of a stupid kiss. He never did stuff like this. A woman kissed him or she didn't. She slept with him or she didn't. Her choice, always. He never got hung up over it one way or the other. That Deanna had him weighing the meaning of it all was a very bad sign. It was time to run for the hills.

But he didn't want to run anywhere…except straight back to the restaurant so he could kiss her again and make sure that the wicked wonder of the first time had been real.

Deanna sat at Ruby's kitchen table with her jar of tips and began sorting the money. She did it once a month, then deposited the cash into her savings account, the one she'd started when she'd been convinced that if she planned ahead she could put enough money aside to buy a little house someday for herself and Kevin. The costs associated with getting back on her feet after the fire had wiped out every last penny she'd accumulated to that point.

Kevin wandered into the kitchen, his eyes widening at the sight of all the wrinkled dollar bills and change. "Wow," he said, climbing into a chair opposite her and propping his elbows on the table for a closer look. "That's a lot of money. Are we rich finally?"

She smiled at the question. "Hardly."

He studied her thoughtfully. "Do we have enough to get our own place yet?"

Deanna's head snapped up at the plaintive note behind the question. "What's wrong? I thought you liked staying here with Ruby."

"Sure," he said at once. "Ruby's the best."

"Then what's the problem?"

"I was thinking maybe if you and me had our own place, Sean would come to see us."

It wasn't the first time Sean's name had come up around the house. Kevin had been quoting him nonstop since the fire. Going to the fire station and then seeing him at Joey's had only reinforced his hero worship. In Kevin's view, Sean Devaney pretty much hung the moon. Deanna knew allowing that to continue carried risks, but she didn't want to steal the one bright spot in her son's life. Still, she had to caution him against expecting too much.

"Honey, you can't expect Sean to come around. He has his own life."

"But he likes me. He said so."

"He's also a very busy man. He has an important job, and I'm sure he has his own grown-up friends that he likes to spend time with when he's off. I don't think he's staying away because we live with Ruby."

"But I'm his friend, too," Kevin said reasonably. "And if we had our own place, I could invite him to dinner. He'd come. I know he would, especially if you fixed spaghetti like Joey's."

"Then he did like it?" Deanna asked. She'd wondered about that. She'd intended to ask him, but they'd gotten sidetracked in the kitchen. She nearly groaned at the understatement. They'd gotten more than sidetracked. Every rational thought in her head had flown straight out the window when he'd kissed her. Even now, just thinking about the way his mouth had felt on hers, she had to drag her attention back to Kevin.

"Uh-huh," he said. "Sean said it was the best spaghetti he'd had since he was a little kid. So if you promised to fix it, I know he'd come for dinner."

Deanna sighed. "Kevin, you know that I'm not even home for dinner most nights. That wouldn't be any different if we had our own place."

His expression turned mulish. "You never want me to have my friends over."

A headache was beginning to pound at his relentless complaining. "Sweetie, that's not true," she said, trying to keep her voice even.

"It is so true," he insisted. "You always say I can

have them over when you're here, but you're never here."

Deanna considered the accusation and realized it was possible Kevin had gotten it exactly right. She always meant to let him invite his friends over, but there were simply too few free hours in her week, and she didn't want Ruby to have to babysit Kevin's friends. It was enough that she was willing to look after Kevin.

"Why don't you go call them right now and ask them to come over?" she suggested. "We can order a pizza."

"I don't want a pizza. I want Sean to come over," Kevin said, clearly impatient that she'd missed his point.

"Not today," she said flatly.

"Then can I go see him at the fire station again?"

"No."

"Why not?" he asked, clearly warming to this new idea. "I could call first and ask if it's okay. If you can't go, Ruby would probably take me. She probably wants to see Hank, anyway." His expression turned serious. "I still don't get why they fight so much, but I think she really, really likes Hank, don't you? And he's kinda cool, not as cool as Sean, but okay."

Deanna wished she could be as sure of Ruby's feelings as Kevin seemed to be, but Ruby never mentioned the man's name. That might be a dead giveaway that she cared…or it might mean the opposite, that she hadn't given him a thought. It wasn't as if he was hanging around, at least not while Deanna was around. And since Ruby didn't have a phone at the apartment, the two of them couldn't be spending hours on the phone talking, either.

When she didn't respond to Kevin's question, he slid his chair closer. "So, is it okay? Can I call Sean?"

Deanna knew she ought to nip this whole thing in the bud, but the hopeful expression in Kevin's eyes kept her from saying no outright. After all, Sean was a grown man. If Kevin was making a nuisance of himself, Sean could find some way to tell him not to come by the station. And Ruby knew how to protect herself if she wanted to steer clear of Hank. She certainly hadn't seemed all that upset that he'd joined her after dinner the other night at Joey's. Every time Deanna had glanced their way, the two of them had been laughing.

She reached over and brushed Kevin's hair off his forehead. He needed a haircut, but he'd refused, telling her he wanted his hair to be as long as Sean's. "Okay," she relented. "If Ruby doesn't mind taking you, ask her to go to the pay phone with you and you can call." She tossed him enough change for the phone.

"All right!" Kevin said, bounding out of the kitchen. "I'm gonna call right now."

"Ask Ruby first!" Deanna shouted after him. "And take her with you. Do not go to the corner by yourself."

"Ask Ruby what?" Ruby inquired, appearing in the kitchen doorway.

"If you're willing to take him to the fire station for a visit if Sean says it's okay." Deanna studied her reaction. Ruby's expression remained completely neutral. "You're not answering me."

"Sure, I'll take him," Ruby said with a shrug. "It's no big deal. Why can't you take him, though?"

"Because that's a bad idea," Deanna said without thinking.

Ruby regarded her with sudden fascination. "Oh, really?"

"I meant that I have things to do."

"That is not what you meant," Ruby accused. "You meant that you don't want to see Sean Devaney again. Why is that? He seems like a perfectly nice guy to me."

"He is a nice guy," Deanna conceded reluctantly.

"Then what's the problem?" Ruby studied her face. "Or do I even need to ask? Are you beginning to see that he's more than just a nice guy? Are you maybe just the teensiest bit attracted to him?"

"If I admit that I am, will you leave me alone?"

Ruby's grin spread. "For the moment," she agreed. "I will, however, point out that that makes you a complete and total coward for refusing to take Kevin to the fire station."

Deanna looked straight into Ruby's eyes. "Maybe I'm just playing hard to get."

"As if," Ruby scoffed. "You don't play at that. With you it's the real thing." She regarded Deanna with evident fascination. "Have you kissed him yet?"

Deanna was debating the technical accuracy of a negative response, when Ruby gasped as if she'd just read her mind. "My God, I've got that backward, haven't I? He's kissed you."

"Once," Deanna admitted reluctantly.

Ruby studied her with undisguised curiosity. "Well, tell all. How was it? Was it awful? Is that why you don't want to see him?"

"No, it was not awful," Deanna said. "How could it be? We're talking about Sean Devaney here."

Ruby held a hand to her chest. "Oh, my, that good, huh? When did it happen? Never mind. I think I know. It was when he followed you into the kitchen at Joey's. That's why you looked completely dazed when you finally wandered out of there, isn't it?"

"I did not look dazed," Deanna said with exasperation.

"I just call 'em like I see 'em," Ruby retorted. "Well, well, well…this is definitely a fascinating turn of events. Is Sean the first man who's gotten close enough to kiss you since Frankie?"

"Don't be absurd. Frankie's been gone for more than five years. Of course other men have kissed me." Joey. Old Mr. Jenkins at the restaurant. Even one of the law partners at work had given her a friendly peck on the cheek once when they'd said goodbye after an office party.

"Why is my head screaming 'Technicality' when you say that?" Ruby demanded. "I'll rephrase. Has any sexy man kissed you with mind-blowing passion since Frankie?"

Deanna sighed. "You've been hanging out with lawyers for too long."

"Dee?"

"You're relentless."

"Yes, as a matter of fact, I am," Ruby said with pride. "Well?"

"Okay, no."

"You did kiss him back, didn't you? You didn't freeze up or, worse yet, slug him?"

"Oh, no," Deanna said, feeling her cheeks flood with heat. "I definitely kissed him back."

Ruby beamed. "This just gets better and better."

"It was a kiss," Deanna reminded her. "It lasted all of thirty seconds, tops. Then he apologized and bolted out of the kitchen."

"Smart man," Ruby said with approval.

"Smart?"

"Always leave 'em wanting more. I think that's especially applicable in your case. If he'd swooped in for another kiss, you probably would have slugged him."

Deanna regarded her with dismay. "I do not make a habit of slugging men."

"Only because none prior to this have been brave enough to ignore the Do Not Touch warnings posted all around you."

Deanna took an exaggerated look around. "I don't see any signs."

"Trust me. Men do. Our Sean is a very brave man. He gets my vote."

"Vote for what?"

"Guy you're most likely to sleep with."

Deanna ignored the fluttering that Ruby's words set off in the pit of her stomach and held up her hand. "Hold it right there. It's a pretty big leap from letting the man kiss me once to hopping into bed with him."

"Sometimes yes, sometimes no," Ruby replied knowingly. "I'm betting it's not much more than a baby step for Sean."

"Then isn't it a good thing I don't intend to see him again?" Deanna shot back.

"Coward," Ruby accused softly.

Deanna met her friend's direct gaze without flinching. "Darn straight."

For nearly a month now, Deanna had been going out of her way to avoid him, Sean concluded when Kevin and Ruby showed up at the fire station without her yet again. It was getting on his nerves. So was watching this bizarre dance Hank and Ruby seemed to be doing. They barely spoke. Hank merely watched her as if she possessed the key to eternal youth.

After observing this same ritual for an entire afternoon, Sean finally decided he'd had enough. Since Hank wouldn't answer his questions, he decided to try Ruby. He sent Kevin off to the kitchen to bring back sodas for all of them.

"You and Hank have a fight?" he inquired as casually as possible.

Ruby regarded him with an unflinching gaze. "No. Why do you ask?"

Sean shrugged, uncomfortable in his unfamiliar role as meddler. "Seemed for a while as if you two were really hitting it off. Now it doesn't."

Her expression brightened. "Sort of like you and Deanna?"

He frowned at that. "Who said anything about Deanna?"

"Since we're discussing our personal lives, I figured it was a fair question. You going to ask her out?"

Sean was flustered by the question. "I hadn't thought about it."

"Why not? Didn't you enjoy kissing her?" Ruby asked bluntly.

He groaned. He'd thought that was a relatively well-kept secret. "She told you about that?"

"Not willingly," Ruby admitted with a grin. "I pried it out of her."

He shoved his hands in his pockets and wished he had the power to make himself sink through the floor. "Yeah, well, that was probably a mistake."

"Me prying or you kissing?"

He chuckled despite himself. "Probably both."

"You regret kissing her?" she asked, clearly disappointed. "Because I don't think she does. I think she's scared, not sorry."

Sean was intrigued by her interpretation. "Why would she be scared?"

"Because she hasn't dated much since Frankie left. The scumbag really destroyed her self-confidence, if you know what I mean. She doesn't trust her own judgment when it comes to men, so she avoids all of them."

Sean studied her with a narrowed gaze. "Is there a point to all this insight you're sharing with me?"

"Just that you're the first guy she's shown any interest in. Add to that the fact you're a nice guy, and that makes you the perfect candidate to help her get her feet wet." She surveyed him closely. "Unless that kiss scared you, too. Is that it, Sean? Are you as much of a coward as she is?"

Sean ignored the taunt. "Who told you I was a nice guy?"

"Nobody told me. I *am* a good judge of men. Not

that you could tell it by the one I married, but I learned a lot from that mistake. My standards have improved."

"Is that why you ended things with Hank?"

She regarded him with surprise. "Who said I ended things with Hank?"

"I just thought..."

"You thought I'd dumped him because I figured out that he's a big flirt."

"To be honest, yes."

Ruby patted his cheek. "Honey, that just makes him a challenge," she said.

Shaking his head, Sean watched her as she sashayed off toward the kitchen in search of Kevin. He had to give her credit. She understood Hank probably better than Hank understood himself, which raised an interesting point. Did she understand *him,* too? *Was* he avoiding Deanna because he was a coward?

Yep, no question about it. With his reputation on the line, he picked up the phone on the wall, took a slip of wrinkled paper from his pocket and dialed her number at the restaurant. He was relieved when Deanna was the one who answered on the first ring.

"Ruby, is that you?"

"No, it's Sean."

"Oh."

"I thought maybe we could go out for dinner sometime. Are you interested?"

Silence greeted the blunt question, then she finally demanded, "Did Ruby put you up to this?"

Sean chuckled. "Sweetheart, Ruby may be able to manipulate your pal Joey, but she doesn't get to me."

"That doesn't mean she didn't try. I know she and Kevin are over there."

"Look, leave Ruby out of this. It's a simple question. Would you like to have dinner with me sometime or not? Yes or no?"

"You could come by Joey's," she conceded eventually. "We could eat together when I take my break."

Sean bit back a grin at her attempt to avoid being on a real date with him. "As attractive as that offer is, I think I'd prefer a time and place when I can have your undivided attention."

"Why?"

Sean barely smothered a laugh. He was tempted to suggest that she must not date much if she couldn't figure out the answer to that one herself, but he decided that would probably just infuriate her. If Ruby was telling him the truth, she really *didn't* date much.

"So we'll have time to talk," he said instead.

"About what?" she asked suspiciously.

This time he did laugh. "The weather. Kevin. Hank and Ruby. The Red Sox. Whatever we decide we want to talk about. We're adults. We have varied backgrounds. The possibilities are endless."

"Oh."

"Deanna, this isn't a trap," he said gently. "I just thought you might enjoy a night out with somebody waiting on *you* for a change. There's no hidden agenda." He hesitated, then, unable to resist teasing her just a bit, he added, "I won't even kiss you again unless you ask me to."

He waited for a response, but she remained perfectly

quiet. "Would you be more interested if I said I *would* kiss you?" he asked.

She laughed, although it sounded to him as if her laughter was a little choked.

"That's what I was waiting to hear, of course," she said gamely. She drew in a deep breath. "This invitation of yours—it's not very specific. Are you just testing the waters, or did you have a particular night in mind?"

"First night we're both free," he said at once, ridiculously pleased that she was considering the invitation. "I'm off tonight and tomorrow night, then again over the weekend. How's your schedule?"

"I'm working tonight and tomorrow night and over the weekend," she said.

"Including Sunday night?"

"No. Actually I'm off by three on Sunday afternoon, but I'm usually pretty beat. I don't know what kind of company I'd be. And that's usually the time I reserve for Kevin."

"Then bring him along," Sean said, seizing on the excuse to avoid risking another one of those sizzling kisses. "I don't mind."

"You don't?"

"Of course not," he said with total sincerity. "He's a terrific kid. Besides, you know I'd be the last person to want to steal some of your time with him."

"Then Sunday sounds good," she said.

"I'll pick you up at five. We'll make it an early evening, since Kevin has school the next day." It also meant less time with Deanna on a sultry spring night when the senses tended to take over.

"Perfect," she said, sounding oddly relieved, as well.

If they weren't a sorry pair, Sean thought wryly as he hung up. He wasn't sure which of them was worse. Bottom line, they were both cowards.

Which raised an interesting point. Neither of them would have a thing to fear if there were no attraction at work between them. That meant they were both terrified for a reason. And it went back to that kiss.

So, he concluded happily, he had absolutely nothing to fear as long as he didn't kiss her again.

Of course, as soon as he hit on that as the perfect solution, the desire to do the exact opposite and kiss her senseless slammed into him and wouldn't let go. Sunday night began to loom as a monumental test of his willpower. He had this gut-deep feeling he was going to lose.

6

Ruby listened to Deanna's announcement that Sean was taking her and Kevin out to dinner on Sunday without saying a word.

"Well, say something," Deanna finally said. "I thought you'd be dancing around the room. This is what you've been hoping for, isn't it?"

"Actually, what I was hoping for was you and Sean, all alone in some romantic setting where you could pick up where that kiss left off," Ruby retorted. "Have you lost your mind? The first sexy man you've been attracted to in years asks you on a date, and you're taking your five-year-old son along?"

Deanna frowned. "Sean didn't seem to mind."

"No, I don't imagine he did," Ruby scoffed. "He may be the only person in Boston more terrified than you are of having a real relationship."

"And you reached this conclusion how?"

"By talking to him," Ruby explained with exaggerated patience. "It's a fascinating concept. You should try it sometime."

They were interrupted by the sound of the buzzer from downstairs.

"That's probably Sean," Deanna said, actually relieved by the interruption. For once, seeing Sean seemed preferable to listening to any more of Ruby's analysis of her cowardice. "Will you get it, while I go and hurry Kevin along?"

"If it weren't for the fact that your son would be disappointed by having to stay home after you've promised him an evening with his hero, I would never let you get away with this," Ruby said, her expression grim.

Deanna frowned at her. "It's not your call."

Ruby sighed. "No, sadly, that's true." She waved Deanna out of the room. "Go. Fetch Kevin. I'll get the door. Maybe I'll have more luck explaining to Sean how real, grown-up dates are supposed to work."

"Don't even think about it," Deanna warned, almost afraid to leave her friend alone with Sean. Ruby rarely hesitated to speak her mind.

"Oh, go on," Ruby ordered. "I promise I won't embarrass you."

Deanna left the room reluctantly. To her relief, when she returned—without Kevin, who was still in the bathroom—Ruby and Sean were discussing baseball, not the rules of dating.

"Hank's a big baseball fan, too," Sean said, his expression completely innocent. "Maybe we could all go to a Red Sox game sometime."

"Sure," Ruby said easily, surprising Deanna with her ready agreement.

Sean seemed taken aback, as well, but he rallied

quickly. "I'll talk to Hank and work on getting the tickets, then. You and Kevin up for it, Deanna?"

"Kevin would be thrilled," Deanna said honestly.

Sean's gaze locked with hers. "And you?"

She flushed under the intensity of his gaze. "Sure. I'd love to go." What could be safer than a ballpark, surrounded by thousands of screaming fans, one of them her five-year-old son? If there was a way for Kevin to continue seeing Sean from time to time that wouldn't put her heart at risk, she was willing to consider it.

She caught the knowing glint in Sean's eyes and realized he had a pretty good idea of exactly what was going through her mind. Before she could think of some way to extricate herself, Kevin thundered down the hall and launched himself at Sean.

"This is so cool," he said from his perch on Sean's shoulder. "Where are we gonna go?"

"That's up to you and your mom," Sean told him. "What kind of food do you like?"

"I like pizza," Kevin said at once.

"I think we can do better than pizza tonight," Sean said, his gaze steady on Deanna. "How about seafood? Or Chinese?"

"Mom likes Chinese," Kevin admitted, his face scrunched up in disgust. "I think it's yucky."

Sean laughed. "Okay then, no Chinese food. Steak? Burgers?"

"A great burger sounds good to me," Deanna said. That would mean the kind of casual place where Kevin would feel comfortable and she wouldn't have to worry quite so much about him misbehaving. They hadn't been to a lot of fancy restaurants, not on her income. Joey's was the cream of the crop, and most of the regulars there considered Kevin a surrogate grandson.

"Then I know just the spot," Sean told her. "It's not too far from here. We can walk."

For the life of her Deanna couldn't think of a single good hamburger place in the neighborhood, but she trailed along beside Sean, content to listen to her son's nonstop barrage of questions and Sean's patient responses. She tried to imagine Frankie showing such patience and couldn't. It was a solid reminder that those occasional regrets she had about his absence from his son's life were wasted.

"Here we are," Sean announced as they reached an apartment building half a dozen blocks from her place.

Deanna gave him a quizzical look.

"There's no place in town that makes a hamburger any better than mine," he said. "And it just so happens that I went grocery shopping earlier." He studied her intently. "You okay with this?"

She managed to nod. The truth was that she felt a small quiver of anticipation in the pit of her stomach at the prospect of seeing where he lived. The building was certainly unpretentious, but the lawn around it was well tended. There were flowers blooming in pots beside the front door. A half-dozen children were playing catch on the stretch of grass. She saw Kevin studying them enviously.

Apparently, Sean saw the same thing. He waved at the kids. "Hey, Davey, Mark, come on over here."

Two dark-haired boys broke away from the others and ran to Sean, regarding him with the same adulation that was usually evident on Kevin's face, though these boys were around ten or twelve.

"This is my friend Kevin," Sean told them. "Would you mind letting him play with you guys while I'm getting our dinner ready? Is that okay with you, Deanna? He'll be fine. Davey and Mark are very responsible. They look out for their kid brothers all the time."

"It's okay with us," one of the boys replied.

"Please, Mom?" Kevin begged.

She grinned at his eagerness to abandon the adults—even his beloved Sean—in favor of playing catch with some older boys. "If Sean thinks it's okay and the boys don't mind, it's fine with me."

"All right!" Kevin said, racing after the others as they loped back to their game.

Deanna stood looking after him. He was growing up so fast, and she was missing so much of it, thanks to her work schedule. In that instant she could see as plainly as she ever had that she was shortchanging not only Kevin but herself. Unfortunately, she couldn't see any way around it, not unless the courts managed to track down the errant Frankie and extract all the child-support payments he'd missed over the years.

"You don't need to worry about Kevin. Davey and Mark live right downstairs from me. Their mom keeps an eye on them out her window, and you'll be able to see them from my kitchen window, too."

Deanna forced a smile. "I'm being silly and over-protective, aren't I?"

"No, of course not. You can never be too careful in this day and age, but this neighborhood is as safe as any in town. I wouldn't have suggested letting Kevin play if it weren't. And there's always a parent within earshot."

Deanna studied him closely, realizing with a sense of amazement that he took the safety of all these children as personally as if they were his own. "Something tells me you keep a close eye on things when you're around, as well."

He shrugged. "I do what I can. Now let's get out of here before we cramp their style." Reaching for her hand, he led her inside and up the narrow stairs.

"The kitchen's this way," he said as soon as they'd walked into his apartment.

Deanna wondered at his eagerness to keep her from looking around. "Did you forget to straighten up this morning?" she asked, deliberately lagging behind him.

Sean stopped and stared at her, evidently bewildered by the teasing question. "What?"

"You seem to be in a rush to get me into the kitchen. I figure that's because you left your underwear scattered all over or something."

"Hey, I'm no slob," he protested with feigned indignation. "I thought you'd be in a hurry to look outside and check on Kevin, make sure you could keep an eye on him."

"You told me he'd be safe," she reminded him.

"And you trust my judgment?"

"When it comes to my son, yes," she said, surprised to realize that it was true. If there was one thing she believed with all her heart, it was that Sean would never deliberately put her child—any child—at risk. She was surprised by the expression that washed over his face. Relief, maybe. Even a hint of wonder.

"Just like that?" he asked.

"Not just like that," she countered, astounded that he would doubt her faith in his reliability. "I've seen you with Kevin several times now. I saw how those boys outside look up to you. And I've talked to you myself. You're a good guy, Sean, especially when it comes to kids."

"Thanks. It means a lot to hear you say that."

"Why? You have to know you're great with kids."

"I don't know about that," he said.

"Of course you are," she insisted. "You know what surprises me, though?"

"What?"

"As much as you obviously love children, I can't believe you don't have some of your own."

His expression promptly shut down. "Not going to happen," he said tightly.

"Why on earth not?"

"You know why," he said. "What the hell does a man with my background know about raising a family?"

Deanna met his tormented gaze directly. "It seems to me if anyone knows what *not* to do when it comes to raising kids, it's you," she said, gently but with complete conviction.

He seemed startled by her statement. "Doesn't mean I could stick it out, any more than my folks could."

"You're not giving yourself much credit," she accused.

"For good reason. Those are the genes I've got running through me."

"You said you've been in touch with one brother recently. Does he feel the same way?"

"Pretty much," he said, then hesitated. "Or at least he did."

"What changed his mind?"

"He met someone, fell in love."

"And got married?" Deanna guessed.

Sean nodded.

"And he's braver than you are? I doubt that," she scoffed.

"It's not about being brave," he retorted.

"Sure it is. Every marriage requires a leap of faith, even for people who don't have lousy examples all around them. The same holds true for having kids. They don't come with instruction manuals. Even the best baby books don't really prepare you for the day-in, day-out realities. But thousands—probably even millions—of people have babies for the first time every year. These parents survive, and so do the kids."

He grinned. "All this talk about bravery from a woman who didn't even want to go out on a date because the prospect scared her," he teased.

Deanna winced at the accurate accusation. "I'm not scared of dating," she muttered.

"Oh? Must be me, then. Are you scared of me, Deanna?" He stepped closer as he spoke, then reached out and traced the curve of her jaw, sending a shudder through her.

"No," she whispered, but it was evident to both of them that it was a lie. She was sure he could feel her trembling, feel the heat climbing into her cheeks.

"I want to kiss you again," he said, as if he weren't especially happy about it.

Because she had something to prove, she faced him with her jauntiest expression. "Then why don't you?" she dared him.

He rubbed his thumb across her lower lip. "You mean that?"

The truth was, she thought she might die if she didn't feel his lips on hers in the next ten seconds. She nodded.

"Well then, I suppose it would be wrong of me to let a lady down," he said, slowly lowering his head until his mouth was a scant fraction of an inch above hers.

"Very wrong," she agreed as his lips met hers.

The explosion of need was every bit as violent and overwhelming as it had been the first time he'd kissed her. Deanna lost herself in the swirl of dark, tempting sensations, letting herself rock forward until she was crushed against him. Heat from his body surrounded her, pulling her in, making her crave more.

What on earth was she doing? This was exactly what she'd told herself to avoid at all costs. Her senses were swimming, filled with the taste and feel of Sean as he devoured her with that kiss. He shifted, and she felt the edge of the counter at her back, the hard press of his arousal against her hip. There was an odd sense of comfort in knowing that he wanted her as desperately as she wanted him, that he had as little control over his responses as she did.

"Mom! Sean!"

The sound of Kevin's shouts and the thunder of footsteps on the stairs tore them apart. Deanna barely resisted the urge to turn and splash cold water on her face before her son ran into the room. She noted that Sean deliberately turned his back to the room, dragging in deep gulps of air to steady himself before facing Kevin.

"In here," she called, her voice shaky.

Kevin raced through the door, then skidded to a stop. He studied her worriedly, then looked at Sean. "You guys aren't fighting, are you?"

"No, of course not. Why would you think that?"

"'Cause you look all funny, kinda like Hank and Ruby when they're fighting."

Now wasn't that telling? Deanna thought, resolving to ask Ruby just how much *fighting* she and Hank were doing lately. "Everything's fine," she reassured Kevin. "Did you come up here for a reason?"

"I'm starving. The other guys had to go in for dinner, so I came up to see if the burgers are ready."

"Not just yet," Sean said.

Deanna barely contained a chuckle at the gross exaggeration.

Kevin looked around the kitchen, clearly noting that the table wasn't set and that there was no evidence that dinner had even been started. "What have you guys been doing?" he asked.

"Talking," Deanna said at once. "We lost track of time."

"Oh," Kevin said, apparently placated. "Can I have a soda?"

"Sure," Sean said eagerly, reaching inside the fridge to retrieve one, then glancing at Deanna. "Okay?"

"Sure," she said. She would have given Kevin anything he'd asked for at that point, if it would have gotten him off the embarrassing topic of what she and Sean had been up to.

Kevin took his can of pop and climbed onto a chair. "What have you been talking about?" he asked, clearly settling in.

"Grown-up stuff. Nothing that would interest you, kiddo," Sean said, when Deanna remained completely mute, unable to think of a single response.

"Oh," Kevin said again, a bored expression crossing his face. Finally he asked, "Can I watch TV?"

Sean again glanced at Deanna. She nodded. "Just until dinner's ready," she told him. "You turn it off and come when we call, okay?"

Kevin looked at the unopened package of hamburger meat sitting on the counter and rolled his eyes. "It's not like that's gonna be anytime soon, is it?"

As soon as he'd left the kitchen, Sean looked at Deanna and grinned. "Scolded by a five-year-old," he lamented. "How embarrassing is that?"

"Not as embarrassing as trying to explain what he almost walked in on," she said. "I felt as if I were sixteen again and my father caught me making out on the front porch."

He studied her with undisguised curiosity. "Did you get caught a lot?"

"Probably not nearly as much as you probably did," she said.

"Nobody much cared what I did," he said in a matter-of-fact way that said volumes about how much that still hurt.

Deanna avoided any hint of pity. "Not even the fathers of the girls you dated?"

A smile tugged at his lips, apparently at some nearly forgotten memory. "You have a point. They did care quite a lot, but I was a smooth operator. I almost never got caught kissing their precious daughters."

"Lucky you."

He winked. "Luck had nothing to do with it. I knew enough to steer clear of their front porches. I did all my kissing in the back seat of a car, blocks from home."

Deanna felt a little thrill of excitement at the image he'd created. She wouldn't mind spending an evening in the backseat of a car with him. But given their age and experience, she doubted they'd be able to confine themselves to kissing.

"Don't even go there," Sean said.

"Where?" she asked innocently.

"I am not going to make out with you in the backseat of a car," he said firmly, his eyes twinkling and his lips struggling to hold back a grin.

She frowned at the obvious teasing. "Who asked you to?"

"Come on. You know you want to. It's written all over your face."

She shook her head and regarded him with a stern expression. "Given what you're telling me, I'm more amazed than ever that you made it to the age of twenty-nine without having at least a brush with fatherhood."

Sean's humor promptly died. "Ever heard of birth control?"

"Sure, but it's not fail proof."

"It is when I use it," he said, his expression grim.

She should have found that reassuring, but for some reason all she felt was sorrow that a man with as much parenting potential as Sean was more terrified of becoming a father than he was of walking into a blazing building.

Sean thought things had been going just great until Deanna had started pushing him about being a father. Why she couldn't see that he was a lousy candidate for such a role was beyond him. He liked kids. He got along with them. But that wasn't enough to prove that he had what it took to nurture one the way a real dad was supposed to do. Hell, he didn't know the first thing about making that kind of lifelong commitment to another human being.

He pounded the hamburgers into patties with more force than necessary, scowling as he went over their conversation in his head. He'd been honest with her, but she hadn't believed him. Like too many women Deanna apparently saw him the way she wanted him to be, not the way he was. The faith she apparently had in him was scary stuff, worse than any fire he'd ever faced.

When she'd gone into the living room to check on Kevin, he'd finally breathed a sigh of relief. He'd thrown open the window to get some air into a room that had suddenly gone claustrophobic.

A faint prickle of unease on the back of his neck told him she was back.

"You trying to tenderize that meat by pounding it to death?" she inquired lightly.

Sean stared at the hamburger patties that were less

than a half inch high. "Just working in the seasonings," he claimed, molding them back into balls before flattening them on the already hot skillet.

"What can I do to help?"

"Not a thing. I've already dished up the potato salad and coleslaw. We've got tomatoes, onions, ketchup and mustard. Anything else you need?"

"Buns?" she asked, glancing around.

"In the oven warming."

"Sounds as if you have everything under control, then."

"Kevin okay?"

"He found the cartoon channel. What do you think?" she asked wryly. "We don't have cable at our place."

"That's probably a good thing. Kids spend too much time in front of TV or computers these days. They're better off outside in the fresh air, getting plenty of exercise." Even as the words left his mouth, he realized it was something he'd heard his foster father say on more than one occasion. Evan Forrester had obviously taught him more than Sean had realized.

"Amen to that," Deanna said. "I only wish there were more places for them to play in our neighborhood. Some of the kids play in the street, but I refuse to let Kevin do that, and the nearest park's too far away."

"Ruby could bring him here in the afternoon. There's plenty of room outside the building, and there are usually a bunch of kids out in front. I could introduce her and Kevin to some of the moms."

"You wouldn't mind doing that?"

"Why would I?"

"It might mean you'd be bumping into Kevin more. I'm sure it's flattering to be idolized the way he idolizes you, but it can take a toll after a while. You might start to want your privacy back."

"Dee, don't worry about it," he said, using the nickname he'd heard Ruby use. "Kevin's a great kid. He's not getting on my nerves. I like having him around. And it's not as if I'm here all that much, anyway. If it'll make you feel better, have Ruby call me before they come by, to make sure it's not an inconvenience, but I can tell you right now that it won't be."

Deanna didn't look totally convinced.

"Okay, what else is on your mind?" he asked.

"I'm not sure it's a good idea for him to start to count on you too much," she admitted. "It's not as if you're always going to be available for him. Despite what you think now, you could eventually meet someone, get married, have your own family. Where would that leave Kevin?"

He carefully flipped a burger as he considered his response to that. "We've already discussed the likelihood that I'll never get married, so that's not an issue." He met her gaze. "Dee, I'm not going to let him down. I'll make it very clear that we're just buddies. I won't set up any false expectations."

"That all sounds very reasonable to me, but I'm an adult, not a five-year-old boy who desperately wants a dad."

Sean swallowed hard as her quietly spoken words hit home. Of course she was right to be worried. How many times as a boy had he watched with envy as his friends went off to do things with their dads? Evan

Forrester had done things with him, but it had taken years before Sean had allowed himself to begin to count on his foster father really being there for him. If anything had happened to jerk the rug out from under his feet once he'd finally started to trust his foster father, it would have been devastating. Kevin had none of those defenses in place. The kid was still innocent enough to wear his heart on his sleeve.

"Would you prefer it if I steered clear of him completely?" he asked, feeling an odd sense of loss even before she replied. Though he spent time with a lot of kids, there was something about Kevin's cocky self-assurance and his vulnerability that struck a chord with Sean. Maybe he saw himself in the boy.

Deanna stood there, clearly weighing her answer for what seemed to be an eternity before she finally shook her head. "No, that's not what I want, and I know it's not what Kevin wants. I just don't want him to get hurt."

"Sometimes it's not possible to protect the people we love from getting hurt," Sean said. "But I'll do my best not to hurt Kevin."

"I know that, or we wouldn't be having this conversation," she said. "We wouldn't even be here."

Sean tucked a finger under her chin and forced her to meet his gaze, "I'm going to do my best not to hurt you, either."

She shrugged as if her feelings were of no importance. "Yeah, well, like you said, you can't always protect people from pain. It's part of living."

"You learned that lesson from your ex?"

"Among others," she said tightly.

"Care to elaborate?"

"Not really. The important thing is that I survived." She met his gaze. "So did you."

Long after Sean had walked Deanna and Kevin back home, her words lingered in his head. He doubted she realized the significance of what she'd said. She'd managed to remind him that for most of the past decade—no, even longer than that—Sean had not only survived, he'd worked hard to keep himself safe from being hurt.

But only today had he realized that he—very much like Deanna, whether she realized it or not—had also kept himself from really living.

7

"What the devil is this?"

From her place at the reception desk Deanna heard the shout of the senior law partner in his office. She exchanged a glance with Ruby.

"Mr. Hodges sounds like he's on a real rampage," Deanna said in a whisper. "I wonder what it's about."

Before they could even speculate, the intercom on her desk buzzed.

"Deanna, Mr. Hodges would like to see you," Charlotte Wilson said, her tone somber. "Have Ruby cover the desk for you."

"Yes, ma'am," Deanna said, her palms sweating. She gave Ruby a shaky smile. "Pray for me."

"Don't let the man bully you," Ruby advised.

Stomach churning, Deanna walked down the corridor to the suite of offices belonging to Jordan Hodges. A glance at Charlotte's face was not encouraging. The secretary, who usually maintained a facade of icy reserve, looked as if she wanted to cry.

Deanna stepped inside the office and waited.

"Don't just stand there. Come in and close the door," her boss said, regarding her with a scowling expression.

She shut the door and crossed the room. "Is something wrong?"

"I'll say something's wrong," he said, his expression grim. "I found these papers on my desk just now." He waved an envelope in her direction. "They were supposed to be across town on the desk of opposing counsel. Care to explain why they're not?"

Deanna stared at the envelope in confusion. True, it was her job to see that the outgoing mail went out each day, but she wasn't the one who addressed it. "I have no idea. What does it say on the envelope?"

"The address label is quite clear," he said, waving it under her nose.

She snagged a corner of the envelope and studied it. Sure enough, it was addressed to a lawyer in downtown Boston. "Sir, I know I've been a little frazzled lately, but if this envelope had come across my desk addressed like this, it would have gone out," she said confidently. "It wouldn't have gotten mixed up with the incoming mail."

The color in Mr. Hodges's face had finally begun to return to normal. He sank into his chair. "It's not like you to make a mistake like this," he agreed, studying her with concern. "You say you've been frazzled. Is something wrong I should know about? Your boy's okay?"

She was surprised by the question. She rarely mentioned Kevin around the office. "Kevin's fine."

"Something else, then?"

Deanna hadn't wanted to get into her personal problems at work. She never wanted her boss to think that she had so much going on that she couldn't concentrate on her job. It was a sure way to get fired.

"It's okay," he encouraged her, pinning her with a steady gaze. "Just tell me."

No wonder the man was considered a shark in court, Deanna thought. He was relentless and he managed to cross-examine a witness with that same look of compassion on his face that he had right now. She could almost believe that he really cared about what was going on in her life.

"I really don't think there's any need for me to burden you with my problems," she said.

"Nonsense. Tell me," he said even more emphatically.

"It's just that there was this fire a couple of months ago," she said hesitantly.

"A fire? Where?"

"My building."

"How bad was it?"

"Pretty bad," she admitted, then added with some reluctance, "We lost everything."

Shock spread across his face. "Why on earth didn't you say something?"

"We've been doing okay. We're living with Ruby temporarily. I've been adding hours at Joey's to try to get enough money so we can move into our own place. To be honest, it's possible that it's catching up with me."

"You're working a second job at Joey Talifero's restaurant?" he asked, clearly shocked.

"Actually I have been for some time."

He shook his head. "Well, one thing at a time. We'll deal with your need to work a second job another time. As for the fire, why wasn't I told about it? I assume you told Charlotte."

"Actually, no." Mr. Hodges's executive secretary was the last person she would have shared her personal problems with. "I don't like to bring my problems to work. I never want you to get the idea that this job doesn't have my full attention."

He regarded her with unmistakable dismay. "Deanna, how long have you been here now? Five years, isn't it? Ever since your son was born."

She nodded.

"And every single evaluation has given you high marks for being a responsible employee, correct?"

"Yes."

"Then why on earth would you be afraid to come to me when you lose your home? I think that qualifies as the kind of thing your boss ought to know. We could help you out, give you a loan, represent you if you want to sue the landlord."

Deanna stared at him in astonishment. She had never considered asking him for free legal assistance. The kind of cases he normally handled involved hundreds of thousands of dollars, not what would amount to pocket change in his world. "You would do that?" she asked.

"Well, of course we would," he said with a hint of exasperation that she even had to ask. "What did you expect? As far as I'm concerned, every employee in this firm is like family. When anyone's having a problem, I expect them to come to me *before* it interferes with their job performance."

"Thank you. I'll remember that in the future."

"Forget the future. What about the here and now? What can I do?"

Deanna refused to ask for more money. He was already paying her a decent wage for the receptionist's job she'd been doing. And she certainly didn't want a loan she would have to struggle to pay back.

"Nothing, really. I'm handling everything."

"Not if this mistake is an example of the way you're handling things," he chided, but more gently this time. "Who was at fault for the fire?"

"The fire inspector said it was the landlord," she said. "But the landlord made it clear when I signed my lease that he wasn't responsible for damages to anything in any of the apartments, that I needed to carry my own insurance."

"Did you?"

She shook her head. "I couldn't afford it," she admitted. "And we didn't have that much. I didn't realize until we lost everything how much it would cost to replace what little we did have."

Mr. Hodges pulled out a legal pad and a pen. "What's the landlord's name?"

"Lawrence Wyatt."

To her surprise her boss reacted with disgust. "Typical of Wyatt," he muttered. "This isn't the first time I've run across him. I'll have a talk with him. I think I can promise you a settlement of some kind. Will that mean you can cut back on your hours at Joey's, maybe start getting some sleep?"

"Yes."

"See that it does," he said sternly. "And, Deanna?"

"Yes, sir."

"Next time there's a crisis, don't wait so long to come to me."

"No, sir," she said, exiting the office before the tears of gratitude stinging her eyes could fall.

Charlotte studied her worriedly. "Did he fire you?"

"No."

"Thank heaven," the secretary said fervently.

"I just can't imagine what happened, though. I'm always so careful. I know how important papers like that are."

"Mistakes happen to everyone," Charlotte said.

It was such a rare attempt at reassurance that Deanna regarded her with sudden suspicion. "You never put that envelope on my desk, did you?"

Charlotte's thin mouth remained clamped firmly shut, but the misery in her eyes was a dead giveaway.

"Never mind. I won't say anything," Deanna promised. "But you owe me, Charlotte."

The woman finally sighed. "You're right. I do. I wouldn't have let him fire you, you know. I would have confessed if it had come to that."

"But you were willing to let the mistake go on my record," Deanna reminded her. "I won't forget that."

She turned and left the suite before Charlotte could respond. When Deanna reached the outer office, she was surprised to find Sean perched on the edge of the reception desk chatting with Ruby. They both regarded her with worry when they spotted her.

"What are you doing here?" she asked Sean.

"I called him," Ruby said. "Mr. Hodges never yells like that unless he's ready to can somebody. I was afraid you were about to get fired, so I figured you'd need a big, broad shoulder to cry on. So, what happened in there?"

"He blew a gasket about a really stupid mistake, but then I explained about the fire and the extra hours at Joey's, and instead of firing me, he's going to talk to the landlord and try to wrangle a settlement for me. Actually, except for Charlotte's role in it, it's pretty amazing," she said, still bemused by the whole turn of events.

"Charlotte?" Sean asked, looking confused.

"The snake who runs Mr. Hodges's office," Ruby said, then turned to Deanna. "What did she do?"

"Turns out she was the one who made the mistake I was getting blamed for."

Ruby regarded her with indignation. "I hope you told Hodges," she said.

Deanna shook her head. "No. I didn't even realize what had really happened until after I'd left his office."

"Why the heck didn't you go right back in and tell the man the truth?" Sean demanded.

"Because it turned out okay. Charlotte won't do anything like that again."

"You're too darned noble," Ruby said.

"Actually, I'm not," Deanna said with a grin. "Now I have something I can hold over her head for years to come. Having leverage over Charlotte is a very good thing."

Ruby grinned. "Then I suggest you start by telling her you're taking the afternoon off and that she's going to cover for you. Then the three of us are going to pick up Kevin and go celebrate."

Deanna glanced at Sean to see how he was taking Ruby's attempt to plan his afternoon. He winked at her.

"Sounds like a plan to me. I don't go back on duty till midnight." He glanced pointedly at Ruby. "Neither does Hank."

Ruby frowned at that. "So?"

"Just thought you might be interested."

"Oh, go on and call him, if you want to," Ruby told Sean grudgingly.

Deanna didn't think Ruby ought to get off the hook so easily. As Sean reached for the phone, she stopped him. "Why don't you make that call, Ruby? I'll go and speak to Charlotte."

"But—"

Deanna cut off the protest. "If I can go in there and face down dragon lady, you can call Hank."

"Oh, for heaven's sake, go. I'll call," Ruby grumbled.

She was still on the phone with Hank when Deanna came back. "How are they doing?" she asked Sean in a whisper.

He chuckled. "The subject of the celebration hasn't actually come up yet. Those two are doing a dance that defies explanation. I'm almost tempted to yank the phone out of her hand and tell the poor guy why she really called."

"She'd never forgive you," Deanna said.

"But Hank would be forever grateful. I like to shift the balance of power in our partnership arrangement from time to time."

Deanna groaned. "You men and your macho games. I thought the two of you were friends."

"We are. That's how we stay that way," he explained in a way that almost made it sound like a perfectly rational way to live.

"Whatever," Deanna said. "Thanks for coming over here when Ruby called. You didn't have to."

He laughed. "You wouldn't say that if you'd heard her on the phone. I expected you to emerge from that office bloodied and defeated."

"But I notice you didn't rush in to save me," she said.

"Only because when I got here and heard the whole story, I got a somewhat different picture of the crisis unfolding." He reached in his pocket and withdrew a package of tissues. "I ran out and got these."

"Anticipating my weeping, were you?" she inquired, amused by his attempt at preparedness. "A lot of men would have run at the prospect."

He shrugged. "Not me. I'm a sensitive kind of guy."

"You say that as if it's a joke, but you are, you know."

"You wouldn't say that if you knew about my plan to go in and pound your boss for making you cry in the first place."

She bit back a smile. "When were you going to do that?"

"As soon as I gave you the tissues and turned you over to Ruby."

Deanna laughed. "I don't need you fighting my battles for me."

"I know. I can see that."

"But I appreciate your willingness to step in, just the same."

He seemed suddenly uncomfortable with her praise. "Don't turn me into some kind of hero. All I did was show up."

She reached up and touched his cheek. "That's quite a lot for a man who claims to know nothing about sticking it out through tough times."

"Dee—"

"Hey, you guys," Ruby interrupted. "Are we going to hang around here all afternoon or are we going to celebrate?"

Deanna met Sean's gaze and held it. "I think we have quite a few reasons to celebrate, don't you?"

For a minute she thought he might prolong the argument, but eventually he shrugged. "Whatever you say. Who am I to argue with a woman who managed to emerge from battle unscathed?"

Satisfied, Deanna turned to Ruby. "Is Hank joining us?"

Ruby shrugged. "Beats me. He was still grumbling a lot of nonsense about being awakened out of a sound sleep for no good reason when I hung up on him."

"But you did tell him where we'd be, right?" Deanna persisted.

"How could I?" Ruby asked reasonably. "I don't know where we're going to be."

Deanna sighed.

"I'll call and give him a heads-up when we get there," Sean said.

"Whatever," Ruby said, setting off down the street

at a brisk pace that left Deanna and Sean trailing behind.

They stared after her, then exchanged an exasperated look.

"Do you have any idea what's going on between those two?" Deanna asked.

"Not me," Sean said.

"Well, he's your friend," she said irritably.

"And she's yours. Do you get it?"

"No," she admitted.

"Why do I think that getting in the middle of it is a very bad idea?" Sean asked.

"Because you're an intelligent man," Deanna said. "But you're going to call Hank, anyway, right?"

Sean nodded. "If only to get a firsthand look at the fireworks."

Brave man, Deanna thought. Then again, he was a firefighter. A hot, noisy skirmish probably wouldn't faze him. After all, he had lots of experience extinguishing out-of-control blazes.

Sean wasn't prepared for Hank's haggard look when he finally joined them at the ice-cream parlor that had been chosen for the celebration. He looked every bit as bad as he had a few weeks ago at the gym. He cast a sour look at Sean, barely managed a smile for Deanna, then squeezed into the booth next to Ruby, who never even looked up from her hot-fudge sundae.

Sean might not know what game those two were playing, but one thing was plain—Hank had it bad for the woman beside him. Sean couldn't think of a single occasion in the past when his pal had been so hung up on a woman. Usually after this length of time, he'd slept with a woman a few times, tired of her and moved on.

Suddenly the answer dawned on him. Hank and Ruby *hadn't* slept together. That was why they were both so cranky and out of sorts. Sean almost laughed at the irony of it. All this time, he'd been half-envious of Hank's success, and Ruby had been keeping Hank at arm's length. She was obviously a whole lot wiser than Sean had given her credit for being. He wondered if Deanna had guessed the truth, but judging from the puzzled way she was studying the two of them, she hadn't.

"Hey, Dee, feel like going for a walk?" he turned and asked her.

She regarded him blankly. "Now?"

"Seems like a good time to me," he said with a pointed glance across the table.

She looked at Ruby and Hank, then nodded with evident reluctance. "I guess so. Come on, Kevin. We're going for a walk."

Ruby's gaze shot up. "You're leaving?" she asked, a faint hint of panic in her voice.

Deanna regarded her worriedly. "Unless you want us to wait for you?"

Hank seemed to be holding his breath as he awaited Ruby's reply. She looked at him, waged some sort of internal debate that Sean couldn't interpret, then finally shook her head.

"Go ahead," she told them. "Hank hasn't even ordered yet. I can stay with him."

"You're sure you don't mind?" Deanna persisted,

as Sean latched on to her hand and began tugging her from the booth.

"You heard her," Sean said. "She told us to go on."

Kevin regarded all of them with impatience. "Are we going or staying?" he grumbled.

"Going," Sean said firmly.

Deanna looked as if she might balk, but then she shrugged. "We're going."

Outside, she scowled up at Sean. "What was that all about? Why were you so anxious to get out of there?"

"Discretion," he said.

"What?" she demanded. Then understanding obviously dawned. "Oh, of course."

"You two are acting all weird again," Kevin declared with disgust.

Sean laughed. "You'll understand when you're older."

"So, where are we going?" he asked. "Is the celebration over?"

"Not yet," Sean reassured him. "How about my place? Want to head over there for a while?"

Kevin's expression immediately brightened. "Will Mark and Davey be there?"

"More than likely."

"All right!" he enthused.

"Deanna, is that okay with you?" Sean asked.

To his surprise, she looked hesitant, but one glance at Kevin's excited expression had her backing down from whatever objections she had. "Sure."

As soon as they reached Sean's apartment, Kevin spotted the older kids and took off without another word. Deanna watched him go with a contradictory mix of dismay and relief on her face. Sean wished he could read her mind.

"What's wrong?" he asked, concerned that he'd been pushing her too hard and overstepping some unspoken boundary where Kevin was concerned. He thought they'd talked that all out, but maybe she'd had second thoughts.

"Nothing, not really. I'm glad Kevin's found some friends. They don't even seem to mind that he's so much younger. It's almost as if he has big brothers. He talks about the two of them nonstop." She grinned at Sean. "Except when he's talking about you."

"There's nothing like having brothers," Sean said. "My parents taking off was bad enough, but in some ways losing my brothers was worse. We were best buddies, especially Ryan and me. Mikey was a couple of years younger than me, four years younger than Ryan, but he trailed around after us whenever we'd let him."

"What about the twins?" Deanna asked. "You never say much about them."

"It was different with the twins," Sean recalled. "They were still practically babies when Mom and Dad left—barely two years old. From the time they came home from the hospital, Ryan and I used to take one each and feed them, first their bottles, then that yucky stuff that passes for real food." He shuddered at the memory. "If I don't ever again see another jar of mashed peas or carrots, it will be too soon. I've never seen a worse mess in my life than those two could make having lunch."

"You sure that's not the real reason you don't want to have kids of your own?" Deanna asked lightly.

"Baby food?"

She laughed. "No. I was thinking of the way babies are when you're feeding them. You realize just how dependent they are on you. It can be scary."

Sean thought back to the way he'd felt holding his baby brothers, as if he really were somebody's hero. If anything, that emotion was the one reason he could see in favor of having kids. It was all the rest—the terrifying fear of letting them down—that kept him single and childless. Instead, he'd settled for being a different kind of hero, one who never had to risk his heart, just his life.

"I suppose," he said eventually.

She seemed to sense she'd pushed him far enough. "So how's the search going for Michael?" she asked.

He shrugged, as uncomfortable with this topic as he had been with the one before. Despite how well the reunion with Ryan had gone, he had mixed feelings about the search for Michael. Most of the time he pushed it completely out of his mind. "I have no idea," he admitted. "I haven't heard from Ryan lately."

Deanna regarded him with obvious surprise. "You could always call him or stop by to see him, couldn't you? Didn't you say he owns a pub?"

"Yes, but…" He really didn't have a good explanation for why he'd been avoiding his brother. He was pretty sure it had something to do with the overwhelming feeling of happiness that had swamped him when Ryan had first come back into his life. He didn't trust that kind of emotion. It never lasted. He supposed a part of him was waiting for his brother to keep reach-

ing out to him. Maybe he needed proof that Ryan was
back in his life to stay.

Or maybe it was flat-out jealousy that Ryan had
found something with Maggie that Sean wouldn't
allow himself to feel.

"I'd like to go sometime," Deanna said.

He stared at her. "Go where?"

"To your brother's pub. I love Irish music. I imagine they have it there."

"On weekends," he admitted, still struggling with
the fact that she'd actually initiated the idea of getting
together with him.

She kept her unflinching gaze leveled on him. "Will
you take me sometime?"

"What are you trying to do, Deanna?"

"Ask you on a date," she said, her expression innocent. "Wasn't I clear enough?"

He studied her suspiciously. "What if I said I'd take
you to some other pub in the city?"

"Then I'd say you're avoiding your brother," she responded. "And you certainly wouldn't want me to get
an idea like that, would you?"

He chuckled at the tidy trap she'd sprung. Until he'd
met Deanna, he'd had no idea how many traces of cowardice lurked inside him. "No, I suppose not. I imagine
you can be a real nag when you set your mind to it."

"I can," she agreed proudly. "I learned from Ruby."

Sean held up his hands in a gesture of surrender.
"We'll go the first weekend I'm off," he said.

To his surprise, instead of feeling trapped, he felt
a faint stirring of genuine anticipation. Maybe Ryan
didn't have to be first to reach out. He'd been the one

who'd searched for and found Sean, after all. And he had asked Sean to be the best man at his wedding. Maybe it was Sean's turn to take a risk and keep the lines of communication open.

He met Deanna's penetrating gaze, saw the warm approval in her eyes and realized that there could be yet another benefit to taking a tiny chink out of the wall around his heart. Eventually there just might be enough room for a woman like Deanna to squeeze through.

8

Joey had promised Deanna she could have Friday night off to go to Ryan's Place with Sean, but on Friday at three o'clock, he called her at the law office and said he needed her to come in after all. Deanna thought of how hard she'd had to work to get Sean to agree to go to his brother's pub in the first place and felt her heart sink.

"Joey, you can't do this to me. You promised," she said.

"I'm desperate," Joey countered. "Pauline's sick."

"What's wrong with her?" Deanna asked, instantly concerned. Joey's wife had struggled for years with diabetes. Sometimes when things got especially hectic at the restaurant, she forgot to take her insulin.

"Just a cold, but it's wiped her out. I don't want her coming in here, and she shouldn't be handling orders and sneezing all over the customers, anyway."

Deanna sighed. She could hardly argue with that. "Okay, I'll work."

"I'll make it up to you, I swear it," Joey promised.

"Next week you can have the whole weekend off. Catch up on your beauty sleep."

"Next week's no good," she said at once, at least not for her plan to get Sean to visit his brother. She knew by now that Sean worked every other weekend. "I want the weekend after next. Guaranteed, okay?"

"Guaranteed. You've got it," Joey said.

"Put that in writing with a penalty clause for cancellation," she said wryly. At least thanks to working in a law office, she'd picked up a few hints about protecting her rights.

"What?" Joey asked blankly.

Deanna laughed as she imagined trying to enforce such a guarantee, even if she got Joey to sign it. "Never mind. I'll see you in an hour." As soon as she'd hung up, she drew in a deep breath, picked the phone back up and called Sean.

"I have to cancel tonight," she blurted when he picked up. "But I think you should go, anyway."

"Why do you have to cancel?" he asked, sounding suspicious. "Did you ever intend to go in the first place or was this all some scheme to make sure Ryan and I don't lose touch?"

"Of course not," she said indignantly. "I don't scheme."

"Okay then, why are you canceling at the last minute?"

Deanna had a feeling he wasn't going to be much happier about the real reason she was backing out. "I have to work at Joey's," she admitted, then added, "His wife's sick."

"And there's no one else he could call?" Sean asked,

his skepticism plain. "There's at least one other waitress there that I know of."

"Adele never works weekends," she explained, referring to Joey's one other nonfamily waitress. "It's usually Pauline and me. With Pauline sick, Joey's in a bind."

"Just this once, don't you think he could have called Adele first?" Sean asked.

She saw no reason to explain why Adele always had weekends off, that she cared for an ailing husband on the days insurance wouldn't pay for a nurse. "It's not a big deal. I don't mind pitching in."

"You need time off," Sean countered. "And we had plans."

There was an odd note in his voice she couldn't interpret. "Are you more upset because I have to work or because I have to postpone our visit to the pub?"

"Both," he insisted. "I told Ryan we were going to be there, and I also know that you're stretched to the limit. You need a night off."

"Sean, you can go to the pub without me. You and your brother can spend a little time together. I'll meet him in a couple of weeks," she said reasonably.

"And the break you need? When are you going to squeeze that in?"

Deanna lost patience. "When I can," she said tightly. "Sean, my life is not one of your projects."

"I don't have projects," he said tightly, clearly exasperated. "And I don't need this."

"Well, neither do I," she retorted angrily. "I have enough on my plate without having to defend myself to you."

She hung up without listening to his response. Judging from the angry tone, it wasn't the apology he owed her, anyway.

All evening long Deanna kept expecting to look up and see Sean walk through the door. When there was no sign of him, she told herself it was for the best. She'd been running her life reasonably well for a long time now. She didn't need some man swooping in and forcing changes on her that *he* thought were for her own good.

Despite her rationalization, she was still feeling sick at heart when Joey dropped her off in front of Ruby's at ten-thirty.

"Thanks again," he said as she got out of the car. "I'm really sorry about having to call you today and ruin your plans."

"Stop apologizing. I told you it wasn't a problem."

"Then why have you spent the entire evening looking as if you lost your best friend? You and Sean had a fight about this, didn't you? I know how upset he gets over the long hours you put in."

Typical of Joey to develop insight and sensitivity when she had something she didn't want to discuss.

"I'll talk to him," Joey offered when Deanna kept silent. "I can explain."

"No, you'll stay out of it," she countered.

"But he's a good guy. I like him. So does Paulie. She'll kill me if she thinks I did anything to mess up your relationship with the guy. And since all this happened because she was out sick, she'll be even more upset."

"Sean and I don't have a relationship," she said, not entirely sure how to describe what they did have. It seemed to be evolving from day to day.

Or at least it had been. She sighed.

Joey frowned. "I really think I'd better talk to him."

"No, absolutely not. Now stop worrying and go home and check on your wife. Give her my love."

"I'll wait till you get inside," Joey insisted. "Blink the lights like always, so I'll know you're safe."

Deanna leaned down and kissed his cheek. "You are such a worrywort. Good night."

As soon as she reached Ruby's apartment, she blinked the lights, then turned and looked directly into Sean's solemn face. Her heart leaped into her throat. She wasn't entirely sure whether it was because he'd just scared the daylights out of her or because she was overjoyed to see him. She decided to go with the fear factor.

"What on earth are you doing inside my apartment lurking in the shadows? You scared me half to death," she said.

"Sorry."

He didn't seem very sorry. "How long have you been here?" she asked.

"About an hour." He'd been sitting on the edge of the sofa, but he stood up now, took a step toward her, then stopped as if he was uncertain what to do next.

"Where's Ruby?"

"She went out with Hank. Kevin's asleep in the bedroom."

Deanna tried to process the fact that Ruby had left her son with Sean without checking with her first. Not that it was a problem, other than the fact that it was one more thing Sean could hold over her head. She recognized the reason for his knee-jerk reaction to anything he considered neglectful, but it always hurt when the accusation surfaced—spoken or unspoken.

"You're pretty high-priced for a babysitter. What am I paying you?"

He frowned at her attempt at levity. "Don't even go there."

Something in his tone warned her he wasn't in a joking mood. She bit back another jibe and said simply, "I'm amazed Kevin went to bed knowing you're here."

He grinned at that. "He was already asleep when I got here."

"Ah, that explains it."

He jammed his hands in his pockets in a gesture she'd come to realize meant he was uncomfortable. "So," he said, not quite meeting her gaze. "You want some coffee? I made a pot. I had a feeling it might be a long night."

"Oh?"

"I figure we've got a few things to hash out."

She studied him curiously. "Such as?"

"Why you get so uptight just because I'm concerned about you. Why I insist on acting like a horse's behind when you don't fall in with my plans."

Deanna bit back a grin. "You're right. I'll take that coffee. If we've got all that to discuss, it could be a long night."

She led the way into the kitchen, took two mugs from the cupboard and poured the coffee. "I brought home a couple of pieces of Joey's lemon meringue pie,"

she said, holding up a takeout box from the restaurant.
"You interested?"

His expression brightened. "Sure."

Deanna set one piece in front of him but put the
second piece in the refrigerator.

"You're not eating any?" he asked.

"Just a bite of yours," she said, pulling two forks out
of the drawer. "I'm not that hungry. Do you mind?"

"Of course not," he said.

He leaned back and watched while she proceeded
to eat most of the slice. A few minutes later Deanna
stared at the empty plate with chagrin. "Why on earth
didn't you stop me?"

"There's something kind of erotic about a woman
with a healthy appetite," he said.

"Even when she's stealing the food off your plate?"

He leaned forward and wiped a crumb from the corner of her mouth. "Even then," he said solemnly, his
gaze locked with hers. "I'm sorry, Deanna."

Her head seemed to be spinning. "For?"

"Trying to run your life. I know it's not my place,
but I hate seeing what all this work is doing to you."
He traced a finger under her eyes. "You're exhausted.
The proof's right here."

"That's no way to lift a woman's spirits," she
pointed out.

"I have to call 'em like I see 'em."

She sighed. "Sean, I realize you only take on my
lifestyle because you care. I suppose I'm just not used
to anyone besides Ruby caring whether I'm worn-out
or not. It makes me uncomfortable."

"I can't promise to stop caring," he said, regarding her solemnly. "But I'll try to stop hassling you."

"That would be nice," she said. "And I'll try to stop overreacting when you lose your head and do it again."

He gave her a rueful look. "You're so sure I'll forget my promise?"

"I'm certain of it," she said. "But, oddly enough, I think that's one of the things I like best about you."

"Care to name any of the others?"

She laughed, suddenly feeling better. "Stop fishing for compliments."

"You know, Deanna, one of these days we're going to have to deal with the real issue between us."

She swallowed hard at the suddenly solemn expression on his face. "What issue is that?" she asked, not entirely sure she wanted to know.

"The fact that I want you," he said simply.

Desire curled through her like the warmth of a fire on a cold winter night. She refused to let herself look away from the heat in his eyes. "I guess that's plain enough," she said, her voice unsteady despite her best efforts to seem blasé.

A smile tugged at his lips. "You're not going to admit it, are you?"

"Admit what?"

"That you want me, too."

She drew herself up and inquired in her best imitation of a haughty princess speaking to a peasant, "Whatever gave you that idea?"

To her surprise, Sean laughed.

"Nice try, darlin', but you're not going to win any prizes for your acting."

"I am not acting," she said irritably.

"One kiss says otherwise."

"Are you daring me to kiss you, Sean Devaney?"

"Yep."

"Well, you can just forget it. I don't have to prove anything to you."

"Then you don't mind if I go right on believing what I want to believe?"

She leveled a look straight at him. "Up to you. I can't control what you think."

"But you can prove me wrong," he countered mildly. "Or rather, you can try."

"That is so…" She couldn't think of a word to describe just how low she thought he'd sunk, but finally settled on the first one that came to mind. "Juvenile. That's what it is, juvenile."

He didn't seem especially offended by the accusation. In fact, he merely shrugged. "I've been called worse."

"I'm not surprised."

"Can I ask you a question?"

She studied him suspiciously. "About?"

"What the hell did your ex-husband put you through to make you so suspicious of all men?"

The question caught Deanna completely by surprise. Sean had never shown any interest in her relationship with Frankie before. And her ex-husband was not a subject she liked discussing.

"Isn't it enough that he walked out before Kevin was born and left me on my own?"

"That's pretty rotten," Sean agreed. "But I have a feeling it was more than that."

"Such as?"

"Why waste time with me speculating? I'm asking you for an explanation."

Deanna thought back to her brief marriage. She'd gone into it with stars in her eyes, convinced she was madly in love and that Frankie felt the same way. Barely eighteen, she had defied her parents, walked away from a promised college education, given up everything and everyone to be with the charming rogue who'd stolen her heart.

But Frankie had been after more than her heart. To Deanna's everlasting embarrassment, she finally realized he'd been after her trust fund. That money was the only reason he'd been willing to make a commitment to her. After the wedding, when he'd finally understood there was no way either of them were going to get their hands on it, he'd lost interest and moved on to someone a little older, a little richer, someone whose parents hadn't disowned her.

The humiliation had been almost unbearable. There was no way Deanna could bring herself to crawl back to her parents to ask for help, which, of course, was precisely what Frankie had assumed she'd do. To this day she doubted he knew the dire straits in which he'd left her.

Despite Ruby's urging her to tell her folks what had happened and that they had a grandson, Deanna had been determined to make it entirely on her own. Though the court had awarded her child support, she'd never expected to see a dime of it, not from a man who'd expected to be supported by her family. So far she'd done a pretty lousy job of triumphing over the past, but at least she hadn't had to listen to an endless tirade of "I told you so." One day, when she was really and truly back on her feet, she would contact her parents, but not now.

In the meantime, there were all those scars, the ones that made her question her judgment, the ones that made her distrust all men. Not that anyone could possibly be after her for her money now, she thought, barely stifling a laugh.

She felt Sean's warm, steady gaze on her and finally lifted her eyes to meet his.

"Where'd you go just then?" he asked.

"Back in time," she said wearily.

"Obviously not a happy time."

"No," she said succinctly.

"Will you tell me sometime?"

"Probably not," she said.

"Because you can't talk about it?"

"That's one reason." There were others, though. She didn't want his pity, and she certainly didn't want him realizing what an idiot she was for being taken in so easily.

"Did you love him that much?" Sean asked quietly.

She had. That was the worst joke of all. She had really loved Frankie, at least the man she'd thought he was. She'd had some sort of Romeo and Juliet fantasy about the two of them defying all the obstacles in their path to live happily ever after.

"Truthfully?" she said wearily. "I didn't even know him."

Sean couldn't forget what little Deanna had revealed about her relationship with her ex-husband. Nor could he keep himself from speculating about all that she'd left unsaid. It was just one more mystery to be unraveled, one more facet to add to this fascination he couldn't seem to shake.

And despite all his promises to stop hovering over her, he couldn't seem to stop himself from worrying about the almost driven way she continued to live her life. It went beyond survival instinct. It had something to do with the past. He was sure of it.

Despite her boss's promise to help her win a settlement from her landlord, as far as Sean could see, Deanna was still working herself to death. He was damned proud of the fact that he managed to keep from butting in, hauling her home and barring the door until she got at least twenty-four straight hours of sleep. But every time he saw her, the circles under her eyes were darker, the weariness in her shoulders more evident.

Even though he'd resolved to keep silent, he couldn't stop himself from doing what he could to keep an eye on her. Something told him she was nearing the end of her rope, and he intended to be nearby whenever possible in case she needed him. What had begun as a resolution to make sure Kevin was well looked after became an obsession to do the same for Deanna.

"You know, Sean, I like Joey's food as well as the next guy, but do we have to eat there every night?" Hank inquired as they left the firehouse.

"Yes," Sean said tersely. He sighed and raked a hand through his hair as he regarded the whole group of firefighters apologetically. "Look, I really appreciate the fact that you guys are willing to go there."

"Not a problem," the others chorused. "Especially if you keep paying."

Sean winced at the reminder. He figured if Deanna found out about that, she'd be furious that he was wasting his money just to keep her under surveillance.

As the other men drifted away, Sean faced Hank. "The truth is, I'm worried about Deanna."

"Why? What's up?" Hank asked, his expression instantly filled with genuine concern. "Her ex isn't stalking her or something, is he?"

"No. But she's tired and on edge. She can't keep up this pace forever."

"And this is your problem because?" Hank asked, though his eyes were dancing with undisguised amusement.

"Because I've made it my problem," Sean returned. "Besides, I don't know what you're complaining about. Tonight is spaghetti night. You're bound to run into Ruby."

Hank looked decidedly uncomfortable at the reminder. Sean studied him intently. "Is that a problem?"

"No," Hank said tersely.

Even though his expression warned against further questions, that didn't stop Sean from asking, "You sure about that?"

"Leave it alone, okay? My relationship with Ruby is none of your business."

"That can cut both ways, you know. I can tell you to butt out of my relationship with Deanna, as well."

Hank's laugh held little mirth. "As if you two actually have one."

Sean's gaze narrowed. "Relationships aren't just about sex, you know."

"Is that so?" Hank retorted sarcastically. "Enlighten me, then. What are they about?"

"I'm not surprised you don't know," Sean said. "Since you've always been a wham-bam kind of guy."

Hank threw up his hands. "Forget it. I ask a serious question and I get wisecracks. Who needs it?" He walked out of the station and slammed the door behind him, leaving Sean staring after him.

Well, well, well, he thought. Hank was neck deep in water and floundering. He recognized the signs because he was pretty much in over his head himself.

Sighing heavily, he went after his partner to make amends. He found Hank sitting on the running board of the fire truck, looking despondent.

"I'm sorry. I didn't realize she was really getting to you," he told Hank.

Hank scowled up at him. "I never said—"

Sean cut him off. "Save it, okay? Just save it. If you can't tell me the truth, who can you tell?"

For a minute he thought Hank might stand up and throw a punch, but he finally shrugged. "Okay, I'm falling for her," he admitted. "There. I've said it. Are you satisfied?"

Sean grinned. "It's a start."

"I don't hear you admitting that you're crazy about Deanna," Hank said sourly.

"Yeah, well, maybe I'm not as in touch with my feelings as you are."

"Like hell. Everyone around here knows you're Mr. Sensitive."

Sean laughed. "Tell that to Deanna."

"Why waste my breath? I've seen the way the woman looks at you. She already knows it."

"Actually, at the moment she thinks I'm an interfering, pushy man, and I'm not too sure which part of that she considers to be the worst crime."

"Then by all means let's get over to Joey's so you can reinforce her opinion," Hank said wryly.

"You think I should stay away, give her some space?"

"If that's what she says she wants, yes," Hank told him.

Sean considered Hank's advice. It wasn't as if he was doing anything more than satisfying his own overprotective instincts by sitting at Joey's watching Dee work.

"Maybe we should eat here at the station tonight," he said, just as a call came in for an ambulance. Though he wasn't involved in the call, he instinctively listened to the dispatcher.

He and Hank recognized the address at the precise same moment. It was Joey's.

Panic swept through Sean, even as he ran for his gear. He frowned at Hank. "You coming or not?"

"It's not our call. Let the paramedics take it."

"Are you crazy?" Sean demanded. "Get the rest of the guys. We're going over there. It could be Deanna. Or Ruby, for that matter."

"More than likely, it's one of the seniors who eat there every night," Hank said reasonably, then shrugged when Sean refused to back down. "I'll get the guys."

"I'm riding with the EMTs. I'll meet you there," Sean told him, shoving his way into the back of the departing ambulance. His scowl kept the paramedics from arguing with him.

The instant they reached the restaurant, he was bolting for the door, scanning the cluster of people gathered over someone stretched out on the floor for some sign of Deanna.

"Please, let her be in the kitchen," he muttered as he raced across the room. But something in his gut told him he wasn't going to find her in the kitchen. When Kevin wiggled through the crowd, his eyes filled with tears, Sean knew even before the boy charged at him.

He scooped Kevin into his arms. "What happened?"

"Mommy fell down," Kevin sobbed, clinging to his neck. "She won't wake up."

Sean held him tightly and rubbed his back as sobs shuddered through him. He would have given anything to put Kevin down and rush to Deanna himself, but he understood that the EMTs knew what they were doing. "It's okay. The paramedics are going to take real good care of her," he promised, saying the words aloud as much for his own benefit as for Kevin's.

When the customers recognized him, they parted, making a path so that Sean could get closer. Ruby caught his eye.

"I think she just fainted," she said, her voice tremulous, her cheeks pale. "We wouldn't have called nine-one-one except she didn't come to right away."

"Can you take Kevin for a second, so I can check on

her?" Sean asked, surprised to hear the husky sound of his voice.

"Of course." She reached for Kevin. "Come here, buddy. Let Sean help your mom."

Sean sucked in a breath when he saw how pale Deanna was. Add to that the bruise already blossoming on her forehead from slamming into the floor face-first and she looked pretty awful. He managed to find a spot next to her that wouldn't interfere with the EMTs and took her hand in his. Hers was icy cold.

"Hey, darlin', wake up," he murmured. "Let me see those pretty brown eyes of yours."

Her eyelids fluttered and a sigh seemed to wash over her.

"Come on, Deanna, you can do it," he coaxed. "Wake up."

She stirred restlessly. "No."

The word was barely a whisper, but it had him grinning. "Why not? You enjoying this Sleeping Beauty routine?"

"Not that," she said, her eyes still clamped shut.

"What then?"

"Don't want to listen to you saying you told me so."

The EMTs regarded him with a grin.

"I think she's back with us," one said. "Or at least she will be if you don't terrorize her into sinking back into oblivion."

"Her vitals are strong," another confirmed.

"You taking her to the hospital?" Sean asked.

Her eyes did snap open at that. "No," she said very firmly. "No hospital. I just fainted, for goodness' sakes."

"A trip to the E.R. wouldn't hurt," Sean said, still holding her hand. "Get you checked out. Have someone take a look at that bump on your head."

Her gaze clung to his. "No hospital, please. I'm fine. See?" She started to sit up, then clutched her head and sank back.

"Whoa, darlin', how about staying real still till your head stops spinning?"

"Where's Kevin?" she asked.

"He's right here. Ruby has him."

"I need to see him. He must be scared."

Sean heard the anxiety in her voice and knew she was worried about more than Kevin's state of mind. She was worried that Sean was going to view this incident as one more example of her not being a good parent. Good parents didn't fall on their faces in front of their kids.

"Kevin's a little worried about you, but he's doing just fine. No harm done," Sean reassured her, hoping that she understood the underlying message. "Hey, Ruby, bring Kevin over here. Somebody's asking for him."

Once again Deanna struggled to sit up, this time making it with Sean's arm to prop her up. When Kevin raced toward her, she enveloped him in a hug that Sean found himself envying.

"Mom, are you okay?"

"I am now," she assured him.

Sean watched the two of them clinging to each other, and for the first time in years, he felt like an outsider again. What had ever made him think that he could fit into their tight little family circle? They had each other and that was all that seemed to matter to either of them.

The loneliness that crept through him now was even worse, somehow, than it had been years ago. He'd gotten used to it then, but lately he'd started to let himself dream. He was an idiot, no question about it.

Satisfied that Deanna was going to be fine, he stood up, took one last look at them, turned on his heel and walked away. Some people just weren't meant to have their dreams come true. It looked as if he was one of them.

9

Deanna was home, tucked beneath the sheets in Ruby's bed with a tray of scrambled eggs, toast, raspberry jam and tea in front of her, by six-thirty. No one had listened to her protests that she was perfectly capable of finishing out her shift. She grinned ruefully. Maybe it had something to do with Joey's liability insurance. He probably wasn't covered for waitresses fainting into people's dinners.

Ruby and Kevin sat beside the bed watching her intently, as if they weren't so sure she wasn't going to pass out again.

"Eat," Ruby finally ordered, when Deanna had yet to pick up her fork.

"I'm not hungry."

"Yeah, right. That's why you fainted, because you were so overstuffed from chowing down all day."

"Very funny," Deanna said, pushing the eggs around on the plate. She lifted the fork to her mouth, then put it down again.

"Nice try, but you have to actually put the food

in your mouth for it to do any good," Ruby commented. She studied Deanna worriedly, then glanced at Kevin. "Kiddo, I knew we forgot something. How about going into the kitchen and getting your mom a glass of juice?"

Deanna started to protest, then caught the forbidding look in Ruby's eyes and clamped her mouth shut.

As soon as Kevin was out of the room, Ruby frowned at her. "Okay, you want to tell me what's going on?"

"Nothing. I'm fine. Really."

"And I'm first lady of the United States," Ruby retorted in a tone heavily laced with sarcasm.

"Okay, it's Sean," Deanna admitted reluctantly. "He just took off. One minute he was there watching me with that worried frown on his face. The next he was gone." She noticed that Ruby didn't even try to deny that there was anything odd about Sean's behavior. Evidently she'd noticed it, too. "Did you see him go? Was he upset?"

"A woman he cares about keeled over while serving spaghetti, what do you think? Of course he was upset," Ruby retorted impatiently. "When he walked into Joey's and spotted you on the floor, I thought he was going to pass out right beside you."

Deanna recalled the gentle, coaxing tone in his voice as he'd tried to draw her back to consciousness. She also recalled something else, the quick glimpse of a totally bleak expression on his face when she was holding Kevin. Then she'd been concentrating on reassuring her son, and by the time she looked Sean's way again, he'd gone.

She was still puzzling over that memory when the doorbell rang.

"Eat your dinner while I get the door," Ruby said. "Unless it's a tall, handsome man, I'm sending whoever it is away." She regarded Deanna with a stern expression and added, "As for you, drink the juice when Kevin brings it."

"Yes, ma'am," Deanna said with a salute that mocked her drill sergeant manner.

After Ruby had gone, she toyed with the now totally unappetizing eggs, then sighed. She couldn't seem to shake the feeling that something just wasn't right about the way Sean had disappeared.

"That's no way to get back on your feet," a disapproving voice chided her.

Deanna's gaze shot to the doorway, where Sean stood regarding her uneasily.

"I'm not hungry."

"Isn't that how you landed in bed in the first place?" He crossed the room, took a look at the plate of cold, congealed eggs and dry toast, and made a face. "Give it to me."

She held tight to the tray. "Why?"

He rolled his eyes. "Do you have to argue about everything?"

"Pretty much. Otherwise, people tend to steamroll right over me."

"This could be one instance when you should let them," he said, gently disengaging her fingers and taking the tray. "I'll be right back."

She stared after him, more confused than ever. He didn't seem angry or even upset, just a little sad.

It was twenty minutes before he returned, carrying the same tray with a plate of steaming French toast with a dusting of sugar and cinnamon. He set the tray across her knees, then stood scowling down at her.

"Now, there are two ways we can do this," he said. "You can eat that like the intelligent woman we both know you are."

Deanna had to fight to hide a smile. "Or?"

He grinned, looking surprisingly eager for her to test him. "Or I feed it to you."

"I'd like to see you try," she muttered, but she picked up the fork and began to eat. After a couple of bites she stared at him in surprise. "This is really good. You made it?"

"With my own two hands," he acknowledged. "When you live on your own, you learn a thing or two about cooking or you live on frozen dinners. And at the station, we all have to take a turn at kitchen duty. Believe me, none of us are slackers. Hungry men take no prisoners."

She grinned at the image. "What else can you cook?"

"Give me a cookbook, and I'll try anything."

"You're going to make some lucky woman a wonderful husband." She'd expected the teasing remark to draw a smile, but instead, that bleak expression darkened his eyes again before he turned away to stare out the window.

"Sean?"

"Yeah?" He turned back slowly.

"Thanks for coming to Joey's tonight. I know it wasn't your call."

"No big deal."

"It was a big deal to me," she insisted. "I heard you."

He turned to face her. "What?"

"When I was still pretty much out of it, I heard your voice. I think it pulled me back to reality."

He shrugged, looking uncomfortable. "You said something like that at the time." A smile tugged at his lips. "You said that was why you wouldn't open your eyes, 'cause you didn't want to have to face me when I said I told you so."

She vaguely remembered saying that. "But you didn't say it, did you?"

"Nope. I figured you'd gotten the message anyway."

"Why did you take off without saying anything?"

"You were in good hands. You didn't need me around anymore."

Deanna heard the casually spoken words, but she was also almost certain that she heard something more, something that sounded an awful lot like pain.

"Sean?"

"Look, I've got to get out of here," he said abruptly. "I shouldn't have left the station, but I wanted to check on you." He bent down and brushed a quick kiss across her forehead. "Finish every bite of that food. If you don't, I'll hear about it."

"You've got Ruby tattling on me again?"

He grinned. "Ruby *and* Kevin. You're not going to get anything past me."

There was something oddly comforting about that, Deanna thought as she finished her meal and slowly drifted off to sleep. Not that she'd ever tell him that.

Something had changed between them, Sean concluded on his way back to the station. He couldn't quite put his finger on it, but he'd left Ruby's with the sense that he and Deanna had a new understanding. He wasn't sure yet whether that was a good thing. He wasn't crazy about the distinct possibility that she was starting to see through his defenses.

Nor was he nuts about this need he had to check up on her, to reassure himself that she was all right. Hadn't he learned anything from that moment at Joey's when he'd been an outsider looking onto the tight-knit world of Deanna and Kevin? Apparently not, because just a couple of hours later, he hadn't been able to stop himself from going back for more.

As it had turned out, he'd been right to go. Deanna evidently hadn't learned a thing from that fainting episode. She hadn't touched the food that Ruby had fixed for her. The woman needed a keeper.

Was he prepared to be that? An image of Kevin flashed through his head. If ever a boy needed a dad, it was Kevin. But he deserved one who was going to be around for the long haul. Sean wasn't convinced that he was that guy. Maybe if it were just Deanna and him, he could take that leap of faith his brother had talked about when he'd married Maggie, but not with a kid involved, a kid who didn't deserve to be let down if things didn't work out.

Sean sighed heavily. Things were getting too damned complicated. He was almost relieved when a call came in not ten minutes after he got back to the station. He dragged on his gear and headed out, eager for the distraction, eager to be doing something he knew he was good at.

Of course, a fire could be just as unpredictable as a woman, no question about that. What should have been a quick run turned into an all-nighter with two more companies involved. A fire that had started on a kitchen stove spread to nearby curtains before the old lady living there realized anything was amiss. She'd run screaming from the apartment rather than calling 911, which gave the fire a few extra minutes to blaze out of control in the old wooden structure.

"What the hell happened?" Hank muttered when they arrived to find flames shooting from several windows on the third floor. "I thought somebody's dinner caught on fire."

Sean latched on to one of the residents. "Is everybody out of the building?"

The man was clearly shaken. "I'm not sure. I just moved in last week. Second floor."

"How many apartments are there altogether?" Sean asked.

"Six, two on each floor."

"Okay, your apartment's accounted for."

"And Mrs. McGinty, it started in her place," he said. "She's right over there. And that's her third-floor neighbor with her."

"That leaves us with three more apartments we don't know about," Sean said, looking at Hank. "One on the second floor, two on the first."

He saw their lieutenant trying to get similar information from the weeping old lady and her neighbor. "What do we have, Jack?" he hollered as he hauled hoses toward the front of the building where the flames were beginning to shoot through the roof.

"Everyone's accounted for except an old man who lived on the second floor. He's hard of hearing. Neighbors tried beating on the door on their way down, but they couldn't wait. It was too hot."

"I'm on it," Sean said at once.

"You can't go in there," Jack protested. "The third floor's engulfed. It could cave in any second. You'd be trapped."

"I'm not leaving the man in there to die," Sean said, not waiting for permission before scrambling over equipment to head inside.

The heat came at him in waves, accompanied by thick smoke that blurred his vision and made him choke.

"Dammit, Sean, are you crazy?" Hank said, on his heels.

"It's one flight of steps. I can make it," he insisted, dropping down to feel his way up the stairs. "You go back."

"No way. I'm not living with guilt for the rest of my life if something happens to you while I'm standing around in the fresh air twiddling my thumbs. Now, stop arguing and move. Let's get in and out while we still can."

When Sean reached the second-floor landing, the smoke was so thick he couldn't see his hand in front of his face. He heard the crackling of flames just over head and the sizzle of the water trying to douse them.

"Come on, guys. Five minutes. Ten, tops. That's all I need," he muttered to himself. Thank God there were only two apartments. The door to the one on the right was ajar. More than likely that was the one the man outside had fled. That meant the old man was probably trapped in the apartment on the left.

He crawled across the landing, reached up and twisted the doorknob. The metal was hot to the touch, but not unbearable. No flames inside the apartment, not yet, anyway. Unfortunately, though, the door was locked.

Sean muttered a curse. "Hank, we're going to have to knock it down."

"Stand back. I'll do it. You be ready to go inside. On the count of three. Ready?"

"Ready." Sean stood up as Hank counted rapidly, then slammed his foot into the door just below the lock. It shattered on its hinges and he was inside, shouting, feeling his way through the thick smoke, coughing despite the gear meant to protect them from smoke inhalation.

He found the old man in the bedroom, next to the window. He'd passed out before he could get it open to call for help. Sean scooped him up and was about to turn around and head back the way he'd come, when wood splintered overhead and flaming beams crashed down around him, blocking his intended route of escape.

"Hank?" he shouted.

"I'm okay, but we're not going out the easy way. Open the window. I'm right behind you."

Despite the confidence of Hank's words, Sean knew his partner better than anyone on earth. He heard the faint hitch in his voice that no one else would have been able to discern.

"Dammit, Hank, what's wrong? Now's no time to lie to me!"

"Just get out of here," Hank shouted back.

He wasn't nearly as close as Sean would have liked. He put the old man down long enough to get the window open. In seconds there was a ladder against the side of the building, and he was able to hand the victim to one of the other firefighters. Still there was no sign of Hank.

Sean looked back through the flames, wincing at the sting of smoke that blurred his vision. Hank was on the far side of the burning beam, on the floor, not moving. Sean had to fight against the wave of panic that crawled up his spine. He was not leaving Hank in here to die, and that was that.

He met the gaze of the firefighter at the top of the ladder. "I'm going back for Hank."

"Dammit, Devaney, there's no time."

"I want you out of there now," the lieutenant shouted up at him.

"No way in hell am I leaving Hank in here." He glanced at the firefighter at the top of the ladder. "Move it. Buy me some time. Two minutes. That's all I need."

The man seemed about to argue, but then he was moving, shouting at the firefighters down below. Water began to splatter down through the destroyed roof. Flames sizzled and sputtered, but didn't die. The smoke grew even thicker and more acrid, the way a doused campfire did just before it died out.

Sean dodged another falling beam engulfed with flames to reach Hank's side. He didn't waste time on questions about his friend's injuries. Hell, he wasn't even sure if Hank was conscious. Sean just picked Hank up as if he weighed nothing and pushed his way back toward the window, oblivious to the heat, just totally focused on getting his partner to safety.

He handed Hank's limp body through the window to another waiting firefighter, then crawled out behind them. On the top rung, he ripped off his gear and sucked in a lungful of fresh air, coughed, then gasped for more.

Not until he was on solid ground again did the rush of adrenaline fade. He barely made it to where the paramedics were working on Hank before collapsing.

"He going to be okay?" Sean demanded, his voice hoarse.

"Looks as if he might have broken an ankle," Cal Watkins replied. "Smoke inhalation, too, but he'll make it." He looked over at Sean. "What about you?"

"I'm fine," Sean insisted.

Cal frowned at him. "Yeah, you sound fine, like you've been smoking for about a hundred years and have no lung capacity left." He slapped an oxygen mask over Sean's face, then peered at him more intently. "A couple of minor burns on that handsome face, too. Don't worry, though, they'll just give you a little character. You can hitch a ride to the hospital in the same ambulance with Hank."

Sean hadn't even felt the burns. Now, though, with the adrenaline wearing off and relief coursing through him that Hank was going to be okay, he was beginning to feel the pain. It wasn't the knock-you-on-your-butt pain some of the other guys had described after burn injuries, but it was bad enough to keep him from arguing about the ride to the hospital. Besides, one glance at his lieutenant's fierce expression told him he'd be better off in the emergency room than facing the storm that was brewing over his decision to go into that burning structure not just once, but twice, in direct defiance of orders.

Thanks to plenty of repeat visits to various fallen firefighters, Sean had a passing acquaintance with most of the burn specialists at the hospital. It was the first time, though, that he'd been on the receiving end of their attention. They were like a bunch of mother hens. He kept explaining that he could go home, but before he knew it he was upstairs in a room with a grumbling Hank in the bed next to his and a male nurse who looked like a linebacker for the New England Patriots stationed at the door.

He tried the phone, but calls were blocked. He turned to the nurse. "I don't suppose you could get this phone turned on, could you?" he asked. He really needed to call Ryan in case word leaked out about his injuries. He debated a call to Deanna, but decided it could wait until after daybreak. She needed her sleep.

"I'll have a phone hooked up in here in the morning," the nurse said.

Sean tried his best smile. "It's almost morning now. What difference will a couple of hours make?"

"The orders are on your chart. No calls. No visitors till morning. You both need some rest."

"What about the old man we pulled out of that building? How's he doing?"

The nurse shrugged. "Haven't heard."

"Couldn't you find out?" he coaxed. "After all, we risked our lives to save him. I'd sleep better knowing he's going to be okay."

The man scowled, but finally relented. "I'll check. You stay put."

As soon as he was gone, Sean slid out of bed, cursing the indignity of the hospital gown that was flapping around him. He made it as far as the door, opened it and peeked out, when a familiar scent caught his attention. He looked up straight into Deanna's worried face. Ruby was right on her heels.

"Going somewhere?" Deanna inquired lightly.

"Looking for a phone that works," he admitted, surprised by how glad he was to see her.

"Not to call me, though, right? It wouldn't occur to you that Ruby and I might hear about the fire and panic."

He frowned at her tone. She was clearly angry. "It's not morning yet. The local news isn't on, and I doubt this fire was big enough to make CNN."

"Actually, your boss called because Hank asked him to," Ruby said. "He also tried to let Ryan know you were here."

Sean didn't even try to hide his shock. "The lieutenant called you and my brother?"

"That's the one," Deanna said. "Nice man. Seems to understand the importance of keeping friends and family informed."

"Of course, the staff has kept us cooling our heels

out here in the hall," Ruby complained. "But now that you've tried to make a break for it, I figure we can come inside and prevent any more attempted escapes. Out of my way, handsome. I need to see for myself that Hank's in one piece."

She pushed past Sean and left him standing there to face a still-indignant Deanna.

"I would have let you know what happened," he swore. "You weren't in great shape yourself last night. I didn't want to worry you."

"Nice try, but I'm not buying it. Who were you about to call? And don't try to pretend it was me."

"Ryan, actually."

She nodded. "Good choice. Give me the number. I'll try him again. I'll tell him to come by in a couple of hours after you've had some sleep."

For a woman who'd collapsed herself not twelve hours earlier, she sounded amazingly strong. And she didn't seem inclined to take no for an answer. Sean didn't know quite what to make of this new, take-charge woman who was facing him down. This woman didn't look as if she needed anyone to rescue her. She looked more like an avenging angel herself.

"Where's Kevin?" he asked.

"Asleep in the waiting room right over there."

"Take him home. As you can see for yourself, I'm fine."

She reached up as if to touch his face, then pulled back, her eyes filling with unexpected tears. "Yeah, I can see that."

"Surface burns," he said, clasping her hand and

pressing a kiss to her knuckles. "They'll heal before you know it."

"It could have been worse," she said with a shudder.

"But it wasn't."

"I heard the whole story. The lieutenant's mad as hell, but he said you saved two lives tonight—Hank's and the old man's."

Sean sighed with relief. "He's going to make it, then. I just sent the nurse out to check."

"Yeah, sure. You sent the nurse out so you could make a break for it."

He grinned. "That, too."

"I thought you said Hank was the danger junkie," Deanna said, her frown back in place. "But the lieutenant says you're the one who took all the chances tonight."

"Calculated risks," Sean insisted. "There's a difference." To his chagrin, the night's events finally caught up with him and his knees almost gave way. He reached for the doorjamb, but Deanna was right there, putting his arm around her shoulder and leading him back into the room, muttering a stream of surprisingly colorful curses all the way. He grinned.

"I hope you don't use that language around Kevin," he said.

"Of course not." She scowled at him. "He never deserves it."

"And I do?"

She settled him onto his bed and pulled up the sheet as if she were tucking in her son. This time when she reached out to Sean, she did touch him, smoothing his hair gently back from his forehead.

"Yes," she said softly. "I think you do."

Sean sighed, relaxing at last. He let his eyes drift shut.

"Not supposed to be this way," he murmured. "Supposed to be looking out for you."

"Oh, Sean, don't you realize you have people who care about you now?" Deanna whispered. "People who would be devastated if anything happened to you?"

Her fierce words drifted into his subconscious and he finally fell asleep, a smile on his lips.

10

Despite assurances that Sean was going to be fine and that he'd probably be released from the hospital by midday, Deanna refused to budge from his bedside. Ruby was just as adamant about staying beside Hank. Deanna left the room only long enough to get her son. Kevin crept in from the waiting room, studied Sean intently as if to satisfy himself that his hero was okay, then fell back to sleep in a chair in the corner.

Deanna had never in her life been as terrified as she had been the night before when the lieutenant had called to inform Ruby about the fire. Nor had she ever seen Ruby as shaken. Despite the lieutenant's reassurances that both men were going to make it, neither Ruby or Deanna had hesitated before dragging on clothes and heading for the hospital to see the men for themselves.

"I've never felt this wiped out in my life," Ruby mumbled from across the room.

"It's been a long night. We should probably go home, shower and go to work," Deanna said half-heartedly.

Ruby looked at her as if she were crazy. "I'm not going anywhere. Give me some change. I'll call the office and explain things to Charlotte the snake."

Deanna managed a weak grin at the venomous but fitting nickname. "You really need to stop calling her that. One of these days you're going to say it in front of her."

"Well, she is a snake," Ruby retorted. "Just look what she did to you, making you take the rap for that report that didn't get mailed to the other law firm. I guarantee she'll never own up to that to Hodges."

"She's been better since then," Deanna said. "Haven't you noticed? She actually says good morning when she comes in, and adds please and thank you to her commands."

"Only because she's terrified you're going to rat her out to Hodges," Ruby insisted.

"Hey, ladies, could you keep it down? My head's killing me," Hank muttered hoarsely.

Ruby was on her feet in an instant, the expression on her face a dead giveaway. Deanna wondered if Hank could see it. Was he smart enough to see all the love Ruby would willingly shower on him, if only he was ready for it?

"Hey, beautiful."

Sean's voice drew Deanna's attention away from the other couple. She smiled at him. "Now I know your injuries were more severe than they're saying, if you think I'm beautiful."

"You are beautiful." He started to sit up, then winced and fell back down. "Have you been here all night?"

"Yes."

"Kevin?"

She gestured toward the corner. "Sound asleep."

"Go home."

"Trying to get rid of me after I've invested all this time and energy worrying about you?" she teased.

"You fainted last night. You need to be in bed, too." A devilish grin crept over his face. He patted the bed beside him. "Of course, there's plenty of room here."

Deanna laughed. "I don't think so. By the way, after you fell asleep I tried to reach your brother. There was no answer at the apartment, so I left a message on the answering machine at the pub. Somebody named Rory called here a little while ago and spoke to the nurse. He says Ryan and Maggie went away for a couple of days, but they'll be back this afternoon and he'll let them know what happened."

"Thanks." He glanced across the room toward Hank. "Hey, buddy, how are you feeling?"

Hank's pithy response had them all grinning.

"Watch your language," Sean said, sobering. "Kevin's here."

Hank winced. "Sorry." He fell silent, his expression unreadable. "Hey, buddy, I owe you."

"You don't owe me anything," Sean said. "You'd have done the same for me."

"Doesn't change the fact that you risked your life to come back after me."

"I'm the one responsible for you being in that building in the first place. If I hadn't been so damned stubborn, you'd never have been in danger."

Deanna heard the unmistakable regret in Sean's

voice and knew that he'd have been tormented for the rest of his life if he hadn't gotten Hank out alive. She reached for his hand and squeezed.

"Just be grateful you're both here to tell the tale," she said. "You can't go back and change the past."

Sean studied her intently. "Something you might want to remember, as well," he said lightly.

Before she could reply, Kevin yawned widely, blinked and stared around the room until his gaze fell on Sean.

"Hey, Sean," he said sleepily.

"Hey, kiddo."

Wearing socks but no sneakers, Kevin padded over to the side of the bed, his gaze immediately drawn to Sean's injured face. "Does that hurt?"

"Not too much."

Kevin nodded, his expression thoughtful. "Still, I'm thinking maybe I don't want to be a firefighter after all. You can get hurt real bad."

"Knocked off your pedestal already," Hank teased Sean.

Deanna saw a flicker of sorrow in Sean's eyes, but he managed a grin. "You've got a lot of years before you have to decide what you want to be," she told her son.

"Maybe it would be cool to be a doctor," Kevin said.

Ruby grinned at him. "Then you'd have to give shots," she teased.

Hank moaned. "Don't go talking about shots, okay?"

Kevin's eyes blinked wide at the evident hint of

panic in Hank's voice. Ruby and Deanna both stared at him, as Sean began to chuckle.

"Don't tell me you're scared of shots," Ruby said to Hank, apparently delighted by the evidence that the courageous firefighter had a very human weakness.

"What if I am?" he retorted defensively. "A healthy respect for needles seems like a perfectly normal reaction to me."

The same nurse who'd been on guard duty during the night appeared just then and overheard Hank's remark. "Uh-oh, don't tell me I'm going to need restraints for this."

Hank frowned at him. "Who the hell are you?"

"Our warden," Sean said grimly. "I remember him from when we first came in. And judging from that tray he's carrying, he's armed."

Ruby leaned down until her face was scant inches from Hank's. "Concentrate on me. I promise you won't feel a thing," she said, then glanced up to wink at the nurse.

Hank opened his mouth to protest, but Ruby swooped in and kissed him just as the nurse administered the shot. Deanna glanced at Sean and saw the speculative gleam in his eyes as the nurse headed his way.

"Forget it," she told him.

"What?"

"You're a big boy. Take your shot like a man."

Kevin frowned at her. "But, Mom, can't you at least kiss it and make it better?"

"Yeah, Deanna, that's not too much to ask, is it?"

Sean coaxed. He bravely held out his arm for the shot, but kept his gaze locked with Deanna's.

"Oh, for heaven's sake," she muttered, after the nurse had finished. She bent down to press a kiss to Sean's arm. She doubted he'd felt a thing. "Better?"

She stared into eyes twinkling with pure mischief.

"Not yet, but I think I'm getting there." He tapped his lips. "How about another one right here?"

She planted her hands on her hips and frowned at him. "Did something happen to your mouth?"

"It hurts real bad," he assured her.

"Liar," she accused, but she was laughing. And oh, so tempted.

"Really, really bad."

Knowing that the room was filled with avid spectators, she had two choices. She could ignore the teasing, plaintive note in his voice and walk right out of the room and wind up labeled as a coward. Or she could kiss him and let the man jumble her senses one more time. It was a no-brainer.

Deanna stepped closer, locked her gaze with his and bent down, stopping just as his lips parted and his breath caught. Let him wonder, she thought. Let him feel that edgy sense of anticipation that he triggered in her.

But before he could wonder or feel much of anything, his hand circled the back of her neck and drew her down until their lips met. The teasing kiss she'd intended got lost in yet another swirl of wild sensations and drugging heat.

Apparently, though, Sean was as aware as she of their audience, because he released her mere seconds after claiming her mouth. As she braced herself on the side of the bed and tried to regain her composure, he winked at her.

"I'm feeling better already," he announced cheerfully. "How about you?"

She leaned close and whispered for his ears only, "I'm feeling an almost overwhelming need to make you pay for that."

His laugh echoed in the room. "I can hardly wait."

Sean was going stir-crazy. The doctors had refused to release Hank, so even though they'd released Sean around noon, he was sticking close to make sure his partner didn't do anything foolish. He'd finally convinced Ruby, Deanna and Kevin to go home for some sleep, so there was no one to talk to except a man who growled the few responses he deigned to make. Obviously, as far as Hank was concerned, Sean was a traitor for not helping him to make a break for it.

The day nurse was a pretty young woman named Susie, a vast improvement over the scowling, muscular night nurse. In the past Sean would have wandered down to the nurses' station and flirted with her to kill some time, but images of Deanna kept him in the chair beside Hank's bed.

He was about to go down to the gift shop in search of some magazines, maybe even a decent book, when the door opened and Lieutenant Beatty walked in.

"Good. You're still here," he said to Sean, then nodded toward the sleeping Hank. "How is he?"

"Cranky but on the mend," Sean said.

"I heard that," Hank retorted, cracking one eye open. "Hey, Lieutenant, how's it going?"

Their boss dragged over a chair, then looked from one to the other with a grim expression. "Here's the thing," he began in a tone that sent a chill up Sean's spine. "There's a school of thought that the two of you deserve medals for bravery for going into that building and getting that old man out safely. If it were up to the mayor, there'd be a damned ticker tape parade."

Sean knew it wasn't up to the mayor. It was up to the fire chief and this man, and the lieutenant definitely did not look as if he wanted to hand out any medals.

"What's the other option?"

"Suspension for defying not one but two direct orders."

Sean winced. "I think I see where this is going, but I've got to tell you, if I had it to do over again, there's nothing I would have done any differently."

"Same here," Hank said loyally.

The lieutenant's scowl deepened. "Couldn't you show even the tiniest hint of remorse? Give me something to work with, guys. You're two of the best men I've got. I don't want to put you out on unpaid leave."

Sean's gaze narrowed. "You don't?"

"Not if I can help it, but chain of command and discipline are essential. I can't have rogue firefighters making decisions that put their lives or the lives of others at risk. If you two had gotten yourselves killed in that fire, the buck would have stopped with me. I was the highest-ranking officer on the scene."

Sean knew he was right. Jack Beatty was a career firefighter who'd risen through the ranks, a man who took his responsibilities seriously. He'd made a tough call under extreme pressure. That Sean's instincts had been right was almost beside the point. He could just as easily have been wrong, and three people could have died inside that burning building.

"I couldn't let that old man die in there, not when there was a chance I could save him," Sean said, then held up his hand when the lieutenant seemed about to argue. "However, I see your point. It wasn't my call to make."

"And next time you'll listen to the officer in charge," the lieutenant coaxed.

"And next time I'll try to listen to the officer in charge, before doing something on my own," Sean said.

Jack uttered a resigned sigh. "Close enough. I'll speak to the mayor. You can have your medals, but he can forget the parade."

"Was he really talking about a parade?" Hank asked.

Sean frowned at him. "Be grateful we're not sitting on our butts doing nothing for a month."

Hank glanced pointedly at the cast on his ankle. "I'm pretty certain I'm going to be sitting on mine, even though Jack, here, has let us off the hook."

"Yes, but you'll still have a paycheck," Sean pointed out. "If you're smart, you'll talk Ruby into going to some romantic seaside cottage while you recuperate."

"You've got plenty of vacation time coming," the lieutenant pointed out to Sean. "You could take a break, too. I know how you hate working with anyone besides Hank, because the other men actually listen to what I tell them to do."

Sean tried to imagine a week on Cape Cod with Deanna and Kevin. The idea held tremendous appeal, but he doubted he could get her to go for it…unless Hank and Ruby went, as well. Maybe they could convince the women this was a real mission of mercy.

"I'll think about it," he told the lieutenant. "And thanks for letting us off the hook this time."

"Self-preservation," Jack said. "Can you imagine the outcry if two men who'd saved an old man's life ended up suspended?" He patted Hank's shoulder, then shook Sean's hand. "You two try to stay out of trouble, okay?"

"We always do," Hank said solemnly.

The lieutenant shook his head. "If only that were true."

After he'd gone, Sean felt Hank's gaze studying him. "What?"

"You've got something going on in that head of yours. Care to tell me about it?"

"I was thinking about Cape Cod," he admitted. "The five of us out there for a week. I could call a couple of people, see if there's a house available. What do you think?"

Hank's expression grew thoughtful. "I suppose Ruby might go for it, if you guys came along."

"I was thinking the same about Deanna. She'll only say yes if you and Ruby agree and we play the pity card, tell 'em we need to recuperate from our ordeal."

"It won't exactly be a romantic getaway with all

of us under one roof," Hank said. "But that's a good thing, right? Keeps things from getting too serious."

"Right," Sean agreed, warming to the idea. "I'm thinking a big house, lots of bedrooms."

Hank grinned. "And if some of them don't happen to get used, well, that's just too bad."

"Hey, watch it," Sean chided. "There will be a kid present."

"I'm injured," Hank said pitifully. "Let me dream."

Sean laughed. "Okay, you dream. I'm going to make some calls. Then we can talk to Ruby and Deanna. You should probably go first. If you can sell Ruby on the idea, she'll help with Deanna."

"Use the kid," Hank recommended. "You talk Kevin into a week at the beach, his mother will never say no."

"That would be sneaky and underhanded," Sean retorted, then sighed. "I'll only use it if I have to."

This trip was going to be perfect. He was going to get a little quality time with Deanna, Kevin was going to get a real vacation at the beach, and Deanna was going to get some much needed R and R. And all of it in the guise of keeping poor, injured Hank company. How noble and selfless was that?

Deanna listened to Sean's entire pitch with a perfectly straight face. It sounded good, noble even. A week on Cape Cod keeping Hank from going completely bonkers while his broken ankle began to heal. Ruby had even bought into the scheme.

"But I'll only go if you will," she'd told Deanna not ten seconds ago.

Now Ruby and Sean sat side by side awaiting Deanna's decision.

"And this is all about Hank?" Deanna asked, her gaze on Sean's face.

"Absolutely," he said. "Taking time off is hard on him, especially when he can't get around all that well. Hank's an active guy. Forced immobility will make him impossible to live with."

She grinned. "So you want us around to be a distraction for an incredibly cranky man? Sounds like fun."

"Oh, I think I can guarantee his mood will improve with you ladies underfoot, Ruby especially."

"Charlotte will have a cow if the two of us ask for vacation at the same time," Deanna said to Ruby. "You know she counts on you to fill in for me if I so much as go to the ladies' room."

"She can hire a temp," Ruby countered. "The firm can afford it. Hodges has won two huge settlements in the past week."

"Not to change the subject, but speaking of settlements," Sean said to Deanna, "what's he done for you lately? Has he managed to get you a dime from that irresponsible landlord of yours?"

Deanna thought back to the conversation she'd had with her boss just two days ago. She'd kept the news to herself, because she could hardly believe it was going to happen. "He settled," she confessed. "The check's supposedly in the mail."

Ruby whooped and ran over to give her a hug. "Way to go, Dee! How much?"

"Not a fortune," she said, trying to caution Ruby

against getting too excited. "But five thousand dollars will go a long way toward getting Kevin and me a place of our own and a little bit of furniture."

"Is Hodges taking a cut?" Sean asked suspiciously.

She shook her head. "Not a dime. I offered, but he said I deserved a lot more, so he wasn't taking any of it."

"Well, well, well, a lawyer with a conscience. I'm impressed," Sean said.

"Don't be," Ruby said wryly. "All he did was make a couple of threatening phone calls to the guy. He didn't even waste any corporate stationery."

"Well, whatever he did, it worked and I'm grateful," Deanna said. She looked at Sean. "So your timing couldn't be better, actually. I was thinking that Kevin deserved a vacation before summer's completely over, and that I'd use a little of this money to pay for a couple of days at the beach."

Sean's expression brightened. "You're saying yes?"

"Yes," she said, unwilling to think about the prospect of spending several lazy nights in Sean's company on a romantic, moonlit beach. "But we're chipping in for part of the expenses."

"Absolutely not," Sean said, his jaw set stubbornly.

"Absolutely yes," Deanna said just as firmly.

"Can we dicker over the finances later?" Ruby begged. "I want to go tell Hank."

"Go," Sean and Deanna said in unison.

Sean chuckled. "I think we can finish this discussion without bloodshed."

Deanna frowned at him. "Don't count on it."

Ruby shook her head. "Can you two play nice, or do I need to send Kevin in here to referee?"

"We're two civilized adults. We'll be fine," Sean reassured her.

"One of us is civilized. The other one is stubborn as a mule," Deanna countered.

When Ruby had gone, Sean met Deanna's gaze. "I'm glad you said yes."

Her heart flipped over in her chest at the heat that rose in his eyes. "Sean, we're not going to be alone out there."

"I know that, but I imagine we can steal a few minutes to ourselves from time to time."

"To do what?"

He drew her to her feet and into his arms. "This," he murmured, kissing her until her toes curled.

"And no more," she said in a shaky voice.

"And no more," he agreed solemnly, then grinned. "At least not the first night."

Anticipation shot through her, tempered only by a stern reminder that this was going to be essentially a family vacation with lots of people under that same roof. Sean would never pressure her into turning it into something else, not with Kevin just down the hall.

But he might tempt her, she thought, glancing into his eyes. They were sparkling with pure mischief. Oh, yes, he was definitely going to tempt her. And she was going to have to draw on an already overtaxed reserve of willpower to resist. Heaven help her! It was going to be a really, really long and dangerous week.

11

The house in Truro was covered in soft-gray shingles that had been weathered by countless storms. The shutters were white, and window boxes full of bright flowers hung on the railing around the porch. The house was within sight of the beach dunes, and, with the windows open, a salty breeze wafted through the bright, cheerful rooms. Deanna had never seen such a lovely place. It reminded her of a house her parents had rented years ago at the Jersey shore, but this one was smaller, cozier.

"Hey, what was that look about?" Sean asked, regarding her with concern. "You looked so sad all of a sudden."

She forced a smile. "Just thinking about a time long ago and far away."

"Did it involve Kevin's father?" he asked.

She heard the tension in his voice and quickly reassured him. "Absolutely not. Frankie and I never went on a vacation."

"Your parents, then?"

She sighed at the accurate guess. "Yes."

"You don't say much about them. Are they dead?"

"To me," she said softly, unable to stop the tears that welled up in her eyes. She'd told herself a thousand times that what had happened years ago didn't matter, but there was an ache in her heart that never seemed to go away.

Sean frowned. "What does that mean?"

"They didn't approve of me marrying Frankie. We haven't spoken since," she said, giving him the short, unemotional version that omitted all of the rage and accusations that had left her feeling raw and anguished on the day she had walked out of their house for the last time. The fact that their concerns had been well-grounded was something she still hated to admit.

Sean regarded her with surprise. "You never told them he'd left you?"

She shook her head. "At first I kept silent because I didn't think I could bear to hear them gloat over having been right about him. Then it became a matter of pride. I didn't want to go to them when I needed help."

"Do they know about Kevin?"

"No."

She saw the war of emotions on Sean's face. "You realize who's hurt most by that, don't you?"

She refused to acknowledge that her son could be hurt by the absence of two people he'd never even known.

"Deanna, you need to contact them," Sean said. "Give them another chance."

She leveled a look straight into his eyes. "The same way you've given *your* parents a second chance?"

Sean winced at the comparison and his jaw set. "It's not the same thing," he insisted. "I don't even know where my parents are."

"One of these days you will. Ryan's determined to find the whole family, isn't he? What will you do then?"

"We're not discussing my family," he said tightly, "we're talking about yours. Kevin ought to have a chance to know his grandparents and vice versa."

"You're setting a double standard, and you know it," she accused, hurt that he, of all people, didn't understand why she might never want to see her parents again. They'd made the decision to turn their backs on her. She'd asked nothing from them but their love, and they'd withheld it. How was that any better than what his parents had done?

Hurling the one comment guaranteed to infuriate him, she said, "Besides, this is none of your business."

With that she whirled around, shouted for Kevin and headed for the beach at a brisk pace. She wasn't surprised when Sean didn't bother to follow. After all, she'd just slammed a door very firmly right in his face.

Sean had had no idea that he and Deanna had so much in common. Granted the break with her parents had come when she'd been an adult, and she'd made her own choice about it, choosing Frankie Blackwell over her family, but the fact was, they were both facing a future without the people who had given them life. If he wasn't anxious to change that in his own situation, why was he so insistent that Deanna should be?

Was it because he wanted for her—for Kevin—what he wasn't willing to fight for for himself?

He heard the thump of Hank's cane hitting the porch, but he refused to turn around. He wasn't sure how much his friend had overheard, but knowing Hank, it had been enough to ensure that he'd have an opinion to offer. Probably one Sean had no desire to hear.

"It's going to be a long week, if you don't go after her and apologize," Hank said, coming up to lean on the railing next to him.

"Why should I be the one apologizing?" Sean grumbled, even though he knew the answer as well as Hank did.

Hank grinned. "Maybe because she's right. You set impossibly high standards for everyone else when it comes to family, but you don't exactly apply the same rules to yourself. How many times have you even seen Ryan since you were best man at his wedding?"

"We're both busy," Sean said defensively.

"The man owns a pub," Hank retorted. "You know where to find him any night of the week."

Sean had no argument for that. "Deanna just took me by surprise. I had no idea that she was on the outs with her family. I assumed she didn't have any, since she'd never mentioned them."

"You don't mention yours, but they're out there," Hank reminded him.

Sean scowled at him. "You are so damned annoying when you find a chink in my armor."

Hank grinned. "We live to serve. Go after her. I don't think I can stand an entire week of you two dancing around each other. Besides, it'll ruin the romantic vibes."

Sean glanced pointedly toward the door. "Speaking of romantic vibes, where is Ruby?"

"Hiding in her room," Hank said. "Upstairs. She refused to take the one next door to mine on the first floor. She left it for you."

"Sorry."

"Me, too. The thought of looking up into your ugly mug if I call out in the middle of the night is not exactly the scenario I envisioned when we came out here." His expression brightened. "But I'm confident I can get her to change her mind eventually. I'm impossible to resist when I really put my mind to it."

Sean studied him curiously. "Is this just about sex? Is that all you were hoping for this week?"

Hank shrugged, looking more at a loss than Sean had ever seen him. "Hell if I know. That woman has more excuses for keeping me at arm's length than any female I ever met."

Sean chuckled at the confirmation that Ruby wasn't sleeping with Hank. "She still has your undivided attention, though, doesn't she? In my book, that makes her the smartest woman you've ever dated."

Hank didn't seem impressed by his analysis.

"What about you and Deanna? Anything going on?"

Sean wasn't particularly happy at having the tables turned on him. "No," he said succinctly. "Mutual decision."

"Yeah, right," Hank said skeptically. "If it's mutual, it's only because you're scared. Are you finally in over your head?"

Sean thought about the feelings that welled up in him every time Deanna walked into a room. Some were familiar—attraction, heat, lust. And some were emotions that usually sent him racing in the opposite direction—vulnerability, protectiveness, a longing for the kind of future he'd never allowed himself to imagine before.

"Getting there," Sean admitted aloud for the first time. He sighed heavily. "Guess I'd better go find her and apologize."

"If you want to do it right, you can always send Kevin back up here. Ruby will be glad of the chaperon."

Sean laughed. "Poor kid. He has no idea the heavy burden he's carrying on his shoulders this week."

"Probably best to keep it that way," Hank said. "Or you'll have something else you'll need to apologize to Deanna for."

"I think there's enough crow on my plate for now," Sean said, then headed off to get his first taste of it.

He found Deanna walking along the beach, shoulders slumped, hands tucked in the pockets of her light windbreaker. Kevin was running head of her, ducking in and out of waves as they splashed against the shore. The look on his face was one of pure joy. Whatever else came out of this week, Sean was glad he'd been a part of giving the boy this happy memory. As a kid, he'd always managed to get sick on the day everyone in school was supposed to talk about their summer vacation. He'd hated that he never had anything to talk about while everyone else shared stories about their weeks at camp or trips to the beach, to ball games or amusement parks.

Kevin looked up, spotted Sean and gave a shout, then began racing toward him. Sean saw Deanna's shoulders stiffen perceptibly, but she stopped and turned to wait for Sean. Even if she wasn't quite literally coming back to meet him halfway, it was something. He had to give her credit for not backing down from the encounter.

"I'm sorry," Sean mouthed silently as he scooped Kevin high in the air and perched the boy on his shoulders.

Deanna's serious expression didn't acknowledge the apology, but some of the tension seemed to drain out of her.

"How's the water?" he asked.

"Cold," she said, just as Kevin shouted, "It's great! Can we go swimming?"

Sean looked to Deanna.

"I'm not going in there," she said with a shiver.

Sean laughed. "Then I guess it's just you and me, buddy. You wearing your suit?"

"No," Kevin said, clearly disappointed.

"Run on up to the house and change, then," Sean said. "Your mom and I will wait right here."

A flicker of dismay crossed Deanna's face, but she didn't argue.

After Kevin had gone, Sean repeated his apology, trying to explain his attitude toward his own family, an attitude he admittedly tried never to examine too closely.

"I know your heart's in the right place, that you're

thinking about Kevin," Deanna conceded when he finished. "But when it comes to my folks, you don't know what you're talking about."

"I know."

"Then you'll drop it?"

"If it will wipe that frown off your face, yes."

A smile trembled at the corners of her mouth.

Sean reached over and touched a finger to her lips. "Much better." Then he leaned down and kissed her, just a quick, gentle kiss to remind himself of the taste and feel of her mouth beneath his.

Huge mistake. He wanted so much more, but Kevin was screaming his name and tearing across the sand, dragging a towel behind him. Sean's only consolation was the unmistakable shadow of regret in Deanna's eyes, too.

"I don't see why anyone would want to dig for clams," Kevin grumbled. "It's hard work, and they're yucky."

"Not when they're in a big bowl of New England clam chowder," Sean assured him.

Deanna grinned at the pair of them. The clam digging had been Sean's brilliant idea. She was stretched out on a blanket nearby listening to the two of them grumble. The sun was warm against her skin. After only a couple of days, Kevin's hair was turning lighter and his skin was developing a faint tan, except for his nose which had gotten sunburned the first day out. He looked healthy and happy as he knelt on the sand beside Sean, digging haphazardly with his small shovel.

The setting was idyllic, even if being around Sean

24/7 was beginning to take a toll on her nerves. It had been difficult enough to resist him in the city, where she only had to contend with the sight of him in tight T-shirts and snug jeans. Out here, even on the chilliest mornings, he was usually wearing shorts and a T-shirt. More often than not he wore only his bathing suit, exposing more taut, bare skin than she'd been exposed to in years. The temptation to rest her hand against his bronzed chest, to trace the hard muscles in his arms or the six-pack of sculpted muscles on his abdomen was nearly irresistible.

If Sean was having similar difficulty keeping his hands to himself, she wasn't aware of it. He seemed perfectly content jogging along the edge of the water with Kevin running along beside him or engaging in a cutthroat game of cards with Kevin and Deanna in the evening while Hank and Ruby disappeared into town.

This was what marriage to a man like Sean would be like, Deanna realized with a sudden burst of awareness. Slow, quiet days together as a family, accompanied by the edgy thrill of anticipation. Of course, if they were married, there would be an end to the sensual torment. They could spend the entire night making wild, passionate love to each other, satisfying this longing that never quite left her.

Deanna was so shaken by the image that she inadvertently dropped the can of soda in her hand. It spilled over her bare thigh, soaked the blanket and sent her scooting onto the hot sand.

"You okay?" Sean asked, appearing beside her.

She forced a smile. "Just dropped my soda all over myself. It was cold."

"You need to go in the water or you'll be all sticky," he said.

"Not me. The ocean's freezing."

By then Kevin had joined them. "No, it's not, Mom. You'll love it once you get in."

A mischievous grin spread across Sean's face. "Kev, I don't think your mom's going to become a believer unless we prove it to her."

She shot a wary look at him and backed up a step. "Meaning what exactly?"

Before she could react, Sean had scooped her up until she was resting against his bare chest. The sensation of being next to all that sun-warmed skin was so intriguing that for a moment, she completely forgot about his obvious intentions. When she finally remembered, they were already at the ocean's edge.

"Put me down, you idiot," she demanded, trying to wriggle free and escape before he dunked her in the Atlantic. He simply held on more tightly and kept walking.

The icy water skimmed the bottoms of her feet. "It couldn't be any colder if there were ice cubes in here," she squealed. "Sean Devaney, put me down right this instant."

He looked steadily into her eyes. "Now?" he inquired lightly. "You want me to put you down right now?"

Deanna saw the trick, but it was already too late. Sean released her. She hit the water with a splash. It was no more than three feet deep, but she sank into it with a shriek of dismay. It was like stepping under the shower and belatedly realizing that she'd forgotten to turn on the hot water. The shock of cold nearly paralyzed her.

The instant she managed to get on her feet, she brushed her soaking wet hair out of her eyes and faced Sean with a determined look. "You are in so much trouble," she said.

Her indignation was enough to heat her up as she went after him, diving neatly below the surface and aiming directly for his knees. She took him by surprise, managing to knock him off his feet. Satisfied with her sneak attack, she surfaced just as he stood up, sputtering.

"So, that's the way you want to play," he said, a glint in his eyes as he came after her.

Deanna tried to evade his reach, but Sean was quicker. He had her off her feet and in the water before she could plead for mercy. Then Kevin was in the middle of things, splashing them both. When he managed to hit Sean squarely in the face with a handful of water, Deanna saw her chance. She ran for shore.

Sean caught her just before she hit the beach, carried her right back out and sank down in water to his shoulders, still holding her cradled against his chest.

"Ready to concede yet?" he inquired, his gaze locked with hers.

Deanna was aware of every single spot where their bodies were in contact. Given the temperature of the water and the heat they were generating, she was amazed that this part of the Atlantic hadn't turned into a steam bath. She tried to respond to Sean's taunt, but she couldn't seem to form the words, couldn't even think.

Suddenly Sean's eyes darkened as if the heat had finally gotten to him, as well. His hand slipped higher, brushing against the already hard bud of her nipple. Even through her suit the sensation shot fiery heat straight through her. His knowing gaze held hers, daring her to protest or move away.

But Deanna didn't want to move. She wanted that almost innocent caress to last forever, wanted the wild flaring of need to build and build until she was writhing beneath Sean and he was burying himself deep inside her.

Oh, no, she thought with a moan. What was happening to her? She was turning into a bundle of exposed nerves, sensitive to every brush of Sean's fingers across her flesh. If she could react like this with her son just a few feet away and Sean doing practically nothing, what would happen if he truly set out to seduce her?

"We're going to finish this one of these days," he told her quietly, still holding her gaze.

She shuddered at the certainty in his voice. There was little point in denying his claim. They were destined to finish this. They had been for weeks now. Only old fears and uncertainties, which ran deep in both of them, had kept the tide of their wanting in check.

His lips curved. "No argument?"

She solemnly shook her head. "Why waste my breath?"

"Geez, Dee, why not torment me a little more?" he muttered hoarsely. "I thought you'd at least tell me I was crazy to think for one minute that you and I..."

His voice trailed off and he glanced toward Kevin who was splashing nearby, safe with his colorful floating device twisted around his waist. "Well, you know."

Deanna smiled at his attempt at discretion. "I know." She rested her hand against his cheek, loving the way the combination of stubble, heat and icy salt water felt against her palm.

Eyes locked with hers, he lowered her slowly to her feet, letting her feel the tension in his body, his unmistakable arousal. With water swirling around them up to their waists, he held her tightly against him, rocking his hips just a little, just enough to make her wish they were out here all alone, under a moonlit sky.

She swallowed hard. "I'd better...I need..."

"What do you need?" he asked, amusement in his eyes.

"Heat," she blurted.

He laughed. "This isn't making you hot enough?"

"Sun," she insisted, refusing to concede. She waved in the general direction of the beach. "I need to get back."

"Because?"

She opted for total honesty. "Because, Sean Devaney, you scare the daylights out of me."

He seemed genuinely shocked by that. "Me? Why?"

"Because you make me feel things, want things, I'd never expected to want again."

He regarded her with a commiserating look. "Tell me about it. This—you and me—it was the last thing I expected."

"Or wanted," she guessed.

"Or wanted," he agreed.

Somehow knowing that he didn't want this—didn't want to want her—hurt more than she'd anticipated it would. Of course he didn't. How many times had he made it plain that commitment was the last thing on his mind? She remembered another man—Frankie—who'd hedged about the future, but she'd been so confident that they could defy the odds. Was she willing to take on another man with doubts?

"It doesn't have to go any further than this," she said stiffly, gathering her pride around her.

He touched a finger to her lips. "I think you and I both know that it's impossible to turn back now."

"Not impossible," she insisted.

He shrugged. "Unlikely, then."

Yes, she thought, refusing to waste her breath arguing. It was definitely unlikely that they could turn back now. If only she could be equally certain just what the future held.

12

The rest of the week in Cape Cod was pure torment. Sean's desire was a palpable thing—with him whenever he was in a room with Deanna, with him at night when she was in her own bed in a room upstairs. Not even the presence of Ruby and Hank or Kevin's constant chatter could take his mind off Deanna and his insatiable need for her.

He was unable to put a name to it that he could live with. Calling it lust diminished it. Describing it as love terrified him. Better just to acknowledge its existence and not label it at all.

Adding to his level of frustration was the fact that Deanna didn't seem the least bit unnerved by the simmering passion between them. It was as if that moment in the ocean had never happened. She was perpetually cheerful. She didn't seek him out, but neither did she avoid him. She seemed perfectly content with the blasted status quo, while Sean was about to tear his hair out.

He wondered if his brother had gone through any

of this when he'd fallen for Maggie. Had Ryan been even half as reluctant as Sean was to make a commitment? Had he struggled with the past, with their parents' inability to stay the course, as Sean seemed to be struggling? He'd have to ask him one of these days.

Right now, though, he was so edgy, he was snapping at everyone except Kevin. He probably would have bitten the boy's head off, as well, but one look at that innocent face with its new freckles and peeling, sunburned nose had him cutting off the sharp words on the tip of his tongue. No child should ever have to pay for the craziness going on in the lives of the adults around him.

Sean could hardly wait to get back to Boston and back to work, even if it was going to be a few more weeks before he'd have Hank back as his partner. In fact, he was so relieved by the prospect of being alone in his apartment, he dropped Deanna, Kevin and Ruby off first with barely a word of goodbye, then headed for Hank's, hoping to escape from there without an interrogation about his sour mood.

He should have known better. It became obvious the minute they were alone that Hank intended to poke and prod the same way Sean had nagged at him during his divorce and was still nagging at him about Ruby.

"You going to tell me what's wrong?" Hank asked when Sean pulled to a stop in front of his place.

"No."

"You and Deanna have a fight?"

"No."

"You and Deanna have sex?"

Sean whirled around and glared at Hank. "You know damn well we didn't."

"Hey, I wasn't watching the two of you every minute. I had my own problems to deal with." He gave a rueful shake of his head. "If this isn't pitiful. The two of us, who have the reputation of being the hottest studs at the station—"

"Speak for yourself," Sean muttered.

"The guys enjoy having their illusions about the two bachelors among them," Hank chided. "The point is, we're supposed to be able to get any woman we want, and neither one of us is getting a damned thing."

Sean sighed. "It's not about sex with me and Deanna," he said. "I don't know exactly what it is about, but it's definitely not the same-old same-old."

Hank's expression turned grim. "Same with me and Ruby. The woman scares me to death. She sees straight through me. The hell of it is, she seems to like me, anyway."

Sean grinned at his apparent astonishment. "Maybe that's because underneath all that flirting and bragging you enjoy, you're a likable guy."

Hank frowned. "But I don't want to get married again, and Ruby's anxious to have kids."

"Has she said that?"

"She doesn't have to. I can read between the lines. She loves taking care of Kevin. She goes all maternal when she talks about him. And you should see her if we happen to run across a baby. The look on her face…" He shook his head. "I can't even begin to describe it. A part of me wants to give her what she wants. Another part…well, you know how I am."

"I know how you are about marriage," Sean agreed. "But children, no. Are you that opposed to having kids? I thought it was in your plans when you and Jackie were together."

"It was—till she made me see that someone risking his life all the time was a bad bet as a dad."

Sean frowned at him. "Hank, you know that's not true. If it were, then firefighting wouldn't be the kind of profession that is just about handed down from generation to generation. Half the guys we work with are the sons of firefighters. And many of them have kids of their own, some of whom will grow up to be firefighters, too."

Hank's expression turned thoughtful. "I never thought of it that way."

"Because you've been too busy trying to prove that Jackie was right to divorce you. Otherwise, it would have hurt too much." He punched Hank in the shoulder. "Face it. The divorce was all about her fears. Some were rational. Some weren't. But getting out of the marriage was the only way she could see to deal with them. Ruby's not Jackie."

"That's for damn sure," Hank said. "The woman's fearless. Last night she suggested we try bungee-jumping as soon as my ankle heals. Said she thought it would be a real high."

Sean had to bite back a laugh. Hank was an intrepid firefighter, but he claimed to be terrified of heights. It was one reason he didn't work at a station with skyscrapers in the area. "What did you say?"

"Are you kidding me? I told her she was out of her

ever-loving mind." He shook his head. "She said she'd go without me."

"Think she will?"

"Probably, just because she knows it will make me crazy," he said with a sigh.

"You are so hooked," Sean said, delighted with this latest turn of events. Hank had enjoyed the heck out of being single, but being married had grounded him, given him a much-needed stability. That was why it had rocked him back on his heels when Jackie had walked out. He'd realized he was losing something important. He just hadn't known how to prevent it, short of giving up his career.

"In fact," Sean taunted, holding a hand to his heart, "I think I hear the faint sound of wedding bells."

Hank swore at him. "Don't laugh, buddy. Seems to me that you're just as bad off as I am."

Now it was Sean's turn to sigh. "You've got that right."

Deanna wasn't sure what to expect after the trip to Cape Cod. A part of her wanted Sean to make good on his promise to haul her off to bed at the first opportunity. A part of her knew that once that happened, she'd no longer be able to deny the feelings he stirred in her. Even that wouldn't be such a problem if it weren't for the unresolved issue of his need to control her life.

Maybe now that he'd seen to it that she had an entire week of rest, it would be a nonissue, she thought hopefully, just in time to look up and spot him strolling into Joey's and heading for a booth in the back. It was nearly 10:00 p.m., two hours later than she was scheduled to work, but Adele had had a headache. She'd gone home early, and Pauline hadn't come in at all. Pauline still hadn't fully rebounded from her bout with the flu, so she'd been taking more time off than usual lately. Joey was relying on Deanna to fill in.

One look at Sean's scowling face told Deanna that maybe she shouldn't have agreed quite so readily to stay. Bracing herself for an argument, she walked over to the booth, pad and pencil poised to take his order.

"You're here late," he said, his tone neutral. "I went by the apartment, but Ruby told me Joey had talked you into working till closing."

"He was in a bind," she said, instantly on the defensive.

Sean scowled. "Joey always seems to be in a bind. Do I need to have a talk with him?"

She slapped her pad down on the table and placed both hands against the edge as she leaned down to scowl straight into Sean's face. "Don't...you...dare."

He actually winced under the intensity of her gaze. "Crossing the line?" he inquired mildly.

"Oh, yeah."

"Come on, Deanna, you know I'm right," he said reasonably. "You're going to wear yourself out."

"I just got back from vacation."

"Which will be wasted if you plunge right back into a back-breaking schedule. And what about Kevin?"

She frowned at him. "Don't use Kevin to try to make me feel guilty. He's getting plenty of attention. In fact, if you were so worried about him, you could have stayed at the apartment and kept him entertained. This is about your need to control me."

He seemed genuinely shocked by the accusation. "Don't be absurd. I don't want to control you."

"That's not how it looks to me."

"I'm worried, dammit. Is that a crime?"

Deanna studied his face and realized he was dead serious. She sighed and slid into the booth opposite him. "Sean, I'm healthy as a horse. There's no need to worry about me."

"You fainted," he reminded her.

"That was weeks ago," she said, dismissing the incident. "You landed in the hospital the same night. You don't hear me fretting about *you* being back at work."

"It wasn't even three weeks ago," he said. "And it was different for me. I had a couple of minor injuries."

She rolled her eyes at his dismissal of his burns. "And I've had a vacation since then, and you saw to it that I ate everything in sight and got plenty of sleep."

He frowned. "You actually slept?"

"Sure," she said cheerfully, realizing exactly why that annoyed him. "Didn't you?"

"No," he all but growled.

"Sorry."

His gaze swept over her, lingered here and there, then came to rest on her mouth. "We could solve my sleepless nights fairly easily."

She couldn't seem to swallow past the sudden tightness in her throat. "Oh?" It came out as a croak.

"My place. Tonight."

"I thought you were anxious for me to get home to my son," she said.

He grinned. "Not that anxious. He'll be asleep soon, anyway."

"How convenient for you."

"It could be," he agreed. "So? What do you think? My place? I have a chilled bottle of wine. Some cheese and crackers."

The invitation had seduction written all over it. There wasn't a doubt in Deanna's mind that if she went to Sean's, that wine and cheese would still be untouched come morning. A huge part of her was tempted to throw caution to the wind and say yes. Another part held back.

"Another time?" she suggested, not even attempting to hide her regret. "I have an appointment first thing in the morning before work."

His frown slammed back into place. "An appointment at that hour? To do what?"

"I'm looking at an apartment."

"You're leaving Ruby's?"

"It was always a temporary solution. And I really think she'd like to have a little more privacy. Plus, then I wouldn't be the buffer she needs to avoid dealing with her feelings for Hank."

Sean chuckled. "That cuts two ways, you know. You haven't had to decide what to do about me, either."

Just then the one remaining customer beckoned for his check. Deanna stood up, winked at Sean and said, "I wasn't aware you'd given me anything to decide."

She could feel his gaze on her as she gave the man his check, then took his money up to the register. By the time she'd finished, she found Joey sitting in the booth with Sean.

"If he's trying to convince you to work me fewer hours, ignore him," she said as she joined them.

"Actually, I was suggesting he fire you," Sean said, his gaze unrepentant.

Deanna immediately bristled.

"Settle down," Sean advised. "I was only teasing." He glanced at Joey. "See what I mean, though. She's edgy."

Joey held up his hands. "I'm not getting in the middle of whatever is going on between you two. You figure it out, let me know. Now get out of here. I need to close up and get home to Paulie."

Deanna was very aware that Sean's gaze never left her as she took off her apron and grabbed her purse from the cupboard under the register. "You coming or not?" she asked as she headed for the door.

"Right behind you," he said. Outside, he caught her hand. "Where are we going?"

"I don't know about you, but I'm going home," she said emphatically.

"I'll walk with you," he said, falling into step beside her. "Dee?"

"Yes."

"Do you have any idea what we're doing?"

"Driving each other crazy?" she suggested.

"I'm serious."

"So am I."

He stopped and drew her around to face him. "Good crazy or bad crazy?"

She looked deep in his eyes and saw the genuine confusion. It mirrored her own. She lifted her hand to his cheek. "I'm still trying to figure that part out."

Sean sighed heavily. "Let me know when you do, okay?"

Deanna smiled at the plaintive note in his voice. "Believe me, you'll be at the top of the list. You do the same, okay?"

He nodded. "Will do. So, what time's your appointment in the morning?"

"Seven-thirty."

"Mind if I tag along?"

"Why?"

He seemed to be debating the answer. She had a feeling it was because he didn't want to admit that he felt some crazy sense of responsibility for seeing to it that she and Kevin had a decent place to live.

"Curiosity," he said finally.

Deanna nodded. "In that case, I'll see you in the morning."

She was about to go inside when he stopped her. His gaze on her face, he tilted her chin up and touched his lips to hers. Light as a breeze, the kiss was still enough to send a shudder through her.

For a man who worried so darned much about how little sleep she was getting, he certainly didn't seem to mind doing the one thing guaranteed to keep her awake all night.

Sean hated the whole idea of Deanna hunting for a new apartment. He knew just how limited her resources were, even with that settlement from her old landlord. He also knew that despite what she'd said about using some of the cash for the new place, she'd tucked most of the money away in a savings account she didn't intend to touch except in an emergency.

When he arrived in the morning, he discovered he

was just part of the entourage going to check out the new apartment.

"Mom and me are looking at a new place to live," Kevin said excitedly. "Once we move, you can come to dinner."

Sean noticed that Ruby didn't look nearly as cheerful as either Kevin or Deanna.

"Sean can come to dinner here," she grumbled, sending a scowl in Deanna's direction. "I don't know why you're so anxious to move."

"Because we're in your way," Deanna explained patiently.

"You are not. This has been fun." She turned to Kevin. "Hasn't it been fun?"

"Sure," he said, apparently sensing the need not to hurt Ruby's feelings.

Sean gave Ruby a sympathetic look. "You're wasting your breath."

"I know," she admitted.

"If you're going to be a sourpuss through all this, then don't come with us," Deanna told Ruby. "I want objective opinions on this new apartment, not self-serving criticism."

When Sean started to say something, she scowled at him. "That goes for you, too."

"Yes, ma'am," he said, sharing a commiserating look with Ruby. "Where is this place?"

Deanna looked at a piece of paper on which an address had been written. She read it to him. "It's only a few blocks from here."

Sean winced. "And another world," he said. "That area's not that safe."

"Would you stop with the grumbling before we even look," she demanded. "Now, let's go."

Sean sighed and followed along as she and Kevin set out at a brisk pace. Ruby fell into step beside him.

"Can't you stop her?" she asked in a low voice.

"You heard her. She doesn't intend to listen to reason. She'll only hear what she wants to hear. She's in an independent frame of mind this morning."

"No kidding," Ruby muttered bleakly.

"Maybe the place will really be a dive, and she'll have to admit it's a bad idea," he suggested, even though he knew that unless it was tumbling down, Deanna wasn't going to back out of making this deal. He and Ruby had pretty much backed her into a corner.

When they found the address, Sean was relieved to see that the building was an old brownstone. It wasn't especially well kept, but from the outside at least, it didn't look like a fire hazard. That was something in its favor.

Kevin, however, was regarding it with a doubtful expression. "Mom, it's kinda ugly," he said hesitantly, still clinging to Deanna's hand.

"That's cosmetic," she said. "It doesn't matter, as long as it's clean and the pipes don't leak."

Sean frowned. "You might want to raise your standards just a little to include a lack of drafts. Boston winters can get pretty cold."

She scowled right back at him. "The real estate agent said she'd meet us inside," she said, entering the unsecured foyer and starting to climb the stairs. "The apartment's on the top floor."

"Great," Sean said. "It'll give us a chance to see if the roof leaks."

Ruby barely managed to smother a chuckle as Deanna whirled around to glare at them. "You two want to wait outside?"

"Not a chance," Sean said, staying right on her heels.

The door to one third-floor apartment was open, so they trooped inside. The real estate agent greeted them and began a spiel that would have sold Sean on the place had he not been standing in the middle of the dreary, cramped rooms. She assured them that the water stains were the result of now-corrected leaks. Ditto, the buckling wood floors near the windows. She didn't seem to have an explanation for the grimy state of the ancient kitchen appliances, but Deanna dragged in her new favorite word—cosmetic—to dismiss the problem.

The two bedrooms were tiny, but they did have tall windows that might actually let in a fair amount of light once years of grime were washed away. The bathroom had a sink with rust stains and a claw-footed tub that had lost a good bit of its porcelain glaze.

It was, in Sean's opinion, fairly awful, but Deanna was determined to see it with rose-colored glasses. The price was right and it would be hers.

"I'll take it," she said, even as the rest of them, Kevin included, choked back dismayed protests. She looked at each of them pointedly. "And I don't want to hear one single negative word from any of you."

Sean knew he and Ruby had no one to blame but themselves for kicking Deanna's independent streak into high gear. Nothing short of the roof caving in on their heads before she signed the papers would have stopped her.

The real estate agent beamed as Deanna signed the lease and handed over a check. The agent's day was obviously off to a rip-roaring start, if she could unload this dump before eight o'clock.

Seeing the defiant jut to Deanna's chin as she paid the woman and accepted her copy of the one-year lease, Sean forced a smile. "So, darlin', when do you want us over here to paint?"

She seemed completely flustered by the offer. "I don't expect—"

"Name the time." He'd taken just about as much of her independence as he could handle for one morning.

"Saturday morning."

He nodded. He might not be able to keep her from moving herself and her son into this dive, but he could make damn sure it was livable before she did.

"What color paint do you want?" he asked.

"I'll get the paint," she said.

His scowl deepened. "What color?"

Apparently she finally realized that she'd pushed him as far as she could push him. "Pale yellow for the living room walls, blue for the bedrooms. White woodwork."

Sean nodded as he jotted it down. "Got it."

"I think I should at least come with you," she said. "In my experience men aren't all that reliable when it comes to picking out paint colors."

"Did you just insult my taste?" he inquired.

"Uh-oh," Ruby said. "Kevin, I think you and I ought to wait outside."

Kevin regarded her blankly. "How come?"

"Because your mother and Sean are about to have a discussion."

The boy's brow knit worriedly. "You mean a fight?"

Sean winked at him. "No big deal. Your mom just doesn't seem to respect my eye for color."

"Huh?"

"Go with Ruby. We'll be down in a minute." After they'd gone, he turned and faced Deanna. "You could accept my help graciously, you know."

"It's not your help I'm worried about. It's the color scheme I'm likely to end up with. I'd feel better if I had a say."

"You feel that way about a lot of things, don't you?"

"Because, in my experience, men aren't that reliable."

"Are we talking paint now, or in general?"

She regarded him with an unflinching look. "In general."

"Dee, have I ever let you down?" he asked, his tone softening.

"No, but—"

"But you haven't given me a chance to let you down, is that what you were going to say?"

"As a matter of fact, yes."

Sean wanted to defend not only his honor but the honor of all men, then decided not to. His father certainly hadn't been that reliable. Maybe everybody generally sucked at relationships. Of course, his brother and Maggie seemed to be doing okay, but there were exceptions to every rule.

Deanna looked at him intently. "You're not arguing."

"No," he said flatly. "I'm not arguing."

That didn't mean he didn't want to kiss her and protect her and swear that he was different. He just didn't have any solid proof that that was so.

13

The little set-to over paint at the new apartment was just one more example of Sean trying to control things, Deanna concluded after he'd left with Kevin and she and Ruby had gone on to work at the law office.

"If I don't like the paint he chooses, I'm taking it back," she muttered under her breath.

Ruby regarded her with amusement. "I'm pretty sure he understands that. Did either one of you ever consider the idea of compromise? Did you even suggest meeting him at the home-improvement store on your lunch break?"

"I said I wanted to take care of this myself," Deanna said defensively. "It is my apartment, after all. I'm perfectly capable of selecting paint, brushes and whatever else I need to fix things up. I can also handle whatever work needs to be done. I haven't had anyone to do things for me since I left home."

"Knowing Sean, I imagine he thinks he's just being helpful," Ruby explained quietly. "He's merely offering to take on something that would cut into your little bit of free time."

Deanna tried to see it from Sean's perspective. She was forced to admit that Ruby was probably right. That didn't mean his presumption didn't grate. Once she'd left home, she'd been forced to learn to rely on herself. She'd no longer been able to pick up the phone and hire someone to do whatever needed doing. She'd learned to be plumber, painter and basic mechanic. That necessity had only deepened after her divorce, when money was even tighter.

"If this is going to drive you nuts, call him," Ruby suggested. "Errands are the third best use you can make of a lunch hour after sneaking off with your honey for a quickie or eating something totally decadent. Heck, Sean might even buy you lunch." A grin spread across her face. "Or go with you to pick out a bed."

He'd probably insist on it, Deanna thought irritably, then sighed. Why did she find it so annoying that Sean wanted to help? The answer was easy. It was precisely what she'd alluded to that morning. After Frankie— heck, even after her father's rejection—she didn't trust any man in her life to be reliable. Maybe it was even worse with Sean, because she wanted so badly to be proved wrong in his case.

She settled at her desk, handled the first few incoming calls, took a few messages, then when the phones were quiet, she called Sean.

"I've been thinking," she said quietly. "I can get away from here for an hour at lunchtime. How about if I meet you to pick out the paint?"

"Since you asked so nicely," he said, clearly teasing, "is noon good for you?"

"Perfect."

"I'll pick you up in front of your office."

"It's only a few blocks. We can walk."

"I know you think of me as a big, strong guy, but I am not hauling gallons of paint around. We need the car."

He had her there. "I'll meet you out front at noon," she agreed.

Sean laughed. "See how easy that was?"

"Only because I agreed with you," she retorted.

"That goes without saying. You should consider making it a practice. We'll see how you do when it comes to picking out furniture."

Even as Deanna deliberately hung up on him, she chuckled at his completely unrepentant attitude. She couldn't deny, though, that she was looking forward to the trip to the hardware store as if it were a date for champagne and caviar. Heck, maybe more. Given her family background, she'd long ago discovered that she wasn't really a champagne and caviar kind of woman. That was her mother's domain.

Deanna could just imagine what Patricia Locklear Tindall would have to say if she knew her daughter was going on a date to pick out paint at a neighborhood hardware store. Truthfully, her mother probably wasn't even aware such stores existed, and she surely wouldn't have approved of Deanna dating any man whose idea of a good time was taking her to such a place. Add to that her mother's opinion of any home that hadn't been fully decorated by an interior designer before the move, and Deanna was pretty sure her actions would have her mother's head spinning. And that was even before she discovered that all Deanna's furniture was likely to come from thrift stores.

Sean realized he'd made a mistake in agreeing to let Deanna accompany him when she spread ten different shades of yellow paint chips out on a counter and started pondering them, musing aloud about the advantages of one over the others. As far as he could tell, yellow was yellow. Maybe that was why she'd insisted on coming along.

She finally turned to him, a perplexed expression knitting her brow. "What do you think?"

"This one," he said at once, choosing one at random.

"Really? Don't you think it's a little bright?"

He shrugged. "Looks fine to me, if cheerful's what you want."

"I want cheerful, but not overpowering." She picked up a lighter shade. "How about this one?"

Eager to end the process, he nodded. "Fine. I'll have 'em start mixing it."

Before he could move, she picked up a second paint chip. "Then, again, this one is nice. It's kind of soothing, like warm sunshine."

Sean sighed and waited as a third chip was debated. "Could you at least rule out a couple?" he inquired. "You only have an hour for lunch, and we still have to look at all the blues."

She frowned at him. "This is an important choice, one Kevin and I will have to live with for years and years."

A knot formed in Sean's stomach that had nothing to do with her disinclination to make a decision. It was the "years and years" comment that got to him. She was making a commitment to paint, for heaven's sake. Why should that bother him?

He answered the question himself. Because it implied that there was going to be no place for him in her life, not for "years and years." She had more faith in the endurance of paint than she did in their relationship.

So what the hell was he supposed to do about it? Was he supposed to ask her to marry him just to keep her from choosing a paint? Of course not. The whole idea was ridiculous, but damned if he wasn't tempted to do just that.

Because the temptation was so real and so disturbing, he fell completely silent and let her struggle on all alone with her debate over the new apartment's color scheme. He wasn't going to be a party to it, no matter how ridiculous that made him feel. It was better than admitting to her just how badly he wanted her to forget all about this whole move and stay with Ruby.

Or move in with him. He was so stunned that such a thought had even crossed his mind, he had to clutch the edge of the counter to steady himself. That notion was even more absurd than marriage. She had a child. She had deeply held values. She wasn't going to move in with him on a whim, not when she was gun-shy about relationships to begin with. Nope, with Deanna it was going to be permanence or nothing.

Sean sighed.

"Sean, what do you think?" she prodded, holding out what were apparently her two final choices.

Since one was right under his nose, while the other was barely in the air, he assumed there was a subliminal message there. "This one," he said reluctantly, pointing to the closest choice.

Her expression brightened. "I think so, too. Now for the blues." A frown puckered her brow. "Or do you think the bedrooms ought to be more neutral, maybe a soft cream color?"

He couldn't do it. He could not debate the virtues of cream over blue, or vice-versa. Instead, he swooped in and kissed her to shut her up. He threw himself into the task, too, feeling the heat that spread through her almost at once, the way her knees buckled, so he practically had to hold her up. When he finally pulled away, she stared at him with dazed eyes.

"What was that for?"

He grinned and shrugged nonchalantly. "Just felt like it."

"We don't have time to go home and do anything about it," she told him.

As if she'd even consider the notion in the first place, he thought, but encouraged by her teasing, he decided to push the point a little more. "We would if you'd finish picking out the paint."

She laughed. "Nice try, but if you think I'm racing out of here to make love with you for the very first time with barely ten minutes to spare, you're completely bonkers."

"Fifteen minutes, if you let me come back and get the paint later," he coaxed.

She patted his cheek. "Not a chance. I want lots and lots of time when we finally make love."

When, not if. He made note of the distinction. Intrigued, he met her gaze. "Just out of curiosity, what do you intend to do with all that time?"

A blush crept into her cheeks. "Use your imagination."

"Sweetheart, the way my imagination's working overtime, we wouldn't have enough time if we locked ourselves away for a month."

She grinned. "Precisely."

Sean stared at her. The woman had a wicked streak he'd noticed only once before, way back when she'd taunted him with that ice-cream cone. It was now clear that hadn't been an aberration. It was also evident that boredom would certainly never be a problem. Now if he could just shake this overall terror that the thought of marriage and forever instilled in him, he might actually work up the nerve to propose.

In the meantime, he'd just have to settle for getting her to decide on the paint before the store closed for the night.

Deanna was slamming pots and pans around in the kitchen when Ruby got home that night. Ruby stood in the doorway and watched her warily.

"You and Sean have a fight?"

"Nope."

"You did go to pick out paint at lunchtime, right?"

"Yes."

"And?"

"And nothing," Deanna grumbled, then sank onto a

chair. "The man is making me crazy. Out of the blue, right there in the middle of the hardware store, he kissed me as if there were no tomorrow."

Ruby stared. "Oh, my. Were you embarrassed?"

"No, not really."

"Mad?" Apparently, curiosity won out over wariness, because Ruby risked coming in and sitting down at the table.

"Only because there wasn't time to finish what he'd started," Deanna admitted. "I have never wanted a man to make love to me so badly in my life. If he'd pushed just a little harder, I would have gone home with him then and there. Instead, he gave up."

"You mean he took no for an answer," Ruby teased. "Isn't that what a gentleman's supposed to do?"

"Well, of course it is," Deanna conceded impatiently. "But it was annoying just the same. He should have figured out what I really wanted."

"Men who think they know what a woman wants when she's saying no tend to get themselves in a whole lot of trouble," Ruby pointed out. "I'm sure Sean knows that. I think you'd better be a little more specific if you really want him to make love to you. Maybe set the scene, light some candles, put some flowers on the table, cook him a fabulous meal, kiss him till he can't breathe."

Deanna sighed at the suggestion. "Oh, yeah, that's easy for you. You date all the time. You have confidence in yourself. I've been dumped by the only man I ever made love with. Maybe I'm really lousy at sex. Maybe I send out hands-off vibes."

She knew that wasn't entirely true. She had evidence that Sean wanted her, verbal evidence and solid proof, so to speak. His arousal today—and on other occasions, for that matter—had been unmistakable.

"Oh, please," Ruby said. "Frankie Blackwell was a selfish, inconsiderate rat. He left because he was an irresponsible, immature idiot who thought you were going to be his meal ticket, not because you weren't good in bed. He and Sean Devaney are nothing alike." She regarded Deanna intently. "Is it really about being scared you're not sexy, or is it about the fact that you're terrified because you have feelings for Sean, the kind of feelings you'd told yourself you would never have again?"

"I don't have feelings for him, not the way you mean," Deanna insisted heatedly. "I just want to make love with him. He's gorgeous. He's sexy. It's all about lust, nothing more."

Ruby rolled her eyes. "If you were the type to go in for uncomplicated sex, I'd be the first to tell you to go for it, but you're not. You're the happily-ever-after type. You want romance and commitment. You've got a kid. You're not going to indulge your hormones on a whim. If you were, you'd have done it long ago. You've had chances."

"None worth considering," Deanna said defensively. "And I could have uncomplicated sex. I'm not opposed to it."

"Oh, please," Ruby said dismissively. "How many times have you told me that you don't even like to date because it might be confusing for Kevin? Now you're willing to go to bed with a guy because you're in lust with him? I don't think so. It's more than that. You're completely crazy about Sean. You're at least half in love with him, if not head over heels. Why not admit it and go from there? Men like Sean Devaney don't come along every day, you know."

Deanna flatly refused to consider that possibility. She didn't want to be in love, therefore she wasn't. Period. "I'm not going to admit to anything, because you're wrong," she said emphatically.

"I have one word for you—*denial*."

"You don't know what you're talking about," Deanna insisted. But the sad truth was, Ruby had pegged it.

And that was the crux of the problem. Deep down, buried in a part of her heart she hadn't listened to for years, were feelings she wasn't ready to acknowledge, not aloud, not even to herself. Deep down she knew she wanted more from Sean than sex. A tiny untested part of her wanted the one thing he'd vowed never to do. She wanted to get married, have a family with him and live happily ever after.

Those were the kind of feelings, hopes and dreams that led to heartache. It was far better—safer—to pretend they didn't exist. It was far wiser to accept that there were limits to the relationship. Sean certainly thought there were. His reasons were valid. So were hers.

Deanna might believe with all her heart that Sean was capable of making that kind of commitment to a future, that he was steady and dependable and would never abandon his family the way his father and mother had abandoned him—the way Frankie had abandoned her.

Unfortunately, she wasn't the one who needed to have faith in him. Sean had to have faith in himself. Without that, it didn't matter what she wanted or what she needed. Thinking she could control Sean's emotions—could heal old hurts for him—was a surefire way to get her own heart broken.

She met Ruby's worried gaze and forced a smile. "Stop looking at me like that. I know what I'm talking about."

"You're deluding yourself," Ruby insisted, clearly unconvinced. "Stop making assumptions about what Sean does or doesn't want. Tell him how you really feel. Total honesty is the only way to get what you want."

Deanna regarded her curiously. "Have you told Hank what *you* want?"

The question clearly flustered Ruby. Bright patches of color burned in her cheeks.

"You haven't, have you?" Deanna said triumphantly. "You're pretty good at dishing out advice, but not at following it."

"Two different situations," Ruby said tightly.

"Meaning you have no interest whatsoever in pursuing a future with Hank?" Deanna asked skeptically.

"I didn't say that."

"Well, then? What are you waiting for?"

Ruby's expression turned thoughtful. "I suppose you and I could make a pact. We could vow to jump off this particular bridge together. That way, if we crash land, we can always console each other. What do you think?"

Deanna studied her with a narrowed gaze as she

considered this so-called pact Ruby was proposing. "I tell Sean how I feel, and you tell Hank how you feel, is that the deal?"

"Pretty much."

If it would give Ruby the shove she needed to be honest with Hank, Deanna was willing to agree to just about anything. "Okay."

Ruby stared at her with obvious shock. "You'll do it?"

"If you do," Deanna said.

"Okay, then. It's a deal. When?"

"First opportunity. You're seeing Hank tonight, right?"

Ruby swallowed hard. "I said I'd call him if I was free."

Deanna grinned at her. "Then make the call." Her grin spread. "I guess I won't bother waiting up for you to get home tonight."

"You're being a bit overly optimistic, aren't you?" Ruby grumbled.

"No way. I've seen the way Hank looks at you."

"That doesn't mean he wants any more than a quick roll in the hay. He probably wants it a lot, since I've been keeping him at arm's length all these months."

Deanna regarded her with a pitying look. "Ruby, think about it. If sex were the only thing on Hank's mind, he could have dumped you weeks ago and moved on to someone more willing. He never had any trouble finding playmates in the past, at least not to hear Sean tell it. He's stuck around because you fascinate him. You're unpredictable. You keep him on his toes.

Honey, you're a terrific woman. Any man with half a brain would know he's lucky to have you in his life."

Ruby grinned as she stood up and headed out of the kitchen. "Nice pep talk. But if he says yes to going out tonight, I think I'll put on something outrageously sexy, in case you're wrong. What about you? When are you seeing Sean?"

Deanna shrugged. "I'm not sure."

Ruby stopped in her tracks. "Hold it. I'm going out there with my heart on my sleeve, and you're what? Curling up with a good book?"

"A couple of decorating magazines, actually."

"I don't think so," Ruby protested. She handed the phone to Deanna. "Call Sean right this second. Invite him over. I'll run downstairs and see if Kevin can spend the night at Timmy's."

"Timmy's out of town," Deanna said, not even trying to hide her relief at the excuse to put off the promised encounter with Sean. She'd never intended to make good on her end of the deal, anyway.

Ruby frowned at her and came back into the kitchen. She held out her hand. "Give me one of those magazines."

"Why?"

"Because we made a deal to do this together."

Deanna stared at her suspiciously, suddenly aware that Ruby had had no more intention of following through than she had. "You never had any intention of talking to Hank tonight, did you?" she demanded.

Ruby ignored the question and began flipping through the magazine.

"Did you?" Deanna persisted. "It was a trick to get me to talk to Sean."

Ruby peered over the top of the magazine. "Would I try to trick my best friend?"

"In a heartbeat," Deanna said.

"Only if I thought I was acting in her best interests," Ruby retorted.

"That's no excuse."

Ruby laughed. "Is your heart one bit purer? Were you really going to spell things out for Sean, if not tonight, then whenever you do see him?"

"Of course," Deanna said, working hard to maintain a pious expression.

"Yeah, right."

Deanna sighed. "We're quite a pair, aren't we? At this rate, we'll be 102 and still talking about what might have been."

"Now there's a thought that ought to terrify both of us into action," Ruby said.

They exchanged a look, then chorused with heartfelt sincerity, "Tomorrow."

"Soon enough for me," Ruby added.

"Me, too."

In the meantime Deanna had a hunch they both ought to be praying that tomorrow didn't turn out to be too late.

14

Sean had already passed the point in his relationship with Deanna when he would normally call it quits. She was getting under his skin. Not a minute went by that he wasn't desperate to kiss her, even more desperate to make love to her. If the reaction had been purely physical, he would have run with it, but it was more than that. Which was why he ought to be giving her a wide berth instead of putting himself smack in the way of temptation by going over to that disgustingly shabby new apartment later this morning.

Then again, how much trouble could he possibly get into while they were painting? As far as he knew, she hadn't picked out any furniture, so there wouldn't be so much as a sofa, much less a bed, to give him any ideas about what he'd prefer to be doing with her today. Besides, Hank and Ruby would be there. Kevin would probably be underfoot.

Sean grinned whenever he thought of Kevin with his wise-guy tongue and the expression of total adoration that crept across his face whenever Sean came around. Kevin was a very big part of what was going on between him and Deanna. The boy needed a surrogate dad, and so far Sean hadn't seen any evidence that anyone else was going to step up to the plate and fill in. He tried really hard not to think about what would happen if his relationship with Deanna ended. Or, worse, if she found some other man who was eager to play daddy.

Sean clenched his jaw. That wasn't going to happen, not unless he'd checked the guy out every which way, to be sure he was worthy of the two of them. He was still frowning over that when the doorbell rang. He jerked the door open and found his brother on his doorstep.

Ryan held up his hands and backed up a step. "Hey, whatever it is, I didn't do it."

Sean's scowl deepened. "What the hell are you talking about?"

"The look on your face, the one that says you're looking for someone to punch," Ryan explained. "What's that about?"

Sean couldn't quite manage a smile, but he forced a neutral expression. "Sorry. I was in a bad place."

"I could see that. Want to talk about it?"

"No time. I'm on my way out," he said, hoping to forestall a cross-examination on his mood.

"Then I won't keep you long," Ryan said, ignoring the lack of invitation and stepping inside the apartment. "Where are you off to, anyway?"

Sean studied his brother intently. There was still a certain wariness between them. After so many years apart, it wasn't as if they could just pick up the brotherhood bit where they'd left off as kids. They'd made some progress, but there was still some natural uneasiness over revealing too much, taking too much for granted based on their closeness as kids. A lot of water—a lot of anger—had passed under the bridge since the old days.

Maybe, though, this was the perfect opportunity for another round of long-delayed bonding.

"I'm helping a friend paint an apartment," he told Ryan as he led the way into his cramped kitchen. Since Ryan wasn't going anywhere till he'd said his piece about whatever had brought him by, they might as well be comfortable.

"The coffee's still warm," Sean said, after testing the pot. "Want some?"

"Sure."

Sean poured two cups, handed one to Ryan, then straddled a chair, waiting for his brother to explain what he was doing there. When Ryan remained quiet, Sean found himself filling the silence. "You know," he began, feeling awkward about asking Ryan for anything. "If you've got the time this morning, we could always use another pair of hands. It's no big deal if you can't, but I thought it might be fun to hang out for a while."

"I've got a couple of hours to spare," Ryan said at once, seizing on the invitation as the peace offering it had been intended to be. "Who's the friend?"

"Deanna Blackwell."

Ryan studied him curiously. "Girlfriend?"

Sean debated how to answer that. He supposed that was as close a description as any, but he didn't want to admit to it and then listen to the barrage of questions that was sure to follow. He opted for evasion. "Not exactly," he murmured.

His brother grinned. "Maybe I can help you clarify that. How is she paying you back for recruiting a painting crew?"

"Not like that," Sean protested. "She's just a friend, who happens to be a woman." And whose kisses could melt a steel girder.

"Sure." Ryan's expression was doubtful.

"She is."

"Whatever you say, bro."

Determined to change the subject before Ryan got him to say more than he intended about his relationship with Deanna, Sean asked, "Okay, other than hassling me, what brought you by this morning?"

Ryan seemed to debate whether to let him get away with the obvious ploy, then finally said, "I wanted to let you know I have a lead on Michael."

Sean swallowed hard at the news. The search for the rest of their family was Ryan's idea. Sean was less enthusiastic. Every time he thought of the family he'd lost, he wanted to start breaking things. He hated what his parents had put them through. He tried never to think about them, or about the brothers he hadn't seen since first grade.

But he couldn't deny that since meeting Deanna, he'd been thinking a lot more about the meaning of family. He was a little more open to the possibility of discovering answers to all the questions that had haunted him through the years.

"You know where Michael is?" he asked, his chest tight.

Ryan shook his head. "Not exactly. He's apparently in the Navy, but when I try to find out where he's stationed, I keep hitting a brick wall."

Sean suddenly recalled the four-year-old who'd trailed after him and Ryan, eager to do anything they'd let him do just to be around them. The image was so vivid it nearly made his heart stop. Something about that early case of hero worship had stuck with him. It was the last time anyone had looked up to him…at least until he'd become a firefighter. Maybe that need to be somebody's hero was even one of the reasons he'd chosen the dangerous profession in the first place.

Every once in a while when he saw the way Kevin looked at him, it reminded him of the way Michael had once looked up to his two big brothers. Brothers, who, when things got tough, hadn't been able to do anything to make them better. Maybe it hadn't been their doing, but in a way he and Ryan had abandoned Michael, the same way their parents had abandoned all of them.

He sighed and looked up to find Ryan studying him with concern.

"You okay?" Ryan asked.

"Just thinking about how we let him down," he admitted, unable to keep a note of self-loathing out of his voice.

"I know how you feel. I lived with the same guilt for years where both of you were concerned, but Maggie's made me see that we were just kids, too," Ryan said. "There's nothing we could have done differently to change things. When it comes to kids our age, adults are always in charge. We had to go along with what they decided. Now we have to go on from where we are. There's no point in looking back and wishing we'd done things differently."

"I suppose."

"Hey, you forgave me," Ryan said lightly. "Maybe Michael will forgive both of us."

"Maybe he won't even remember us," Sean said. "Hell, he was only four when we were split up."

Ryan sighed. "Definitely a possibility, but I can't stop looking now. Any idea how we can take this information and use it?"

Sean didn't want any part of the investigation. It was one thing for Ryan to conduct his search, maybe turn up this family member or that one. Then Sean could see them…or not. But the memory of Michael, his lower lip trembling as he was led away by a different set of foster parents, made him want some resolution, too. And one look at Ryan's expression told him he couldn't sit on the sidelines, especially when there might be a way he could help.

"There's a guy in the department whose brother is at the Pentagon. Maybe he'd be willing to do a little digging around for us," Sean conceded reluctantly. "Want me to ask him?"

"That would be great," Ryan said enthusiastically. "I know you have your reservations about all this, but seeing me again hasn't been so awful, has it?"

Sean grinned. "Hardly. How many times have I actually seen you, though? You could start to get on my nerves yet."

"Very funny. Now tell me about this woman we're helping this morning," Ryan coaxed, circling right back to the topic Sean had been hoping to avoid. "How'd you meet?"

Sean told him the story of the fire and all about Kevin. When he was finished there was a broad grin on his brother's face.

"You are so hooked," Ryan declared happily.

"Don't be ridiculous."

"Is she pretty?"

"I suppose."

"Sweet?"

He thought of Deanna's sharp edges and feisty independence, all of it tempered by a surprising naiveté. "Sweet enough, I guess."

"Vulnerable?"

Sean's gaze narrowed. "Yes," he confirmed tightly.

"And she's a struggling single mom?"

"Yes. What's your point?"

"Damsel in distress. Kid desperate for a father. Firefighter with a need to play hero. You do the math."

Sean didn't like the way things were adding up in his brother's head. "Oh, go to hell," he muttered.

His brother grinned. "Not till I get a look at this woman. And before you tell me what a pain in the butt I am, consider this—it could be worse."

"I don't see how."

"Maggie would be all over this," he teased. His face took on an odd expression, and then he met Sean's gaze. "She's got all these nesting urges." He hesitated, then added, "She's pregnant."

Sean studied his brother, trying to gauge how he

felt about the news. He didn't know him well enough to read him with any accuracy. "You sound dazed," he said finally. "You are happy about this, aren't you?"

"Happy. Terrified."

"What are you terrified about?" Sean asked, even though he could guess the answer. He opted for being supportive, saying the words he'd want to hear if he were in Ryan's place. "You're going to be a great father. And Maggie's amazing. She'll be a wonderful mother."

"Oh?" Ryan said, his expression skeptical. "Maggie will be a terrific mother, but me as a dad? I don't know. It's not like either you or I had a sterling example set for us."

"Which means you'll try all the harder to avoid making the same mistakes," Sean reassured him, stealing words Deanna had once expressed to him.

"The same way you're trying with this kid? What's his name? Kevin?"

Sean sighed. "Yeah. Something like that."

"A word of caution," Ryan said. "If what you're saying is true, that you're not interested in his mom—not that I believe that for a second—then be careful. Who knows better than the two of us what it feels like to be abandoned? You may not officially be this kid's dad, but if he's come to think of you that way, it could be devastating if you take off."

"Yeah, I know," Sean said. "It's not something I'm likely to forget."

With that thought hanging in the air, they fell silent. Ryan had managed to hit on the one flaw in Sean's plan to keep Deanna at arm's length. He needed to make a decision to stay—or go—before it was too late.

Unfortunately, he knew in his heart it was already too late on all counts. There was no question that he already loved that boy. What was more important, like it or not, he was in love with the kid's mom.

Admitting that to himself was one thing. Acting on it—doing what was right—was entirely another. But there was no question about one thing, he was running out of excuses and out of time.

Sean had been in an odd mood all day. Deanna glanced at him now and found that he was still wearing the same brooding expression she'd found troubling the second he'd shown up with his brother in tow.

The fact that he hadn't reacted at all to the discovery that she'd already managed to find a few pieces of furniture was especially telling. She'd expected a scathing glance at the sofa, maybe a remark about the bed, but there'd been nothing at all.

Maybe it was because his brother was with him, she concluded. She'd liked Ryan Devaney at once, even when she'd realized that he was subtly sizing her up. In fact, a part of her liked him even more for that. She thought it was great that he was looking out for his kid brother, even after all the years they'd been separated. Though the byplay between them was awkward at times, there was an unmistakable undercurrent of love and a bond that was growing stronger as time went on.

Apparently she'd won Ryan's wholehearted approval, because he'd kissed her cheek when he'd left and whispered, "Hang in there."

She still wasn't entirely certain what that had been about, but she suspected it had something to do with Sean's weird mood. He'd offered to give his brother a lift, but Ryan had turned him down flat, hitching a ride with Hank and Ruby instead.

Kevin was spending the weekend with a friend, so he hadn't been underfoot during the painting, which meant Deanna was now all alone in her new apartment with Sean.

"Thanks for helping today," she said as she gathered up empty pizza boxes and hauled them off to the trash can in the kitchen. "You want a beer or soda or something?"

"Nothing."

She came back into the living room and studied him intently. He was sprawled in an easy chair she'd found in a thrift store the day before. Even with paint spattered on his T-shirt, jeans and even on the tip of his nose and eyelashes, he made quite an enticing picture.

If only there weren't that dark scowl on his face, she thought, barely containing a sigh.

"Okay, that's it," she announced, standing over him, hands on hips. "What's going on with you? You've been acting weird all day."

He seemed vaguely startled that she was calling him on it. He straightened up and looked as if he might claim that everything was just fine, but she cut him off.

"Did something happen before you and Ryan got here?" she demanded. "I know he's been searching for Michael. Has there been some news?"

"He has a lead," he admitted.

Deanna frowned. He'd answered a little too quickly, almost as if he were relieved that she'd asked about the search for his family. "That's good news, right?"

"Yeah, of course it is," he said, though without much enthusiasm. "I'm going to see if a friend in the department can help us follow up on it."

"So it's not that," she concluded. "Come on, Sean. Talk to me. I thought we were friends."

To her shock, his expression turned even darker. "Yeah, that was the plan, all right."

Her heart began to thud dully. She ran a mental movie of everything that had gone on while they were painting, but nothing out of the ordinary struck her. "And something's happened today to change that?" she probed. "Did I do something to upset you?"

The corners of his mouth twitched. "You could say that, though probably not in the way you mean."

"Tell me."

He faced her with an anguished expression. "Okay, since you asked and I don't want to lie to you, here it is. I'm in love with you."

Something that felt a whole lot like heady exhilaration swept through her. Still, she noticed that he didn't look all that happy about the discovery that his feelings ran that deep.

"But?" she asked cautiously.

His gaze held hers. "That's it. I know you aren't interested in having a relationship, and I'm not convinced I'm any good at them, and here I go changing the rules."

Despite his somber tone, she couldn't contain the

rush of pure joy. Until she'd heard the words leave his lips, she hadn't realized just how desperately she'd been wanting to hear them. She laughed and launched herself into his arms. "It's about time, Sean Devaney. The wait was getting on my nerves."

He caught her and clasped her to his chest, then leaned back to scan her face. "You're not furious?"

She was almost as stunned by that as he seemed to be, but there it was. She was ecstatic, not angry.

"Furious?" she echoed, not even attempting to disguise her own amazement. "I guess not." To prove it, she kissed him, not pulling back until their breathing was ragged.

A grin tugged at his lips. "Do you have any idea how much I want to make love to you, Deanna Blackwell?"

She wriggled against him. "As a matter of fact I think I do," she teased.

"Well?"

"The bed's made. There's nobody around to interrupt. I'd say we have all the time in the world."

Sean's expression turned serious. He reached out with fingers that trembled slightly and brushed a stray curl away from her cheek. "You're absolutely certain this is something you want?"

She touched a finger to his lips. "Not if you intend to talk it to death."

He laughed. "No more talking?"

"Nope. I think all the important stuff has already been said."

"Not all of it," he said. "You haven't said how you feel about me, about us."

"Haven't I? I thought I had," she said, kissing him thoroughly. "Not clear enough? I love you, Sean Devaney. I never thought I would say that to another person, but it's true. Not even *I* could be stubborn enough to go on denying it, when it's staring me in the face. I love you."

His expression brightened. Before she could guess what he had in mind, he rose to his feet, still holding her in his arms, and headed for the freshly painted bedroom. At the doorway he hesitated.

"Shower first," he said. "Of course, I won't have any fresh clothes to change into afterward."

Deanna grinned. "I don't think clothes are going to be a necessity for the rest of the night."

"You going to join me in the shower? Or do you want to go first?"

Normally she would have wanted to go first, maybe use the time to steady her nerves before she took this next step, but right this moment she couldn't imagine being separated from him even for a second. Despite his claim to love her, there was still a chance he could change his mind about making love. Obviously, he knew, as she did, that they were about to cross a line from which there would be no turning back.

"I'll scrub your back if you'll scrub mine," she said lightly.

His eyes darkened. "Deal," he said, his voice suddenly hoarse.

The bathroom was fairly large, with an old-fashioned claw-footed tub with a showerhead installed above. The tile floor was cool beneath her bare feet. Deanna suddenly shivered, overcome with an attack of jitters.

Sean studied her. "Change your mind?"

"No," she said staunchly. But the transition from fully clothed to buck naked intimidated her.

Sean seemed to guess what was going on in her head. Eyes locked with hers, he reached for the faucets and turned on the water, then faced her and reached for the hem of her T-shirt. Ever so slowly, his gaze never leaving her face, he lifted it over her head.

Then he skimmed his knuckles across her bare skin, avoiding her breasts, on his way to releasing the snap on her cutoff jeans. A leisurely push had the shorts skimming over her hips and sliding down her legs.

Then she was standing before him in bra and panties, watching the desire darken his eyes. He kicked off his sneakers, then shucked his T-shirt and jeans and stood before her in briefs that did nothing to conceal the full state of his arousal. A smile played across his mouth.

"If it would help, we could jump in like this, pretend we're going swimming," he suggested.

One tiny part of Deanna wanted to do just that. In fact, there was something amazingly provocative about imagining how they would look with damp cloth clinging to her curves and the evidence of his desire. Another part of her cried out at being a coward. If this was what she wanted—and it was—then there shouldn't be anything halfway about it. And there shouldn't be any hesitation or embarrassment.

Because she couldn't seem to summon a single word, instead she reached down and unclasped the hook on her bra and let it fall away. Sean sucked in a sharp breath as his gaze fell to her breasts. He reached out and with one finger, slowly circled first one tip, then the other. The gesture was enough to send heat spiraling through her.

Then his hands slipped past the elastic waistband of her panties and slid them off. It was no more than a quick, skimming touch and yet she was shuddering with need somewhere deep inside.

Sean saw her reaction and when she reached for his briefs, he caught her hands. "Something tells me I'd better do this myself if we're actually going to get a shower."

She grinned at the admission that he was as close to the edge as she was. It made her feel something she hadn't felt in a very long time. It made her feel desirable. For too many years now, she'd concentrated on being a mother. She'd forgotten how to be a woman.

Finally undressed, Sean held out his hand and helped her into the tub, then stepped in to face her. Keeping his gaze focused on hers, he picked up the soap and began to lather it all over her with quick, slippery passes that tried to avoid being provocative. Deanna almost laughed at the concentration knitting his brow. She could have told him all that restraint was wasted. Every place he touched was on fire. Her heart was pounding as if she'd just run a marathon.

"My turn," she said, stealing the soap and using it to work up a creamy lather which she spread slowly across his solid chest. The white foam against bronzed skin made her want to linger there, but there was so much more of him to explore—broad shoulders, muscled legs, a powerful back and tight butt. She could feel his skin heat beneath her touch, felt the tension in his muscles.

"Enough," he whispered, his voice tight.

He turned around and drew her against him, slick skin against slippery heat. His arms loosely circling her waist, he moved slightly until the shower was cascading over them, the water in the old pipes turning cool, but not cold enough to temper the fire burning inside them both.

When they'd been rinsed clean, he shut off the water, reached for a towel and rubbed her skin until it glowed. He barely made a pass with a towel to dry himself before scooping her into his arms and heading for the bedroom.

By then Deanna was restless with wanting, desperate to feel him deep inside her.

Sean apparently felt the same urgency, because he hesitated above her for no more than a heartbeat, gazing deep into her eyes as he slowly entered her, stilled and sighed with obvious contentment.

But being together wasn't enough, not for long. Sean began to move, the strokes slow and leisurely at first, then deeper and more intense. Deanna's hips rose off the bed to meet him, desperately seeking a release that remained just beyond reach. The rhythm teased and tormented, promising so much but holding back until Deanna was about to scream.

Just then Sean's fingers glided intimately over her, sending shock waves ripping through her. The scream came then, but Sean's mouth covered hers, capturing the sound as he held her tight. Then he was moving again, carrying her beyond where she'd thought she was capable of going, until together they fell off the ends of the earth.

15

In Sean's past, the morning after making love with a woman had always meant a hurried escape to safer emotional waters. Even on those rare occasions when he'd lingered for breakfast, he'd been careful to retreat to more neutral turf. He'd done his best not to give confusing signals that might suggest that the night before had been a prelude to forever.

This morning he awoke to the discovery that he was exactly where he wanted to be, where he *intended* to be, for the rest of his life—in bed with Deanna curled next to him, her breath fanning across his bare chest.

Even as he made that mental admission, he waited for the panic to follow. He expected some sort of fight-or-flight instinct to kick in that would have him bolting for the door. Instead, there was…an unbelievable sense of inner peace. Genuine contentment stole through him.

Gazing down at soft-as-satin cheeks still flushed from the last time they'd made love, he felt a smile curving his lips. He could do this. With Deanna he

could face the future with the kind of faith that commitment required. He couldn't imagine a time when
he wouldn't want to wake up next to her, when he
wouldn't want to play ball with Kevin, maybe even
hold a baby of their own.

There it was, he thought, as the first hint of anticipated panic crept in at the thought of babies. *That* was
the image destined to send a little tremor of fear racing
through him. His pulse raced and his stomach knotted.

A baby, for heaven's sake. What was he thinking?
What did he know about babies? The last time he'd
spent any extended time around babies, he'd been a
kid himself. He remembered the twins' homecoming
from the hospital, how he and Ryan had held them as
if they might break, excited by the prospect of having
two more brothers.

Unfortunately, that thrill hadn't lasted. He remembered that the twins had cried more, been more difficult to pacify than Michael. One cranky baby would
have been stressful enough. Two caused sleepless
nights and frayed tempers. He remembered the strain
on his mother's face, the impatient complaints from his
father that escalated into shouting matches that often
sent him, Ryan and Michael running from the house
to hide until the furor was over. He remembered feeling scared and, worse, resentful of the two tiny beings
who'd come into their midst and ruined everything.

What the hell was he doing, thinking about having
a baby with Deanna or with anyone else? How many
times had he wished back then that the twins had never
been born? Now guilt and anguish welled up inside
him at the hateful thoughts he'd once harbored for

those two innocent boys. How could he have been so selfish? he reproached himself.

With the long-forgotten memories flooding in, he wondered how he could have buried all of that for so long. Obviously he'd buried it as deep as the fear that those childish wishes had been the cause of his parents taking the twins and leaving.

He wasn't aware that tears were sliding down his cheeks until he felt Deanna hesitantly touch the dampness, her expression worried.

"Sean, what is it? What's wrong?"

He shoved her hand aside and swiped impatiently at the telling tears, embarrassed at having been caught crying. "Nothing," he said brusquely.

She laid her hand over his. "Don't try to tell me that. I don't believe you."

Her steady look told him she had no intention of letting him off the hook. He took a deep breath and forced himself to admit at least part of what had reduced him to tears. "I just slammed headfirst into a slew of old memories."

"Not very pleasant ones, I gather."

He shook his head.

She smoothed her hand over the stubble on his cheek. "Tell me."

Her tone was gentle, but it was a command. He knew her well enough to see that. She wasn't going to rest until he'd spilled his guts to her. What would she think of him then? Maybe, despite what she'd said last night, she would be the one who'd flee from the relationship.

With a sinking sensation in the pit of his stomach,

he began slowly, describing the upheaval the twins' arrival had caused in his family. As he described how the situation had worsened month by month, Deanna nodded, her expression filled with understanding and compassion, not the disgust he'd feared.

"I wanted them to go away," he said, his voice barely above a whisper as he admitted the shameful sentiment.

"Oh, Sean." She didn't seem shocked or appalled, just very sad. "Don't you imagine that's exactly how every sibling feels when a new baby brother or sister comes home from the hospital? You had two brothers thrust on you all at once. Worse, they weren't easy babies."

"But Ryan didn't resent me. Neither of us felt that way about Michael."

"Do you really remember that clearly? You were only two when Michael was born," she reminded him.

"I remember…" he insisted, not ready to let himself off the hook "…as clearly as I remember the tension that began the second Patrick and Daniel came home from the hospital."

Deanna didn't seem entirely convinced, but she said, "You mentioned the twins were difficult babies, and they caused problems between your parents. It was natural for you to be afraid that your world was about to be disrupted. Just look at what happened— your family was torn apart. Maybe that was because of the twins or maybe it was something else, but the bottom line is, your fears had some basis in reality."

"That's no excuse," he said, refusing to let himself

off the hook. "They were babies. What kind of man blames a baby for anything?"

She laughed then and pressed a kiss against his lips. He was so surprised by the reaction, he didn't move, didn't even automatically deepen the kiss as he might have another time.

"Sean, you weren't a man," she reminded him. "You were a six-year-old boy, younger than that when they first came into your life. I'm sure there are plenty of other things you did at that age that you would never consider doing now."

He started to argue, then slowly grasped the wisdom in her words. She was right. He was blaming himself for things that had been far beyond his control. Whatever had happened back then, it was because of decisions the adults had made, not anything he or Ryan or even Michael or the twins had done. The blame, if there was any, belonged with their parents. It had been up to them to cope with the disruptions, to reassure their sons, not to simply take off when things got to be too difficult.

He and Ryan had talked about that before, had agreed on it, but until now he hadn't let himself believe it. Having Deanna, an objective third party, provide a fresh perspective helped more than he'd imagined possible. A sigh of relief shuddered through him as he finally let go of some of the guilt.

Deanna regarded him with surprise. "You really were blaming yourself, weren't you? Have you been doing that all these years?"

"Not consciously," he said. "But somewhere in the back of my mind, I suspect it was always there."

"What made you think about it this morning?"

He started to keep the answer to himself, but she deserved to know where his head was. "I was thinking about babies. Yours and mine."

The expression on her face was priceless—a mix of shock, wonder and something that looked a whole lot like panic. Sean could relate to that.

But he wasn't scared anymore, because when he looked deep into Deanna's eyes, anything seemed possible.

Deanna didn't want Sean to see just how deeply she'd been affected by his off-the-cuff remark about the two of them having babies. They'd spent one night in each other's arms and he was talking about a family. How could she even think about that? How could he? Wasn't admitting that she loved him a huge enough leap for now?

Because she was so completely disconcerted, she scrambled from his embrace with the excuse that she was starving, that he must be, too. She was dressed in her robe and out the bedroom door before he could blink, much less reach out and haul her back into bed.

Her hands shook as she made the coffee. She had just grabbed the edge of the counter to steady herself when she felt Sean come up behind her, bracing his hands next to hers, trapping her in place.

"Okay," he said quietly. "Your turn. Why did you take off like that?"

"I'm hungry," she insisted.

"Turn around, look me in the eye and tell me food is the only thing on your mind," he said.

She swallowed hard and forced herself to turn around and level a look straight into his eyes. "I want pancakes," she said, managing to keep her voice steady. She was impressed with her acting, if not the blatant lie.

Sean didn't seem quite as taken with her proclamation. "Pancakes? You'd rather have pancakes than me?" he asked lightly.

She laughed despite her tension. "I didn't know you were even on the menu."

"Oh, yeah," he said softly, his mouth covering hers. "Always."

One hand cupped her breast, causing the nipple to bead beneath the soft fabric. Just like that, the panic fell away.

This was Sean. This was the solid, steady man who had befriended her son and protected her, even when she didn't want his protection. Sean would never run out on her the way Frankie had, not after he'd committed to staying. Sean would never take such a commitment lightly. He'd lived through the pain of abandonment, just as she had. If he could take a giant leap of faith into the future, so could she.

Couldn't she? Her heart hammered at the thought.

Then she met his gaze, saw the man who made her pulse race, the man who *loved* her, who loved her enough to face his own fears and move forward.

She shrugged out of the robe, let it slide to the floor as she moved into his waiting arms. Just as he swept her off her feet, she reached out and flipped off the coffeepot. Coffee, pancakes, everything else would have to wait. The future was right in front of her, and she intended to reach for it and hold on tight.

After they'd finally recovered from the most incredible, spontaneous explosion of sex Deanna had ever experienced, she met Sean's gaze and caught the spark of amusement lurking in his eyes.

"What? I'm completely out of breath, and you're laughing at me?"

"Not at you," he insisted, smoothing away her frown. "It just occurred to me that we wasted an entire day painting this place."

She looked around at the bright, cheerful walls. "How can you say that? It's beautiful."

"But you're not going to be living here more than a week or two."

She stared at him. "Excuse me?"

"Isn't it usual for a husband and wife to live under the same roof?"

She went perfectly still. "What are you saying?"

"That I want you to marry me. Today. Tomorrow. As soon as possible."

She stared at him. "A few hours ago we were just friends, and now you want to get married right away?" She couldn't seem to help the incredulity or the panic threading through her voice. "Isn't that a little sudden?"

The earlier talk of babies had been one thing. That had been a sometime-in-the-future sort of discussion. This talk about a wedding had an immediacy that terrified her. Sean had kept her senses spinning all night long. Now he was making her dizzy, moving their relationship along at the speed of light.

He regarded her with understanding. "I know it's scary," he soothed, cupping her face in work-worn hands that were astonishingly gentle, hands that could make her tremble with the slightest caress. "But I love you. You love me. And this isn't sudden. We've been getting to this point since the day we met. If you think about it that way, we've already been courting for months now. And we owe it to Kevin to let him know that what we feel for each other is permanent."

"Let's leave Kevin out of this for the moment."

"How can we?"

"Because this is about us," she protested weakly. "We have to do what's right for us first, or it will be all wrong for Kevin."

"Okay," he said slowly. "Then what are you saying?"

"That I'm still stunned about the fact that we made love."

It was his turn to go still. "Do you regret it?"

How could she? She met his gaze. "Of course not."

"And you do love me, right?"

She nodded.

"And Kevin thinks I'll make an okay dad," he said.

"That's an understatement," Deanna acknowledged.

"Then what's the real problem? Are you going to love me any more if we wait six months to get married? A year?"

Deanna thought about the logic of that. He was right. Her feelings might deepen, as love tended to do with time, but they wouldn't change. Not really. The love she'd finally admitted feeling was as real today as it would be months from now. So, why wait?

"You're that sure?" she asked, studying his face, astonished that all of his doubts could have disappeared overnight.

He regarded her solemnly. "I'm that sure," he confirmed.

The last of her own doubts vanished. Her heart began to sing. She glanced around at the freshly painted apartment. It was lovely, but it was hardly a reason to delay the inevitable. If there was one thing life had taught her, it was to seize happiness when it came around, for herself, for her son. Summer was almost over. A fall wedding could be beautiful.

"October?" she asked tentatively, thinking of the changing leaves that could provide a palette for the wedding.

Sean's expression brightened. "Is that a yes?"

She refused to give in so easily. He needed to understand that he couldn't get his way about everything in their new life. "That's a maybe," she corrected. "October's awfully short notice to pull a wedding together. Maybe *next* October would be better."

"That's more than a year from now," he protested. "What if we get cold feet?"

"I won't," she said with certainty. "Will you?"

"No, but—"

"If what we're feeling is real, it won't hurt to wait."

Sean regarded her with obvious disappointment. "Isn't there anything I can say to persuade you to move things up? How about if I promise to spend every day of my life making you happy, building a family with you that can't be broken?"

She touched a finger to his lips. "I already believe that with all my heart."

Sean sighed. "Then there's nothing I can say?"

"I can't think of anything," she said.

"I guess there is a bright side," he said finally. "At least Hank won't win a few hundred bucks from the guys at the station."

She stared at him blankly. "What does our wedding date have to do with Hank winning a bunch of money?"

Sean hesitated, then shrugged. "Now don't get too upset, but he's got a bet going at the station. He thinks I don't know about it, but nothing stays secret down there for long. He bet that you and I would wind up married by fall."

"He what?"

"I told you not to get upset," he scolded. "All the other guys thought it was a sucker bet. Hell, even I thought it was a sucker bet. I'd have put my money on Hank and Ruby getting to the altar a whole lot faster that the two of us." He shook his head in disgust. "I can't believe those two are still dillydallying around. Anybody with two eyes can see they're meant for each other."

Suddenly Deanna saw the humor in the situation. "And if we're not married by fall, *this* fall, Hank loses, right?"

"Exactly."

"Maybe I should re-think this," she said, her expression turning thoughtful. "Winter officially begins December twenty-first." She snuggled just a little closer to this man who'd taught her to dream again. "I know it's not quite as soon as you were thinking, and it's a whole lot sooner than I was planning, but actually I've always thought it would be wonderful to get married on New Year's Eve."

"New Year's Eve," he repeated slowly, his gaze locked with hers. "*This* New Year's Eve?"

"Seems like the perfect time to commit to a fresh start, don't you think?" she asked solemnly, trying to keep a grin from spreading across her face.

For a minute Sean seemed to be absorbing the comment, interpreting it, and then he let out a whoop. Deanna wasn't entirely sure if Sean's delight was at her sneaky way of winning the bet or at his success in getting her to say yes to a very short engagement.

Then his mouth was covering hers, and none of that mattered. In fact, she didn't have any more doubts about anything at all.

Epilogue

Hank was still grumbling about having been cheated out of hundreds of dollars by a few short weeks, but he was decked out in a tuxedo and standing beside Sean as they waited for Ruby and Deanna to walk down the aisle of a church in the neighborhood. They'd considered the same church where Ryan and Maggie had wed, but the reality was that Father Francis's hands were tied, because Deanna was not only divorced, but Protestant.

Once the old priest had heard the whole story, though, he'd said, "That doesn't mean I can't participate in a service held at another church, if that's what you two would like."

Sean had grinned at his clever way of skirting the rules. It was little wonder Ryan and Maggie adored the man.

Now, as the organist began to play, Sean's gaze shot to the back of the church. Kevin appeared first, wearing a tuxedo that was already wrinkled, a cowlick of hair sticking straight up despite the gel Sean had used to tame it. When he spotted Sean, a grin split

his face and he started forward, holding tightly to a
pillow bearing the rings as if he'd been entrusted with
a priceless piece of fragile crystal. Sean gave him an
encouraging wink.

Beside Sean, Hank sucked in a breath as Ruby appeared in a gown of black velvet that clung to every
curve and yet managed to have a totally proper and
regal look to it. Sean knew that an engagement ring
was all but burning a hole in the pocket of Hank's tux.
If he was any judge of anything having to do with love,
Ruby was bound to say yes. New Year's Eve was going
to be a night to remember for all of them.

Then Deanna appeared, framed by splashes of red
and white poinsettias, her white satin gown shimmering in the candlelight. Every single thought in Sean's
head vanished at his first glimpse of her. She was stun-
ningly beautiful, but there was an unmistakable hint
of sadness in her eyes that he suspected only he could
see. He also thought he knew the cause.

He held his breath before finally catching a move-
ment just to her side. He heard a whisper, saw her gaze
shift and a look of wonder spread across her face. Until
that moment Sean hadn't been sure he'd done the right
thing. Now he knew he had.

A tall, distinguished-looking man stepped into
place beside Deanna and held out his arm. After the
slightest hint of hesitation Deanna linked her arm
through her father's, and together they walked toward
the front of the church.

When they reached Sean's side, her father, his eyes
misty, bent and kissed her, then placed her hand in
Sean's. His gaze held Sean's for just a minute and then

he moved to take a seat beside a woman who was un-ashamedly crying in the front row.

Apparently hearing the faint sound, Deanna gasped. Her gaze flew toward her mother, and for an instant Sean thought she was going to burst into tears, too, but she rallied and turned back to face him, her eyes shining.

"Thank you," she whispered. "I know you did this."

"I wanted this wedding to be perfect." Then he leaned closer to whisper, "Don't cry. People will think you don't really want to marry me."

She blinked back the threatening tears and smiled. "Better?"

"Beautiful," he assured her. "The most beautiful bride ever."

The service went by in a blur. Sean spoke the vows he'd written himself, amazed that he didn't stumble even once, not even over the promise of forever. In fact, believing in an eternity rich with love was becoming almost second nature to him.

Deanna's voice was steady and clear as she promised to be steadfast in her love. "Nothing, not sorrow, not crises, will shake the foundation of the family I am committing to give you today. I take you as my husband, my son takes you as his father, from now through all time."

Sean hadn't expected his heart to be so full. He knew as well as anyone that words could be too easily spoken, that promises could just as easily be broken, but his faith in Deanna and this marriage was strong.

Then the minister stepped aside, and Father Francis rested his hand on theirs. "I ask God to bless this union," he said. "Now and for all time." His mouth curved into a serene smile as he added, "And I now pronounce you husband and wife."

"And son," Kevin chimed in.

The old man grinned. "And son," he added, putting his blessing on the adoption that would officially take place as soon as the papers could be signed.

Sean hoisted Kevin into his arms, then turned to take Deanna's hand for the rush down the aisle and into a future that looked brighter than anything he'd ever imagined.

Deanna still couldn't believe that Sean had somehow managed to convince her parents to be a part of this day. If he'd searched the world's finest stores, he couldn't have found a more perfect wedding gift.

There were still a lot of old wounds that would need time to heal, but this was a start, and she owed it all to a man who had virtually no relationship with his own family. Maybe no one could understand better than Sean how bereft she'd felt all these years. She hadn't understood it herself until she'd looked up into her father's face as he'd joined her for the walk down the aisle. The emotions had almost overwhelmed her.

"You've married a fine man," her father said approvingly, his gaze shifting to the other side of the room where Sean, Ryan and Maggie were huddled together. "He made it clear to me that this was a chance to make things right between us and that if I blew it, I didn't deserve another chance."

"He does tend to be plainspoken," Deanna said, amazed that her strong-willed father had taken such an ultimatum so well. Perhaps he'd been waiting for an excuse to mend fences and Sean had simply given one to him.

Beside Deanna, her mother seemed less impressed. She was gazing around Joey's restaurant with a disdainful lift to her chin. "I just can't imagine what he was thinking, picking a place like this for the wedding reception."

Deanna laughed. "Don't blame Sean. I insisted on it. Joey and Paulie would have been heartbroken if I'd had it anywhere else. Besides, the price was right. They refused to let us pay for a thing."

"We would have—" her mother began, only to have Deanna's father cut her off in midsentence.

"This is what Deanna wanted," he reminded her. "It's her wedding."

Her mother sighed heavily, but a glance in Sean's direction brought a half smile to her lips. "He is a handsome young man."

"Better than that, Mom. He's a good man," Deanna said. "If you'll excuse me, it's been too long since I've let him steal a kiss."

The truth was she was worried about the intense expression on Sean's face as his conversation with Ryan and the obviously pregnant and glowing Maggie went on. Deanna slipped up beside him and pressed a kiss to his cheek. "Everything okay?"

Ryan's expression immediately turned guilty. "Sorry. Sean and I have been discussing family business. It could have waited."

"Don't be silly." She studied her husband's stony expression. "Is this about Michael?"

Sean nodded. "Ryan's located him."

"That's wonderful," she said, but neither brother seemed to agree with her. She looked at her sister-in-law. "Isn't it?"

"He was injured in the line of duty a week ago," Maggie said. "He's in a hospital in San Diego. He hasn't regained consciousness."

"Then go to him," Deanna said at once. "Tonight, if there's a flight available."

Sean searched her face. "You wouldn't mind?"

"We're not taking an official honeymoon until later, anyway. This is important. You need to go."

Ryan seemed to be waiting for Sean's response. At Sean's nod, a weight seemed to lift off his shoulders. "I'll make the arrangements. You enjoy your party and see to your guests. As soon as I have flight information, I'll find you."

When Ryan and Maggie had gone, Sean stood looking at her as if he couldn't get enough of the sight. "You're remarkable. You know that, don't you?"

"Why? Today you gave me back my old family and started a new one with me. How could I not do anything necessary to see that you get yours back, too?"

"I love you, Deanna Devaney."

"I love you, too." She touched a hand to his cheek. "And when you see your brother again, tell him that we can't wait for him to come home."

* * * * *

Read on for a sneak peek at
Sherryl Woods's upcoming SWAN POINT,
available in stores and online soon!

* * * * *

Gabe Franklin had claimed a booth in the back corner of Rosalina's for the fourth night in a row. Back in Serenity for less than a week and living at the Serenity Inn, he'd figured this was better than the bar across town for a man determined to sober up and live life on the straight and narrow. That was the whole point of coming home, after all—to prove he'd changed and deserved a second chance. Once he accomplished that and made peace with his past, well, he'd decide whether to move on yet again. He wasn't sure he was the kind of man who'd ever put down roots.

"You're turning into a real regular in here," his waitress, a middle-age woman who'd introduced herself as Debbie a few nights ago, said. "Are you new in town?"

"Not exactly," he said, returning her smile but adding no details. "I'll have—"

"A large diet soda and a large pepperoni pizza," she filled in before he could complete his order.

Gabe winced. "I'm obviously in a rut."

"That's okay. Most of our regulars order the same thing every time," she said. "And I pay attention. Friendly service and a good memory get me bigger tips."

"I'll remember that," he said, then sat back and looked around the restaurant while waiting for his food.

Suddenly he sat up a little straighter as a dark-haired woman came in with four children. Even though she looked a little harried and a whole lot weary, she was stunning with her olive complexion and high cheekbones. She was also vaguely familiar, though he couldn't put a name to the face.

He watched as the intriguing woman asked for several tables to be pushed together. He noted with disappointment when a man with two children came in to join them. So, he thought, she was married with six kids. An unfamiliar twinge of envy left him feeling vaguely unsettled. Since when had he been interested in having a family of any size? Still, he couldn't seem to tear his gaze away from the picture of domestic bliss they presented. The teasing and laughter seemed to settle in his heart and make it just a little lighter.

When his waitress returned with his drink, he nodded in the woman's direction. "Quite a family," he commented. "I can't imagine having six kids. They look like quite a handful."

Debbie laughed. "Oh, they're a handful, all right, but they're not all Adelia's. That's her brother, Elliott Cruz, who just came in with two of his. He has a baby, too, but I guess she was getting a cold, so his wife stayed home with her."

Gabe hid a grin. Thank heaven for chatty waitresses and a town known for gossip.

"Where's her husband?"

The waitress leaned down and confided, "Sadly, not in hell where he belongs. The man cheated on her repeatedly and the whole town knew about it. She finally kicked his sorry butt to the curb. Too bad the whole town couldn't follow suit and divorce him." She flushed, her expression immediately filled with guilt. "Sorry. I shouldn't have said that, but Adelia's a great woman and she didn't deserve the way Ernesto Hernandez treated her."

Gabe nodded. "Sounds like a real gem," he said. In fact, he sounded like a lot of the men who'd passed through his mom's life over the years. Gabe felt a sudden surge of sympathy for Adelia. And he liked the fact that his waitress was firmly in her corner. He suspected the rest of the town was, too, just the way they'd always stood up for the wronged wives when his mom had been the other woman in way too many relationships.

Still, he couldn't help thinking about all the complications that came with a woman in Adelia's situation. He had enough on his own plate without getting mixed up in her drama. Much as he might enjoy sitting right here and staring, it would be far better to slip away right now and avoid the powerful temptation to reach out to her. Heaven knew, he had nothing to offer a woman. Not these days, anyway.

Gabe followed the direction of her gaze and found the very woman in question glancing his way. His heart, which hadn't been engaged in much more than keeping him alive these past few years, did a fascinating, anxiety-producing little stutter step.

No way, he told himself determinedly as he headed for the door and the safety of his comfortable, if uninviting room at the Serenity Inn. He'd never been much good at multitasking. Right now his only goal was to prove himself to Mitch and to himself. Complications were out of the question. And the beautiful Adelia Hernandez and her four kids had complication written all over them.

#1 *NEW YORK TIMES* BESTSELLING AUTHOR

sherryl
woods

swan point

A Sweet Magnolia Novel

"Sherryl Woods writes emotionally satisfying novels about family, friendship and honor. Truly feel-good reads!"
—#1 *New York Times* bestselling author DEBBIE MACOMBER

$14.95 U.S./$17.95 CAN.

Limited time offer!

$1.⁵⁰ OFF

#1 *New York Times* bestselling author

sherryl woods

brings readers back to Serenity, South Carolina

Available July 29, 2014,
wherever books are sold!

HARLEQUIN® MIRA®
™ www.Harlequin.com

$1.⁵⁰ OFF the purchase price of
SWAN POINT by Sherryl Woods

Offer valid from July 21, 2014, to August 25, 2014.
Redeemable at participating retail outlets. Limit one coupon per purchase.
Valid in the U.S.A. and Canada only.

5 2 6 1 1 4 2 9

5 65373 00078 6   (8100)0 11912

Canadian Retailers: Harlequin Enterprises Limited will pay the face value of this coupon plus 10.25¢ if submitted by customer for this product only. Any other use constitutes fraud. Coupon is nonassignable. Void if taxed, prohibited or restricted by law. Consumer must pay any government taxes. Void if copied. Millennium1 Promotional Services ("M1P") customers submit coupons and proof of sales to Harlequin Enterprises Limited, P.O. Box 3000, Saint John, NB E2L 4L3, Canada. Non-M1P retailer—for reimbursement submit coupons and proof of sales directly to Harlequin Enterprises Limited, Retail Marketing Department, 225 Duncan Mill Rd., Don Mills, Ontario M3B 3K9, Canada.

U.S. Retailers: Harlequin Enterprises Limited will pay the face value of this coupon plus 8¢ if submitted by customer for this product only. Any other use constitutes fraud. Coupon is nonassignable. Void if taxed, prohibited or restricted by law. Consumer must pay any government taxes. Void if copied. For reimbursement submit coupons and proof of sales directly to Harlequin Enterprises Limited, P.O. Box 880478, El Paso, TX 88588-0478, U.S.A. Cash value 1/100 cents.

® and TM are trademarks owned and used by the trademark owner and/or its licensee.

© 2014 Harlequin Enterprises Limited

MSHW1642CPN

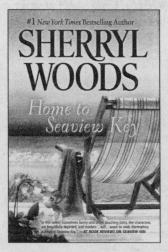

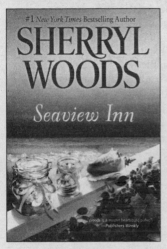

SHERRYL WOODS

HARLEQUIN® MIRA®
™ www.Harlequin.com

MSHW0414BL